ANTIQUE

A Novel

BY SETH PANITCH

New York Boston

This book is a work of fiction. Names, characters, places, and incidents are the product of the author's imagination or are used fictitiously. Any resemblance to actual events, locales, or persons, living or dead, is coincidental.

Grand Central Publishing
Hachette Book Group
1290 Avenue of the Americas, New York, NY 10104
grandcentralpublishing.com
@grandcentralpub

First Edition: February 2026

Grand Central Publishing is a division of Hachette Book Group, Inc. The Grand Central Publishing name and logo is a registered trademark of Hachette Book Group, Inc.

The publisher is not responsible for websites (or their content) that are not owned by the publisher.

The Hachette Speakers Bureau provides a wide range of authors for speaking events. To find out more, go to hachettespeakersbureau.com or email HachetteSpeakers@hbgusa.com.

Grand Central Publishing books may be purchased in bulk for business, educational, or promotional use. For information, please contact your local bookseller or the Hachette Book Group Special Markets Department at special.markets@hbgusa.com.

Interior design by Taylor Navis

Library of Congress Cataloging-in-Publication Data
Names: Panitch, Seth author
Title: Antique : a novel / by Seth Panitch.
Description: First edition. | New York : GCP, 2026.
Identifiers: LCCN 2025037622 | ISBN 9781538772942 hardcover |
ISBN 9781538772966 ebook
Subjects: LCGFT: Magic realist fiction | Novels | Fiction
Classification: LCC PS3616.A536 A85 2026
LC record available at https://lccn.loc.gov/2025037622

ISBNs: 978-1-5387-7294-2 (hardcover), 978-1-5387-7296-6 (ebook)

Printed in the United States of America

LSC-C

Printing 1, 2025

To my wife; my Grail

ANTIQUE: something old, rare, of great value

Also used as a pejorative:, out of fashion, washed up, dead

Part I
Shape

One

It was Old.

Five thousand years old. And what it contained was older still. It had been worn as a necklace by the high priestess of Sin, the Babylonian god of wisdom, whose many eyes peered through the Great Void, illuminating the night sky for those curious enough to contemplate it. At one time, the necklace's six strings were threaded with the riches of Empire, but they had been stripped clean by greedy fingers over the millennia, leaving only the first string, the original artifact: twelve cylindrically shaped stones of pure black onyx spaced with Nubian gold nuggets of unequal size and shape.

And fastened in the very center, between two crimson bloodstones, hung the celestial globe itself: a marble-size stone of the finest lapis lazuli, mined in the ancient limestone beds of Pakistan. It emerged from the earth a perfect sphere, and those who unearthed it averted their eyes, awed by the golden pyrite inclusions that shimmered like starbursts across the deep blue face of the stone. To hold the globe was to grasp the Cosmos, and it was of such infinite value, a great stepped ziggurat rose in the Sumerian city of Ur to protect it.

But the ziggurat fell when Ur fell, and the high priestess smuggled the globe out of the smoldering city. She ran afoul of the wilderness and might have failed in her task, but for the kindness of a small tribe of nomads. They took her in, and although they nursed her body to health, her soul succumbed. With her last breath, she placed the globe about the neck of Sarah, the wife of their leader, Abraham. And so the necklace was passed from mother to child, from generation to generation. It ventured to Egypt with Joseph, it hung about the shoulders of Moses on Sinai, and as he gazed up for the last time into the wonders of the firmament, he gifted it to the Bedouin sheep herder who tended his final rest. The Bedouin returned to his tribe, and the necklace remained with them for thousands of years, passed down from generation to generation, while cities and peoples and nations rose and fought and fell.

In the year 1917 of the Common Era, an American spy stole behind the Ottoman lines to gather intelligence on the Turks. The mission failed—the spy traded his cover to save the life of an innocent Bedouin caught in the crossfire—but they escaped together and hid out the war under the protection of the Bedouin's tribe. When he was free to go, the American left with a gift from the wife of the man he had saved. It was an old, tarnished necklace, but quite stunning to behold; a single string of onyx and bloodstone housing a stone of the deepest blues and golds he had ever seen.

He brought it home to his wife, and she wore it for a time, but boxed it when her eyes lit upon newer, finer things. Her daughter wore it at her wedding, but children and the cares of home gave her little chance to bring it out into the light, so it remained in the dark for many years, the once glittering starbursts long since burned out beneath the dust and debris of neglect. It no longer shined because it had no need to shine. It had no purpose, and was content to remain purposeless for the eternity to come.

Until.

Two

The great tent rose like the unfurled mainsail of a nineteenth-century frigate, its pearl white canvas flapping in the humid Massachusetts breeze. Wherever it appeared, whether in botanical garden or trash-strewn parking lot, it was recognized as a beacon to those who worshipped oil and pastel and platinum, who felt the keen tug of provenance and history. They came by the hundreds, sometimes thousands, seeking answers from a traveling oracle that was, to them, no less profound than the one at Delphi. Two twin cardboard monoliths stood sentry outside, identical in text to the thousands of fliers that had been mailed, posted, stuffed in mailboxes, slipped under windshield wipers, and taped to every road sign in town by the show's local brigade of dedicated volunteers:

THE APPRAISAL EXPERTS ROADSHOW
WANTS **YOU**!

BRING YOUR CHERISHED, YOUR CHOTCHKES,
YOUR HUDDLED GLASSWARE!

FREE CONSULTATIONS TO THE FIRST 100 VISITORS

AT THE:
MEDFORD ART CENTER,
SATURDAY AND SUNDAY MARCH 25 & 26
ONE WEEKEND ONLY! HOPE TO SEE YOU THERE!

The huge signs funneled the hopeful multitudes into the cool confines of the great tent, where they were greeted and their cherished wares evaluated for admittance to the show. Some were directed to the Antiquities Table, others to Clocks and Watches. English tea sets followed the yellow spike tape to the Silver and Jewelry Desk, dog-eared (and nibbled) baseball cards took the express train to Toys and Collectibles. There was Arms and Militaria from wars both Civil and foreign, Textiles and Rugs for those hung in dining rooms and trampled in playrooms, Books and Photographs and Carnival Glass, and when all else failed, the all-inclusive come one, come all Decorative Arts.

And so the faithful filed in, armed with moth-eaten boxes and overstuffed shopping carts brimming with the cherished legacy of generations. They came from mansion and mobile home, from dorm and apartment, from condominium and convalescent hospital. They came from near and far and high and low, but mostly they came from the nooks and crannies of an America that felt just a little bit forgotten, just a little bit left behind. They came, not for an appraisal, but for an answer:

What's it worth?

Brenda Almond had no idea as she turned the old cedar box over in her hands. Fifty dollars? A hundred? That would be nice. Not that she'd sell it. Unless they said a thousand—for a thousand, sure. She could fix her daughter's brakes and replace that damn dryer that still smelled like her ex-husband. *What if it's worth more, though?* she thought, her mind swirling with dizzying possibilities as she crossed the threshold into the buzzing, thrumming heart of the show.

She was greeted by a Grand Central Station of chattering humanity. Eight tightly packed lines of guests fanned out toward the Appraisal Desks, like a promenade of ants nosing their way down diverging lines of pheromones. She took her place in line, shuffling ever closer to the Antiquities and Tribal Arts Table, its green fabric sign flapping at her like a matador's cape. The wait was agony—the closer she drew, the slower she moved—until finally, the line froze altogether.

Brenda's spirits sagged, and she wondered if she had spent her last sick day of the year for nothing—until she noticed an expert behind the neighboring Paintings, Prints, and Photographs Table waving her over.

"I can help you over here, miss," the woman said.

The woman was striking—tall, a bit lanky, but gracefully so—and when she gestured, there was a familiarity to it, as if Brenda were an old friend at a chance meeting. There was an effortless elegance to her, an unforced confidence that intrigued Brenda, so she shuffled over to the nearby table. "They told me 'Tribal Arts,'" she said, holding up her green station pass.

"That's all right." The woman puffed out the chest of her charcoal pinstripe pantsuit in a mock show of pride. "We all know a bit more than just our *own* bit, if you know what I mean." She smiled, a lovely smile; unforced, genuine. It wasn't just kind, it was kindred. "I'm Grace," said the woman, whose name tag confirmed this, just above the name of her gallery: SCHAFFER & SCHAFFER, LTD.

"I'm Brenda." She pointed at Grace's name tag, joking: "What happened to the other Schaffer?"

Grace paused, but the smile remained airborne. "There's just me today," she said, shifting her attention to the box in Brenda's hands. "Now, what lovely treasure do you have there?"

Brenda set it down on the table between them, making a few adjustments until it was just so. "I was hoping you'd tell me. I know very little about it."

Grace switched on a desk lamp, bathing the little box in sharp white light. Brenda was riveted—not on the reveal, but on Grace, on her reaction. Her ex-husband had told her it was worthless. That she was a fool to buy it. *Tell me it's rare*, she thought, willing it so with all her might. *Tell me it's beautiful. Just please—don't tell me he was right.*

Grace opened the box, dipped her fingers inside, and lifted out a fist-size shrunken head—eyes bulging, nostrils flaring. "Oh, Brenda." She grinned. "I'm absolutely smitten." And she was—taking the utmost care as she set it down on a soft felt doily. "How did you come across this whimsical little character?"

"I was on my honeymoon," Brenda said, the words tumbling out. "Me and my husband—well, ex-husband—spotted this poor little guy at a street fair in Puerto Plata, all alone at the end of a table. I don't know if I wanted to buy him, as much as I wanted..."

"To rescue him?"

"Yes!" This woman knew, thought Brenda. She understood.

"Well, let's take a closer look at your *tsantsa*, shall we?"

"*Tsantsa*," said Brenda. "I like that." Much better than "shrunken head," which was what her ex-husband called it; and what her ex-husband had, so far as Brenda was concerned.

Grace tilted the tiny skull into the lamplight, turning it this way and that, as if searching for a trapdoor into the mysteries within. "*Tsantsas* go all the way back to the ancient Jivaro tribes of Peru, although the practice was outlawed in the 1930s. This isn't to say we don't see authentic ones every now and then, but they are incredibly rare."

"Is this one...?" Brenda couldn't even say the word.

"Authentic?" Grace turned it over in her hand with reverence. "If he is, we'd be in the audience of something quite special. Would you mind if I take a closer look?"

"Please!" she yelped, instantly covering her mouth. "Sorry."

"Oh, don't be." Grace chuckled. "I'm excited myself." She ran her fingers through the stringy black hair of the *tsantsa*. "The hair is nice and glossy—that's a promising start."

Brenda nodded, her heart racing.

"There's a telltale incision on the back of the skull, here," Grace said, running the tip of her index finger over a faded suture line. "And the lips," she said, turning the head back over, "they're sewn up in the exact pattern we'd want to see."

I never dreamed, thought Brenda—but of course she had. And here it was, revealing itself before her very eyes. She willed herself to be present, to enjoy the moment—she'd want to remember this for the rest of her life.

Grace withdrew a magnifying glass from the armory of tools before her. "And in terms of the skin itself..." She trailed off, spying something in the glass that gave her pause.

"The skin...? Yes...?"

Grace started to speak, and then took Brenda's hand instead, brushing it over the *tsantsa*'s cheek. "You feel that?"

"It's smooth."

"Too smooth, I'm sorry to say. Real skin—animal or human—has texture, imperfections. I can't spot any, not even under extreme magnification."

The excitement drained from Brenda's cheeks. "Does that mean...?"

"It's synthetic," sighed Grace. "Probably worth ten dollars. Maybe twenty."

"Twenty dollars?" Brenda deflated, shrinking herself about an inch. "That's all?"

Grace nodded, offering a sad smile. "I'm so sorry, Brenda."

And Grace was, but that didn't make Brenda feel any better. "Thank you," she said, gathering the head and plopping it back into the box without ceremony.

"But I'm sure there's tremendous personal value in it, isn't there?" asked Grace.

Brenda took one last look inside the box before slapping the top back on.

"No," she said. "Not really."

Grace Schaffer sighed as she watched Brenda disappear into the crowd. She felt tired. No, she felt old. She was only in her forties, well mid-forties, that's what she told people. But forty-six was no longer mid-anything, was it? It was the other side of middle. It was past middle.

It was Old.

Maybe it was the appraisal. She should have known it was synthetic the moment she opened the box. First show back or not, it was unforgivable—she had given that poor woman a false hope, and that had made the reveal that much harder. The show's director had assured Grace it would be just like getting back on a bike, and if it was, hers was in serious need of a tune-up. It wasn't just the missed signs of counterfeit. Even when she had the facts straight, they sounded so odd coming out of her mouth. Off-key. Which was exactly how Grace felt—off, flat, behind the beat. Worst of all, when appraisals ended like this one (as they all had right before her *hiatus*), they always felt to Grace like a breakup—not a nasty one, like her marriage had been—but sad nevertheless. To see the hope drain out of someone's eyes, and know it was your call that had pulled the stopper. It used to feel so common; an ordinary part of her everyday business. Now it just felt cruel.

Then again, maybe it wasn't just the appraisal that troubled her. Aside from antiquities appraiser Jerome Zwick, who could boast (but never did) of a massively successful career spanning over fifty years, the batting order of her new team looked less like the New York Yankees and more like the Hartford Yard Goats. These were not the bow-tied, high-heeled celebrity superstars of *Antiques Roadshow*, nor the appraisal aristocracy that dominated the acquisition departments of Sotheby's, Christie's, Bonhams, and Heritage Auctions. These were the no-names, the working stiffs of the Antique World; all of them in business, none of them known outside of it. They were here, not for the small fee they received from the show for their appearance, but to drum up much-needed business for their struggling galleries. That was reason enough for them to return, year after year, many of them for their entire careers.

But it was not the reason.

All of them, Grace included, were on the trail of a Lost Ark, of a Loch Ness Monster. They called it a *Grail*, and every appraiser, every gallery owner, every auctioneer had one on their career bucket list.

That one undiscovered treasure, that misplaced masterpiece—whose unearthing had the power to rekindle a small spark of wonder into a world that had been bled dry of it. But the flow of fresh discoveries had slowed to a trickle, and then dried up completely. Without the possibility that something mysterious was waiting on the other side of monstrous student loans, and endless degrees, and a lonely lifetime spent in the gloomy corners of cavernous libraries, their spirits sickened and, for some, died off completely. Those who remained found their talents no longer needed, unnecessary in a market that thrived no longer on new discoveries, but on recycling past finds until they spit out higher and higher values. Worth was no longer calculated by age or provenance, but by dollar and cent, and so the experts turned on one another, picking at each other's scholarship like a murder of crows.

Grace's thoughts were interrupted by a red-cheeked woman in an orange muumuu. "Paintings, Prints, and Posters?" she asked, rushing up to the table with a large painting wrapped in a sheet no less colorful than her outfit.

"At your service," said Grace, switching gears as best she could. "Can I help you?"

"Prepare to have your mind blown!" Before Grace could even get a scent of what was beneath the sheet, the woman yanked it back, revealing a blue-and-green-pastel painting of the woman herself, naked—her arms and legs spread wide like Leonardo da Vinci's *Vitruvian Man*, her hands wrapped around two un-da-Vinci-like battery-operated, bullet-shaped devices.

"Pardon me," said Grace, grabbing her phone and grimacing at the blank screen as if an important call were coming in. "I'm terribly sorry. I have to take this. It'll only be a moment."

Grace ducked out the rear of the tent into the blissful relief of the fresh morning air. It was not blissful for long.

"That head wasn't worth ten dollars, Grace," said a voice behind her. "And certainly not twenty."

Grace turned to find Jerome Zwick scowling at her from the tent entrance, his thick, stocky frame locked in position like the bolt of a sniper's rifle. He had a nickname (they all did), and his was well earned: *Torquemada*—the Grand Inquisitor. On anyone else, a three-piece gray tweed suit and yellow bow tie might evoke a favorite grandfather; on Jerome Zwick, it evoked the Third Degree. Although he only stood five and a half feet, Grace felt him tower over her like a bald skyscraper.

"I know it's been a while," he said. "Shake the rust off, kid."

Grace thought of arguing the point, that it was her first mistake, to cut her some slack, and she would have with anyone else, but not Jerome Zwick. Their orbits had only occasionally crossed at conferences and auctions, but his reputation was unblemished by the usual inflammation of ego that afflicted many in the field. If he lowered the boom of his bushy white eyebrows on you, you probably had it coming.

"I'm trying, Jerome," she sighed. "But I feel a bit wobbly in there. Maybe I came back too soon. But there's only so many ways I can rearrange the furniture in my living room before I go stark raving mad."

Jerome eyed her, and Grace felt the heat of his stare. He was appraising her like a five-hundred-year-old pottery shard, which was pretty much how she felt—a faded, unremarkable piece of something that used to be spectacular.

"You can't be here because you don't want to be anywhere else," he said. "That's no good for you." He pointed at the small crowd milling about in the garden. "Or them."

She nodded. "Please don't tell Elaine." Grace winced at how pathetic it sounded.

"Tell her what, Ms. Schaffer?"

Grace laughed. "I owe you one."

Jerome cracked a sly grin. "Mind if I claim it now?" He pointed at her name tag. "That second 'Schaffer.' I'm curious—why not 'Schaffer & Karlin'?"

"God, no." She chuckled. "Victor wouldn't have been caught dead sharing a billboard with me."

"Of course not. He wouldn't deserve it," said Jerome, and Grace fell just a little bit in love with him.

"No, the second Schaffer, that's always been—" Grace hesitated. "That's my dad," she said, and even that tiny mention of the man made her chest tighten. "It's been nearly a year, and I still can't bring myself to take his name off the door. I shouldn't be surprised—it took me thirty years and half a dozen therapists to stop calling him 'Doctor.'"

"I didn't know you and Albert were in business together."

"We weren't," said Grace. "Not officially. But he was always... there."

Jerome, ever the Inquisitor, leaned in slightly. "He still is, isn't he?"

Grace looked back at him—and reminded herself to be more careful around him. "Yes," she said, "I suppose he is."

He waited for more, but for Grace this was a stone best left unturned. "Are we square?" she asked.

Jerome nodded and slipped back into the tent, leaving Grace alone outside with the dwindling line of buzzing, hopeful visitors. No matter how small the heirlooms they carried, how distressed, how shattered, how smudged, they bore within them the infinite weight of their owners' expectations. And Grace felt that weight, felt it press down, its iron grip digging into her, for she knew—rust or no rust—it was her job to reward those expectations, or dash them all to pieces. She stood and watched them crowd into one side of the tent, bursting with excitement, filing out the other in a slow trickle of disappointment.

Grace knew that procession well. Ever since she was a little girl. It wasn't a tent, of course. It was an office in Jersey. But the journey was the same—excitement in, depression out.

Oh yes, she thought. *There's no place like home.*

Three

Gracie Schaffer was tired of hearing it, although her mother never tired of saying it: Sit at the kids' table. Go to bed early. Eat your carrots. Go out to play. *Play?* There was no time to play! She had books to read, and mysteries to uncover, and who the h-e-l-l would she play with? Phoebe Archer? Phoebe was a *kid*, for God's sake. Not Gracie—no Girl Scouts for her, no slumber parties, no giggling about Tommy Mains and his stupid feathered hair. No, Gracie was different. It was impossible to miss—all anyone had to do was look at her fingernails.

Gracie adored her fingernails. Not because they were sparkly, like Dinah Cole's, or perfectly manicured like Reba Geer's. No, Gracie's twelve-year-old fingernails might as well have been twelve hundred years old, what with the thick layer of soil and soot beneath them. Her mother could sigh *Oh, Gracie* until she was blue in the face, but as soon as she cleaned out the dirt beneath Gracie's nails with that dreaded metal file of hers, those fingernails were once again wrapped around the handle of her little red shovel, digging into the forbidden treasures of their sprawling New Jersey backyard.

And what a collection they curated! The other girls in her sixth grade class had their My Little Ponies and Dream Glow Barbies and Easy-Bake Ovens. Gracie had limestone and sandstone and quartz that changed color when the sun shone through the open blinds of her bedroom window. She had animal bones and snakeskin and shotgun shells and Michelob bottle tops, and even an old cigar box with a parrot skeleton inside. She had the entire history of her backyard on those shelves.

But none of it compared to this.

Gracie knew it as soon as her shovel struck something hard and unforgiving beneath the barren topsoil. It was small and white as ivory, like an animal's tooth, but Gracie knew different. She was sure it was stone the moment she plucked it out of the protesting earth—but it had been fashioned. A scraper, a tool, perhaps? No, this was too sharp, too pointed. This was a weapon. But whose? She couldn't imagine.

But *he* could.

Gracie dropped her shovel and ran across the yard, jumping over her mother's flowerbeds, up the splintering wooden stairs, and into the air-conditioned blast of the family room. Her mother, sitting primly in her favorite armchair in the corner, pried her eyes up from a large hardcover book, took one look at Gracie's mud-caked shoes, and slapped the book face down on the coffee table.

"Gracie," she gasped. "Shoes off, young lady."

Gracie groaned and kicked off her shoes, booting them across the room to join a small squadron of similarly adorned Keds in the corner, before bounding toward the hallway.

"He's working, Gracie."

"This is an emergency."

"What kind of emergency?"

Gracie spun around as if her mother had spoken in tongues. How on earth could she possibly understand? This was History (*Living, Breathing History*; that's what he called it), and only True Art Historians could handle this sort of emergency. "Sorry, Mom," she said. "You wouldn't understand." She expected her mother to yell at her. Maybe raise her voice a little—just enough for Gracie to work up a stink and storm off down the hall. But she didn't.

"Well," said Shirley, picking her book up off the coffee table and settling back into her armchair. "Perhaps I wouldn't."

Gracie stared at her mother, and her mother stared back, wavy-chestnut-haired mirror images of the other—but Gracie knew from experience the similarity was skin deep at best. "It's not your fault, Mom," she said. "You're just not that into it, is all."

"No, dear," said Shirley, submerging back down into the depths of her book once again. "I suppose I'm not."

Gracie hesitated. Her mother may have always had her head in a book, but the woman herself was unreadable. Gracie had tried, over and over, but like an empty canvas, there was just nothing to keep her attention for very long.

"Whatever, Mom," she said, and off she went, tearing down the hallway, around the corner, flying toward the double doors at the end of the hall. She skidded to a halt at the threshold and, with just the very edge of one knuckle, knocked softly on the door and placed her ear against it—but nothing stirred within.

"Dr. Schaffer?" she called.

"Working," said the basso gruffness within.

"I think I found something."

Silence, save the crisp Gatling gun of her father's typewriter.

"It'll only take a second."

The typing stopped. A chair slid back, and hard-soled shoes clacked their way toward the door. A lock snapped and the doors swung wide.

Albert Schaffer stood in the doorway, which appeared to retreat from his massive frame, unable to restrain him. He towered before Gracie, his legs and arms dangling down from a barrel-chested redwood trunk of a torso. His face was likewise long and thin—not gaunt but sharply chiseled, framed by a short, jet-black beard shot through with thin brushstrokes of silver and ivory. His eyes were hooded by the broad cliffs of his brow, but they simmered and crackled with irritation, hot enough to liquefy Gracie's resolve.

"Grace," he said, and the very hardwood beneath her feet vibrated with the sound. "I am not to be interrupted."

"I know, I'm sorry," she stammered, smacking her tongue against the dry roof of her mouth. "But this is important, I promise."

"It will have to wait." He began closing the door.

"It's an arrowhead," she said, blurting it out. "I think it's Native American."

Albert paused; eyes narrowed. "You *think*?" he said. "What's your *proof*, Grace?"

"Shape, for one," she said, her trembling voice settling, calming, for he had opened the door. He had challenged her. And she was ready. "And you can see the faint fluting on the edges, it's ay-ay-asymmetrical."

"More, Grace," he said. "I need more."

She had saved the best for last. "Strike scars," she said. "From flintknapping."

He paused, his face unreadable. "Show me."

Gracie opened her hand to reveal the arrowhead, which looked humongous in her tiny, mud-streaked palm. Her father raised his gold-rimmed spectacles and peered down at it, silent for an excruciating eternity. Finally, he let his glasses fall and trained his cold, hard gaze upon her.

"Come in," he said, walking back into the mahogany depths of his office. "And close the door behind you."

Gracie replayed it in her mind, to be sure she had not imagined it. She glanced down at the threshold—the one she had only ever crossed in secret—and stepped inside, closing the door behind her, sealing her inside a forbidden world. The entryway sparkled with gold leaf commendations: Summa cum laude Brooklyn College, MA/PhD Columbia, letters of tenure, associate and full professor (from Columbia as well). The walls beyond disappeared behind bookshelf after bookshelf, and there, on the top shelf nearest his desk, Gracie spied *his* books—stretching from the dawn of his career to the precipice of the present. She had read them all, some of them often enough that she knew a few of the lines by heart.

Gracie was in one of them, too—well, her name was—right there in the Dedication, the year she was born. Gracie had it bookmarked on her nightstand, and she read it out loud to herself on the nights he worked late, when she was denied that brief but cherished goodnight kiss: *My Daughter, Grace.*

And there he was, looming over that huge expanse of a desk, which was devoid of any personal pictures or items, no mail, no magazines. Only his typewriter held court in the middle of the desk, pages upon pages piling up beside it.

To Gracie's amazement, her father pushed the typewriter aside and placed her arrowhead in the very center of the desk, switching on a fluorescent magnifying light and bending it over the stone. He transformed before her, his icy demeanor collapsing like the crumbling walls of a glacier, caressing the stone with his eyes as they swept back and forth over every flint stroke.

"Sit," he said.

Gracie sat on a small leather bench by the door.

"No, Grace. Beside me." He turned his leather desk chair, opening it toward her. "Let's take a look at what you've found, dear."

Gracie walked toward it as if in a trance. She lowered herself into the soft leather, and he eased her around until she was directly over the arrowhead. Her nose twitched with the sweet smell of his aftershave as he leaned over the side of the chair, his arm around her. He began to speak, and Gracie wished to God she could hear him over the pounding of her own heart—she did catch the occasional date and possible identities of tool and tribe—but by the time the words were spoken, she had forgotten to listen. There was just that one single word, repeating in her mind, over and over.

He had called her *dear.*

Four

The Appraisal Experts Roadshow awoke from its overnight slumber. There was no hangover—there was no time with only two days to satisfy the demands of each location. Volunteers in their smart red vests scurried about in an anxious swarm of preparation, dressing the appraisal tables, replacing burned-out bulbs, hanging banners, and vacuuming yesterday's disappointment out of the crisscrossing red carpets beneath the big top.

"So what do you think?" asked Elaine Courtney, the show's long-serving (and long-suffering) director, as she made her final check of Grace's appraisal table. "Any second thoughts?"

Grace laughed. "Second chances don't get second thoughts. Let's just hope I don't give *you* any."

"Don't be silly, Grace."

"I'm not exactly anyone's pot of gold these days, and you know it. Things are so quiet back home, I had someone call the gallery to make sure the phone still rang. If you hadn't thrown me a lifeline..." She hesitated, afraid to finish the thought.

"You would have been fine, Grace."

"I don't think so." Grace paused, and when she spoke again, her voice was thin and quiet. "That was a dark place, Lain. I've seen my share—you know, we all have—but I couldn't see a way out of it.

It felt like forever, like I'd be there forever, and after a while I just gave up and stopped fighting. I didn't see the point. Even if I had crawled out, I knew there wasn't anyone or anything waiting for me on the other side. I owe you, Lain. And I intend to pay you back, with interest."

"Friends don't owe," said Elaine, giving her arm a squeeze. "And good friends get their fannies swatted for even suggesting it. Besides, I wet my knickers when you called. You're going to be the jewel in our crown."

"Oh, I'm anything but." Grace chuckled. "My shine's dimmed to a dull whimper."

"Not to me. And not to anyone else—even if they're too jealous to admit it. I don't see anyone else around here on *Antiques Roadshow*."

Grace flinched, as if she'd been nicked by a razor. "I'm not on it either, Lain. Not anymore." It was a fact, of course, and she'd repeated it often enough, but for some reason it still twisted around in her gut.

"That was stupid of me." Elaine reached out, taking her hand. "I shouldn't have brought it up. I'm so sorry, Grace."

"Don't be." Grace gripped back. "I'm over it."

"I'm not. You were a fucking star—he forced you out."

"He didn't force me, Lain. I left."

"Well, you've here now," said Elaine. "And you're still a jewel to me, whether you like it or not."

Grace worked up the best smile she could as she scanned the tent for a change of subject. She found it in the timely arrival of Jerome Zwick, who began unpacking his leather satchel at the neighboring Antiquities Table. "I'm amazed he's still at it at his age, still pounding the pavement," she said. "Didn't he retire?"

"He can't retire."

"Why not?"

Elaine leaned in, dropping her voice to a whisper. "He lost one, poor guy. Right there in his own gallery."

"A *Grail*?"

"Damn thing came in on consignment. He sold it to some looky-loo before he'd even taken a good look at it."

"God, that's heartbreaking." Grace watched him set up his wares, arranging his tools with military precision, as if he were preparing for battle. "He thinks he'll find it here, doesn't he?"

"Nice appraisal, Grace." Elaine grinned. "Told you, you're our jewel." She suddenly burst out laughing. "Eureka! Found your nickname on the very first weekend!"

"No, Lainy, please."

"The Crown Jewel!"

Grace groaned. "Oh God. The other appraisers will love me for that one."

"They better." Elaine took her hand. "Or I'm going to fire them." She gave Grace a peck on the cheek and hustled off, herding the volunteers to the entrance, preparing them for the opening rush.

Grace hoped it would be a rush. Not just for Elaine, but for all the experts standing at attention behind their tables. To Grace, they looked like anxious kids waiting to be picked at their first school dance, all smiles and bow ties on the outside, all agony within. Antiques had appreciated over the centuries because people had taken the time and effort to appreciate them. But time had grown short, and effort shorter in an age when most things were bought with a mouse and a click. Art had always maintained a wary alliance with commerce, but it was dangerously unprepared for the rise of the influencer, which, one live stream at a time, ground down the textured palates of an entire generation. The Appraisal Experts Roadshow, then, would be their last stand. They needed this show.

And so did Grace. This was indeed her second chance. It was also her last. The very act of calling Elaine and asking for a job had made her hyperventilate, for if she did venture back out into the world, if she attempted another ascent and failed, no one, not even Elaine would take her calls, and art would slip away from her grasp once and for all. For oils and pastels were not merely her passion, they were instrumental to the woman she had become, as necessary as any organ or limb or digit; to be stripped of them would feel like an amputation, a dismembering of her very spirit. She braced herself against her appraisal table and steadied her breathing, in and out. *Easy does it, Gracie*, she thought. *The climb starts with a single step. Just don't trip.*

Elaine gave the order, the tent flaps flew wide, and the first guests hurried in. Some carried cuckoo clocks with laryngitis, others their cherished collections of *MAD* Magazine, others moth-eaten blankets with the moths still nibbling on them. All of them carrying one thing in common: hopes of such buoyancy, they seemed to strain the canvas of the tent itself.

The anxiety faded and a huge grin spread across Grace's face—appraisals always did this to her. If her father's prolific writings had built his reputation, if Victor's sharp wit had made his, it was Grace's eye that carved out her niche. She saw things, things others had missed—a faded manufacturer's mark, a hidden signature, that tiny quiver in a client's voice that provided the key to unlock the whole. Yes, Grace had missed the warning signs with Victor, but she had much better odds behind an appraisal desk. Not lately, of course. It had been nine long months since she'd had the courage to work, and her appraisals so far had felt brittle and tight, like an atrophied muscle. But Grace knew if the winds of chance were ever to shift for her, it would be here.

She welcomed her first guest of the day—a thin, grandfatherly fellow with a *Peanuts* comic strip lithograph; signed, it appeared, by Charles Schulz himself. Unfortunately, both strip and signature were copies, and the poor man left as dejected as Charlie Brown after yet another disastrous kick of the football.

She was sure her next appraisal would be more fruitful, and it was: a pastel sketch of an earthen fruit bowl, brimming with glistening apples, pears, and bananas—but not with value. There were copies and forgeries, promising pieces unmarked and unsigned, and even when her heart fluttered at the sight of a Winslow Homer seascape, the mounting board had cracked and the canvas had frayed—lowering a fifteen-thousand-dollar estimate to less than three hundred dollars.

One after another, the attendees bounded up to her appraisal table, flushed with anticipation, and one by one, the spark within them fizzled and died. It weighed heavily on Grace, but the market was the market. Trends shifted, as did the value of arts and antiquities, but appraisers were subject to the market's momentary whims, no matter what their own personal appreciation of a painting or a pocket watch might be. Grace could stretch a value here, massage a number there, but when all was said and done, there was little more she could do.

She noticed she had a few more guests still queued up. *A few more hearts to break before lunch*, she thought. She gestured for the next in line to approach, but before the woman could get to the table, Jerome Zwick stepped directly in front of her.

"I know, I know," said Grace, rubbing her face as if she might massage the last appraisal out of it. "That last painting's worth half that, maybe less."

"Can you come with me for a moment, please."

Grace sighed. "Look, if you have a problem with my appraisals—"

"It's my problem," he said. "I have something I need your eyes on."

"Oh," said Grace, relieved. "Sorry. Of course. What do you have?"

"A necklace, old necklace."

"Uh-huh." Grace gestured toward Lennie Reno at the Jewelry Table. "Why don't you ask Lennie?"

"I don't need Lennie," he said. "I need you."

Grace glanced at Jerome's Antiquities Table. A middle-aged woman and her daughter were waiting there, a small black felt box in the older woman's grasp. "A necklace, yes?" she asked.

"Egyptian, maybe Ptolemaic."

"Well, that's worth a pretty penny."

"Not this one. It's a mess."

"Did you tell them that?"

"No." He avoided her eyes. "I was hoping you would."

"Why?"

He hesitated. "I can't."

Grace was still confused, but nodded anyway, excusing herself from her station and following Jerome over to his. Aside from Elaine, Grace had not made any friends at the show yet, but she preferred not to make an enemy, particularly of him. His reprimand outside the tent had not felt personal—it was protective; of the show, of the guests, but most of all, of the antiques they carried with them.

"Sorry about that, ladies," he said, approaching the women. "I wanted another eye on this intriguing piece." He moved aside so Grace could take center stage behind the table.

"Hello there," said Grace, stepping forward. "I'm Grace Schaffer."

"Mary Turner," said the older woman. "And this is my daughter, Rebecca."

Grace shook Mary's hand and instantly understood why Jerome had asked her to pinch hit for him. Mary held on so tightly, so desperately, to Grace's hand, as if Grace were holding her over a yawning chasm. The woman smiled with her very best effort, but it quivered on her face, ready to crumble at any moment. This was not a woman at the end of her rope. This poor woman had no rope at all.

"Pleasure to meet you," said Grace. "How can I help?"

Mary hesitated and turned to her daughter, who spoke for her. "We'd like to know what it's worth—just the ballpark, you know. We have an estate sale coming up."

"Estate sale?" Grace looked into Mary's eyes and found the answer. "Your mother?"

Mary nodded.

"I'm so sorry," said Grace. "May I take a look at it?"

Mary shut the lid, gripping the box so tightly her knuckles turned pale. "I'm not sure I want to sell."

"That's perfectly all right," said Grace. "We're not allowed to buy anything at the show, are we, Jerome?"

"Not if we want to stay hired," he said.

"Good," said Mary. "Not that I want either of you fired."

"Well, you might reconsider if you knew us better," he said.

The four of them laughed and the tension settled to a dull roar.

Mary lowered the box onto the table before Grace. "I found it in the back of my mother's closet," she said. "She hadn't worn it for years, not that I can remember, but..."

"It's hers," said Grace.

Mary nodded. "A piece of her, yes."

"May I touch it?"

Mary hesitated, then nodded again.

Grace gently touched the soft felt of the box and lifted the lid, but it hesitated at first, as if it was straining against Grace, denying her access. Mary had shut it with some strength, and the piece was old enough that a touch of inflexibility was not unexpected. Grace put a bit more force into her fingertips and as the hinges gave way, the suction broke, and the box cracked open, releasing the pent-up acrid smell of dust and stone. Grace sniffed at something caught in her nostrils; not an aroma, but a tingling, as if something sharp and cold had brushed past the tiny hairs in her nose. There was always something about opening an old box like this that made Grace feel as if she were uncovering buried treasure, but this felt more like the opening of a tomb. She shook off the feeling and peered inside.

Jerome was right. It was a mess. The stones of the necklace were faded and chipped, some of them flat-out missing, like the gapped front teeth of a toddler. It was impossible to tell what their original colors were, but Grace figured they were onyx. Not pure black, but it was in such poor shape, it was hard to tell. There was a spherical gray-blue stone in the center, set with two dull dark red stones that Grace could not place.

She reached into the box and slowly removed the necklace. It was far heavier in her hands than it looked, a surprising weight; almost as if it were metal or steel, or tungsten. The stones revealed no more of their secrets in the light; in fact, if anything, Grace thought they looked even duller. She ran her finger across the central gray stone. It was slick as a billiard ball, perfectly smooth; she pressed harder, searching for the mark of a jeweler's tool, for any imperfection and—

Grace drew back her finger. Something had pricked her. But there were no marks upon the stone, no sharp edges, and her finger was unmarked, although it was ever so slightly pink.

As if I'd been burned.

She slowly touched the tip of her finger to the stone, but the heat—if heat there'd been—was gone. *Basalt?* she thought. Basalt held heat for hours, as did red granite, soapstone; but this was neither.

Grace smiled—the stone was playing hard to get. *Don't be bashful, my dear*, she thought. *Talk to me.*

She traced her finger around the edges of the gray rock. It was suspended in the setting by a delicate gold filament that ran through the center of the stone. Grace wondered if it had been mobile once but had been soldered shut by time and neglect.

Did it rotate? Grace thought, as she spun the piece around in her mind.

"Jerome," she asked. "Do you have any bicarbonate?"

"In my medicine cabinet at home for indigestion," he scoffed, and passed her a small vial with a denim polishing cloth. "My own concoction. Try this instead."

Grace opened the vial and sniffed. Light vinegar and dish soap—simple. Then again, simple was best when it came to restoration, so she tipped a few drops onto the cloth and gently polished the central stone. The grease and grime held fast for a few passes until they slowly gave way to a deep, rich blue color, so deep Grace thought she was seeing into the stone, not glancing at its surface.

"This is lapis lazuli," she said, unable to keep the awe out of her voice.

"Is that expensive?" piped Rebecca.

"It depends on the cut," said Grace. "And the quality." She polished the stone in one specific spot, intrigued by the golden pyrite inclusions. "These look like constellations."

"Stars?" asked Mary, her eyes filling with them.

"Yes, look here," said Grace, picking up Jerome's pointer and leaning over the table. She ran the sharp end of the pointer across one of the golden structures. "See this?"

"What am I looking at?" asked Mary.

"Look closer."

Mary gasped. "That's the Big Dipper!"

"It is indeed," said Grace, running the pointer over the face of the stone. "And there's the Little One, and there's Taurus and Gemini and Cassiopeia."

"Amazing," Mary whispered. "What is it?"

"A celestial globe," said Grace. "Our very first attempts to record the Cosmos. Some were sculptures, some jewelry. There's one—the Farnese Globe—in the, uh..." Grace turned to Jerome for help.

"National Archeological Museum in Naples," he said. "That one dates all the way back to the third century BCE—but the first recorded ones date all the way back to the sixth."

Mary put a hand to her chest to keep her heart from leaping out. "Is this one that old?"

"I'd be surprised if it was," Grace said, feeling its weight, its mass. "But it's certainly special." She hovered above the shimmering golden celestial signs once again with her pointer. "It's something in the signs themselves," she said. "I can't tell the nature of the craftsmanship, but the stars of the constellations have been made to appear naturally existent within the rock, not added after extraction, which of course is impossible."

"Why not?" asked Rebecca.

"Well." Grace chuckled. "No rocks naturally exist pre-stamped with every constellation of the Cosmos."

Rebecca shook her head. "No, of course not."

"Some might appear to possess one or two, but not—"

Every constellation? Grace looked closer, and her heart sank.

"What's wrong?" asked Mary.

"Well," Grace sighed. "Although this appears on the surface to be Middle Kingdom Egyptian, or Assyrian."

"Or Babylonian," added Jerome, peering over her shoulder.

"Yes, perhaps," she said. "And if it were, that would make it most rare, most rare indeed."

"But it's not?" asked Mary, begging Grace for a different answer.

"It can't be," said Grace. "This globe has dozens of constellations on it, maybe all of them."

"Isn't that a good thing?"

"The Babylonians only knew fourteen," said Grace. "If some of these were added later, perhaps we could make a case for an earlier creation, but I can't spot any signs of revision. I wish I had better news, but this appears to be a modern construction."

The color drained from Mary's face; there would be no magic. "I thought," she sighed. "I thought it might be valuable."

"I didn't say it wasn't," said Grace, although she knew that was a lie, just something to buy her a little time. It was, unfortunately, anything but valuable.

What a pity.

But pity didn't enter into it. This was a commodity, an exchange, and there was quite simply nothing desirable in that scuffed-up, crumbling rock.

And yet there was, Grace was sure of it. Not something measurable by scale or instrument or auction, but wasn't there some sort of value in that necklace? Wasn't the memory of their mother and grandmother, bound forever within this blue-gray hunk of earth, wasn't that worth something?

Mary asked her the same question. "How much do you think it is worth, then?"

Grace turned to Jerome, and he avoided her eyes. This was why he had brought her. Not to let them down, but to let them down gently.

Grace took the woman's hand, and for a moment, it felt so eerily familiar to her. It was so weak, so fragile, as if the life beneath was fading away. As if Mary were fading away. Like Albert's memory. Like her mother, wasting away in that home. Like Grace, slowly seeping out of her very pores, unable to grasp herself as she spilled out. It wasn't right. It wasn't fair. But the television channel had been turned away from all of them—Grace, Jerome, Mary, Rebecca, the guests, the experts, the artworks themselves. No one was watching, not anymore.

Pity.

Deep down in Grace's chest, a single drop of blood wormed its way into a dark corner of her heart; a place where blood had not flown for many, many years. It was as gray as the unpolished face of that stone, and just as lifeless. But one solitary cell pierced the dead muscle, and deep within it, something soft and kind and immensely sad began to pulse.

No, Grace thought, fighting against it. *It's worth nothing—average quality at best, ten carats, maybe twelve.* What could she do? *Fifteen dollars, I could tell her. Maybe sixteen.*

She checked with Jerome. His eyes said seventeen.

Eighteen, she thought, *I'll tell her eighteen.*

Eighteen sounded fair. Eighteen sounded more than fair.

But it didn't sound right.

"Twenty-five hundred," said Grace.

The words went off like a grenade; both women flinched from the shrapnel.

"Excuse me?" Mary asked, gripping Grace's hand, hard.

Grace gripped back, as stunned as Mary at the outburst. It had sounded like her, the words were hers, but she couldn't remember thinking them.

Twenty-five *hundred*?

She thought of all the ways she could laugh it off, take it back, defer to Jerome, and she tried, but she couldn't, because, for some inexplicable reason—

I'd be lying.

"Twenty-five hundred," she said once again, amazed at how sane it sounded. She glanced down at the stone and noticed she had been stroking it unaware, tracing her finger back and forth over the sparkling constellations. "At auction, and with the right buyer, I believe this necklace would bring twenty-five hundred dollars. And not a penny less."

"Well, that's..." Mary's words deserted her. "Twenty-five *hundred?*"

Jerome's eyes fastened around Grace, as if they might pull her back from the precipice. She knew he was right, so very right, and she was so very, very wrong. But she also knew somehow, without a shadow of a doubt: "Twenty-five hundred," she said, with absolute finality. "And that's a conservative estimate."

Mary grabbed her chest, right there where her mother was with her, still. "My mother," she said, her voice cracking, "she didn't have a lot, you know? She only bought nice things for me, for my sister, never . . . never for herself."

"But look what she had, all this time." Grace pressed the globe into the woman's palm and her hand began to tingle, like gossamer needles of static electricity, but warmer. Such a pleasant warmth. "She had this."

The tears finally broke free, washing over Mary's eyelids in sheets. She batted them away with her fingers, but they just kept coming. "She did. All this time." She smiled through the tears. "She had this."

She reached out for her daughter's hand, and they folded into one another, so relieved, so vindicated, as if this alone could make up for the loss they had borne. As if that dusty string of stone could somehow bind and define all three of them, grandmother, mother, and child.

Because it did.

Five

Grace didn't smoke, but she could have used a pack or two, unfiltered. She was spent, physically and emotionally (and professionally, if Elaine got wind of the appraisal). Her fingers still tingled from gripping Mary's hand, from the emotional current that had passed between them. She looked at her own hand, searching for some sort of residue from the moment, some mark by which she could remember this, so she could store it and crack it open on a gloomy day. She did not see any. No sign of anything, in fact. Anything at all.

Pity.

"Twenty-five hundred, Grace?" said Jerome, storming out of the tent after her.

"What did you want me to say?"

"Not twenty-five hundred," he said, exasperated. "I figured fifteen, maybe twenty dollars, but—"

"Twenty-five hundred, I know. That's about twenty-five hundred more than it's worth. I don't know what happened in there. I'm such an idiot."

Jerome sighed. "No, you're not. I asked you. I'm the idiot." He shook his head, troubled. "What's going to happen if they go to auction, Grace?"

Grace groaned. In the whirlwind, she hadn't even considered it. "Oh shit."

"A whole bucket of it. Up to our eyelids, I'd say."

"My appraisal, my eyelids," she said. "I promise."

He fell silent for a moment.

"What?"

"Not sure I want you taking all the credit for what happened in there."

"You better. If I go down, you really want to go down with me?"

He waved around the show with a grand gesture. "And give up all this?" He grinned. "The horror."

Grace laughed. "Well, next time, I'll try to be more conservative."

"Just move the decimal point two places to the left, okay?"

"Deal."

He tipped an imaginary hat and slipped back into the tent.

Grace needed that cigarette, even more than before. Jerome was right. If that necklace went to auction, and brought what Grace knew it would bring, Mary and her daughter could lodge a complaint with the show, and Grace would be fired. They could post the misappraisal all over the antique chat boards, devastating Grace's gallery. They could—

"Ms. Schaffer?"

Mary and Rebecca rushed over from the guest entrance. Grace could not believe her good luck.

"Hello, ladies," she said, a plan brewing. "I'm so pleased you're still here."

"We weren't planning on it." Mary laughed. "We were almost home, but turned around to see if we could catch you one last time."

"I'm glad you did," said Grace. "There's something I forgot to mention about auctions."

"We're not going to auction," said Mary.

"Oh," said Grace, as sweet relief cascaded down her face. "Well, I think that's wise."

Rebecca checked in with her mother before speaking. "The piece is too important to Mom," she said. "And to me."

Grace smiled. The women were now clearly of one mind. At least Grace could be proud of that. "I can see why. I think it is a most extraordinary object."

"Which is why we'd like to sell it to you."

Grace cleared her throat. "To me?"

"We're not going to lie," said Mary. "We don't have the time for auctions. We need money, right now. The funeral, getting rid of the house, her possessions."

"Uh-huh," said Grace, racking her brain for an exit strategy.

"Besides, I couldn't bear to see strangers haggling over it," Mary said. "People who don't appreciate it. Who don't appreciate Mom." She took Grace's hand. "You're no stranger, Grace."

"Thank you, Mary. But I'm really not allowed to—"

"And if someday you decide to sell it," said Rebecca, "don't worry about us. You said twenty-five hundred was conservative, and we believe you, but we don't need any more than that. Just enough to cover Grandma's expenses. I think that's what she'd want."

"Okay, but..." Grace felt herself backing farther and farther into the corner of the ring, flinching before the knockout blow.

Mary opened Grace's hand and slipped the black felt box into it. "It's yours to sell, but I hope you won't," she said. "If anyone would have it, other than us, I think she'd want it to be you."

And that was that. There would be no exit strategy. Twenty-five hundred dollars was a tall price to pay for Grace to keep her place on the tour, but it was a pittance to pay for *this*—for someone to place that kind of faith in her. Grace had never experimented with drugs, but she couldn't imagine anything equaling the rush she felt in that moment, that intravenous injection of pure, distilled confidence coursing through her. She removed a business card from the pocket of her suit jacket and handed it to Mary. "My email is at the bottom. Just contact me with your address and I'll send a check."

Mother and daughter thanked her and walked off, light of foot and heavy of wallet. At least until their debts were paid.

As Grace watched them leave, she suddenly grew jealous, not because they had her next paycheck, but because they had each other. There had always been an invisible barrier between Grace and her mother; a wall without edge, no top to climb over, no bottom to plumb. It was impregnable because it was magnetic—Grace and Shirley had always simply repelled.

But at least Grace had a new necklace, well, new to her. She removed it from the box and held it in her hand. The stone was cold now; gone was the warmth that had so intrigued her. Even the golden pyrite inclusions had dimmed, receding into the dull gray background of the stony surface. There was something protective about it. Defensive. Coiled. Grace suddenly had the feeling she should put it back, box it up, wrap it tight, stuff it in a darkened corner in the back of an unused drawer. That she shouldn't disturb the dead.

But it didn't feel dead, not really. It felt dormant.

Grace knew the feeling. She rolled it around in her palm. It felt oddly familiar to her. It felt good.

And her palm felt good to *it*.

Six

It was a Queen Anne highboy; elegantly designed, expertly crafted. Grace ran an outstretched hand down the face of the varnished wooden cabinet, her fingers caressing the corkscrew finials that crowned the stately bonnet top, the exquisitely carved inlaid fans, the silk mahogany veneer of the drawers. She hiked her black skirt and dropped to her knees, craning her neck under the bottom of the lowest drawer to spy the hidden mark of the maker if she could.

And that's when the door opened behind her and Dr. Charles Lee entered the office, hesitating at the curious sight before him.

"If you're hiding from me, it won't work, ma'am," he said. "I've tried crawling into every nook and cranny of this office at one time or another, believe me."

Grace bolted to her feet with an unsuppressed gasp, smoothed her skirt over her hips, and yanked on the embossed lapel of her taupe blazer as if it were a ripcord. Realizing no parachute was forthcoming, she turned around, flushing an elevated shade of crimson.

"Please excuse me, Doctor. I'm terribly sorry."

"Please don't be." He smiled. "I assure you, there are far worse ways to be greeted at a new resident's intake."

Grace thought the medical director of Mary Elwood Estates couldn't have been much older than forty. He looked far younger than he had sounded on the phone. And far kinder, considering the awkward introduction she had just given him.

"Forgive me," she said. "I traditionally greet people with the appropriate *façade*, but you caught me in the midst of—"

"Admiring my furniture?"

Grace eyed the highboy. "That furniture, yes."

"Really?" he said, raising an eyebrow. "You like it?"

"I adore it. How long have you owned it?"

"I'm not sure," he said, joining her beside the highboy. "It's been here as long as I have."

"A bit longer, I suspect."

Lee laughed, rearranging the unruly bag of golf clubs that leaned against the piece before gesturing for Grace to sit in one of two chairs facing his desk. He watched her sit with the sort of giddy fascination Grace had become used to, as if she bore some sort of mystical stigmata.

"We don't often have celebrities in our midst," he said, grinning at her as he sat down across from her, perching himself at the edge of his chair.

Grace wondered if she should just smile and take the compliment, but somehow that always fingered the padlock on her memories, and she found herself back on set once more. The prickling flush of anxiety before a taping, the way she fed off it, how it focused her down like a telescoping gunsight. God, it hurt. To be so far from the molten core of the art world. And to be drifting still, ever farther and farther away. No, better to come clean and take whatever punishment came her way. It tended to be the lesser of two agonies.

"You mean *Antiques Roadshow*," she said. "I'm not on it anymore."

"Oh," he whispered like a gravesite mourner. "I'm so sorry."

Grace hated doing this to people. Bad enough she had to take her spoonful—no need for them to have to choke it down as well. "That's all right," she said, flashing a camera-ready smile. "More time to visit my mother, right?"

"Of course." He settled back into his chair, relieved for the change of subject. "She's getting settled into her apartment with Nurse Dow as we speak. She'll take very good care of her, I assure you."

"I'm sure," said Grace. "She seems lovely. Everyone does." She glanced out the large bay window as a clean-cut male attendant in a pressed blue uniform wheeled an elderly man onto the veranda. The old man turned to strike up a conversation, but the attendant had already gone back inside. For some reason, it absolutely broke Grace's heart.

Lee noticed the sudden change in her demeanor. "This is never easy, Grace."

"I know. Thank you."

"She won't ever be alone here. Unless she wants to, of course."

Grace laughed. "Oh, she'll like that. Mom has always been..." What had she been? Grace drew a blank. "Mom's a pretty private person."

"Oh?" Lee tilted his head. "Truly?"

"To a fault." Grace chuckled. "Closed Book—that's what Dad and I called her."

Lee opened a thin blue file on his desk. "Your father passed last year, is that correct?"

Her smile faded. "Yes," she said. "Almost to the day."

"And you're becoming concerned about her living alone?"

"This wasn't my idea, Doctor. It was hers."

Lee paused. "Is that so?"

"I wasn't crazy about her moving here. No offense."

"None taken," he said. "Do you mind if I ask why?"

"She was fine," Grace said with great conviction. "She was managing."

Lee chose his words carefully and with great compassion. "Her Parkinson's is extremely mild, Grace. But at some point, it's going to be challenging for her to live without some form of assistance, don't you think?"

"Of course," said Grace, inwardly cursing her—what was it, denial? Self-absorption? "I'm sorry, Doctor. Of course, you're right."

Lee eased the file across the desk to Grace. "Your mother has already signed her lease, but I do suggest another family signature, in the event an additional voice is necessary in her care." He offered her a small pen elegantly inscribed with MARY ELWOOD ESTATES, which felt surprisingly heavy in her hand.

"Thank you," she said, refusing to look directly at her signature as she signed. She finished without comment and slid the contract back across the desk.

Lee made one final notation in the file and stood up, offering his hand. "Very good, Ms. Schaffer. I hope my earlier indiscretion about the show hasn't caused you any additional duress."

Grace laughed. "Quite the contrary. You've been most patient with me." Grace rose and grabbed her soft leather briefcase. "Besides, I'm sure my mother will be happy to pass along any duress you may have missed." She lifted the strap onto her shoulder and started for the door.

"Thank you for the free appraisal, by the way," Lee said, tilting his head at the highboy.

"My pleasure," she said, admiring it one last time.

"What do you think we might get for it, if we ever chose to sell it?"

"What do *you* think it's worth?" Grace asked, arching an eyebrow.

"Gosh, I don't know. Twelve hundred? Fifteen hundred?"

"Seventeen."

"Wow," he whistled. "That much? Seventeen hundred?"

"Thousand." Grace grinned. "Seventeen thousand." She pointed at the bag of golf clubs leaning up against it. "You might want to find a better spot for the clubs, Doc."

She slipped out of the office as Lee jerked around at the dresser, mouth and mind wide open.

The old man on the veranda perked up like a child in a darkening movie theater just as the sun began its long slide into the evening sky. He cast a glance over his shoulder, perhaps in hopes someone might emerge to join him for the day's final encore. When no company appeared, he sighed and settled back into his wheelchair, turning his attention once more to the setting sun.

Grace felt a sharp twinge of loneliness herself as she watched the solitary figure from the open doors of the lobby. It was still new to her, that feeling of isolation, even after six months of being locked inside the sense deprivation chamber of divorce. She had gotten wind of the affair just a few weeks after her father's death, so perhaps she had hung on to Victor longer than she should have. Victor had been her husband, but he had also been her dearest friend—someone who saw the world as she did, who loved what she loved. Losing him had felt like losing her balance point; but losing her father . . . well, he was her magnetic north. Whenever Grace found the way unclear, she need only look for some small trace of him, some remnant of the choice he had made, and the fog would lift.

But now she'd been cast adrift in a dark and windless sea, without a star or current to guide her out. There was her mother, of course, but Shirley was just as lost. So that left Grace with just . . . Grace. And after being swept up in the atmospheric rise of Albert Schaffer—as his child, his student, his *colleague*, her name on his articles, her seat beside his at panels and conferences—Grace alone just plain didn't feel like enough. It didn't feel like anything. Just lonely—like that poor man on the veranda.

Grace walked past the open doors, careful not to disturb him. She made it all the way to the far side of the entryway before she hesitated.

It's not right, she thought, fiddling with the new necklace around her neck. *My twenty-five-hundred-dollar necklace*, she mused, barely suppressing a laugh. The old man deserved a kind word, for God's sake. She could spare that, at the very least.

Grace walked out onto the veranda and smiled down at the old man.

"Hello," she said.

He glanced up, squinting just a bit. "Do I know you?"

"I'm Grace."

"Max."

"Pleasure to meet you, Max." She shook his hand, noticing his eyes possessed a few of the same milky clouds as the horizon. "Looks like you grabbed the best seat in town."

"Every chance I get," he said, turning back to the sunset. "Never had the time to do this when I was young." He paused, before adding, "Too busy painting my face."

Grace blinked, surprised. "Your face?"

"Every night," he said, a wry smile spreading across his face.

Grace smiled back, unable to resist—and so the appraisal began.

His posture was exquisite, regal; his hair thin but combed back perfectly, as if each hair were a perfect brushstroke across his high forehead. But it was his voice that drew her most. His eyes may have been failing him, but not that voice. Still deep, after all the years. Resonant. Grace imagined it could have carried far distances in his youth.

All the way to the back row.

"You were an actor."

"Guilty as charged."

"Stage, not film."

"How can you tell?"

"Diction, voice—both highly trained. And your gestures; there's a shape to them, they're beautiful—like dance, almost."

He grinned, impressed. "Well, one of us is certainly cataract free."

"Don't give me too much credit. I might think you're flirting with me."

"Am I that obvious?"

She laughed. "You can take the boy off the stage..."

"But you can't keep him out of Mary Elwood Estates." Something dimmed in his eyes, and he turned away, gazing back out at the horizon. Grace kneeled beside him, looking out across the orchard that lined the entrance to the stately colonial residence. An orange haze had descended, making the trees and flowers appear to be glowing from within.

"It's so beautiful," she said.

"Things are always at their most beautiful right before sunset," he said. "I see so clearly now, even with the cataracts. I see the juniper trees—all the way in the distance, birds vanishing into inkblots on the horizon, snowcapped clouds sailing off into the arms of the endless sky. I see what I've done in much the same way: Hamlet, Shylock, Cyrano, Lear. I'm not sure I appreciated the opportunities I was given at the time, but looking back, I sure as hell appreciate them now."

The grand history of Max's life sparkled in his eyes: the great roles, the historic stages, the ovations, the failures. Grace wondered what she'd see through her mother's eyes. Another lunch date with her friends, perhaps? Maybe a daytime soap or late-night game show? It would be a front row seat to a life measured not by victory and defeat but by the ticking of a clock. Although that was unfair, wasn't it? Shirley was as Shirley did, and Grace would have to accept that—particularly now, with her mother entering the postscript of her life.

Grace wished Max a good evening and tucked his sweater up around his neck. Although the evening had begun to chill, Grace felt a tiny warmth in the center of her chest. Perhaps it was a buzz from the conversation with this fascinating, accomplished man. Perhaps it was the stone of the celestial globe against her skin, warmed by Grace's own perspiration. She shifted the necklace beneath her shirt and the tingle dissipated, soon forgotten.

Grace left the veranda and entered Mary Elwood Estates, walking the linoleum halls of Purgatory. It was an intricately choreographed dance—the well-meaning efforts of the staff, the residents' attempts to schedule some momentary excitement into their day; but it was all just a performance, a masquerade. Something to pass the time while they waited for things to run their course. Grace held her nose against the constant stench of ammonia and bleach, the futile attempt to wash away the astringence of age, but there was no escaping it. No matter how hard she pinched, age found its way in.

As silly as it sounded, Grace had always hoped it might somehow skip over her, forget to take her in its wrinkled embrace, but Victor's affair with a younger woman had been the middle-aged wake-up call Grace had always feared, and now the sleep had fallen from her eyes. She'd be here herself, soon enough—life was a one-way street.

And when she stepped into the shaded gloom of her mother's private apartment, she could tell Shirley Schaffer was circling the cul-de-sac. Her mother was sitting at the far end of the living area in a large fabric chair, facing the window, although with night falling, nothing could be seen outside. She stared out into the gray evening anyway, her hands resting across her lap with nothing to occupy them. For a moment, Grace saw not her mother but herself sitting in that chair, gazing out at a life unlived. If only she had found that Grail, if only Vic had left her when she was younger and better equipped for the unapologetic savagery of online dating, if only she'd been able to swallow her pride and stay at *Antiques Roadshow*.

"Grace?" Shirley sprang to her feet with a sudden burst of energy. "What are you doing here? Didn't the season just start?"

"I wanted to make sure you were settling in."

"You could have called, dear."

"You would have lied, Mom."

Shirley smiled, but that was as far as it went. It had always tantalized Grace—that thin twist at the corners of her mother's mouth was the only hint that something else lurked beneath the surface. Grace had always poked around that smile as a child, trying to pry it open, but it always vanished as quickly as it had appeared.

"Come in," Shirley said, walking to Grace with her thin arms outstretched. They hugged, and Grace was struck by how slight and delicate her mother felt. And how her hands lightly trembled against Grace's back.

"What a pleasant surprise," said Shirley, placing a brief kiss on Grace's cheek. "Let me show you around." She took Grace's arm and drew her deeper inside. "Here's my kitchen," she said. "Be careful—if you blink, you might miss it."

The kitchen—a short L-shaped counter, a single sink, and an oven—was a far cry from the granite counter expanse of her mother's kitchen at home. Grace had to remind herself that it was no longer a home, but a house she must sell, and soon.

"And here's my living room," Shirley said, drawing her a few steps into the center of the apartment, where a small fabric couch and a large reclining chair were angled around a glass coffee table. "It's nice, don't you think?"

Her mother was putting on such a brave face, beaming with pride at the tiny end table and the thirty-three-inch flat-screen television and the electric fireplace. Grace turned away, her nose twitching with the beginnings of a tear.

"It's okay, Gracie," Shirley said, taking Grace's hands in hers without a trace of her previous awkwardness. "This is for the best, I promise. It's just new, that's all."

"I'm sorry," said Grace, taking an offered tissue seemingly conjured out of thin air.

"It's really not so bad. Besides, it only takes ten minutes to clean the whole damn thing."

Grace laughed and blew into the tissue. "Thanks," she said, folding it up. "Where's the trash?"

But the tissue was already back in Shirley's hand and on its way to a silver trash can in the kitchen.

"I'm almost old enough to do that myself, you know."

"And I'm still young enough to do it for you."

Grace sighed, but this battle had never been won before, nor would it be today.

"Let me show you the bedroom," said Shirley, disappearing into the adjoining room. Grace followed her inside—as usual, the little that had been unpacked had been meticulously arranged on the built-in bookcase. But there was a tall stack of boxes still unopened in the far corner of the room.

Shirley noticed Grace eyeing the boxes. "I'm taking a break, Grace. Just settling in."

Grace didn't buy it. Shirley usually unpacked before locking the front door. *She doesn't know if she's coming or going*, Grace thought. *She's lost.*

"Let me help," said Grace, moving to the stack of boxes.

"I'll do that later. Please, Grace, let's just have a nice visit, okay?"

Grace chuckled to herself. They were good at awkward visits. Silent visits, sure. But a nice one?

"Why don't we sit down and talk about your new tour?" Shirley sat on the edge of the bed and patted it. Grace sighed, beaten, and joined her mother. The mattress felt surprisingly comfortable.

"Not bad, Mom."

"The show or the bed?"

"The bed." Grace laughed. "The show? Jury's still out on that one."

Shirley gazed at her for a long moment. "I'm proud of you."

Grace looked away, fidgeting. "For what? Hiding in a hole?"

"For starting again."

Grace caught sight of a picture on her mother's nightstand: a teenage Grace and graying Albert on the stairs of the Metropolitan Museum of Art; Grace all smiles and braces, Albert stiff and stern, anxious to return to the creation of some great work. "He never had to start again."

"He had his struggles, Grace."

Grace scoffed. "With what? Which publisher to choose?"

Shirley fell silent. "He struggled, sweetheart."

Grace shook her head. Albert Schaffer never struggled. He worked—hard; and she loved him for it. Even when he was sick, even at the very end, he taught, he published. He fought to the last breath. No, Grace's father did not struggle. And if he saw Grace now—saw her treading water, saw her struggling—he'd be anything but proud.

And he'd be right.

Grace felt something small and sharp prick her right in the middle of her chest, like the tiny shard of a jagged fingernail. Something had stung her. She reached up, searching for the eight-legged culprit, but her fingers wrapped around the necklace instead—it had caught on something, chafing against her skin. She would be glad to be rid of it. "Say, Mom," she said, sliding the necklace up over her head. "I almost forgot. I bought something for you." She placed the tarnished necklace in her mother's palm.

Shirley cupped it in both hands, as if it were some precious elixir. "My God, Grace," she said, tracing her thumb over the faded golden inclusions. "This is far too nice for me. Don't you want it?"

"I don't think so." Grace rubbed her chest. "It irritates me, for some reason. Maybe you'll have better luck with it."

Shirley held it up to the light; her hands were as solid as the stone itself. "It's the most beautiful thing I've ever seen. Don't you think?"

Grace just smiled. She was no longer worried about her mother's hands. She was worried about her eyes.

Grace slid behind the wheel of her car in the Mary Elwood parking lot, breathing a huge sigh of Clorox-free air. She reached over and fumbled inside her purse, searching in vain for her phone. Grace cursed herself—she always carried far too much: a penlight, a magnifying glass, polishing cloths, a library's worth of business cards, a tiny book of antique marks...

Her hands locked around something odd at the bottom. She groaned and drew it out.

It was the celestial globe.

"Jesus, Mom!" That woman was as stubborn as kudzu. Grace shouldn't have been surprised. This was par for the course—buy her a coat and it somehow ended up in your closet; treat her to dinner and she'd mail you a crate of Omaha Steaks.

What a martyr, Grace thought, fingering the faded blue-gray stone. If her mother had invested as much energy into a career as she did refusing presents, she'd be…

She'd be me.

Grace chuckled and tossed the pesky necklace back into her purse.

Yeah. Right.

Seven

Ten years younger—that was Grace's line in the sand, her Dating Rubicon. If any of her gentlemen callers were the smallest division of a hair less than ten years younger, they were immediately confined to the dustbin of history. Yes, they were young. And pretty. And flawless, like the Paragon Diamond. Not a blemish, not a mole, not a hair out of place.

Grace glanced over this evening's companion as if she were appraising Michelangelo's *David*, which was not far off. A taut waist, gently curving up to a toned trapezius, and not a single gray hair to ruin the ensemble. In fact, Grace was unsure if he had *any* hair below his perfectly drawn hairline. He didn't even snore, for God's sake, not a whisper. And the way he slept? Like a baby on Benadryl.

How? she thought, more than a little outraged. *I did all the work.*

Grace shifted around, rocking the bed to see if she could break his deep REM trance. Nothing. This one would sleep through the Apocalypse. Grace sighed (that didn't wake him, either) and closed her eyes, but she just couldn't fall back asleep.

It was too bright in her bedroom.

She threw aside the covers and slipped out of bed (no reaction from Rip Van Winkle) and padded over to the window, peeking behind the curtains. No moon, not even many stars to speak of. Grace wondered if it had been the lights from a passing truck or car, so she closed the curtains and looked back into the room.

Still too bright, she thought. She fumbled about in the shadows, searching for her phone on the dresser, but found its screen as dark as the room should have been. *Bizarre*, she thought, and wondered if it was just ambient light reflecting off her guest's freshly shaved derriere. She laughed out loud and quickly covered her mouth, although she knew that was probably an unnecessary precaution.

She resigned herself to yet another sleepless night and set her phone back down on top of her dresser. It knocked against something, making a small clinking noise.

The celestial globe.

It glowed, a pale, moonlight blue in the darkness, pulsing from some unseen source of light, almost as if, Grace thought—

As if it's breathing.

She looked closer at the necklace, coiled about itself in a twisted lump on the dresser, where Rip Van had discarded it in his rush to begin the evening's calisthenics. The light played off the black onyx, and the stones appeared to ripple in waves across the chain, ever so slightly, like the scales of a snake swaying to and fro, plotting its revenge for the indignity it had endured.

Grace reached out, half convinced it would rear up and strike her, sinking its fangs into her soft skin, but she pressed forward, cradling it in her hand, smoothing out the knotted string. She felt sorry for it—he had tossed it aside so quickly. Would he do the same to her if she gave him the chance? Would she blame him if he did?

She cradled the dull blue-gray stone in her hand, which now appeared more blue than gray. *Must be the light*, she thought. Reflecting off the surface of the lapis lazuli.

But it wasn't, and Grace knew it. The light had nothing to do with what she was seeing.

It was the stone.

Grace padded down the stairs, tying a soft silk robe about her waist. The final landing curved to the right, depositing her in the front parlor, with an open view of the living room beyond.

Victor sat in front of the red brick fireplace in his favorite spot—a deep-seated dark green Victorian lounge chair with thick twin-tower arms that made him look a little like Jack in the Giant's armchair. His blue silk pajama legs were crossed atop the matching settee, and his bare feet rubbed against each other as he pored over his laptop, typing away on what Grace knew would be another splendid *Roadshow* introduction. From his very first show as host, Victor had always written his own scripts, and Grace had always sat beside him, hypnotized by his fingers dancing across the keys as the facts and folklore of the next location sprang out of him. Although she yearned to sit beside him once again, to wrap herself in the comfort of his companionship, Grace was loath to step any closer, because she knew the spell would break and he'd disappear from her life once again.

She blinked and he was gone; as was his chair, but not the settee nor the rest of the furniture they had purchased together. He had let her keep it all, and although she was relieved to have had some continuity in the transition from "married" to "divorced," she soon realized her inheritance was cursed. The sofa was harder, the lamplight harsher, even the oils they had purchased together had dulled within their frames. Everything was as it had been before; yet nothing was the same. It felt to Grace as if the colors of her life had slowly drained out, leaving her to haunt the halls of a cold, empty husk of a home.

But there was one place that had always been hers alone, that had never shed its color, so she crossed through the parlor, past the double doors, and into her office. She eased the doors closed behind her and flipped on the light, illuminating the wood-paneled walls of what Grace had always called her Time Machine. In here she could travel to the Golden Age of Athens, to the passionate heart of the Renaissance, to the very center of nineteenth-century Impressionism. The machine's primary destination, of course, was neither Athens nor Florence nor Giverny.

It was New Jersey.

Grace's office was an exact carbon copy of her father's: from the wall-to-wall bookshelves to the choice of leather furniture, to the same gold leaf diplomas from the same gold leaf institutions. Aside from a framed *Roadshow* poster from her first season (which she couldn't bear to remove, even though the sight of it still stung like a canker sore), there was only one thing missing in this room, one single variation from the one in New Jersey—her father.

He was here in two dimensions, though—in a small silver-framed photograph beside her computer, always within eyesight while she worked. It was a picture of her as a young child, sitting between her father's legs on the steps of their home. Grace was leaning forward, chin out, all teeth and joy; and how could she not be, enclosed as she was on either side by her father's knobby knees. Albert's eyes had wandered away from the picture taker (her mother, Grace assumed), focusing instead on the gleaming arrowhead in Grace's palm. It shone in his eyes as well—her great discovery—and for a glorious snapshot second, they were fused together, father and daughter, bound within the ancient stone of that artifact.

Grace needed him now. The necklace made her uneasy. There was something dissonant about it; like a single note in a concerto struck ever so slightly sharp. She sat down at her desk and clicked on her strongest infrared lamp. The stone remained dull, its features muted. Instead of reflecting light, the stone absorbed it, barring Grace from teasing anything out of the blue-gray mass. Grace waited for the piece to reveal itself under the relentless infrared glare, but no answers rose to the surface. The stone was a blank, a cipher.

Grace sat back in her chair and sighed. Sometimes, appraisers projected their own desires onto an object, and Grace realized she was doing just that. She wanted the globe to mean something, and that was unfair to the object. Sometimes, as they say, a cigar is just a cigar, and an old stone is just a—

Grace shook her head. She had broken her own golden rule: Don't blame the object, blame the observation. She leaned forward once again, seeking not form but inconsistency. She started simply: a necklace consisting of a single string—an oddity in itself, as even a half-hearted copy would sport numerous chains, as was the custom. Why had this single string endured? Something on it had to have a special value—either to the wearer or the market for which it was made. The regular spacing of the black onyx set a visual rhythm to the piece, but that was not the melody of the thing.

It has to be the lapis.

The answer was hidden there, somewhere within that rock. Grace angled the lamp and inspected the central stone again, but it stood firm against her, as immovable as the rusted clasps that affixed it to the necklace.

That allowed the stone to rotate on the necklace.

That was the inconsistency, wasn't it? It was designed to spin on an axis, like a planet or a star or the great celestial galaxies themselves. But over time, the clasps had fused to the stone, halting its rotation, imprisoning it in space.

Poor thing, she thought. *It just gave up, didn't it?*

Grace sighed—she could sympathize. And although a few drops of white vinegar and baking soda might not remedy Grace's present situation, she knew it would dissolve the oxide of the clamps and release the bonds restraining the globe. Grace opened the top drawer of her desk and removed a small eyedropper, delicately squeezing out a few drops onto each side of the globe. It hissed as the oxide dissolved into a bright white salt, which Grace brushed away with a thin, delicate mohair brush.

She picked up the necklace with her left hand and the celestial globe dangled down, still frozen in space, immobile. But something about it had changed; Grace was sure of it. She touched the very tip of her right index finger against the lapis.

It's warm, she thought. Had it always been warm? She thought it had, but not like this. Ever so gently, for fear of breaking it, she pressed downward, but the stone refused to budge. Perhaps it was too far gone, too neglected for too long. Perhaps if she'd gotten to it sooner. Perhaps if she were smarter, a better appraiser. Perhaps if she were her husband—he was so good with jewelry. Perhaps if she were her father—he was so good with everything.

Perhaps if I were enough.

All of a sudden, Grace felt something deep within the stone . . . give.

The globe shifted beneath her finger, just a fraction of an inch. Grace gasped—even if it was just a copy, there was something, well, celestial about it. She spun it, just a little bit harder, and the globe began to rotate. The movement pleased her; there was a distant echo of something within it—an echo from her childhood—the first launch on a swing set, the first dive into a pool.

She spun again, harder this time, and it rotated faster, faster than Grace's finger pushed it, as if gaining its own momentum. Faster and faster it spun, and the golden pyrite inclusions began to ebb and flow, metamorphosing into dizzying, impossible constellations unlike any Grace had ever seen. The moment another one appeared on the face of the lapis, it instantly fractured, reanimating into a new system, spinning wildly, giving birth to another, then another. It was impossible to keep up, and Grace's eyes blurred with the speed of the globe as it strained against the chain, nearly ripping itself from her grasp.

Grace yanked her hand back and the globe slowed, coming to rest. She laid it back down on the desk, eyeing it as if it were an angry scorpion, stinger raised. She heard herself hyperventilating, her breath short and sharp. She had a sudden urge to back away, put some distance between her and whatever it was she'd released, but she'd been captured by it already; she had to know. Grace leaned over the globe, peering closer, breaking it apart in her mind, sifting through its mysteries: the sharp geometric angles of the stone, too perfect to be rough-hewn by clumsy human tools; the precise sparkle of the golden celestial shapes; at what appeared to be three dimensions within the blue stone itself.

But where do they lead? The closer she looked, the farther the constellations receded, as if she was the one pushing forward into that deep, terrible blue; as if it was giving way, yielding to her. No, not yielding.

Fusing.

Grace gasped and pawed at her eyes—something had burst within them, blinding her. She shut her eyes tight against it, as a hailstorm of color erupted with such violence it seared her, and she cried out. *Oh, dear God*—she thought—*macular hole?* Although it felt more like something sharp had torn through both retinas. The pain whirled about within her, slicing through the soft jelly, and her temples swelled, straining against the mounting pressure like the thinning skin of a Mylar balloon. It would rip any second. She would never see the sun again, no art, no oil, no color, no love.

And then, it was gone. The storm had simply vanished.

Grace stood frozen in darkness for a moment, terrified to open her eyes, unable to face the thick black curtain of blindness that waited patiently for her on the other side. Finally, she cracked open one eye and then the other. The occasional white floater still danced about before her, but her vision had mostly returned to normal. For a moment the reprieve seemed unreal, but then her stomach unclenched and her lungs filled with sweet breath. She felt her chest rise and fall, slower and slower, until all was still once more. It was over. Whatever had happened, it had passed. Everything was exactly as it had been.

Except the lapis lazuli of the celestial globe. It was still tarnished, it was still old, it was still everything that had led Grace to believe it was worthless. But it was nothing of the kind. Grace knew that, as sure as she knew that she had not experienced a phantom loss of vision. She had seen something deep within the pyrite inclusions of the necklace.

And it was brighter than the sun.

Part II
Line

One

Even after three days, Grace still saw the occasional floater, but her vision had otherwise returned to normal, so she decided the worst of whatever had happened was past.

Her recovery was in stark contrast to the declining fortunes of the Appraisal Experts Roadshow, which had set up shop in its second location of the season (and perhaps its last) in a crumbling parking lot across the street from the Sparta Avenue Stage in Sparta Township, New Jersey. The sixty-seat Sparta Stage specialized in magic shows, which Grace hoped might rub off on the show over the next two days. If not, they would be forced to perform the only trick they'd have left—disappearing back into the empty confines of their own galleries, which would, in turn, vanish as well.

Grace winced as she passed the few tiny pockets of dedicated antiquers who milled about outside the registration tent. Usually, a healthy crowd queued up for the hundred free appraisals given at the start of each show, but this group was in no danger of missing that cut. Grace counted no more than two dozen people as she passed into the main tent, where Elaine had gathered the eight appraisal experts for a pre-show strategy session.

This was the first time Grace had been this close to them, all together. She had kept to herself for the most part—not because she felt in any way superior to them—quite the contrary. Reputations contaminate by association, and Grace's still radiated with her humiliating retreat from *Roadshow*, the hermit-like withdrawal that followed, and the collateral damage her gallery had suffered as a result. She yearned to be part of a whole again, to feel a sense of belonging, but it wasn't worth the possibility she might be the cause in others of the very thing she'd been through herself. It made her feel terribly isolated, but just as Jonah hurled himself into the waters to calm the seas for his fellow crew, Grace remained aloof to spare her fellow experts the radioactive cloud that had gathered about her.

But the mandatory gathering made it impossible for her to keep her distance, so Grace sat down beside Patricia Rosenberg, their rare books and manuscripts expert. Pat's fellow experts had nicknamed her "Kenny Rogers," and like Mr. Rogers's song by the same name, Pat was a gambler; notorious for betting the farm on just an initial hunch, winning big and losing bigger. Grace knew her well enough from the conferences they'd attended—Pat worked hard and lived harder. She had grown up in a rough part of the Bronx in a broken home, but she was raised in the streets by the toughened kids who thrived there. Pat was roundly considered One of the Boys, and she could drink them under the table or take them upstairs, or both. Somehow, though, she was always surprisingly comfortable with the younger children who approached her at a show or conference. Grace knew it had nothing to do with any lack of maturity, and it was a mystery among the experts, but for some reason, Pat reserved what kindness she had for them.

She certainly hadn't saved it for Grace. When Grace arrived and gave Pat a nod and a smile, she was greeted with a side-eyed glare and stony silence.

"You all right, Pat?" Grace asked.

"Fine," she grunted, stalking off to the other side of the circle.

Grace turned to her left, to see if Henry Manfred had witnessed the outburst. Grace had met him only once before, but it was easy to remember his nickname: "Groucho." Henry was the spitting image of Mr. Marx, from the melodic burlesque tremolo of his voice to his jet-black mustache and fluttering Hershey Bar eyebrows. Henry handled toys, dolls, games, and collectibles, and always hitched a double entendre or raunchy joke to the caboose of every appraisal, making him a natural favorite to children of all ages.

"What's up with Pat?" Grace asked.

"Nothing a good company enema can't solve," he growled, before stalking off to the other side of the circle to join Pat. Grace wondered what she might have done to offend them—until she realized nearly everyone in the tent was glaring at her.

"One last thing," said Elaine as she wrapped up the morning meeting. "I know things look a bit on the bleak side right now, but bonding with our guests in a nonprofessional way will not make our state any better. It may even make it worse."

There was a good deal of grumbling in response, and Grace noticed a few more evil eyes come her way.

"We all massage a value every now and then," Elaine went on, looking directly at Grace. "But gross overvaluing of objects is not only unprofessional, it is a dereliction of duty. It hurts our clients when they insure their possessions, or God forbid, go to auction. It hurts this show—it sullies our reputation and puts the entire season in jeopardy. And it hurts you. Those foolish enough to do this will lose their professional memberships, the respect of their colleagues, the trust of their clients, the health of their galleries, and might even lose their license to auction. I strongly urge you—all of you—to respect your sacred responsibilities as good faith appraisers and resist the temptation to please your clients. You risk more than your career, I assure you."

The experts nodded and dispersed to their stations, leaving Grace alone and confused. Who had tattled on her? Certainly not Zwick—he had promised.

"I'll be watching you," snarled Pat as she stalked past. "Miss Crown Jewels."

"I'm really sorry, Pat. Honestly, I didn't mean to—"

"I saw you, Grace. You meant it." She leaned down, nearly close enough for their noses to touch. "You want to flush your career down the toilet more than you already have? Fine by me. Just don't flush ours, understand?"

Grace nodded and Pat huffed over to the Books and Manuscripts Table. Pat was right—Grace had meant it. Her value of the celestial globe was obscene, but to Grace, the numbers that had spewed out of her mouth had somehow felt...right. Something was terribly out of sync.

Grace had never been so thrown by an object before, so transfixed, and it had clouded her judgment. It had even clouded her eyes, conjuring visions that had thankfully evaporated in the sensible light of day. Besides, ever since her dramatic midnight encounter with the celestial globe, it had shown no signs of being anything other than what it was: a necklace. A strange necklace, yes, and she had initially boxed it back up until she could take the time to properly revisit its mysteries.

It was certainly pretty, though, she had to admit; far more attractive than she had originally thought. And every time she peeked into its box, just to make sure it had not gotten tangled or jarred, it looked that much lovelier. It seemed a shame to lock it up like that, such a pretty thing, which was probably why she'd recently found it dangling around her neck every now and then. She reached up and felt the smooth shape of it beneath her blouse.

Yes, she thought. *Lovely.*

"I pulled this off the marquee myself in 1973," said a wiry middle-aged man as he unrolled an old but expertly maintained concert poster across Grace's table. At the top of the poster, a beflowered hippie goddess held court, arms open and welcoming, her blue-and-yellow hair cascading down the sides of the print in psychedelic waves, forming an alphabet soup of headline groups, the theater name, and the dates of performance.

"I was working the concert that night," he said, his eyes twinkling with the memory. "And when the lights went down, I snuck inside to watch the whole thing."

"Incredible," said Grace, looking it over. This was something, finally. "It's a gorgeous print, in perfect condition. I see one or two bands of note listed on the poster, but the real star is your headliner—Jefferson Airplane." This was exciting, indeed, and the list of collectors who would be interested in an original poster of Airplane before they changed their name to Starship was far longer than the ponytail that wound down the aging hippie's back.

Grace leaned over the poster as the numbers clacked around inside her head. This was worth $800, $900, at the very least. "In terms of value," she said, drawing him closer. "If this was a poster from a larger, well-known venue, we'd be looking at a few hundred dollars, but this is even more impressive. To have a record of Jefferson Airplane playing to such a small house, when they were still at the very top of their popularity."

"But they didn't," he said.

"Didn't what?"

"Play. They canceled. Can't remember why."

Grace's shoulders slumped. "They didn't perform?"

"Nope," he said, smiling. "But who cares? It was the greatest thing I'd ever seen. I'd never heard music like that, not in Murfreesboro, that's for sure." He fiddled with an empty finger on his left hand. "I met my wife that night. She was an usher, too, and she snuck in right after I did. We huddled together in that back row, terrified we'd get caught, giggling like a couple of kids—which, I guess we were."

Now it made sense. Grace looked closer at the poster, at something she had thought to ask about, but had been distracted by the headlining group. "This is her, isn't it?" she said, pointing to a tiny, nearly invisible signature in the bottom-right corner.

He nodded, his bottom lip slightly trembling.

"Eleanor." Grace smiled. "What a beautiful name. And this is your first memory together."

"Yes," he said, rubbing his naked finger. "My favorite memory." He looked away, lost for a moment before shaking it off. "You were saying?" he asked, excitement rising. "What's it worth?"

Nothing, Grace thought, the word twisting around in her gut. It wasn't right. All that history, that miraculous curve of coincidence, that love—Grace could feel the sheer weight of it bearing down on her. But she laid it on the scale, and the scale said, *Nothing.*

But the scale was wrong; it was broken, it was foul. This relic of ink and paper had altered the direction of this man's entire life. It had brought two total strangers together and bound them in a love that endured half a century, surviving even the iron grasp of death itself. That poster was four hundred and twenty-three square inches of pure, distilled, unadulterated magic. That's what Grace thought.

But that thought was hers, his, and Eleanor's alone. Not the market's. And certainly not Patty Rosenberg's, who had taken great interest in Grace's appraisal from across the tent. They locked eyes (well, Pat's were locked and loaded), and Grace blinked first.

She's right, Grace thought. *You know she's right, so tell him.*

"Well, sir," she said, the words rising in her throat with the sting of acid reflux. "As much as I am personally moved by this incredible artifact of your life, posters like this—without any significant historical figures—do not actually carry a market value."

"So, then..." The smile slid from his face. "Nothing?"

"Well, no, not exactly." She felt a heat, warmth, again on her chest. *That rock*, she thought. That strange, beautiful rock. She touched it through her shirt, fingering the globe. *Maybe*, she thought, *Maybe if I...*

But Grace was wrong. And the market was right.

"But, yes—for the purposes of auction or sale," she said, deflating, "it has no monetary value. Less than a dollar."

The man sighed and stuffed the poster back into a frayed cardboard tube, tossing his ponytail back as if it were a mosquito buzzing about his neck.

Grace felt like a thief—she had stolen something dear and beloved from that poor man. But she was determined to be a Good Girl, and so she was, all morning long, deflating expectations one broken heart at a time. All received the value of their antiques by book, chapter, and verse (to the cruel red cent), and all left Grace's table with their heads held low and their possessions held lower. Grace felt she had failed them all—they had placed their faith in her and she had ground it to dust. But at least she was accurate. And employed. Grace would keep her job, maybe pick up a client or two for her gallery, and the rest of the experts would stop glaring at her as if she had left a puppy on the side of a rural highway.

Besides, her appraisals had begun to feel familiar once again; the initial awkwardness was gone, the facts flowed freely, and her heart stopped racing with every new object. And now that she had stopped sweating so much, particularly between her breasts, the stone between them had grown as cold as her appraisals. Grace had wrapped her fingers around it, desperate for the calming touch of it, but she was unable to revive it. Grace Schaffer had even disappointed a stone, for God's sake. And although that might have been her cruelest trick of all, if it meant she had finally settled into her rightful place at the show, it was probably for the best.

Soon Grace forgot all about what was fair and what was unfair, and all was well until Pat decided to spend her break leaning against the support pole just behind Grace's table, sipping her coffee and mumbling the occasional snarky comment. Grace was in the midst of explaining to a bespectacled woman that her cherished velvet painting of Elvis and Jesus might have been worth more without the savoir himself in frame.

"*Without* Jesus?" the woman asked in absolute incredulity.

"Well, there are indeed collectors for these types of paintings, but they really do prefer the subject remain the King himself."

"But that is the King," the woman said. "Both Kings."

"Of course," agreed Grace, treading carefully. "But Elvis collectors are understandably focused on the King of Rock and Roll."

"Well, that's a one-way ticket to Hell, if you ask me," she said, gazing down with great affection at the velvet glory between them. "So then, what might this be worth?"

Pat called out from her perch, "A fill-up at your local Chevron station."

The woman straightened the spectacles on her quivering nose. "A fill-up?" she gasped. "Is that all?"

"No, of course not," said Grace, desperately trying to regain control. "The value would depend on any number of things."

The woman snatched the painting up off Grace's table as if saving it from the fires of Perdition itself and stormed off, stroking the back of the painting as if to comfort the bruised egos of the velvet Kings within.

Grace spun back on Pat, incensed. "That was unnecessary and cruel."

Pat scoffed. "She was a quack."

"I was handling it."

"You were flailing—I saw you. You felt sorry for her."

"So?"

"That's not your job."

"My job is to give her a value, and I was—in my own time. Not your time."

"My time?" Pat stood up, off the pole. "What the hell do you mean, my time?"

Grace stood tall herself. "There's a way to do this without being an asshole."

"Not for you," said Pat, coming closer. "You'd light a match under the whole show just so you could feel better about yourself." She tossed her coffee cup into the trashcan beside Grace's station, leaning in for one last dig. "And if you think a smile or two from a thankful guest is going to erase the mess you've made of your life, you're as screwy as that Velvet Elvis."

Pat marched back to Books and Manuscripts, leaving Grace seething. If Peppermint-Mouthed Patty wanted to compare messes, Grace was happy to oblige. She excused herself from her next customer, grabbed her own cup of tasteless black coffee, and planted herself on the metal pole behind Patricia's station.

A woman in her late thirties was first in line, and she placed a colorful book with a frayed dust jacket before Pat. It was a children's book, clearly well read, and the cover was dominated by a blond-haired jester in a red-and-blue motley outfit, laughing freely atop a medieval castle.

"Hmm," said Pat, checking the inside jacket. "I'm not familiar with this one."

"*The Jester Has Lost His Jingle*," Grace catcalled from her perch.

"Yes," Pat said, jaw clenched. "We can all read the giant title. Thank you, Grace."

"What else can you tell her about it, Patty?" Grace asked, flashing a Cheshire grin.

Pat fumbled for her laptop.

"I'll give you a hint," said Grace. "It's by David Saltzman, both words and illustration."

"Thank you, Grace. I can see that myself, right here on Google," Pat said, clicking about, trying desperately to catch up with the appraisal. "As well as its... well, it won quite a few awards, didn't it?"

"Yes," said the woman, perking up. She pointed to the inside cover, which Pat had left open. "And it's signed, as you can see."

"By the author?"

The woman hesitated.

"No, Pat," said Grace. "David died writing that book. His family completed it after he lost his own battle with cancer, which is what the book's about." Grace halted, struck herself by the book's message: "How to recover your 'jingle' when life wrests it away." Grace took a few steps in, leaning over the book. "I think that's actually his mother's signature, yes?"

"It is," said the woman. "We saw her read it at a hospital and she was kind enough to sign it for us."

"Well then," said Pat, elbowing Grace out of the way. "It's not signed by the author himself, not a first edition, its condition ranks it as a 'Fair Book' at best, so unfortunately—"

Pat froze as a small figure emerged from behind the wide skirt of the woman. It was a young girl, about nine years old. She was wearing a skirt herself, the twin to her mother's, and a frilly blouse brimming with flowers the same deep red as the Jester's motley. The girl's skin was white as porcelain, perhaps too white, and her eyes were a brilliant, expectant blue. Those eyes would have been enough to grab anyone's attention, but it was not what grabbed Pat's.

It was the shine of the girl's clean, bald head.

"Hello there, miss," said Pat, her voice softening. "What's your name?"

"Jody," said the girl.

"It's very nice to meet you, Jody." Pat hunched down, bringing herself closer to the girl's eye level. "Are you making sure your mother doesn't get into trouble?"

"Trying." Jody giggled. "It's not easy."

Grace stood back, fascinated. This was a very different Pat, as if the venom had suddenly drained out of her.

The girl's mother took Jody's hand. "You were saying, Ms. Rosenberg?"

Pat's lips tightened against her smile. "Saying?"

"The book isn't what?"

"Oh." Pat faked a cough, buying time. "Yes, well, the book isn't exactly..."

Grace had never seen her struggle like this. She leaned back against the tent pole, enjoying the view of Pat roasting on a spit—until she caught a glimpse of the girl, resplendent in frills and hope.

So much for revenge, she thought.

"Pat means to say it isn't something we've seen before," Grace said. "We probably need another once-over before we hazard a guess as to its value. Wouldn't you say, Pat?"

"Absolutely," she replied, relieved for the extra time. "Let's take another look." She scanned the dust jacket, her fingers gravitating toward the small tears and folds that marred it. "So there are, you know, a few blemishes on the jacket."

The girl's smile sank.

"But that's okay," said Pat. "That's not all we have to go on. Let's look at the cover." She unfolded the front sheaf of the jacket to check the condition of the cover, which was in even worse shape than the jacket. "Let's not look at the cover." She replaced the jacket and smoothed it with her hand, unable to meet the child's eyes.

"It's okay, miss," said Jody. "I've heard worse things, I promise."

Grace watched in silence, stunned by Pat's inability to finish the appraisal. Pat, who could handle anything short of a gang fight, and probably come out with a push there as well. Pat, who grew up between a sewer and a prison cell.

That's it! thought Grace. "Why don't you tell her the kind of things you heard, Pat? When you were a little girl."

Pat glared at Grace, offended and confused, until something clicked into place. She turned back to Jody, walking around the table to kneel beside her. "You've heard some bad things recently, haven't you, Jody?"

The girl nodded.

"I did, too, when I was your age. People called me a loser. Said I didn't belong in school, didn't belong out of jail, didn't even belong in this job." She took the girl's tiny hand in hers. "So I know a little, I think, maybe just a little bit of how you feel. And that's why I don't want to disappoint you. But if I do, maybe your mommy can make it all better?"

Jody nodded.

Pat took in a huge breath, the breath that would surely break the little girl's heart, but it stuck in her chest. "I got a little problem, though," she said. "You see, I never had anyone I could turn to for help myself, so I'm not very good at asking for it. In fact, I'm pretty awful at it." She turned around, glancing up at Grace.

Oh, no, Grace thought. *That's not fair.* Grace would play footsies with the numbers. Grace would take the fall. Grace would get fired so

Pat could go home knowing she had brightened the ever-darkening days of that desperate little girl. But seeing the battle between hope and despair that raged within that little girl, Grace decided she'd had enough of what was fair and what was unfair.

"Say, Pat," Grace said, taking Pat's spot behind the appraisal table. "Would you mind if I took a look?"

"Not at all," said Pat, looking like she'd rather hug than kill Grace for the very first time.

Grace placed a hand on the book, lightly brushing her fingers over the rips, the cuts, the marks on jacket, cover, spine, and page. "It appears our hands are a bit tied here," she said. "We judge a book, any book—published today or two hundred years ago—by the same criteria. Its condition must be absolutely perfect."

"And this isn't?" asked Jody.

"No," said Grace, lowering her voice to a whisper. "Then again, there are always exceptions."

"There are?"

"Of course," said Grace. "If I were to bring a valuable book that had been in the possession of, say, Julia Child—that's a very famous chef, Jody—I'd expect it to be—"

Pat smacked her forehead, as if she should have thought of it herself. "It'd be covered in sauce."

Jody giggled. "That's totally gross!"

"But totally valuable," said Grace. "Now, where did you get this book?"

"In the Cancer Center. Mrs. Saltzman came and gave it to us."

"And what happens in the Cancer Center?"

"They give us a bunch of stinky pills, and chemo, and a million blood tests."

"Not exactly a kitchen, but..."

"But totally gross, too!"

"That's right," said Grace. "So if we take that into consideration—"

Jody gasped. "We're as good as a dirty cookbook!"

"We're better." Grace opened the book to the inside cover end-paper, where Barbara Saltzman had signed the book. "Do you see this signature?"

"Sure, that's David's mom."

"Can you tell me what it says?" Grace spun it around for the girl.

" 'Never lose your jingle! Love, The Jester's Mother, Barbara Saltzman.' "

"That's right, *The Jester's Mother*," said Grace. "My cousin has a copy, and it's signed by Mrs. Saltzman, too. I was there the day she signed it, and she signed dozens that day." Grace leaned forward, speaking just for Jody as if it was their little secret. "But she signed it the way she always signs it: 'The Jester's *Mom*.' "

"Not '*Mother*'?"

"Nope."

Pat broke in, "This is a one-off?"

"One of a kind," said Grace. "But this book—your book—is more than the signature, more than the pages, more than the illustrations or the verse or the funny hats."

Jody giggled. "The hats are pretty funny."

"They made you laugh?"

"Yeah."

"In the Cancer Center—in that scary place. This book made you laugh?"

"Yeah, it did." A smile broke across her tissue paper cheek. "It still does."

"Then I'd say this book has extraordinary power. A power people would pay dearly for." Grace closed the book, winding up for the finale. "So you see, Jody, your book is as well maintained as a totally gross cookbook, it has a one-of-a-kind signature, and it has the power to make us laugh, even in our darkest moments."

"Do you know what it's worth?"

"I do." Grace instinctively put her hand to her chest. The stone of the celestial globe felt warm again, hot beneath her blouse. She took it out, hoping it might cool away from her skin.

"Oh," cooed Jody. "That's awfully pretty."

"Isn't it?" Grace spun the lapis lazuli slowly on its axis. The tent lights flickered off its tiny-angled faces, and for a moment, Grace fell into it, into the shimmering blue. She could hear it too, just above the silence, a hum so low, but all around her, passing through her as if her body were no bar against it, and with every turn of the lapis, it wound around her, tighter and tighter. It should have scared her, but it felt strangely comforting, even pleasurable, so she continued to rotate it as she placed her other hand upon the book. "Well then," she said, aware the eyes of Jody and her mother and Pat and the crowd in line behind them were all fixed upon her. "Taking everything into account, at auction, with the right buyers in the audience or online, I'd place the preliminary estimate on this book as . . ."

Jody's eyes said, *A hundred dollars.*

Her mother's said, *Higher.*

Pat's said, *As high as you can.*

Grace said, "Five thousand dollars."

The girl's mother gasped and dropped to her knees, right beside her daughter. "Five?"

"Thousand," said Grace.

"Oh my gosh!" Jody cried, jumping up and down. "Thank you, thank you, thank you!" She leapt into her mother's arms, and the two of them whirled around, laughing so hard and spinning so fast, even cancer could not keep up.

Pat looked stunned, misty-eyed and speechless for the first time in her life.

I'm as good as fired, thought Grace.

But as she watched mother and daughter twirl around the room as if it were their own private ballroom, she wondered if the view alone might almost be worth it.

Oh yes, thought Grace. *It's more than worth it.*

As sweet as it was, though, it stung; just a little. Grace's parents had never been liberal with their hugs. It wasn't that Albert never hugged, but it was terribly rare—his heart string vibrated at a frequency that very few things could pluck. Her mother... well, she always seemed a little afraid to hug, as if Grace were a blowfish and might sting. Grace had wondered if that would change as she aged, if the two of them might move past the blank white noise of an awkward childhood.

But childhood ended, and the white noise played on.

Two

Stephens Academy was one of the most prestigious private schools in eastern New Jersey, which is precisely why Grace hated it. The New York Public School System had been good enough for her father, so naturally, it was good enough for her. Although her mother had waxed poetic (or at least repeatedly) about the glory of private school, Grace had successfully avoided it throughout kindergarten, elementary and middle schools, but high school had become her Waterloo. Her mother wanted Stephens, Grace wanted nothing to do with it, and her father wanted nothing to do with either of them during the slugfest, so Shirley won the field. Grace's only consolation was that her mother would have to accompany her to Freshman Open House the Saturday before classes began, and no one felt more uncomfortable on such an outing than Shirley Schaffer.

Except Grace. She hung back and watched, nauseated, as a crowd of obscenely over-proud parents inched down the receiving line of teachers, who hugged the new arrivals as if welcoming them to a therapy support group—which Grace presumed she would need if this kind of Kumbaya campfire was what Stephens had in store for her. She had expected stiff bow ties and high-neck collars, hard pews and harder lectures from stentorian octogenarians, but the clothes were casual, the seats were padded, the conversation familiar, and the headmistress looked as imposing as a labradoodle. If Grace was being dragged away from the path her father had followed, she at least deserved some good old-fashioned academic menace in return—rules, regulations, the challenge of an impossibly stacked schedule, perhaps the inferred threat of a paddle hung over a teacher's desk—not a gentle squeeze from a cardigan sweater. She overheard one teacher chortle on and on about how she learned as much from her students as they learned from her. Grace could scarcely wait for that Intellectual Valhalla.

She had lost contact with her mother when Shirley was mauled by the biology teacher, so Grace withdrew and planted herself by the entrance, waiting for her father to arrive from his office at Columbia. She couldn't wait to see his response to all the chest thumping and back stroking. Perhaps he might even relent and let her resume the schooling of her choice.

He would not arrive soon enough. One of the teachers spotted Grace and made a beeline straight for her, arms cranking open for a mighty hug.

"Welcome!" she said, clamping her arms around Grace's shoulders. There was no way to avoid it; before she knew what was happening, Grace found herself planted nose first into the woman's hair bun, which reeked of incense and potpourri.

"Thank you," Grace said, leaning back to get a look at the woman's paper name tag, which read: VIRGINIA ANDERSON, UPPER SCHOOL ART. "Mrs. Anderson."

"*Dr.* Anderson," she said, her chest puffing up like a pigeon's.

So this is my art teacher, Grace thought, a young woman condemned.

"You're Gracie Schaffer, aren't you?"

Grace pointed to her name tag, suddenly pleased to have it. "Grace."

"Grace, yes, very good, very good." Anderson looked Grace over as if she were an exotic creature. "I recognized you from the photo roll. I'm terribly excited to have you in class next week."

"I'm excited, too." And she was—even if *Dr.* Anderson was teaching it. It was an advanced class in the Italian Renaissance, which had scared away enough juniors and seniors that Grace was able to add it to her schedule. "Thank you for adding me."

"How could I not?" she asked, incredulous. "The daughter of Albert Schaffer?"

Grace smiled—perhaps Anderson wasn't so bad after all.

"I was fortunate enough in college to see him present a paper on Rosetti at the Tate. I'd never seen anyone so passionate about art. I'm not sure I have since."

Grace agreed and told her he was just like that at home. That fatherhood lit the same fuse beneath him that John Everett Millais's *Ophelia* did. The more you repeat a lie, she figured, the closer it bends toward truth.

Before she swooned from an overdose of incense, Grace politely excused herself to find her mother. She threaded through the boisterous crowd of Stephens's newest citizens as they exchanged names and numbers, the parents all handshakes and smiles, the students clustered in tight-knit packs of twos and threes. But Grace knew from experience she would not find her mother here, so she scanned the periphery of the auditorium, along a line of empty chairs, until she spotted the telltale sign of a beehive hairdo.

Shirley sat still as a statue in one of the chairs, ramrod straight, hands crossed atop her crossed legs. Her eyes flickered from student to parent, from teacher to teacher, as if she were looking through thick glass at animals in a zoo. But the longer Grace watched her, the more she began to wonder exactly which side of that glass her mother occupied. It felt wrong to study her like that, an intrusion, so Grace broke the spell and walked over, plopping down beside her. "What'cha doing all the way over here, Mom?"

"Oh, you know," she said, snapping out of the trance with a blink of her eye. "Just waiting for your father."

"You could have mingled while you waited. Introduced yourself to a teacher or two."

"Oh lord, no," she said, as if Grace had mentioned an ancient taboo.

"I wasn't suggesting you sleep with them, Mom."

They both laughed and the awkwardness broke, for the loveliest of moments. Then Shirley's smile waned and her nose twitched. "Is that a new perfume, dear?" she asked.

"Lovely, isn't it?" chuckled Grace. "It's my art teacher. I think she moisturizes with frankincense and wood chips. Want to meet her?"

"Mrs. Anderson?"

Grace was impressed; her mother had done her homework. "*Dr.* Anderson, if you don't want to get paddled. Come on, I'm sure she has a big hug waiting just for you."

"Oh no, dear. Not without your father."

"He can meet her when he comes. She'd love a private audience with him, believe me."

"No, that's a special moment for the both of you. I can wait."

"Okay, fine," sighed Grace. She thought of suggesting they take a walk, tour the campus, just talk. But she couldn't imagine what that might look like. They did things, accomplished tasks, but other than that, they didn't really share anything. Except—

"Ah, there he is," Shirley said, perking up.

Albert strode through the double doors of the auditorium, his spit-shined black shoes cracking like gunfire on the parquet floor. As he swept through the crowd, he appeared to Grace like a lofty peak, high above the fray, and he easily spotted them over the heads of the other parents. Grace could not wait to show him off to teacher and student alike, but he pressed right past her, taking Shirley's hand in his.

"I'm so sorry, Shirl," he said. "I was struggling with that damn proposal. I lost track."

Shirley cut him off with an easy wave of her hand. "Of course, dear. I know."

Albert turned to his daughter. "Lead on, Grace. I follow."

Grace's heart thumped against her breastbone. Too giddy to speak, she simply nodded and started off toward the receiving line.

They did not make it very far. Virginia Anderson had been lying in wait behind the punchbowl, and swooped over, sliding in between Grace and Albert.

"Excuse me, Dr. Schaffer," she said, rising slightly on her tiptoes to greet him. "I'm Dr. Virginia Anderson, Chair of Upper School Art. What a sincere pleasure to meet you."

She tilted forward at the waist, diving in for a hug like a drinking bird toy, and Albert stepped back, deftly avoiding it. "The pleasure is all mine, Dr. Anderson," he said, nostrils flaring as if he smelled a gas leak.

"As I'm sure Grace has told you, I was able to sneak her into my upper-level Renaissance class this fall." She turned to Grace with a self-important grin. "I very much look forward to teaching her," she said, patting Grace's head as if she were a dog in need of encouragement.

Grace reddened as a brushfire of hot anger raced across her chest. She couldn't bear to look at her father, but she could feel his gaze upon her. Then she felt it shift back to Anderson.

"Is that so?" he said, every word sharpened to a pinprick. "Teach her what, if you don't mind my asking?"

Anderson coughed up an anxious laugh. "Excuse me?"

"What precisely do you intend to teach my daughter?" he asked. "I perused your biography on the Stephens website. You studied Modern and Contemporary Art at the University of Southern Vermont, which, I believe, is neither a university in the truest sense, nor the southern part of Vermont in any sense." He stepped in, braving the noxious cloud of potpourri. "My daughter has studied—not read, but studied, mind you—every significant volume on the Italian Renaissance from—" He paused, turning to Grace. "Well, I've lost track. What have you read, my dear?"

The shame drained from Grace's cheeks, and she stepped forward, right beside her father, feeling so tall, almost as tall as he. "Well, Baxandall, of course," she said.

"I read Baxandall in high school," Anderson snapped. "Everyone does."

"I started with Baxandall." Grace smiled. "In fifth grade. Then I went on to Vasari, Cennini, Alberti—"

"That exquisite paper on Brunelleschi's Dome," Albert added.

"I'd forgotten King, that's right," Grace said.

"And Plumb."

"And Unger."

And on they went, back and forth, playing off each other like two instruments tuning to the same key. And as they neared the last title, Grace wished she had read one or two more, just to sustain the thrill of vibrating beside him on the same string.

"And I just finished Gilio's *Dialogue on the Errors and Abuses of Painters*," she said, putting a reluctant coda on their performance. "But it's really more a treatise on the rise of the Counter-Reformation."

Albert reached out and nearly—very nearly—took Grace's hand. "You see what I mean?" he said, turning back to Anderson, the right edge of his lips curling up into something that looked suspiciously like a grin. "It's easy to lose track with Grace. I'd say you have your work cut out for you . . . *Doctor*."

"Yes," said Anderson, a bit dazed. "I look forward to the challenge."

She did not look forward as she excused herself, however, running smack into an empty chair, and then a passing teacher before stumbling off into the crowd.

Her father's hand had fallen away, but Grace didn't care. For the first time in her life, he hadn't treated her like a daughter; he had stood beside her as a fellow academic. *As an equal*, she thought, and her vision blurred. She felt dizzy, perhaps even tipsy.

She was hooked.

Grace turned and noticed her mother was smiling at them, and although it looked quite alien, stretching as it did across a canvas unused to such displays, it somehow looked very much at home. Their eyes met for the briefest of moments, and in a flash, Shirley looked away.

But Grace had caught something. Something her mother—who

had always been so careful, so guarded—had not wanted her to see. This was not the glance behind a thick glass window, no survey or examination. But Grace's gifts were still in their infancy, and before she could excavate any deeper, the evening was called to order by the headmistress, and all attention turned to the podium in the center of the auditorium. Grace would have to solve her mother's puzzle another day.

It wasn't going anywhere.

Three

Grace stared at an uneaten plate of food in the company lunch tent. Her stomach growled in distress at the chicken parmesan, but she didn't feel the least bit hungry—she was still digesting the *Jester* appraisal.

Pat plopped down directly across from her and slid a Styrofoam cup toward her. Grace took a sniff, and her nostril tingled with the sharp aroma of cheap whiskey. "Thanks," she said, taking a sip and savoring the sudden warmth that spread across her chest. For once, it wasn't the necklace.

Grace reached for it—it was cold now. She figured she'd leave it out; it went well with her outfit. In fact, Grace thought it went well with a number of her outfits. Maybe it was just the light in the break tent, but it sparkled against her blouse, as if lit from within.

"Don't expect me to apologize," said Pat.

"I'm not asking you to."

"And I'm still not sure I like you. Not even a little."

"Right back at you."

Pat lifted her cup, saluting Grace. "You're one cool bitch, Schaffer."

Grace laughed. "I can't tell you how much more I prefer that to 'Crown Jewels.' "

They both laughed as Jerome Zwick came over with a full plate.

"Is it safe to sit, or are you two still hovering on the brink of a China Syndrome?"

"Sit," said Pat. "Before you get too old to bend those knobby knees of yours."

Jerome sat as Elaine came over, plopping down at the table. "You two sure made a few fans today," she said. "That sweet mother and daughter couldn't stop raving about you."

Grace and Pat shared a quick, anxious look. "What'd they say?" asked Grace.

"Just how kind you were."

"This was *Pat* they were talking about, right?" asked Jerome.

Elaine continued, spearing a piece of chicken, "And how knowledgeable." She popped a large piece in her mouth.

"And?" Grace leaned in, preparing for the worst.

Elaine held up her hand and continued chewing, and chewing, and chewing.

"Just swallow the damn thing, Lain!" said Pat.

"Jesus," Elaine mumbled, before finally swallowing. "And nothing. That was all they said about you, okay?"

Grace shot a relieved look at Pat, whose face was beet red from holding her breath.

Elaine dabbed the side of her mouth with a napkin. "Then they asked me where they should go to auction."

Four

Grace, Jerome, Pat, and Elaine stood shoulder to shoulder outside the entrance to Bonhams Skinner Auctions, lined up as if to defend a penalty kick. The unassuming gray building rose behind them, a modest, single-story structure that would not be out of place in an industrial park. The auction houses of America, like the majestic and mundane objects within them, came in all shapes and sizes—from the palatial towers of Sotheby's and Christie's in Manhattan to the strip malls and office parks of Main Street. Some specialized in farm equipment, others real estate or autos, but the larger regional ones—whose reputation reached across state lines and tax brackets—were the lifeblood of the industry. Over the years, these historic houses carved out their own niches within the market: Heritage with collectibles, Swann with rare manuscripts and papers, Doyle with jewelry, and Bonhams Skinner with Americana, furniture, and fine art. Bonhams had earned a particular reputation as a house for unique and unexpected treasures—but you'd never know by looking at it. Its corrugated cement walls could have held anything from auto parts to office supplies, but hidden within sprawled a seventy-thousand-square-foot series of auction rooms, galleries, and warehouses, teeming with eight-figure oil paintings from European and American masters, rugs and lush carpets from exotic times and places, and jewelry from the Far East, Near East, Southwest, and any other direction where a precious stone was only a fraction of the value. More importantly to Grace, it held the auction room that Jody and her mother, Gloria, would soon visit; the room that would spell doom for the Appraisal Experts Roadshow and, with it, the end of her career. Perhaps, Grace thought, even the end of her.

"Any sign of them?" asked Pat, sneaking a quick tug from a small, shiny flask.

"Not that I can see," said Elaine, squinting through the line of buzzing people that threaded around them.

"Maybe they're already inside."

"Not likely," grumbled Jerome. "We've been here since noon, for God's sake."

"Quit bitching," said Pat. "No one asked you to come."

"No one asked you to put a four-figure value on a four-dollar book."

"Wasn't me." Pat jerked a thumb at Grace. "Talk to Crown Jewels over there."

"Who put her up to it?" snapped Elaine.

"No one," said Grace. "I knew what I was doing. Look, I appreciate you all coming here, but none of this is necessary. This was my call. Why don't you let me handle it?"

"Fine by me," said Pat.

Jerome yanked the flask out of her hand. "If she goes, you go, Patty. It was your table. You could have jumped in at any time and corrected her. Why didn't you?"

Pat snatched the flask back. "'Cuz she was fucking right."

"There they are!" said Elaine, pointing to the far end of the parking lot.

Although it was a full week and a half later, Jody and Gloria were dressed identically once again, in twin powder blue flower printed dresses. The girl's smile was resplendent, shining even brighter than her bare head in the sunshine. It made Grace's task all the more unbearable.

"C'mon, Pat," said Grace. "Let's get this over with."

Pat fortified herself with a pull from the flask as they started off, but after a few steps, Grace noticed her lagging behind. The closer they came to the little girl, the paler she became. All the bravado had drained out, leaving only the blank resigned look of the condemned.

Grace placed a gentle hand on Pat's shoulder, halting her. "Why don't you let me take it from here?"

Pat hesitated.

"You can still hate my guts if you want."

Pat sized her up with what looked just a little bit like awe. "You're taking all the fun out of it, Grace." She nodded her thanks and held back as Grace continued on, directly into the path of Jody and Gloria.

"Mrs. Schaffer!" Jody screamed, skipping over to Grace. "Do you work here, too?"

"No," said Grace, gathering her courage. "I just came to speak to you and your mommy."

"Can you speak to us on our way in?" asked Gloria, checking her watch. "The auction starts in fifteen minutes."

"That's what I wanted to talk to you about."

"Is there something wrong?"

"Not with the auction," said Grace, not daring to look at Jody. "With my appraisal."

"Oh, don't worry," said Jody, taking Grace's hand. "Even if we get half of what you said, I get to keep going to the Cancer Center."

Grace hazarded a look down at the little girl. "Keep going?"

"Yup," Jody said. "For as long as I need. Right, Mom?"

"That's right, sweetheart," said Gloria, lowering her voice for Grace's ears only. "You came to us just in time, Ms. Schaffer. If you hadn't..."

Gloria trailed off, unable to say what Grace had already surmised. Without a sale today—and a big one—Jody was not returning to the Cancer Center. She was returning home, which would almost certainly be her final destination. Gloria had placed her happiness and Jody's health in Grace's hands, and Grace had failed them both before the first bid.

"What'd you want to tell us, Mrs. Schaffer?" asked Jody, walking between Grace and her mother.

Grace looked at them, so hopeful, so blissfully unaware. "I just want you both to know—I meant what I told you, about your book. But that's me. That's how I see it. And I'm not everyone."

"I wish you were," said Jody. "You're a very nice lady."

I'm a very foolish lady, she thought. *And you're about to learn just how foolish.* "Good luck in there, Jody," she said, knowing all the luck in the world wouldn't raise the value of that book by a single penny.

Jody thanked her and gave Pat a rapid-fire hug on her way past. "See you inside, Patty!"

Pat opened her mouth to protest, but all that came out was: "Sure thing, kid."

Gloria hustled her daughter out of the parking lot, up the short path, and in through the double doors, easily splitting the porous picket line of Elaine and Jerome, both of whom simply moved aside and waved.

Grace and Pat walked back and joined them, beaten.

"Sorry, folks," Grace said.

"Don't be," said Elaine. "You didn't see either of us throwing ourselves in front of that bus."

Grace turned to Jerome. "Looks like you're our only hope. Any last tricks up your sleeve?"

"Maybe," he said. "If I know the auctioneer."

Elaine thumbed through the Bonhams Auctions Announcement web page on her phone. She clicked on *Fine Books & Manuscripts, Marlborough, Mass., 6 May, 12:00 EDT* and raced down the various lots until she found what she was looking for. "How about Nanette Bouchard? Do you know her?"

"Yeah. I know Nan." Jerome sighed, turning toward the front door. "Let's see if she still hates my guts."

Five

Nan Bouchard still hated Jerome Zwick's guts.

And she told him so, repeatedly and enthusiastically. After three decades in the business, Nan had grown the thick skin required to be a head auctioneer, so she could forgive and forget most things—particularly with Jerome, who had fought beside her in the trenches for many years. She might even have forgiven him for leaving her without a tribal arts expert during a tremendous spike of public interest. But there was one thing she could not, would not forgive.

"You ran," she whispered, her words stalactites as they stood together on the steps that led up to the auction dais. "Off to a no-name show in the middle of nowhere."

"I needed to slow down. And you needed a younger expert."

"Bullshit. You ran."

"It was tough, after Nora passed. You know that."

"You gave up," she said. "She would have hated that."

"What's the point?" he said. "I'm never going to find it, Nan. I had my chance."

She halted, her words defrosting a few degrees. "You're not a quitter, Jer—at least I thought you weren't. You never quit on Nora. Not even at the end."

"Nora was worth it."

"Aren't *you*?" She shook her head and sighed. "Look, I have to start us up, okay?"

"Just one last thing," he said. "About Lot 22—"

"Too late, Jerry. It's in the program, so we're going fishing. If nothing comes of it, nothing lost, nothing gained, right?"

"Not in this case, Nan. Please."

"I have to go." She brushed past him, ascending two steps to the stage of the auction dais: a large, raised platform at the front of the hall. She took her place at a cherry wood lectern embossed with SKINNER MARLBOROUGH in raised bronze letters, flanked by two shorter lecterns. Behind them sat two assistants flittering away at their laptops, ensuring the video transmission was up and running for the hundreds of online bidders who preferred to battle from the comfort of their own homes. The dais overlooked a modest-size hall, seating just about fifty people, who sat in rows of thinly padded black chairs with their heads in their programs, all making furious notes about which lots they would bid, and how high they might be prepared to go.

These people would not go very high.

These were not the crowds of the historic Skinner House in Boston, or Christie's, and certainly not the Brahmins of Sotheby's. These were everyday Janes and Joes, who arrived not by town car, but by train and Prius, dressed not in suits and cocktail dresses, but in polos and sensible slacks. But just like their distant cousins at Sotheby's, they had all heard the call—a siren song that could, for an afternoon, draw the curtain on their everyday lives as realtors, teachers, or insurance agents, transporting them to a dazzling realm of art, artists, and those like-minded pilgrims who had acquired a soul-depth appreciation of both. They had learned a little bit about the little bits that fascinated them—dipping their toes in an online auction, sneaking into the back row of a live auction or two, and when their fascination overwhelmed their insecurities, attending an auction at Bonhams. It's not that they didn't have money, they just didn't have it to burn. But burn they did, with a desire to acquire something that might bring them that little touch of the glitter lacking in their lives.

The online bid center to the right of the dais was already buzzing with bubbling chat windows and frantic last-second questions. Bonhams Skinner staffers clacked away at their keyboards, while others manned the phone banks, their hands resting just above the receivers, fingers as itchy as gunfighters.

Grace, Jerome, Elaine, and Pat sat slumped in the back row like death row prisoners, watching lot after lot, drawing ever closer to the dreaded Number 22. To Grace, each gavel strike felt as if another nail was being pounded into her coffin. Lot 21 was a first edition of John Updike's *Rabbit, Run.* Grace was tempted by the title and crossed her legs to prevent her chasing that rabbit right out the front door. When Nan banged her gavel, the book sold for $500, a steal for such a classic pillar of prose.

"Isn't that a little low?" Grace whispered.

"Not for this crowd," moaned Pat.

Grace sat back, her troubles mounting. Not only did Jody's book not bring any market value to this auction, the bidders themselves brought even less.

"We'll be lucky if they can get enough money for a trip to McDonald's on the way home," said Elaine, and Grace thought her optimistic.

"I'm sorry," said Pat, bolting up. "I have to watch this outside." She excused herself, disappearing out the double doors and into the lobby.

"I think I'll join her," said Elaine, grabbing her purse and falling in behind Pat.

Grace thought that a brilliant idea. She could watch on the lobby screen and wait for Jody and Gloria outside. That might allow them the time to mourn in peace before she apologized and explained. She stood up and turned to Jerome. "Shall we?"

"No," he said with a firmness that surprised Grace. "We take our medicine."

"It's mine to take—or not, Jerome."

"No, it isn't." He reached up, taking her hand, his voice softening.

"We take what's ours, Grace, the good and the bad," he said. "Especially the bad. Gives us the right to take the good when it comes—if it comes."

A thin curtain of shame descended over her face. "Okay," she said, sitting back down beside him. "Bring on the castor oil."

"Mrs. Schaffer?" Jody stood at excited attention in the aisle before them. "There's an open seat next to us, if you'd like."

Grace took a moment to think, although she already knew what the answer was. "Of course I'd like," she said, taking the girl's offered hand and following her down the aisle.

Jerome watched after her, without a trace of triumph or pride or even grudging respect. It was a small, cautious look, the kind he gave to a withered tapestry or pottery shard when first he laid his eyes upon them. The look that said, *What do I have here?*

Nanette Bouchard took the podium and nodded to the assistant on her right. She punched a few keys on her laptop and a large slide with the words LOT 22: THE JESTER HAS LOST HIS JINGLE displayed on a ninety-inch screen behind them. Nan drew her navy blazer taut around her slim shoulders and leaned forward, her lips close to the microphone.

"Next lot. Lot 22," she said, in a professional, neutral tone.

Grace peeked down at Jody, who sat grinning beside her, her little bare legs swinging back and forth as if she were about to explode like a grenade and spray anxious shrapnel all over the auction hall.

Here it comes, thought Grace. *Down the hatch.*

"*The Jester Has Lost His Jingle*, by David Saltzman," announced Nan. "Second printing. Signed by the author."

The assistant on Nan's left spoke up. "Author's mother."

"Apologies," said Nan, with a bit of a sour look on her face. "Author's *mother*." She checked the notes on her laptop. "No reserve requested."

Grace bit down on her lip to stop herself from groaning. Why hadn't they at least set a minimum bid? If they had, and had asked for a minimum of $5000, it would have been enough of a red flag for Skinner to reject the sale, and that would have been that.

"We'll start the bidding at fifty dollars," Nan said. "Do I hear fifty?"

Grace did not hear fifty, or anything else for that matter, save for a smattering of coughs and the crisp turning of a program page.

"Forty, then," said Nan. "Is there forty in the room?"

Silence.

"Twenty-five. Do I hear twenty-five?"

Silence.

Nan turned to the staff on the computers and phones. "Twenty-five online?"

The three staffers on the computers shook their heads.

Grace reached up and ran her fingers over the celestial globe. What a pair they were, the stone and the stone-cold fool of an appraiser. Grace thought perhaps they deserved each other. Maybe that's why it felt so strangely comforting to hold.

"Ten dollars?" said Nan, with an unprofessional but unavoidable sadness.

Grace glanced around the room and not a single eye met hers; they were either checking their programs, their phones, or their watches. *They're not looking*, she thought. *They don't see.*

Nan took a deep breath and prodded the crowd one last time. "This is well under the cost of purchasing at retail. Last call for this lot. Do I hear ten?"

Nan raised her gavel to end the bloodshed.

Grace raised her hand.

Nan hesitated. "Is that a bid, ma'am?"

A few people glanced up from their programs.

"If you are making a bid, please use the bid card in your program."

Grace slipped the bid card out of her program. But she couldn't bid; she couldn't inflate the price artificially. She wouldn't.

"Yes or no, ma'am?" Nan asked, her patience running on empty.

"Do you happen to have a slide of the cover?" asked Grace. "To check condition."

Nan sighed and nodded to an assistant. A high-definition photograph of the cover flashed onto the large screen above the dais.

Grace gasped, in honest awe at the life-size Jester and the shimmering tangerine sun that hovered in the sky above him. "That's so beautiful," she said, astonished by it all over again.

A young, professionally dressed woman sitting just across the aisle from Grace glanced up from her iPad with tired eyes.

"Amazing, isn't it?" Grace said. "You can't tell if the sun's rising or setting."

"It's setting," sighed the woman, returning to whatever drudgery nagged at her from her tablet.

"Is it?" Grace nudged the woman to look closer. "Are you sure?"

"Unfortunately, it appears this lot is 'bought in,'" said Nan, closing the auction. "Bought in, once... twice..." Nan raised the gavel.

"Ten!"

Grace spun around, scanning the room for whoever had swung to her rescue. She caught Jerome's raised brows in the back row—but he wasn't raising them at Grace. He was raising them at the professional woman across the aisle from her. Grace blinked to make sure she was not imagining it—the woman held her bid card high above her head, her gaze locked tight on the projection screen above.

Nan lowered her gavel. "Very well, I have ten," she said, clearly relieved. "Selling at ten. Any advance?" She quickly raised the gavel, as if in fear the woman would withdraw her bid.

"Twenty." A man in the back row thrust his bid card into the air.

"Twenty in the room," said Nan. "I have twenty, looking for thirty."

Another arm shot up across the aisle.

"Thirty," Nan said, rising up behind the podium. "Thirty on me, looking for fifty."

Another arm.

"Fifty to you, sir."

Grace struggled to keep pace, her head ricocheting back and forth.

A staffer's hand shot up at the computer desk, his index finger raised. "One hundred!"

Grace yelped and covered her mouth.

Nan put a finger to her lips to shush her, but the smile behind it was unmistakable. "One hundred on Dominic," she said.

The room erupted with the frantic rustling of programs, as the bidders thumbed backward to find the lot description, desperate to catch the wave that had swelled within the auction hall.

"I have one hundred online." Nan gathered speed, her voice rising in pitch. "I'm looking for two hundred."

Another bid—behind Jody, who spun around and whispered, "Thank you."

Grace pulled her back around. "Shhh," she said. "Let it ride."

Jody faced front, grabbing her chair as if she were strapping in for a roller coaster. And it had been for the poor girl, all downhill.

Not anymore, thought Grace.

"Two hundred in the room," said Nan, her pace quickening. "The bid is five."

Dominic's hand shot up from behind his computer.

"Five hundred to Dominic. Can I see one thousand?"

A staffer in the last row of the phone bank raised her hand.

"One thousand on Tiffany," Nan said, exhilaration creeping into her voice. "I have one thousand dollars."

Someone in the crowd cheered; another joined her. They were all aboard, everyone in the room, from amateur to expert. Something grand and wonderful, invisible but alive, had crackled to life, and they all wanted a ride.

"One thousand," said Nan. "I'm looking for—"

A hand shot out to the left.

"Fifteen hundred! I need two thousand."

Another hand.

Grace tried to catch Zwick's eyes but couldn't see through the flesh and paper swarm of arms and cards. *It's impossible*, she thought, salt tears stinging her eyes. *Don't stop. Don't stop!*

"Two thousand, looking for—"

Dominic held up three fingers.

"Three thousand on Dominic."

Grace leaned back in her chair, the room spinning.

Another hand, in the back row.

"Four thousand?" confirmed Nan.

The entire crowd craned their necks this way and that, looking for the bidder.

"Did I see four?" asked Nan. "Four in the room?"

A thin man with a short salt-and-pepper Afro sat up, as tall as he had ever sat in his life. "Four thousand!" he cried.

"That's four thousand!" said Nan. "I have four thousand in the room."

Jody gripped Grace's hand so hard, she feared she'd break skin. Grace was thankful for the pain; it was the only thing keeping her from screaming out loud.

"The bid is four thousand."

A staffer at the phones raised a fist and five fingers.

"Four thousand five hundred," said Nan. "Four thousand five hundred is the bid."

The professional woman thrust her hand in the air.

"Four thousand six."

If she fainted, Grace hoped someone would notice.

Another hand.

"The bid is four thousand seven hundred," said Nan, breathless. "I am looking for five thousand."

Silence.

"Five thousand?"

Grace looked about. The room had calmed. The storm had passed.

That's it, she thought. *Thank God.*

"Four thousand seven hundred is the bid," Nan said. "Four thousand seven in the room. Any advance? No . . . ?"

Grace sucked in a deep breath, unclenching her jaw. It was over.

"No advance, then," said Nan, raising the gavel. "Lot 22 selling for—"

Grace chuckled to herself; she had half expected it would come to exactly—

"Five thousand!" said Nan, slamming down the gavel.

Grace spun around. Across the aisle, the professional woman held her bid card up so high, she had torn the armpit of her sleeve.

"Sold to Number 7," said Nan to her assistant, who typed the number of the woman's bid card into her laptop, ending the auction.

The woman lowered her arm and turned to Grace with tears in her eyes, eyes as bright and hopeful as the Jester's sun. "I was so wrong about that sun," she said.

"It's rising."

The auction ended and the bidders dispersed, save the Appraisal Experts Roadshow crew, who lingered behind to share their amazement and congratulate Grace in the lobby.

"I don't know if you're one cool bitch, or one lucky bitch," said Pat, giving Grace a playful shove. Grace had never been either but was not in the mood to argue the point; she had other worries on her mind.

Five thousand?

It made no sense. Had she forced the hand in the room? She didn't think so; in fact, she was sure of it. But she couldn't escape the thought that whispered at her from deep within the shadows of her success.

Five thousand. To the penny.

Nan emerged from the auction hall, where Jerome was waiting to say goodbye. Instead of shaking his outstretched hand, she took it in both of hers.

"You quitter," she said. "How dare you."

He backed away, but she held him tight. "I was never attracted to you," she said. "But you still found a way to break my heart." She dropped his hand and planted a soft kiss on his cheek. "Good to see you, Jerry. Well, what's left of you."

She shook her head and walked away, leaving Jerome alone in the corner of the room. Grace walked over to console him.

"She had no business calling you that," she said.

"Of course she did. I am a quitter."

"No, you're not. You're working your tail off."

"I'm at the show, sure, but I'm not working." He'd drifted off, perhaps, Grace thought, to a gallery counter where a foolish, split-second decision had cost him a Holy Grail.

"I'm envious," she said. "The way you keep looking for it. It's nothing short of heroic."

He shook his head. "Inertia, my dear. Nothing more."

"Then why hang around just to torture yourself? You're clearly miserable."

"Well, that is my resting pulse, Ms. Schaffer."

Grace chuckled. "That's funny, but it's not an answer."

His grin faded, and he gazed at Grace with scalpel eyes. She had let her guard down with him, and could feel they were inching toward friendship, but the intimacy of it unnerved her.

"Why are you looking at me like that?"

He hesitated. "You'll take care of me, if I tell you?"

"Promise."

Jerome drifted off once again, into wounds that had skinned, but never scabbed. "Nan was right. I did quit. Maybe not on my clients, but after I lost Nora, I quit..." He pressed his hand to his heart. "In here."

Grace nodded. She understood that particular ache far too well.

"A foundational truth had been stolen from me," he said. "And in its place, I had learned, in the very cruelest of ways, that there are no such things as miracles."

His eyes came back into focus, sharpening around Grace. "Now I'm not so sure."

Six

The comfortable leather chair in Grace's home office felt anything but. She scooted this way and that, reclined it, raised it, lowered it, but nothing felt quite right.

Like that auction, she thought. That felt anything but right.

Kovels' Price Guide, the very bible of the business, confirmed it, as had *Miller's* and *Warman's*. Grace raked through WorthPoint's online archive and found a few recent sales of *The Jester Has Lost His Jingle*, ranging from five to twenty dollars, LiveAuctioneers had one listed from just the previous week that sold for twenty-two dollars, and there were three on eBay, yielding three, four, and thirteen dollars.

Not five thousand.

But in her heart, that was exactly what it was worth. And exactly what it sold for.

Grace snapped her laptop shut and grabbed her phone, thumbing open her Tinder profile. She swiped through blond and brunette, dolt and distinguished, but the more she looked, the less she saw the point in it. Thirty minutes or so of carnal calisthenics sounded lovely, but when the sweat dried, the thought would remain.

Five thousand dollars.

She tossed the phone aside and slid the silver-framed picture of her father and her younger self closer. His eyes had always mesmerized Grace; always seeking, never resting, like the threshing propulsion of a shark. It stirred something deep within her, stronger than admiration, beyond jealousy—that relentless drive to learn, to grow; even as a little girl, she dreamed of being dragged along with it, swept up in the whirlwind of his ambition. And so she clung to him, her steps tracing the blueprint he had left for her—MA, PhD, auction porter, gallery owner—until she saw through those same eyes, until her own propulsion ran at his breakneck speed. Even when her course was altered by the lush oils of the Impressionists, when the eloquence of her appraisals landed her on *Antiques Roadshow*, it was always his engine that powered her. But one day, a single seditious blood vessel burst within his brain and that tether dissolved, leaving Grace stranded in the middle of a gray and gloomy wasteland. She felt like a child again, as if the world was too big, too large for her, and Grace shrank from it. There were too many paths before her, too many mistakes to be made, and she could not see her way out. She had lost her father's eyes.

She needed them now. *Five thousand dollars.*

There was a clue she was missing, a mark only he would see. She'd ask Jerome, but he was as mystified as she. In another life she'd have asked Victor, but she was left with this life, which meant she was left alone. She could always ask her mother, but she knew exactly what Shirley would say: She'd tell her that lightning had struck at Skinner's and lightning doesn't strike the same spot twice, so move on. But Grace couldn't move on. Something was odd; something was out of balance. And it wasn't luck, or the winds of fortune, or a momentary market surge. Something had placed a finger on the scales of commerce and pushed.

Something unnatural.

It was just a whisper at first, a distant echo, but she felt it dig into her, its long slender tendrils teasing her eyes to the right, over her laptop toward the far corner of the desk, where Grace had placed the celestial globe.

It lay there, a faded clump of metal and stone. Playing dead once again, sedating Grace with the gentle assurance that it was all in her head, that sometimes a necklace is just a necklace. And Grace had given in for a while, had closed her eyes tight, because if she opened them, she might see it was anything but a necklace. But Grace had closed her eyes too many times in her life, so she opened her mind wide and looked closer. This time, she was determined not to blink.

The lapis had been cold when she unclasped it, colder than any stone should be. And it hadn't radiated with the heat of her skin at the auction, as she'd told herself, and it wasn't playing dead now. It was gathering strength, and she knew—she *knew* it wasn't a copy or a counterfeit, or anything other than what it was.

Five thousand dollars.

It had turned a fifteen-dollar keepsake into a rare and valuable commodity. Could it do ten thousand? Twenty? And if it wished, could it take as well as give?

Could it destroy?

She wanted to lock it in a box, bury it deep in the desert sands, let it sink to the bottom of the earth, all the way down to the hell from which it had risen. But Grace Schaffer was Albert Schaffer's daughter, and Albert may have fled from Grace's persistent attempts at a closer relationship, but he never ran from a challenge. And this time, neither would Grace.

If this is lightning, she thought, *I dare you to strike me twice.*

Seven

It wasn't lightning she awoke to, but it was cataclysmic just the same: The next stop of the Appraisal Experts Roadshow would be the last.

Grace sipped on an increasingly bitter cup of coffee in the early morning gloom of her kitchen, reading the email she'd been dreading but expecting just the same. The crowds had dwindled, the coffers had dried up, and Elaine—who had bankrolled a portion of the last show with her very own money—could carry on no longer. Grace shut her laptop and laid her head on the marble counter while the kitchen clock ticked away, time itself moving on without her. The show had been a return to square one for Grace, and after a few short weeks, she had only made it to square one and a quarter. It would be a much shorter fall to the pavement this time, but that didn't make it any easier. At some point, the bones don't heal. At some point, you stay down.

And maybe Grace had come to that point, but she couldn't bear thinking of what it would mean for the others. The show was Elaine's baby, the work of an entire decade; if she had to bring down the big top after only three locations, it might not live to rise again. Jerome was on his last legs; who knew if he'd hitch up to another show. Pat would probably drown herself in the bottom of a bottle, and maybe she'd like it there; maybe she'd like it enough to stay.

So Grace would put on a great big smile, and make the rounds, and commiserate and cry and do whatever she could for every one of them. During her withdrawal from the profession, the profession had returned the favor. Grace *needed some time*, they said; it was best to let her be, give her some space until she cleared her head—not that anyone believed she had the capacity to do so. So the art world spun on without her, and after a few months when Grace sent up a flare or two that she might like to return, no one seemed to notice, and if they did, they didn't seem to care. Elaine and the Appraisal Experts Roadshow extended their hands to Grace when hers were leprous, and it was time to repay that debt—with as much interest as they'd accept. She packed a heartfelt card for Jerome, a gift bag of treats for Elaine, and a framed picture of Jody for Pat. But when she arrived for their final show at Merwin Meadows in Wilton, Connecticut, she realized she should have packed something else.

Smelling salts.

"What the hell is that?" asked a mystified Pat, staring at the Welcome Tent.

Elaine rubbed her eyes, but the strange sight remained. "Is anyone else having an acid flashback?"

"I don't think so," said Jerome. "Even LSD can't produce that kind of hallucination."

Grace stumbled over, joining her slack-mouthed friends outside the tent's main entrance. "Where'd they come from?"

"You, I guess," said Elaine.

"I'd have hired them if I could, Lain, but I had nothing to do with it."

"Don't tell *Good Morning Wilton*," said Elaine, pointing to an amateur camera crew unloading a truck in the parking lot. "Local access must have done their homework—the *Jester*—and you—are all over Bonhams' website."

Grace refused to believe it, but she couldn't come up with any better explanation for the massive line of visitors materializing at registration, long enough that some at the end of the line might actually have to pay for their appraisals.

"Well, folks." Elaine grinned. "Looks like we better get our asses to work."

Pat laughed and walked off, arm in arm with her, chattering like a giddy teen, not the jaded proto-alcoholic Grace knew.

"Pat's happy," said Grace.

Jerome nodded, surveying the experts filing into the main tent. "Yes, there certainly is a bit of that going around today."

Grace caught a flat note in his voice. "But not for you?"

He hesitated. "I'm Russian, so let me put it this way: *Doveryai, no proveryai.*"

Grace shrugged, not following.

"Trust... but verify."

Grace laughed. "Is that a dare?"

"Possibly," he said. "I'm still not entirely sure how I feel about the *event* at Bonhams."

"I haven't slept since," admitted Grace.

"It's unnerving, to be sure," he said. "Then again, if it's only a one-off, a one-and-done sort of thing, I might..." He cleared his throat. "Not in any sort of patronizing way, of course, but... I might worry about you."

Grace blinked, surprised. It felt as if Jerome was attempting to cross the 38th parallel into full-fledged friendship. She had friends—she didn't lose them all in the divorce—but she was unused to concern. This, too, would require *doveryai* and *proveryai.*

Just then, the Welcome Tent opened for business behind them, and the guests filed in. Grace could hear the chatter of expectation, even from their distant vantage point. What was stranger, she felt it, too, like a pleasant buzz. Maybe an addictive one.

"But what if it's not a one-off?" she asked, lightly brushing her fingers over the outline of the celestial globe beneath her shirt. "What if there's another *event?* What happens then?"

"I'm not sure." Jerome thought it over for a moment. "It's tough to tell how thin the ice is here, Grace. Tread lightly."

She nodded and excused herself, threading her way into the main tent. She didn't have to look back. She knew he was watching her.

Jerome wasn't the only one. As she finished organizing her table, Grace glanced up and caught two experts at Clocks and Watches staring at her, whispering out of the sides of their mouths. Some of the other appraisers stole a peek or two as they made unnecessary passes by her table. Even the teenage volunteers had edged their way into the center of the tent, chattering excitedly as if they were waiting for a rock concert, their faces alight with the same expectation Grace had seen on the faces of the guests at registration. Grace felt it crackle across the tent like an electric current; everyone was expecting something special.

Something of me.

What had happened out at Skinner's was impossible. It unmade her. But just as something deep within the dirt had called out to Grace as a little girl, called out for her to dig and dig with the little red shovel her father had given her until she found it, so too did this new voice call out:

Doveryai, no proveryai.

Jerome had wanted her to try again. She could sense it behind the mask of his concern. He, too, heard the voice. But he heard something else, too; something that troubled him. Why was he so worried? If Grace tried again, if she verified and failed, what then? Elaine would have to let Grace go; that was certain. The show would wither away, maybe even close forever. But how long could it survive if this was indeed a one-off? If no local access covered them, if the crowds stayed away?

Jerome had warned her. *Thin ice*, he said, and Grace felt it thinning beneath her feet. She knew that book should not have sold for five thousand dollars. Not at that auction, not at any auction. Grace had made a critical, unforgivable error: She had confused personal feelings with market value. That book was not worth five thousand dollars, or five hundred, or even fifty. Grace had been wrong, dead wrong. Why had she not been punished?

Grace's father had bought her that little red shovel when she was just a little girl. She dug up their entire backyard with it, nearly to bedrock in some places. Grace had lost track of it over the years. Perhaps it had been lost in one of her myriad moves. Perhaps she had thrown it out. She would have to dig without it.

The dirt was calling once again.

"Seventy-five to one hundred and fifty dollars," said Grace as she handed back the small gold frame. It was a Stevengraph—a delicate silk picture woven on a Jacquard loom—signed by Thomas Stevens himself. It was a rare piece, and a good find.

"Oh, that's nice," said the man who had brought it. "One hundred and fifty. Very nice."

Yes, thought Grace. Nice. Nothing more.

Grace had been ready to verify, had been ready to tempt the market fates, but try as she might, the only numbers that made sense were seventy-five and one hundred fifty. That felt right. Because it was right. Grace had consulted a flurry of online auctions, particularly those in England where the sales would be highest. She had given the man a very good price. And he was happy.

And so was the rest of the day's procession. Grace appraised pastels and poster board, oils and charcoal, and everyone left with a smile and one of Grace's gallery cards. None of the appraisals varied from what Grace knew or what she looked up in guide or online.

And that was fine with Grace; not good, not exciting, but fine. Sure, she felt the tug of disappointment, but perhaps that was preferable to the insanity of the last few weeks. Still, Jerome's odd caution remained like a stubborn cobweb in her thoughts—wispy and sticky; she could not quite get free of it. But she needn't worry. *The Jester Has Lost His Jingle* was indeed a one-off—a bolt of lightning in a bottle, and the bottle had been locked away in the cupboard, where it belonged. The rest of the experts had settled down as well. They had stopped peeking over every two minutes and returned to their own appraisals. And that was fine, too.

Grace drew the celestial globe out from beneath her blouse, letting it rest against her chest. For a moment, she was afraid to touch it, lest it awaken and shatter the calm. But she had to know, so she reached up to caress the glass-smooth face of the lapis lazuli. It was neither cold, nor warm, nor anything else but stone; it was fine, too. Everything was just fine. Grace had verified, and the miracle had been unmasked as a fluke. So Grace returned to her appraisals in peace, thankful the world had finally turned right side up. More guests came, and more guests went, and no one was disappointed.

Except Grace.

"It was my great-grandmother's," said a far-off voice.

"I'm sorry?" Grace focused her attention on the man before her—a businessman of some kind, clad in a simple brown suit and tie.

"My great-grandfather sent it to her," he said. "When he was in the war."

Grace glanced down at the heirloom on her table. It was a small silk embroidered greeting card in a glass frame. The colored yarn had faded a few shades, but all the images were still fresh. Roses, lilies, a rolling countryside, and the embroidered message: *A Kiss from France.*

"Ah, yes," said Grace. "These were a popular gift in World War One. The men fighting overseas would purchase these from merchants—oftentimes at the front itself—and they'd write a quick note to send home to their loves."

The man nodded. "My father told me I was obsessed with it when I was a baby. My great-grandfather was already gone, but my great-grandmother used to take it down so I could look at it." He chuckled. "That's why the glass is a little smudged, I guess."

"I can see that." Grace laughed, looking it over. "It's been well loved."

"Oh yes," he said. "My parents gave it to me on my eighteenth birthday—that's actually how old my great-grandfather was when he went to France."

"I take it you've done a bit of research, then."

"A little," he said. "I've looked these up online, and the prices are all over the place."

Grace nodded. "It depends on the condition, of course. We expect some blemishes—we're over a hundred years from their crafting, after all. In good condition, the range is anywhere from fifteen to fifty dollars, although I've seen perfect examples go for over a hundred." She turned on her lamp to get a better look. "Have you had it appraised before?"

"Oh, no." He shook his head. "I'd never thought to sell it."

Grace looked closer at the man. He was dressed for work, not the show. He had either snuck out to do this or taken his lunch hour for the appraisal. This was not recreational—he needed the money.

"Are you thinking of selling now?"

"Maybe," he said, torn. "Depends."

"Well, perhaps I can help, if you like. Would that be okay?"

He hesitated, and his eyes scanned the tent for an open path to the exit. Grace wondered how long he had agonized over whether or not to appraise it, as if he were letting his great-grandparents down in doing so. She did not want to push him, but—

Suddenly, she felt it, a prickling on her skin, a flush in her chest. It crackled within her, ticking over like a hot plate, as if her heart had been shot through with adrenaline, and she felt it swell inside her, expanding against her ribs. It was *happening*, and it terrified her, and it thrilled her, and she reached up, wrapping her fingers around the lapis lazuli. It was warm; pulsing, like her heart, in ever-quickening rhythm, in perfect tune. The surfaces between them, the skin and the stone, fading, dissolving until it flowed into her, draining her, but filling her too, as it surged through her veins like opium, making her head spin from the sheer euphoria of it. What was it doing?

What is it doing to me?

She felt it rise to its full height within her—and somehow, she heard it. Not its voice, not *a* voice, but she heard it, as true and clear as anything she had ever heard in her life:

Something is here, it said.

And it was; Grace was sure of it. "What did he write?" she asked the man. "Your great-grandfather?"

"I don't know. I've never opened it."

"Never? Aren't you curious?"

"Of course, but..." He trailed off.

"It's private."

"Exactly." He relaxed a bit, relieved. "I've always wanted to respect that."

"I admire that," she said. "But you've always had a connection with this yourself, haven't you?"

"All my life."

"Then this is a part of you, too. It is, wouldn't you say, a piece of all three of you?"

He froze. "I never thought of it that way."

"I think you brought it here for a reason—and I don't think it was just about the value of the object," she said. "You came to hear them speak."

He smiled. "I believe I did."

"Then let's hear what they have to say. Do you mind if I remove it from the frame?"

He took a deep breath and nodded. "Please."

Grace laid the frame face down on the table, acutely aware she was unearthing not just a letter, but a body—two of them. Ever so gently, she slid the backing off the frame and eased a thin wood letter opener under the edge of the card, raising it from the depths of its glass tomb, letting the card exhale for the first time in a hundred years.

Without the smudged glass to restrain it, the delicate needlework on the face of the card blossomed before them. The lush green hills; the flowers, glistening with crimson and violet hues; the powder blue message at the bottom of the card—all seemed to levitate off the faded white stock. The letters were frayed, but the message was as clear as any Grace had ever seen:

A Kiss from France.

She heard a collective gasp and looked up to see a small crowd had gathered about them. Grace tuned them out, sliding her finger over a seam on the side of the card until the paper gave way, revealing the hundred-year-old writing within. She had expected a report from the front, a fond memory, perhaps a promise to return home soon. She found only one word, written in faded charcoal pencil, but in that word, an infinity:

Always.

Grace smiled. "Perfect, isn't it?"

The man nodded, his eyes misting over. "My grandfather used to sign cards to me the same way. 'Always.'" He looked closer at the hastily written word, scribbled in between incoming shells. "He must have gotten that from his father."

"And now it's come full circle, back to you."

He nodded, his eyes cleared, and a great peace came over him, easing the wrinkled tension that knotted his face. He was ready. "I'd like to know what it's worth."

Ay, that's the rub, thought Grace, closing the card. *What's it worth?*

She knew the market. She knew the trends and the history and the range. In perfect condition, the card would auction at right around a hundred dollars. But this wasn't in perfect condition, not even close. There were tiny tears all along the edges, some of the flower petals were missing, and then the actual words themselves: *A Kiss from France*. They were terribly frayed. Distressed, as if...

Grace reached up and fingered the celestial globe around her neck, spinning it slowly on its axis. It was so hot now—when had it gotten so fiercely hot?

Distressed...

Grace looked closer. The damage was contained in one area, on one word, in fact.

On *Kiss*.

And then it came upon her, the images as clear as if she were there herself. They had each kissed that word, the husband in his trench, his wife when she received it. The petals had been worn down by her thumb, as she touched what he had touched so that she might somehow touch him. And the tiny tears on the edge of the paper came from her trembling hands as she opened and closed the card, over and over again, cloaking herself in the comfort of that word:

Always.

A promise written by the light of a cannon, a kiss that spanned an ocean, a love that would not yield to Ypres, or mustard gas, or all the engines of a man-made apocalypse. It was embroidered in that card, and it sired a child, and the man who stood before her, and the children who might follow him.

"I'll tell you what it's worth," Grace said.

The man's eyes said: *Something.*

The crowd's said: *Something incredible.*

Grace said: "Nineteen thousand eight hundred dollars."

The man stumbled back, as if hit by a swinging girder. He tried to speak, his mouth trembled, but nothing came out. He shook his head, still mute, no sound, not even breath escaped—the number was too large, too beautiful. Finally, he sucked in a huge breath and steadied himself. "You can't possibly mean," he said. "As high as that?"

"No," Grace said, her hand locked around the lapis lazuli. It was searing now, but she held on, and the tighter she held, the less it stung. "That high. Exactly that high," she said. "That's what it's worth."

He took the card in both hands, cradling it in his arms as if it were the burial flag of a fallen warrior. "Thank you," he said. "I had no idea..." He looked down at the card, at the kiss from France. "I mean, to me, it always had that kind of value, but I never expected anyone else to see it that way."

"Well, I do," said Grace. "And so will any auctioneer." She handed him her card. "Call me tomorrow and I'll recommend a few."

The man nodded in thanks and hurried off as the crowd dispersed, buzzing excitedly.

Grace opened her fist and the celestial globe tumbled out, swinging back and forth until it rested against her chest, cool and calm. She ran a finger over her palm to ease the pain in whatever blister she could find, but she found none, only a small violet impression in the shape of a perfect circle, which seemed to evaporate into her skin, leaving no trace. And no pain either, which was a pleasant surprise. More than pleasant. If anything, she felt...

Good.

And that scared the hell out of her. Lightning had struck twice, even harder this time—and instead of singeing her to a crisp, it had exhilarated her. She could still feel the rush, as if she were coming down from some euphoric fever.

Grace missed it already. She had felt so full, so charged, as if the tips of her fingers had been hardwired to a surging transformer, her entire body a superconductor of some inexplicable, awesome force. It should have hurt, she should have ripped open as it swelled within her, but she rose with it, unfurling herself, expanding into something so powerful and elemental that for a single glorious minute, Grace Schaffer felt indestructible.

But the transformer had gone quiet, and without that current, her limbs went limp, then numb, as the grays and beiges of her life crept back in once again. She had come to terms with the ordinariness of her life, but as she returned to it now, it seemed drained of that, too. Even the people around her looked muted and shapeless, like sheets thrown over furniture in an abandoned home. Abandoned—yes; that's exactly how she felt. But Grace had been to the other side, and now that she had seen behind the curtain, she ached to return.

Grace excused herself from the next guest and walked over to where Jerome, Pat, and Henry Manfred were waiting. Henry's Groucho eyebrows were raised so high, they nearly crawled under his hairline.

"I've seen a lot of kooky things in this business," he said. "But that's the first time I saw an appraiser commit ritual *seppuku*."

"I'll bet you five hundred dollars that's exactly what it sells for," said Pat.

"That's a sucker bet, Patty, and you know it."

"Sure is," she said. "Shake, sucker."

Henry laughed and shook her outstretched hand. "Let me know when it's time to collect," he said. "And then, drinks are on me—well, Pat, I guess." He walked off, shaking his head.

Pat turned to Grace, lowering her voice. "Did that one feel...?"

"Like Jody's?" Grace took a moment. "No. Different. But...it felt right."

"Well, fingers crossed. I'd give anything to see Groucho eat his mustache," said Pat, walking off.

Grace turned to Jerome. The last traces of euphoria had passed, leaving Grace with a sobering thought. "It's wrong—what I'm doing, isn't it?"

Jerome remained silent, patient. Grace adored him for it.

"I don't understand what's happening," she groaned. "I know the numbers—backwards and forwards. I *know* them." She shook her head. "What I told that man was wrong."

"Well, it's certainly something," he said. "Maybe not 'wrong,' though. You can't say your call on the *Jester* was wrong."

"You know the market."

"And I saw the auction," he said. "That price—your price—is what it sold for."

"Exactly what it sold for," she said. "That's what troubles me."

"Well, let's see what happens at the next auction. Then you can worry all you want." He leaned in and whispered, "I might even join you."

Eight

Skinner's historic downtown site dominated the bottom floors of a hulking, three-tower complex of offices and upscale condominiums in the very heart of Boston's Park Plaza. At the base of the central tower, a light blue awning heralded the entrance to SKINNER AUCTIONEERS, and the evening's main attractions were prominently posted on two large marquees to each side. A very different clientele from the industrial park in Marlborough filed through the front door. Cardigans had turned to silk ties, sport coats to suits, skirts to dresses, and flats to pumps. The objects at auction would be rarer, the initial reserves would be higher, and those who competed for them would flinch less as the bids increased.

Inside the auction hall, Grace, Jerome, Elaine, Pat, and Henry staked out their vantage place on the left side of the back row, easing themselves into chairs far more luxurious than the ones at Marlborough.

"Do you see him?" asked Jerome.

"No," said Grace, scanning the room. "Maybe he changed his mind."

"He's probably just nervous," said Elaine.

"Can't imagine why," said Grace, inching her pinky over to Jerome's. Without any hesitation he reached out with his own, clasping hers.

Love this man. She leaned closer to him and whispered, "If I were twenty years older..."

"I'd still be spoken for," he said, eyeing the wedding ring on his finger.

Son of a bitch, she thought. *Where's the mold for this one?*

His eyes shifted to someone at the entrance. "There's your man."

Grace's client walked in through the rear doors looking harried, his hair damp with sweat. Grace wondered if he had not decided to come until the last second. He took one of the last remaining seats on the other side of the hall, just as the auctioneer entered from a side door.

Lynn Martell, the evening's auctioneer, strode onto the dais, which was two steps higher than the one in Marlborough. Everything in the auction hall was that much grander, that much richer. The podium was a darker, deeper cherry wood, its embossed golden plaque proclaiming this to be the selective congregation of SKINNER BOSTON. The paintings and prints that adorned the walls, curated from their own collection of American and European masters, were themselves worthy of display in many museums. The banks of computers for online bids were awash with traffic, the phone banks already humming, each staffed with sharp-eyed, straight-backed staffers primed for the opening bid.

Lynn rapped her gavel, and all conversation in the room abruptly silenced. "Welcome to Arms and Militaria," she said. "We will begin this evening with Lot 1."

A high-definition slide of a dull silver bell stamped USN flashed onto the large projection screen behind the dais.

"A World War Two nickel-plated bronze ship bell from the USS *Lawrence*, Destroyer DD 250," Lynn said. "We have five hundred to open the bidding, I'm looking for five twenty-five."

The room filled with an undulating sea of waving bid cards and the staccato chants of the staff manning the phones and computers. What began in the hundreds quickly ended in the thousands, leaving Grace a little breathless. She gripped Jerome's pinky a bit harder. If any place would yield a nineteen-thousand-dollar bid, it would be here.

"Easy, Grace," he said. "I might need that finger later."

"Sorry," she said, releasing a bit of pressure.

But the pressure continued to build. A pair of eighteenth-century flintlock dueling pistols fetched six thousand dollars. A Civil War snare drum brought eleven. An authentic Japanese *Nihonto* sword that had not seen battle since 1945 saw a bloody one between two collectors—one British, one Chinese—who chased the selling price up above fifteen thousand dollars.

"Moving on to Lot 5," Lynn said as the World War One embroidered card filled the giant screen behind her.

Grace blew out a long breath, but it did nothing to ease the churning anxiety in her chest. If the card didn't bring at least nineteen thousand—*Nineteen thousand eight hundred*, she thought—if it tanked instead, the mistake would be her last. She'd apologize for dashing everyone's spirits, most of all the poor man trying to sell it, and after the smoke had cleared, she'd thank Elaine, pack up her things, and crawl into a box in the basement of her gallery in Manhattan, and that would be that.

"A hand-embroidered World War One greeting card, circa 1918," said Lynn. "*A Kiss from France.*"

Grace leaned forward, trying to catch the eye of the man who had brought her the piece. His head was down but he was leaning forward in his seat, taut with expectation. That letter was not a mausoleum for him—it was the physical incarnation of the beating heart of his entire bloodline.

Grace released Jerome's finger. This was no longer an experiment. This was not a verification. She wanted it. For the grandparents. For the grandson. For the unshakable bond they shared.

Lynn lifted her gavel and hesitated. The bidders gripped their cards, jockeys at the reins. The phone banks lit up like candelabras.

Grace felt time slow, funneling down to the head of a pin. She reached up and grasped the celestial globe, and something ignited deep within it. This time there would be no resistance. She opened herself up, yielding to it, and it snaked its way into her, feasting upon her as she fed on it, one pulse, one breath, one thought:

We are ready.

"We'll start the bidding at one hundred dollars," said Lynn.

There was no pause.

A Gatling gun barrage of bids sent the price up above one thousand almost immediately, then fifteen hundred, two thousand, five, and ten. At fifteen thousand, Lynn Martell, the Iron Lady herself, paused to take a long drink of water.

"What's wrong?" whispered Grace. "Is she rattled?"

"Not half so much as Henry," said Jerome.

At the other end of the row, Henry canted forward, nearly falling out of his chair like a kid watching his very first magic show as the price soared all the way up to—

"Nineteen?" asked Lynn.

The room hushed. Grace held her breath.

"I have eighteen thousand in the room," said Lynn, steadying herself on the podium. "Do I hear nineteen?"

Silence.

Thank God, thought Grace. Eighteen thousand was good enough. No, it was fantastic. Her client would be so pleased. Whatever troubles he faced, this would blunt them, maybe even banish them altogether. Eighteen thousand was an absolutely glorious number.

Because it is not nineteen, thought Grace. Well, nineteen thousand eight—

"Nineteen thousand eight hundred dollars!" bellowed Lynn, slamming the gavel. "Sold!"

Grace blinked, stunned. "Did she say?"

"She did," said Jerome, equally amazed.

"Nineteen thousand eight hundred dollars," stuttered Elaine, as if she were reporting the discovery of alien life.

"Pay up, Grouchy," said Pat.

Henry answered by falling out of his chair, right onto the luxurious Skinner carpet.

Outside Skinner, Grace's client hailed a taxi and slipped into it, turning back to wave at her with a giddy smile, a child's smile, a grandson once again. He had offered to pay her a consulting fee, which she had flatly refused. When Pat asked why the hell not, Grace told her she had already been paid in full.

"Well, I'm about to get paid myself," said Pat, elbowing Henry.

Henry said, for the first time since Grace had known him, absolutely nothing.

"He really needed that money, didn't he?" asked Elaine.

"He did," said Grace. "His bank just restructured, and he's been reassigned to another position at a much lower scale. That card just bought him an engagement ring and a down payment on an apartment for him and his fiancée."

"Amazing," said Elaine.

"'*Always*,'" said Grace.

"I'll drink to that," said Pat. "I'm buying!"

The group began to move toward the pay lot down the street, but Grace hung back. "Oh shit," she said. "Left my phone in the hall. I'll meet you there, okay?"

"Don't be late," said Pat. "Groucho won't shut up forever." She threw her arm around Henry, and the three of them walked off down the sidewalk.

Grace slipped back into the lobby of Skinner's, which was closing down for the evening. Instead of making her way back to the hall upstairs, she sat down on the stairs, rolling the celestial globe between her fingers absentmindedly. It was neither hot nor cold—it was cooling, as if it had released some great and terrible energy that was now slithering back into the depths of the stone. She was tempted to press into it, to tease out one last pleasurable pinprick to sustain her.

Until the next time.

It was a seductive thought, but it wasn't hers.

Grace knew that, as sure as she knew *The Jester* should have sold for twenty and the embroidered card fifty. The globe affected things. It touched the people in that room, and it reached through the phone lines and the internet, and it touched those people, too. Her friends had been astonished by the extraordinary coincidence. But it wasn't a coincidence, and it wasn't a charm, or an heirloom, or a lapis lazuli rabbit's foot. Grace would only guess what it wasn't.

Because she was petrified of what it was.

Jerome Zwick emerged from an executive office, escorted by Lynn Martell. She gave him a sharp peck on the cheek and disappeared back into the office.

"Is there anyone in the world you don't know?" asked Grace.

"When you've been around the block as many times as I have, you get to know where most of the bodies are buried." He walked over and lowered himself down on the carpet step beside her. "Thought you'd be celebrating by now."

"Did you really?"

He cracked a wry smile. "No. In fact, I thought you'd weasel out of it by claiming you left your keys upstairs."

Grace laughed and waved her phone.

"I should have known," he chuckled. "The Hungarian Lost-My-Phone Trick."

"Bavarian," said Grace. "My family was German, until Hitler told them they weren't."

"Well, you don't need a trick—Bavarian or otherwise—when you're seventy years old. You can just go home, which is what I intend to do. That was a very entertaining and surprising evening, and I'm worn out." He gave her hand a tender squeeze before using the banister to hoist himself to his feet.

"It's the necklace," said Grace.

He looked down at her, not understanding.

"I think it's the necklace." She unclasped it and handed it to Jerome.

He held it up to the light, and the golden inclusions sparkled, even in the darkened lobby. "That's impossible," he said.

"What about nineteen thousand eight hundred dollars?"

He sighed. "That's impossible, too."

"It does something, Jerry. It did something to the people in that room." She grabbed his hand. "I think it's doing something to me."

Jerome groaned his way back down beside her. He simply sat there, deep in thought, his eyes ping-ponging about as he ticked off the facts. Suddenly he chuckled to himself, although it was loud enough to worry Grace.

"You don't believe me," she said.

"Oh, no. I believe you. But I think you're only half right."

"How so?"

"Well, something clearly had an effect on the people in that room tonight," he said. "Let's say it's the necklace. Let's say it has the power to encourage people to throw down enormous amounts of money for things that should be bought for next to nothing." He rolled the globe about in his palm, this way and that. "But something had to convince this."

Grace shook her head. "What do you mean?"

"Nineteen thousand eight hundred dollars."

"Yes?"

"How did you come to that?"

She took a deep breath. "It tells me things."

"Okay," he said, taking it in. "Let's say it does. But did it tell you that? Did it tell you nineteen thousand eight hundred dollars?"

Grace closed her eyes and ran back over it in her mind—the appraisal, the card, the eternal eloquence of *Always*, and something stirred within her once again, like a tiny pilot light. "No," she said. "That number was mine. Then it was *ours*, if that makes sense."

"It does, don't you see? The necklace affects the bidding, but it doesn't make the appraisals—it manifests them. And it doesn't choose the objects. *The Jester, the Kiss from France*—those were your calls, Grace." He held it up before his eyes. "The necklace affects the auction," he said, dropping the necklace back into her palm. "You affect the necklace."

Grace held the celestial globe at arm's length, as if it had suddenly turned into a spitting viper. "I didn't try to," she said. "I didn't ask for that."

"That can't be true, Grace," he said in the softest of tones. "I've asked for that power every single day of my career. To set the value—not by a bidder's whim, or the cold calculating machinery of the market—but by the worth."

Grace brought the necklace closer to her, spinning the globe on its tiny axis. *Maybe*, she thought. *Just maybe I could...*

"See where this goes," he said. "Be careful and honorable and sparing, and most of all compassionate. But be on your guard—you've been given an awesome and most terrifying gift."

Grace turned to him. "What if it's a weapon?"

"A weapon in one hand is a plowshare in another." He closed her fingers around the globe until it disappeared into her grasp.

It felt warm.

It felt good.

A gift, thought Grace. She placed the necklace around her neck, fastening it tight.

I accept.

Part III
Space

One

Grace left the baggage claim carousel of Albany Airport and set off down the sidewalk with a small overnight bag, scanning the curb for her ride. As she passed an unmarked black sedan, the back door swung partially open, but no one emerged. Grace peeked inside the shadows but could not spy the driver.

"Are you here for Grace Schaffer?" she asked.

The trunk opened remotely, creaking on its hinges.

He's eccentric, Grace thought, but she had seen eccentric before; from latex glove handshakes to hundred-year nondisclosure agreements, to clients who blindfolded her and drove her around in circles before arriving at their destinations. None of it threw Grace off the scent when she was the go-to scout for *Antiques Roadshow*, and she had a knack for identifying the pieces that would be worth the expense of transporting them to and from set, as well as the ability to charm the owners too anxious to part with them.

But this was more than eccentric—this was creepy. The call had come in right after they announced their upcoming show in Bennington, Vermont. The client would pay the travel for one—and only one—expert, his collection could be viewed only on the day of his choosing, and only between the hours of seven and nine at night, whereupon the expert would be immediately transported back to a hotel by the airport. No lodging on-site would be provided, no pictures could be taken, and the client reserved the right to eject the expert from his premises at any time.

Elaine had told her no, that red flags flew all over it, but things were just beginning to turn around at the Appraisal Experts Roadshow, and Grace had argued they needed to swing at the fences to ensure the hard times were past for good. Elaine was adamant she follow behind at a safe distance, but Grace had all the protection she needed around her neck.

But it wasn't just protection, was it? Grace had a passing thought—a silly one, really—that her desire to be alone with the celestial globe, just the two of them setting off on a grand adventure, sounded just a bit possessive. But nothing like a hand on a bottle, or a needle and the damage done, because the globe was hers, it had chosen her, and together the two of them would find what no one else could, high up in the mountains of Vermont. And Grace would be the one to discover it, and the globe would answer, ticking over once again with that strange and pleasant warmth. She would feed upon it, and it her, as it bloomed within her, and for the first time in a very long time, she'd be full.

And so would the show, of course, and the galleries of all the experts, and anyone else in need of that special something that only Grace and her globe could provide. And so they all agreed the mysterious nature of the call was impossible to resist. As soon as Elaine gave in, Grace and her globe had gotten on a plane.

For what, she had no idea.

Grace placed her bag into the sedan's trunk and doubled back to the open door, peering inside the slick black leather cabin. The windows were so heavily tinted, there was barely enough light to make out the outline of the driver's head, and no sign whatsoever of the limo company itself. But Grace had no intention of letting anyone down, least of all Jerry and Elaine, so she slipped inside and closed the door, which shut with the fabric solidity of a large coffin.

Without a word, the driver put the car in gear, and they drove out of Albany and motored east, ascending into the mountains of western Vermont. Their destination was thirty miles past the show site in Bennington—a large ranch in Woodford. Not exactly a hub of rare antiques, but stranger things had been found in stranger places.

As the car rose higher into the ancient mountains, Grace had the sensation that she was not just leaving civilization, but present day itself. Homes gave way to trailers, which gave way to shacks, many of them charred and roofless. If Grace had seen a young boy with a high forehead and a banjo, she would not have been surprised.

"Do you have any idea what I'll be seeing at the ranch?" she asked, the scenery and silence unnerving her.

"He prefers I not speak to the passengers," said the driver, eyes front.

"I won't tell if you won't."

The driver reached back and pointed to the dome light over Grace's head. It had been replaced by a small security camera, angled directly at Grace.

He's eccentric, Grace thought. *That's all. Just eccentric.* She edged her hand up her shirt, careful not to draw attention as she slipped the celestial globe inside; there was no need to give anyone the incentive to look at either of them any closer.

She wondered if she ought to share her phone's location with Elaine—just as a precaution, of course—but the moment she unlocked it, the last reception bar blinked into oblivion. Whatever lay ahead, Grace would face it alone.

The car drove on, bucking over what felt like a pebbled dirt road. Grace prayed it was not the body of the last appraiser, and she slumped back into the leather seat, reviewing the entirety of her life, one mistake at a time.

Two

The car came to a sudden halt, and the moonlit outline of a large two-story log cabin appeared through a gap in the thick pines. Grace had not noticed it when they pulled in, as the cabin had blended in with the trees around it, making it appear deserted. A dim tallow light from the open front door spilled out onto the wraparound porch, which was completely devoid of any furniture. The windows were caked in a jaundice yellow haze and the log walls were badly weathered, but none were missing or cracked. Grace realized there were no markings whatsoever to identify those who lived within—no signs, plants, flowers, flags, not even a house number. The home was not built to impress or intimidate or make any kind of impression at all; it simply stood.

So did the man gazing at her from the top of the stairs. Grace had expected the traditional uniform of wild eyes, shaggy hair, haphazard eyebrows, and Rip Van Winkle's beard. Stuart Bedford could not have been more, well, bland. His eyes were calm, his gray hair short and unstyled, and not a single blade of stubble stood out on the crags of his angular face. He was dressed in simple clothing—blue jeans, a red-and-white knit shirt, tan work boots, and a thick leather belt; nothing torn or tattered, but nothing new either. His clothes were functional, no more, no less.

He came down the steps and greeted Grace as she emerged from the sedan. "Thank you for coming, Ms. Schaffer," he said in a phlegmy drawl, extending his hand.

Grace shook it—and had to peek at it to be sure she was not shaking a leather glove. "Call me Grace, please."

"I'll call you Ms. Schaffer," he said stiffly.

"As you wish." Grace turned to grab her bag from the open trunk, and wondered if Elaine had been right, and she had been horribly, horribly wrong.

"Robert will get it," said Bedford, starting up the steps to the porch. Grace figured that was the only invitation she would get, so she went up the stairs after him.

She followed him through the front door into an impressive two-story-high living room. It was a huge space—much larger than it appeared from outside. The polished log walls arched up and over their heads, supported by massive timber beams. Stairways to Grace's left and right rose up in wooden switchbacks to identical second-floor wings, which disappeared off in long, low-lit hallways. In fact, there was little illumination in the entire space. A chandelier over the center of the room was turned down to what must have been its lowest setting, and other than that, the only light came from the fireplace, which crackled in the far corner of the room. A large three-section couch stood in the center of the room, flanked by two deep brown leather armchairs. Neither of them sported the usual indentations of body or person—she wondered how often they were sat in. The room was bare of something else—things. There were no magazines out, no books left open on the arm of a chair, no coasters, no pictures, no television remote. Where was Bedford in here, where was his touch? The entire place just seemed... empty. Not stripped clean, for there'd be no need to clean anything that had never been cluttered. Just empty. And cold. Grace drew her sweater close in around her body and wondered if the home had any heating source at all, other than the small, overworked fireplace. Stranger yet, the walls around them were stripped bare, not a single frame or painting to be found. Bedford was an art collector—where was all the art?

"Follow me," he grunted, leading her down a hallway so dark, she had to run her hands over the walls to keep herself moving in the right direction. She tried to glance behind her, but the way back was now an impenetrable void itself. She reached for the lapis lazuli, but even it was cold and dark, as if its power could not penetrate the gloom. She reached out for the wall to steady herself and something hairy and chitinous scurried across the back of her hand. She put her other hand over her mouth to stifle a scream and realized in terror that Bedford's heavy footsteps had halted some time ago. She cringed, waiting for his leathery hands to close around her neck. A wooden door closed behind her, a switch snapped, and Grace was momentarily blinded by a flash of light. She blinked it away to find herself standing in another two-story-high chamber. She assumed there were walls in here, too, but she could not see any of them.

The room was a jumbled warehouse of antiques of every size and shape imaginable: Queen Anne and Victorian Revival chairs were stacked dangerously high atop Federal dining tables, Provincial highboys leaned haphazardly against delicately carved Chippendale chests, and a small phalanx of tall case clocks rose in the distance like the ruins of a distant fortress. Huge splintering crates brimmed over with crumbling clay pottery, fraying tapestries, and rusty silver; and sandwiched between two of the larger crates, Grace saw a stack of at least twenty golden-leaf-framed paintings—the top one a precious oil, glimmering in the low light. It was as if an entire museum had been crammed through a funnel.

To Grace, it was not just a waste—it was a sin. Art truly lived only in the eye of a beholder, and Bedford had denied these precious pieces even a passing glance. No, not denied—he had punished them. Any number of the imprisoned pieces might have had significant value at some point, but they had been tortured on the rack of neglect for so long, it would take an army of restorers to resuscitate them.

"What do you think?" he asked, as if he had opened the gates of a salvage yard.

"You have quite a collection," she said, her voice trembling.

"Well, most of it's crap." He waved a dismissive hand at two hundred years of American culture. "But you know what they say—today's tripe is tomorrow's treasure."

So that was it. He wasn't hoarding; he was hedging. He had amassed a treasure trove of whatever he could lay his greedy little paws on, and now he was biding his time until something appreciated enough to sell. No wonder the house looked abandoned—his last dollar had been spent pirating antiques. No American master would ever grace his walls, no candlestick would ever bear the wax of a single candle, because their purpose was not to enrich his life. It was to expand his bank account.

"Well," Grace said, digging a fingernail into her palm to keep from digging them into his cheek. "I see a great deal of treasure here."

"I suppose." He sniffed. "So what's my best bet at the show?"

Grace looked over the sprawling kill zone of metal, wood, fabric, and canvas. "I wouldn't know where to start."

"My son has a list."

"It might be easier if I check that first and we go from there," she said, averting her eyes from the artistic carnage. "Can I speak with him?"

"I suppose."

He turned to leave and Grace released a huge sigh, relieved to follow him out. Bedford led her back through the darkened hallway and into a small kitchen. A white plastic card table had been set up in the center of the room with paper plate settings for three. Next to one of the plates was a makeshift ashtray made from an anchovy tin. A small orange lamp hung above the table, but three of the four bulbs had gone dark or, Grace thought, had probably never worked in the first place.

Her driver from Albany was leaning into an open oven, spooning gravy over a small roast. The meat looked just large enough to feed one person, but in this house, Grace knew it would need to feed three.

"Where's that list?" asked Bedford.

The driver turned around, and in the tallow light of the kitchen, Grace saw he was young—perhaps eighteen or nineteen. He was dressed like Bedford—jeans, knit shirt, work boots—and shared Bedford's straw-like light brown hair. Grace realized the driver was not only the cook, he was Bedford's son.

"It's upstairs in my room," he said.

Bedford jerked his head at the door and his son got the message, closing the oven and walking out of the kitchen. Bedford plopped down on a rickety stool at the card table.

"Shouldn't we follow him?" asked Grace.

"Robert'll bring it here."

Grace looked at one of the open stools and imagined waiting for Robert with Stuart Bedford, and the excruciating awkwardness that would come with it. "Would you mind if I poked around until he returns?" she asked.

"At what?"

"At what we might bring to the show for you?"

"Yes, I mind." He picked the butt of a used cigarette out of the ashy anchovy tin and lit it up. "Go find Robert. He needs to be there if you're snooping around."

Grace excused herself and walked into the atrium in time to see Robert climb the last few stairs to the landing on the second level. She followed, up the stairs and into the shadowed hallway that led through the east wing of the house. She passed an open door on her right, and although the room was dark, she saw the ghostly specters inside: a dozen filthy white sheets draped over piles of curved and angled shapes—perhaps antique tables or chairs, perhaps dead bodies. Grace had initially thought the house had been turned into a warehouse, but she was wrong. It was a mausoleum.

She shuddered and hurried down to an open door at the end of the hall, stepping into the pale yellow light of Robert's bedroom. He whipped around suddenly, as if something had been thrown at him.

"I'm sorry," said Grace. "I didn't mean to startle you."

He nodded and turned back to the open drawer of a large metal filing cabinet, nearly the only piece of furniture in the room aside from a chipped wooden dresser, a small desk and folding chair, and a lumpy black futon that had been pulled up into a sofa. Grace looked around the bare walls—even in here, a young man's room, there were no pictures or posters of any kind.

This poor kid, she thought—yet another discarded piece of Bedford's collection. Grace had never been discarded by her father, but separation? Isolation? She had certainly made their acquaintance.

"I'm Grace," she said. "Nice to meet you."

He nodded, drawing out a thick file and carrying it over to the futon. He sat down and opened the file, thumbing through handwritten records of Bedford's stash.

"Your father doesn't have any cameras up here, does he?"

The boy glanced up and shook his head.

"No cameras?" Grace gasped in mock shock. "El Comandante can't hear us talking?"

"You didn't ask about microphones."

"Oh shit." Grace covered her mouth, mouthing, *Sorry.*

Robert laughed. "Nah, no mics. I've checked."

"You were smart to do so." She sat beside him on the futon. "I'm Grace. I know I've already said that, but I'm going to keep saying it until you tell me your name."

"Robert," he said. "You can call me Rob if you want."

"I will. There's nothing shorter than Grace, so we're stuck with that one."

"That's okay. Grace is beautiful," he said. "It fits you."

Grace leaned back, touched by the compliment. "Thank you, Rob."

He offered her a guarded smile and returned to the sprawling pile of papers. Grace noticed that Stuart's influence on the boy's appearance ended with the color of his hair. There was a softness to his features that was almost cherubic, with none of the severe lines of Bedford's cheeks. His eyes weren't cold and dead, but a bright shade of blue, and they didn't sit back and judge, they observed—closely. Grace could tell he was deeply interested in his father's art by the care he had taken in compiling the file, and she noticed his fingers seemed to caress each entry as the pages fluttered by. Grace caught brief glimpses of the boy's work, and although his penmanship was poor, Grace could tell his organizational skills were first rate.

"Looks like you run the ship around here," she said.

"Pretty much." Rob angled the file toward Grace with a bit of pride—although even that seemed a guilty pleasure. "I know what he paid for most of it, so I like to know what it's worth." He got up and opened another drawer of the file cabinet, withdrawing a pristine copy of *Kovels' Antiques & Collectibles Price Guide*.

"Good for you, Rob," said Grace, impressed. "You know, *Miller's* is also—"

He reached back in, pulling out a copy of *Miller's Antiques*.

She laughed. "I should have known that I was in the presence of a professional."

He blushed. Grace's heart ached for him. This beautiful boy, locked away up here in the mountains, not with a father, but with a warden, and yet he had somehow found his bliss in this dark cell of a room, digging into the mysteries of Antiquity, just as she had with her little red shovel. He hadn't any of Grace's advantages—a father's footsteps to follow, a mother's encouragement—and yet Rob had clearly found the same path she had. But how much farther would he go, shackled as he was to the deadweight of his surroundings?

"Have you ever thought of going into the field?" she asked. "I could make an introduction for you, if you like."

"Oh, no." He shook his head. "I couldn't do that."

"Why not?"

He blushed again. "Well, uh . . . he doesn't pay me very much, for what I do. It's enough to keep the car running, and buy the groceries, and that sort of thing, but not enough . . ."

"To go your own way."

He nodded, returning the guides to the drawer and easing it shut.

"Well, maybe we can find something downstairs that might help you."

He smiled, but the smile was strained. "That would be nice." He sat back down beside her on the futon and removed a handwritten document from the massive file, its twenty pages held together by a large paperclip. "This is a list of everything in the main room downstairs," he said, handing it to her.

From the very first page, Grace was hooked. It was a spectacularly detailed index, and although the paper was wrinkled and the penmanship poor, it was as eloquent as any archive she had ever seen. Grace felt a sudden surge of guilt. She had come up here on a mercenary mission, to bring back the Golden Fleece, and there was so much that glittered in this house, but none of it shone the way that sweet boy did. She no longer thought about what she could take from here. She only thought—

What can I give?

And something answered.

Look, it said.

Look? she thought. *At the boy?*

Look, it said. *See.*

Grace shifted closer to the boy so they could go through the index together. "Well, let's see what we have here, shall we?" She lifted the first page, but something just above the top edge of it drew Grace's eye. She saw something.

A shining brass knob.

It stuck out from a small door in the opposite wall, and even in the low light of the room, it appeared faintly illuminated, as if from within.

"What's in there?" she asked.

"Oh." Rob waved it off. "Just some things that don't fit anywhere else."

Like me? thought Grace as a single bead of sweat trickled down her chest from the rapidly warming lapis lazuli of the celestial globe. There was something behind that door, calling out to her from the darkness. She felt light, light-headed, as if she were floating, drifting toward the door, downhill like an ever-quickening river toward the rapids, the blood churning and foaming in her ears. "I'd like to take a look just the same, if it's all right," she said, her breath tight in her chest. "I'd like to see."

Rob shrugged and helped Grace to her feet, and the two of them crossed the room. Rob turned the knob, but the door did not open.

"Sorry," he said. "I haven't opened this in a while."

He yanked at the knob and the wood splintered a bit, releasing the door, which swung open with a rusty protest. A musty cloud belched out, and the two of them coughed on the thick gray dust. Grace was reminded again of an open crypt, but this was not like the haunted catacombs below. She sensed a reverence here, a silent presence, as if she were standing on hallowed ground.

"You sure you want to go in there?" he asked, peering inside the darkened attic.

Grace wasn't sure. She reached under her shirt and brought out the celestial globe, rolling it back and forth in her fingers. It was still warm, but it didn't seem to be getting any warmer. It wasn't cooling, either; it was waiting. For Grace.

"That's the prettiest thing I've ever seen," said Rob, admiring it.

"It's my best friend these days." Grace laid it on top of her sweater. "We're inseparable."

"You make a nice pair," Rob said, and Grace was again moved by how sensitive and kind he was—a minor miracle in this house.

"Thank you," she said, poking her head into the inky blackness. A wispy clump of cobweb floated out and she accidentally swallowed it. Grace choked, her eyes tearing up.

"You don't have to go in there," he said. "It's pretty gross."

But Grace knew she was going in. The current was too strong now, and she surrendered, yielding to the darkness as it enveloped her, drawing her inside.

She yanked her shirt up over her mouth, ducked low, and crawled through the tiny doorway into the yawning darkness. Once ensconced within, Grace switched on her phone's flashlight and found herself in a small attic with a sloping roof, tucked as it was into the side of the house. She slowly scanned the light from one side of the room to the other. An old rocking horse emerged from the gloom, then a few splintered sticks of a Belle Epoque rosewood chair, a legless canapé couch, a bent copper candlestick, and a mound of fraying carpets piled nearly to the rafters. There were a few small crates, stuffed with the chubby limbs and decapitated heads of teddy bears and porcelain dolls. Grace sighed, disappointed. *It's not here*, she thought.

See, it said.

She ran her flashlight across the walls once again, and something just beyond the dusty beam twitched, disturbing the darkness like ripples across the placid face of a lake.

Grace froze, her eyes riveted on the dark space, but nothing moved. Had she imagined it, a trick of the shadows? Had she heard something? She thought she had, but the room was so silent.

But it wasn't empty. Grace sensed something inside the silence, and suddenly it reached out, winding about her in invisible tendrils, brushing over her skin like a fine silk.

Then, a sound pierced the silence; not quite loud enough to hear, but Grace felt it resonate within her, plucking the delicate filaments of her inner ear. It was coming from the deepest corner of the room. Grace peered into the darkness, and the outline of a large, flat object breached the black veil. It was leaning up against the far wall, facing away from her.

And it was humming.

It was an alien sound, inhuman but sentient, aware of her presence. Grace wondered if she'd gone too far, too deep into a corner that craved the dark, that didn't want her there. She didn't dare move for fear she might disturb it, anger it, chase it off, but it grew louder, materializing out of the shadows, revealing the back of a gilded rectangular wooden frame, about five feet wide and three feet high. The brown paper that protected the back of the frame was torn and tattered, and Grace could clearly see faded canvas behind it.

A painting. Grace inched toward it, mindful of the cobwebs that dangled from the rafters like ghostly stalactites. This part of the attic was much warmer than Rob's room, and Grace unbuttoned her sweater, but the closer she drew to the frame, the warmer she became.

It was the celestial globe; she could feel it through her blouse. She reached up at the necklace and gasped, flinching. The lapis lazuli was radiating heat, heat she could see—the golden inclusions seemed to flow across the face of the stone in molten rivulets.

What do you want me to do? she asked.

Seek, it said. *See.*

Grace reached out and drew aside a flap of the brown paper that covered the frame. This was definitely canvas—she could see the dark pine stretcher inside the frame and the small handmade nails that held the fabric in place. The frame was old, the canvas old as well.

The globe was blazing now, and so was Grace. It spread over her, prickling her skin, stinging her eyes, her breath reduced to sharp pyroclastic gasps. She pressed her hands against the sides of the frame, and careful not to use too much effort, turned it to face her, easing it back against the wall. She stood back and brought her phone's flashlight up to inspect what she had found.

The gilded frame was a simple carving in the Louis XIII Revival style—the thin tubular perimeter a twisting string of bunched flowers and leafy foliage. Grace could not spy a raised pediment at the bottom for the title of the work, nor any marking from the frame maker. It was not from a museum or wealthy private collection—this was an original frame, commissioned by either the artist or an exhibitor.

She ran her flashlight slowly over the canvas itself. The colors were dulled, muted, slumbering under a thick patina of wood smoke and candlelight. She laid the very tip of her index finger on the canvas and ran it across the surface. Tiny textured lumps tickled her skin—this was a three-dimensional work; an oil.

But whose? Grace leaned closer, pointing the light at the corners of the work, but no signature emerged. Perhaps the patina covering the varnish had grown too thick. She was standing too close—it would never reveal itself like this. She needed to give it room to breathe.

Grace took a few steps back so the flashlight could illuminate the entire canvas. Even in the harsh blue light of her phone, she could make out the bold, thick strokes of paint that swept over the face of the canvas, making the work appear to undulate and breathe within the golden frame. The style was unmistakable.

It's not, she thought. *It can't be.*

Not in Stuart Bedford's cobweb attic. That was silly. She squinted at the painting, and features began to rise off the canvas. A serpentine river, a bank filled with drooping trees, a distant church spire, a stone bridge, a figure on the bridge.

A woman?

Grace's heart thumped hard against her ribs. There was something about her, something so haunting.

But she couldn't *see*. The flashlight was drowning the painting in a blue fluorescence. She became aware of another light—a golden glow radiating off the celestial globe. It seemed natural to her, not like the digitized brutality of the iPhone.

She switched off her flashlight, and a brilliant sunburst of reds and blues and pinks and violets revealed itself. Illuminated by the glow of the celestial globe, the painting opened a portal into a world of colors so thick and liquid, they seemed to surge across the canvas. The river sparkled in a current of tumbling sapphires and foamy, wind-whipped cream-colored crests. Mossy emerald trees lined the banks with rolling blankets of yellow and violet flowers, shielding the scene from the outside world within a fortress of foliage, a hidden paradise. The distant church spire jutted up into a milky sea of cotton clouds like an ivory obelisk, radiating with the burnt orange glow of the setting sun. The sunset itself was a revelation of color, as if the sun had been turned inside out, its every molten gas released in a starburst of oil and paste and powder. The woman, though—

The woman was the painting.

She stood on the bridge, her hand resting lightly upon the railing. It was unclear to Grace if she was momentarily hesitating or had simply brushed her hand against the rail as she climbed the stony steps. Her sky blue skirt fluttered behind her in such a way it appeared she was crossing the bridge toward the far side of the river, but her shoulders were turned, twisting her torso back toward the viewer. She held a white parasol, but instead of shading her face, it illuminated it beneath the glowing fabric halo. As light filtered through and fell upon her features, the colors of the setting sun reversed, as if by reflecting off her face, the light had been reborn.

Grace had to get it outside, had to be sure that it was not just the light of the stone or her own breathless excitement that had lent such color to the faded canvas. She pulled the sleeves of her sweater down over her hands and lifted the frame, shuffling over the dusty wooden floor until she emerged once more into the lamplight of Robert's bedroom.

"What are you doing?" he asked.

"I'm not sure," she said, carefully leaning it up against the wall beside the open attic door. As she set it down, one of her sleeves rode up her wrist, and her fingers brushed once again over the gilded frame. She felt a familiar tingling, then a tiny shock. It raced across her palm, up her arm, into her chest, pumping through artery and vein, across synapse and sinew, and she was back once again in her parents' backyard with that arrowhead, the tactile feeling of flesh on the textured craftsmanship of another era—as if she could reach through time and feel the artist through the delicacy of their work. And she had touched that genius ever since, at auctions near and far, under tents, at civic centers all across the country, but they had all been preludes to this moment. She had stumbled, she had lost her way, but she had found her footing once again, and now she stood on the precipice of a discovery of such magnitude, it had the power to lift her high above the rank fogbank of her existence and set her in the very eye of everything she adored. She stepped back to see what buried treasure she had unearthed.

But . . . it had changed.

It was still an oil, still masterfully done, but the colors had faded. The sapphire crests of the river had disappeared beneath still gray waters. Clouds no longer floated across the sky like ghostly apparitions; they gathered in the upper corners of the frame like hardened dollops of curdled cream. The trees had browned, their leaves wrinkled and crisped by the relentless glare of the sun. The sun itself had lost its soothing glow, its rays now fractured into flaky orange scales from the careless impact of some blunt object. Grace was most crestfallen to see what had befallen the woman who had so drawn her eye. In the harsh light of the room, her face was no longer reflective; it was shaded beneath the parasol, her expression shrouded and inscrutable.

The painting was not what Grace had seen inside the attic. Perhaps the pale yellow light of the bedroom had dampened down the intensity of the paint, perhaps the hazy patina covering the varnish had reacted to the radiating light from the celestial globe, or perhaps Grace had simply imagined the whole thing.

Or perhaps, once again, Grace was just plain wrong.

She reached up for the celestial globe, but it was cold now, silent. Where had it gone—why now, when she needed it most? The thrill of her discovery began to wane, and she grasped about, trying to shake a thought loose, any thought, just to keep the moment alive.

"Where'd you buy this, Robert?"

"I didn't," he said. "It was there when we moved in. I wanted to hang it up, but Dad said I had to keep it in there. He doesn't like things cluttering up the walls." He glanced quickly at the painting, drinking it in as if he were thirsty for the very sight of it. "I better put it back."

"Please don't," pleaded Grace. The moment was drifting away, but it was still so close—*she* was so close. "Not yet."

"Why?" He hesitated. "It's not valuable, is it?"

"It might be." Grace sighed. "Not as much as I thought initially, though."

She gestured for Robert to stand beside her so she could walk him through the appraisal. He took a few hesitant steps, like a child approaching the window of his first aquarium. Grace knew she had to be absolutely sure about the painting. If this boy threw off his shell, he'd be vulnerable, and his pain would be her doing.

"Let's see what you have, Rob," she said, scanning the edges of the painting. "There's no signature or date, not that I can find, so we'll have to get our hands dirty and dig a bit."

"Okay, cool."

Grace felt her heart break into a trot, thumping against her ribs; the game was afoot. "It's an oil painting, oil on canvas. The frame's original, and although I can't see the markings of the maker, that is a very specific Baroque revival style—used mainly by painters in the mid- to late-nineteenth centuries."

"It's that old?"

"The frame is," Grace said, cautioning him. "Not necessarily the picture itself."

Robert's shoulders slumped.

"Which is why we'll check the wooden stretcher of the canvas itself." Grace leaned the painting toward them, pointing at the inlaid wood stretcher poking through the back of the torn paper skin. "Look closely at the age and color of that wood."

He did. "It's brown, dark brown. It looks old."

"Agreed." Grace pointed at the back of the frame itself, where some of the gold had flaked away from the wood beneath. "What do you see there?"

"Looks the same as the stretcher—the same age." His breathing quickened. "Is it?"

"Perhaps, but there's one more test." She leaned the frame farther back, revealing the entire rear of the painting. "The canvas is attached to the stretcher by handmade nails—a good sign—but these stretchers were often recycled."

"Was this one?"

"Do you see any open nail holes?"

Robert scanned the stretcher. "Nope."

"Then it's original."

Robert gasped. Grace put a hand on his arm to calm him. "We still don't know about the canvas," she said. "But the frame and stretcher are a match."

Grace drifted back two steps, and Robert drew back with her, glued to her hip.

"I can't see any dates or marks on the canvas without a magnifying glass, so we have to look to the painting itself, of what stories it wants to tell." She fell silent, her eyes darting across the face of the painting, over hill and river and bridge. Robert glanced from her to the painting and back again to Grace, like a child eyeing his parents during a moment of silent prayer.

The silence was too much for him. "Tell me what you see."

"It's so muted, Rob. We have to peek beneath the layers of tobacco smoke and fingerprints and candlelight."

There's nothing here. Just a hallucination.

But Robert could not sell a hallucination.

The eyes never lie, she thought. *Use something else.*

She opened herself to the paint, allowing the colors and textures to blend before her, to lift off the canvas...

Something stirred, beneath the crust of the oil. Grace stepped back, stunned.

It can't be.

"What?" he asked. "What do you see?"

"It's Impressionist," she said, and as foolish as it sounded, it did not feel like a lie.

"Impressionist? Are you sure?"

"Yes." Grace took deliberate breaths, her heart pounding up into her throat. "Monet, Degas, Renoir, Cassatt—the birth of Modern Art itself."

Robert's eyes bulged with a mixture of awe and fear. "But that's—" He peered into the musty attic. "That's all just... trash."

"It's Impressionist," she said, increasingly certain. "Late-nineteenth century." Grace ran her finger over the surface of the painting as it all fell into place. "The blurred horizon line, full brushstrokes, the stunning juxtaposition of reds and greens and violets and yellows. It's not realistic, not a snapshot—but a sensual impression of the simple things that make our ordinary lives extraordinarily beautiful."

Robert shook his head, struggling to keep up. "Then who painted it? It's not Monet, right?"

"No, not him." Her eyes sought out every nook and cranny in the painting. "Maybe a lesser-known follower of Monet—the style is certainly similar. But I think—" *No, that's wrong.* "I sense this is an original voice."

"Original?" He swallowed hard enough to hear. "That's a big deal, right?"

Grace hesitated. She had no sense of value, not yet. She was missing something. "Well, it's certainly old," she said. "But it's had a rough life." She pointed to the radiating crater over the setting sun. "See this? It might just be *craquelure*—that's damage from alternating exposure to dry and humid air—but it's only in one spot, so it looks more like some careless impact. Unfortunately, it's directly over a major focal point of the painting."

"Yeah." He deflated. "Kind of ruins it, I guess."

"Not at all." Grace ran her hand over the scaling paint. "A true work of art orbits above the sum of its parts. Oil, pastel, watercolor—that's not the painting, is it?"

Robert shook his head, transported by her words.

"The artist has a singular perspective, right? A peculiar angle on the world around them, and they translate that into light and color and shade and pigment, but that's not the life of the piece. It needs us. It needs us to listen, to feel." She paused. "And when I listen to this . . ." Grace gazed deeper into the painting. She could sense something, hear something, hidden within the paint. But it was so faint, so dim, she could not coax it up from the depths of the oils.

"I'm so sorry, Rob," she said. "I think—I *know* there's something here. Something I can't explain, or put into words, and I know that doesn't help you, but I can't shake this feeling. Something's hiding from us—I just can't find it."

"It's okay, Grace," he said. "I believe you."

"Believe what?" said the dry leather voice of his father. Stuart Bedford stood in the doorway, arms and eyes crossed.

Robert froze. All the thrill of the chase, all the childlike wonder, drained right out of him.

"My appraisal," said Grace.

"Of what?" Bedford jutted a tobacco-stained finger at the painting. "That piece of shit?"

Grace bit down on a flood of curse words. "That's right," she said. "I was just explaining to Robert how damage, particularly the kind sustained here, destroys any value it might have brought on the open market."

Bedford nodded as if to say: *Tell me something I don't know.* "I told him he oughta throw that crap out, make room for something worth something. But he's partial to it, so."

Grace hesitated. "This is his?"

"And he can have it," said Bedford. "Along with everything else in there. I even marked it that way on the list, if you'd read it." He snapped his fingers for them to follow. "Now c'mon." He grunted. "Time for dinner. And bring the damn list—we can look through it downstairs."

Robert nodded and Bedford stomped off, disappearing into the darkened hallway.

"Rob," whispered Grace.

He waved her off and walked to the bed, picking up the list of his father's horde.

"Rob, listen to me. I really think you have something here."

"So what?" he said. "I can't sell something."

"Then bring it to the show," she said. "Please. I have a colleague—"

"No." Robert shook his head. "We have to get back downstairs." He slipped the painting back into the darkened attic, sealing it up within its dusty crypt.

Grace felt the room darken. Part of her had been locked away, too, and that painting had set it free, only to drag it back into the shadows.

"That's a pity," she said.

Robert looked at her with eyes far too old for his age. "I know," he said. "But you get used to it."

Three

Grace was relieved that Stuart Bedford kept his word and kicked her out promptly at nine o'clock, as she had run out of creative ways to convince him how close (how very, very close) his treasures were to bringing significant value to the show, if only he could wait a little longer. Perhaps next season would be the perfect time for him to attend. Perhaps by then, Grace would come up with another excuse to keep him far away from the Appraisal Experts Roadshow. If not, perhaps she'd be sick that day, or quit, or set a bear trap for him in the registration tent. Grace hated to think of all that exquisite history locked up in his warehouse, but she knew the more money he made from it, the more he would accumulate. At least she never had to lay eyes on him again. Robert and his mysterious painting, on the other hand—that was a pity. She felt horrible for Robert; he belonged in college, in an internship, in a gallery far away from that artistic wasteland. And so did that painting. Although Robert said she would get used to it slipping from her grasp, Grace did not, could not get used to it. How could she have been so dreadfully wrong?

The celestial globe had been silent ever since, offering no answers. Had it teased her in that cobwebbed attic? Was it teasing her still? She had assumed it was there to guide her, but guide her where? To despair?

The Appraisal Experts Roadshow, on the other hand, had been anything but silent. Even without an heirloom from Bedford to build excitement, the presale for the upcoming Bennington Show looked more like a rock concert than an antique show. The second miraculous auction at Skinner's had thrown fuel on *The Jester*'s fire, and the buzz had spread to the galleries of all the experts as well, including Grace's.

According to Jeff Tangeman, her hyperventilating gallery manager, Schaffer & Schaffer had been roused from its slumber by a steady stream of looky-loos, many there not for a painting, but for an appraisal with Grace. She was absent, of course, but it didn't stop them from making a purchase or two, which had left the shelves looking a little bare. She would have to return soon to give it some tender loving care, but Grace was loath to leave the show just yet.

Her father would understand—he had let his own gallery expire when his writings took off, and now Grace's hard work (*success?*) needed tending to see how far it might go. She could feel things starting to accelerate for her once again, fast enough that even the double loss of Albert and Victor could not completely keep pace. The pain was still there, of course, but it was buried in the landscape, not standing right before her; she had to consciously think of it to give it life, and some days were so busy, she simply couldn't spare the thought. Her phone's inbox was filled with requests for interviews and podcasts, invitations to conferences and shows, and even the occasional old friend who had mysteriously "rediscovered" her number. She had dreamt of it so often—of her return to the limelight—it felt as if she'd been forgiven for some past wrong, welcomed home with open arms. There was a familiar warmth about being in the center of things again, of being necessary. Perhaps even Victor in his lofty peak had caught wind of her revival; perhaps he had smiled, proud of her, just for old times' sake.

So why was she so unsettled? Why couldn't she just be thankful that the dark times were behind her, once and for all? Why couldn't she think about anything other than that painting, hiding up there in the mountains, in that darkened corner, and the hardened pit it had left within her, scratching away?

The Bennington Show was fast approaching, but the interim was torture, so much so that Grace hazarded a quick trip to her mother at Mary Elwood Estates. Even an argument was better than succumbing to the gnawing feeling that roiled within her. As Grace climbed the wooden steps to the double-door entryway, she noticed Max parked in his wheelchair once again at the edge of the veranda. "Afternoon, Max," she said.

Max squinted, not recognizing her.

Grace noticed the haze in his eyes had grown a lighter gray, making them faintly albino. She edged closer so he could see her clearly without straining. "Tread any boards lately, Master Thespian?"

His brow relaxed as she came into focus. "Grace! How are you, my dear?" he sang out in that mellifluous baritone. "Looking for your mom?"

"You know my mother?"

"Shirley?" he said, as if Grace had asked who the current president was. "Of course."

Grace hesitated—was he kidding, or just being kind? Shirley had always flown under the radar; subterranean in most social situations. "Yes. Shirley Schaffer. Have you seen her?"

"She should be back in her apartment by now."

"Thanks, Max." Grace gave him a peck on his forehead and walked inside, immediately assaulted by the thick acrid smell of age. No amount of mopping or polishing by Mary Elwood's dedicated army of orderlies could banish the stench. Grace moved through the halls briskly, so much so she plowed chest first into Dr. Charles Lee as he rounded a corner.

"Oh! Excuse me," she gasped. "I'm so terribly sorry."

"That's all right," said Lee, flashing a winning smile. "It's midday and I'm limiting my coffee intake, so I needed the pick-me-up."

Grace laughed. "Well, you're doing so much for my mother, it's the least I could do."

"Oh, Shirley's already paying us back threefold, I assure you."

Grace tilted her head. "How is that?"

"Oh, you know your mother."

"Yeah," said Grace. "That's why I asked."

He laughed again, as if she had made a fabulously witty joke. Maybe she had; maybe he was just flirting. Then again, he was attractive, he was young, he was a doctor for God's sake. *Let the man flirt.*

"Good to see you, Grace," he said.

"Good to be seen."

He smiled that million-dollar smile once again, striding off down the hall with a physician's purpose. Grace turned and watched him go, but it left her with a strange feeling—not a bad one, just unusual. It wasn't the flirting. The flirting was fine; she'd been on her game and knew she could take it up a notch next time. But—and this was the eerie part—she hadn't gotten the usual buzz from the Tracy-Hepburn back-and-forth. Maybe it was the anxiety of seeing her mother.

Grace shook it off and continued on her way, arriving at the door to her mother's apartment. She knocked, but her mother did not answer. She tried the doorknob, and it was unlocked, so Grace slipped inside and closed the door behind her.

"Mom?"

No one answered.

"Mom? Where are you?"

Silence.

Oh no.

She'd fallen. Or had a heart attack. Or died in her sleep. Grace ran through the tiny kitchen, checking the couch, convinced she'd find her mother sprawled face down on the sofa.

"Mom!" she yelled, tearing into the bedroom. No sign of Shirley, but the door to the bathroom was closed.

God, no.

Grace plunged into the bathroom, to find a counter so clean, you could perform open heart surgery on it, bath towels folded with the precision of basic training, and a full roll of toilet paper with a tri-folded end sheet. If Shirley had died, she had died cleaning.

Grace left the sparkling tiles of the bathroom and walked back into her mother's bedroom. The boxes had been unpacked, and the picture of Grace and her father on the steps of the Met had been placed on the top shelf of the bookcase in a place of honor. The books that lined the shelves were unchanged—her mother always returned books to their proper places every night, rather than leaving them on a nightstand or table.

But one had been left face up on the small desk by the window. Grace immediately recognized it: *Drawing on the Right Side of the Brain*—a literary rite of passage for artists and art historians because of its simple, straightforward introduction to the fine art of shape, angle, light, and shadow.

Grace smiled at her old friend, her old beat-up copy from high school Intro to Art. Her mother must have mixed it in with her own things during the move. Grace walked over and picked it up, flipping through the pages, her eyes scanning over the penciled notes she had taken all those years ago. It was amazing how much clearer her writing was back then, how eloquent her script. When had her handwriting become so messy?

It hadn't.

This isn't my book.

She leafed through it, reading the notes etched in the margins—sharp, precise commentary on how the various techniques might be applied. There was a science to it, a clear development of method assembled step by step within the pages of the text.

Grace shut the book, fascinated. The art world was quite small; perhaps the book had been donated to the Mary Elwood library by an artist she knew or had crossed paths with. It may have been a touch out of character (Shirley had a soft spot for historical fiction and political thrillers), but not terribly surprising she had checked it out—her mother couldn't help developing a passing fancy in her husband's pursuits, in Grace's. Perhaps this might finally give them something to talk about.

Grace grabbed it and left the apartment, scanning the halls for her mother. She wasn't in the library or coffee shop or café, and she didn't see her on any of the scenic verandas that ringed the building. Grace began to grow anxious—where was she? Had she wandered off? Her mother's mind was bulletproof, but her body had begun to rebel. Perhaps she had fallen and been taken to the infirmary?

Just then Grace noticed a few residents in the large open space of the Activity Center, her mother among them. They were busy clearing the center of the room from some event, removing a few chairs and tables and placing them back against the walls.

"Hey, Mom?" Grace waved as she crossed into the carpeted lounge.

Shirley's face was a mask of effort and concentration until she saw her daughter. "Gracie?" A grin spread across her face, but halted at the edges, never quite making it all the way into a smile. "Is everything okay?"

"Yeah, fine," Grace said, hugging her. Their embrace always felt so perfunctory to Grace, like two cardboard boxes leaning up against each other.

"What are you doing here?" asked Shirley.

"Came to see you, Mom." They stood a moment in silence. "Is that okay?"

"Of course, of course," said Shirley, although it sounded like she was convincing herself as much as her daughter. "Come meet my friends." She waved over two women, both about her age.

Friends? Grace was relieved. She had worried her mother's best friend at Mary Elwood would be the wall she was staring at.

"Hi," said Grace, shaking hands with one of the women. "I'm Grace."

"Oh!" The woman's hand locked around Grace's as if it were a rare gemstone. "You're Grace!"

"I am." Grace laughed. "I assure you, it's nothing to get too excited about."

"That's not what we hear."

"Oh?" Grace eyed her mother. "What lies has my mother been telling you?"

The woman patted Grace's hand. "Your gallery, dear. Your articles, your awards, your time on *Antiques Roadshow*."

"I love that show," crowed the other woman.

Grace flinched. *Here it comes.* "I'm not on it anymore."

"Ah," she said, still smiling. "But what a thrilling time you must have had!"

Grace was stumped. Usually, the mere mention of her banishment from the show short-circuited the conversation. Not with these women. "Yes," Grace said, taking a moment to remember the frenetic hustle and bustle of the set. It was so far away now, but these women had invited her to peek back at it, and she greeted it like a cherished sibling she had not seen in some time. "It was a very special time in my life."

"You'll have to tell us all about it."

"She doesn't have time to do that," said Shirley, playfully pushing them back as if they were groupies. "She's very busy."

"That's okay," said Grace, turning to the women. "Maybe next time, okay?"

They cackled excitedly and returned to setting chairs against the wall.

"What were you three up to in here?" asked Grace.

"Oh, you know." Shirley shrugged, as if it was so meaningless, even she could not recall it. "Just a little gathering. Just a few friends."

Grace noticed Shirley grab her wrist, holding her arm close against her hip. She wondered if that was a flash of Parkinson's or just her mother's usual awkwardness. "How are you doing, Mom?"

"Oh, I'm fine. Comes and goes." She smiled. "Mostly goes. It's just acting up from all the heavy lifting. I have to be careful—if they catch me, I might end up on some sort of work detail."

Grace laughed. "I can imagine you on the Mary Elwood chain gang."

Shirley laughed, and this one was free and easy. It was good to hear her laugh like that. Rare, but good.

"Say, Mom?" Grace held up the well-used copy of *Drawing on the Right Side of the Brain.* "I had no idea your library would carry a book like this. How fabulous."

Shirley reached out and took the book, holding it against her chest, face down. "Oh, sure, it's surprisingly well stocked," she said, her hands trembling. "Although I might have borrowed it from one of the other residents. I can't remember."

"It's a great book—you're going to love it," said Grace. "I can talk you through it sometime, if you like. Just the parts you don't follow."

Shirley's smile fractured into a dozen pieces.

Grace cursed herself. "I'm sorry, Mom. I didn't mean to imply—"

Shirley waved it off. "It's okay."

"That's not fair."

"Of course it is," Shirley said. "I'm not a professional—not like you. Or your father, my God. I was just skimming it. For fun, you know?" Shirley made a comical face, as if she were foolish for even reading the back cover. But Grace knew she had hurt her, perhaps by the way her mother tried so earnestly to convince her otherwise.

"I'm really sorry, Mom. That was shitty of me."

"Sweetheart—forget it. Truly." Shirley waved it off as if it were only the barest fraction of a faux pas. "You're probably right. I'm sure most of it went clear over my head."

Grace felt absolutely awful. Her poor mother was just trying to while away the hours, had probably picked out that book just to remind herself of a better time. And Grace had ruined it. She felt a long-forgotten echo of the past rise up like a sharp jet of stomach acid. "Let me apologize, Mom. Please."

"There's no need, dear. Nothing to apologize for."

But Grace knew there was. And it had been a long time coming.

Four

"Tell your father dinner's ready, Gracie."

Sixteen-year-old Gracie Schaffer nodded, head deep in a huge hardcover book on Baroque art, which was spread open on her dinner plate.

"Now, Gracie," said Shirley.

Gracie groaned the plaintive moan of the unappreciated teen and slammed the book closed, stomping out the kitchen and down the hallway to her father's study. The door was closed, as always, and Gracie knocked softly, as always. There was no answer, so she incrementally raised the strength of her knocking until an exasperated voice came from within.

"Working!"

Gracie knew she was already skating on the thinnest of ice. "Dinner, Dr. Schaffer." Then, lest he shoot the messenger: "Mom said."

A large book slammed shut and a chair slid back. Hard-soled shoes slapped against the hardwood floor and the door flew open.

Albert Schaffer crowded the doorway, his wavy salt-and-pepper hair nearly brushing the top of it. Gracie could tell he had been wrestling with something incredibly intense, as his eyes were still burning like hot coals. It always took her father a good ten minutes to return from the exotic intellectual landscapes he visited, and Gracie waited impatiently at the dinner table each evening for the full report of his adventures.

That night, however, he lingered in some other world, all the way through his salad and halfway into the pot roast, scribbling away on a yellow legal pad beside his plate. Gracie had tried tempting him with a few nuggets from her own day, but he remained silent, pencil to pad, circling, revising, striking, streaking down a trail to something that couldn't wait, not for food or drink or a single word to either Gracie or her mother. She'd never been so close to him at this early stage of his work and might never be again—this was her moment—but nothing she did drew more than a monosyllabic grunt. She needed weaponry of a higher caliber.

"We started on Caravaggio today," she said, tossing out *Caravaggio* like an angler baiting a blue marlin. "Mrs. Stephens wants me to do a presentation for the class—like a lecture, she said."

The pencil hesitated. Albert peeked up from beneath a hooded brow. "On Caravaggio?"

"Yes." Gracie grinned. "But I'll need Bernini, too, if I'm doing Early Baroque."

It could have been the light, it could have been the angle of his face, but Gracie could have sworn that he smiled. "You will indeed," he said.

His eyes began tiptoeing back to the yellow pad; her window was closing fast. "Is that an article or a book?" she asked, craning her neck to read his notes.

"Eat, Gracie," said her mother.

"I am, Mom!" Gracie stabbed a piece of roast and gnawed off a chunk of it. "Or a series?" she mumbled through the meat. "Is it a series? Maybe a volume?"

Albert shook his head. "Book, I think."

Grace choked down her roast in one huge gulp. "Can I help? You said maybe I could help out on the next one."

Albert looked up, peering over his glasses with those piercing eyes. "Can you be serious about it, Grace?"

"Oh, Albert," said Shirley. "She's just a kid."

"It's not play, Shirley. It's research. If she wants to do it, she's going to do it right."

Gracie felt her jaw drop far enough she feared it would crack the dinner table. "I'll be serious, I promise!" she said. "I can look things up for you, and do library runs, and get things from your office at school—anything you need."

Shirley sighed. "Come on, Gracie. It's summertime. You don't want to be locked up the whole time, do you?"

"It's *exactly* what I want," said Gracie, eyes afire. "You wouldn't understand, Mom."

Shirley stood up and walked over to a built-in desk in the corner, returning with a colorful brochure. She set it before her daughter. "If you want to do something special this summer, you could always take an art class or two at Union College. Just something fun."

Albert chuckled and reached for the brochure. "I'm always fascinated by the sort of people that teach these 'art' classes."

Shirley laughed with him. "I'm sure, but some of them look interesting."

Albert's eyebrows arched up. "Do they?"

Shirley froze.

"Which one are you thinking of taking?"

"I'm not," she said. "I was just looking."

"Well, I think that's..." He struggled to find the right word. "Sweet."

Shirley fidgeted in her seat. "It would just be for fun, Al."

"There's nothing wrong with that, of course." He opened his hands, yielding the floor to her. "Which one looks good to you?"

Shirley inflated right before their eyes, her cheeks flushing bright red. "Well," she said, sitting that much taller in her seat. "I like the morning one: The Seven Elements of Design."

"Jeez, Mom," groaned Gracie. "We learned about that in middle school."

Shirley smiled, but it quivered. "Well, it's new for me, dear."

Gracie ripped through the elements like third-grade multiplication tables. "Shape, line, space, form, texture, value, and color."

"You see?" said Shirley, deflating like a punctured Mylar balloon. "You're much better at it than I am." She took back the brochure and dropped it onto her dirty plate. "It'd be a waste of time for me. You two are the pros."

"Well, yeah, Mom," sighed Gracie. "Of course."

Albert clamped an iron hand over her wrist.

Gracie gawked at him, shocked and confused. They *were* the pros, weren't they—she and her father? What was wrong with that? She opened her mouth to protest, but Albert cut her off with a sharp, angry look. Gracie immediately shrank back as if he had struck her. He released his grip and turned to Shirley.

"I'm sorry, Shirley," he said. "So is Grace."

"Why?" asked Gracie. "What'd I do?"

"Nothing, dear," said Shirley, clearing the dinner table. "There's no need to be sorry." She took a few dishes to the sink, scraping the food—and the brochure—into the trash beneath it.

Gracie turned to her father and made a face: *What's her problem?*

Instead of agreeing with her, her father stood up and walked over to the sink, joining his wife. Shirley turned to him, and a tear ran down her cheek. Albert brushed it off with the tip of his finger and stared at it for a moment, before he looked into his wife's eyes and froze, unable to speak.

Gracie had never seen her father without a word or insight or solution to anything—not the mysteries of the Renaissance, not the intricacies of academia, not everything in between—but he just stood before her, silent. His mouth opened, his lips flexed, but he was incapable of squeezing out a single word. There was something so delicate about the moment, so paper thin that any tiny thing might tear it to shreds. Gracie watched them, afraid to breathe.

Albert hunched down over the counter and dropped his head, exhausted from whatever agony he had endured. Shirley gazed at him for a moment, then reached out to him. She ran her fingers through his wavy hair with an easy, gentle kindness, and he tilted his face up to hers. She looked into his eyes, and she smiled.

He tried to speak again, and she kissed him, stopping his mouth.

"I'll wash," she said.

Albert nodded. "I'll dry."

And they turned back to the sink in silence; the only sounds the comforting clink of fork, plate, and glass.

"That's a very sweet story, dear," Shirley said, dragging a chair against the wall of the Activity Room. "But it never happened."

Grace followed her over to the corner of the room. "It did, Mom. We were awful to you."

Shirley paused. "It wasn't like that."

"I should never have made fun of that class," Grace said. "Who knows where it would have led you?"

"Here, Grace." Shirley waved her arm around the Activity Room as if it were an island paradise. "It would have led me here."

Grace laughed and grabbed the last chair, dragging it beside her mother's. "Well, either way, I feel absolutely awful every time I think about it."

"Then, don't."

Shirley tucked *Drawing on the Right Side of the Brain* under one arm, took her daughter's arm with the other, and led her out of the room. "I don't," she said with absolute conviction.

"I don't remember that at all."

Five

The Bennington Dollhouse and Toy Museum of Vermont was nestled in an 1850s two-story white-paneled Victorian home that had been crafted with the same delicate whimsy as the miniature galleries within. Two-dozen Humpty Dumpty dolls sat arm in arm in a neat little row, perched on the museum's front banister to greet the weekend visitors. Beneath their dangling fabric feet, all the king's horses and all the king's men had apparently erected the Appraisal Experts Roadshow tents, which covered every green space and open lot on the block, ringing the museum like a canvas horseshoe. Elaine had designed it this way so guests could rotate through the show in a semicircle, creating a flow from entrance to exit that would keep the crowds off Union Street. It was a fine plan if the show had hit Bennington a few weeks back, but the small town was now overrun by a tidal surge of excitable antiquers, fueled by the news that lightning had struck the show and would probably strike again in the mountains of Vermont.

The line of hopefuls stretched so far down the street, Grace could not spy the end of it. Rather than complaining, the industrious locals had set up makeshift refreshment stands in their front yards. Some had gone further, arranging haphazard tables of their own trinkets, and small pockets of guests had drifted out of line to peruse the wares, unable to resist a possible diamond in the very rough.

"Looks like they're selling tickets to Pleasure Island," said Jerome Zwick, glowering at the local barkers with obvious disdain. "I wonder how many of those poor people are going to wake up looking like donkeys."

She laughed. "Well, let's hurry back to Geppetto's, then, shall we?" She took his arm, and they strolled into the thick of the preparations. As they passed the crisscrossing workers, Grace lowered her voice, just above a whisper. "I need to tell you something," she said, scanning about to make sure no one was close enough to hear.

"Is this about your thrilling trip to Deliverance Country?"

"It was a bloody nightmare, Jerry. It took every ounce of self-restraint not to grab whatever I could and flee. Like walking down a row of stray dogs at an animal shelter."

"Say no more."

"But—and this is the strangest part of the thing," she said. "With all that mess, all that cruel distressed jumble, I think I found something."

Zwick froze, eyes narrowed. "What kind of something?"

Grace nodded. "*That* kind."

He started to speak but stopped; his features hardened. "That's a dangerous thing to say, Grace."

"I know it is."

"Is Bedford bringing it down this weekend?"

"It's not his—it's his son's. And the poor kid's too terrified to do anything other than lock it up in his closet."

Zwick nodded, his eyes suddenly distant, deep in thought. "If it is what you think it is, that might be the best place for it."

"How can you say that?" she asked. "This is a once-in-a-generation find. You have to see it to believe it, Jerry. Go back with me after the show."

Zwick shook his head.

"I need to know if I'm right. I need your eye."

"No." Zwick removed her hand from his arm. "I won't give it to you."

"Why not?"

"I'm not bound to give you a reason, Grace. My answer should suffice."

Grace gaped, stunned. More than stunned, she was angry. To shrug it off, to pass on a Grail, as if it were a jury summons? And what's more, to desert her, to ruin her best—maybe her only shot as well? She felt something sharp and hot rise from the darkened pit of her stomach. It gathered speed as it spread across her chest, up the back of her throat, into her mouth, and she could taste it, like brimstone, and the words tumbled out, and even as she spoke them, they tasted foul.

"What's the matter with you, Jerome?" she said. "Isn't losing *one* enough?"

He jolted back as if he'd been slapped.

Grace immediately regretted it. "I am so unbelievably sorry," she said, her fury dissolving in an instant. She reached out to him. "I don't know where that came from, Jerry. That was horribly selfish of me."

"I shall not disagree," he said, leaving her hand untouched in the space between them, which had suddenly grown much wider. There was no anger in his voice, no hurt; only a deep disappointment, which stung Grace all the more. He turned and walked into the main tent, leaving Grace alone with the aftershocks.

That wasn't her. She didn't speak like that—she didn't feel like that. But she had felt it. And said it. And what's worse, she had meant it.

What's happening to me? She reached for the celestial globe, but it brought her little comfort.

In fact, it was cold as ice.

Grace threw herself into her appraisals, hoping to wash away the bitter aftertaste of her outburst at Jerry. It helped, but did nothing to dim the image that painting had burned in the back of her mind; it mocked her every time she blinked, in reds and pinks and exquisite yellows she would never see again. She was almost relieved when Elaine yanked her away in the middle of an appraisal of paraphernalia from the doomed Apollo 13 mission, even if she looked and acted as if the sky were falling.

"Please to God, Grace," Elaine whispered. "Tell me you brought extra powder."

Grace followed Elaine's terrified stare over to a three-person TV crew that was filming over at Pat's Books and Manuscripts Table.

"Where'd they come from?" asked Grace, grabbing her bag off a nearby chair and fishing out a small case for her friend.

"I have no idea," Elaine said, patting her face down with staccato strokes. "That's CAT-TV, local news. I've been after them since January, but they'd never gotten back to me. They must have come across a few of your minor miracles."

"Well, pass the powder," said Grace. "I need a minor miracle myself."

The two women cackled like teenagers, fussing over each other's hair and outfits. For Grace, it conjured other memories, too—the *Roadshow* green room, the experts hyperventilating over their last-minute research, the roving producers doling out golden tickets to one of the camera sets—maybe even the center set. No, this wasn't *Roadshow*, but the thrill was there, and Grace was so thankful to feel the keen sting of anxiety tickling her stomach once again.

They spun back to face the show, armed with their best looks under harried circumstances, and with just a wink and a grin, they separated—Elaine off to introduce herself to the reporter, Grace back to her table.

With one eye on the roving camera, she resumed her appraisal of the Apollo 13 memorabilia. The centerpiece was a six-foot-tall poster of the Saturn V Sa-508 rocket that powered the mission, signed by astronauts Fred Haise and Jack Swigert at final check, right before liftoff. Unfortunately, it was missing Jim Lovell's signature, which hurt the value, and that's what she told the owner, a short but stout Latino man in his early eighties.

"I'm terribly sorry, sir," she said, slipping it back into its tube. "If you'd gotten Lovell's signature as well, you might be looking better at auction."

"I figured," he sighed. "Jim was there, of course, but I didn't want to ask him."

He spoke without any sense of regret, which Grace found odd. "Why not?"

"He offered, of course, 'cause he was Jim, you know, but I didn't want to jinx the mission," he said. "Fred had some muscle on him back then, and when he signed, the pencil snapped right in half. The ground crew, we were a pretty superstitious group back then, so when that pencil broke—"

"Whoever signed afterward—"

"Would have been marked." He nodded. "And that would have been Jim."

All of a sudden, Grace forgot about Grails and cameras and crews and all the sparkling tinsel that came with them. Something far more dazzling was happening here, right in front of her, and she cursed herself for nearly missing it.

"It's a good thing you didn't ask him to sign," Grace said. "Lovell was the glue that held that entire mission together." She paused, transported by the gigantic importance of the little man before her, "And you, sir, are the reason why."

"I'll tell you something, don't nobody know." He leaned in, lowering his voice. "That's exactly what he whispered to me when they got back."

Grace felt a sudden, tingling sensation as a few filaments from the churning arc of history brushed against her. "You're a very special man," she said.

He nodded—not out of any sense of ego or self-importance, but out of gratitude. "Thank you for saying so."

Grace had what she needed, so she sought out the celestial globe nestled in the center of her chest. She felt the needle of a tiny electrical shock when she touched it—it was back, alive and crackling with desire. The world blurred around her, and it was just the two of them once again, seeking the deeper value, the worth. It crystallized deep within her, a marriage of Grace and Globe, like two atoms combining, setting off a chain reaction, until she saw it, clear as day.

"Twenty-five to thirty thousand dollars," said Grace.

The man made no response, his face a blank.

"Would you like me to repeat it?"

"No," he said. "I'm just trying to swallow all those zeros."

He burst into laughter, into tears of laughter, and Grace joined him. She glanced over at Jerome, whose scowl simmered into the thinnest of smiles. He gave her a brief two-fingered salute and returned to his client.

Thank God, she thought. Jerome's doghouse was not only a shitty place to live, it wasn't very nice to visit either.

As Grace helped the man pack up, she caught sight of Henry Manfred out of the corner of her eye. He was hovering at the back of Grace's line, pretending to be quite transfixed by the intricacies of one of the large poles that held up the structure of the big tent.

Grace excused herself and walked to the end of the line, admiring the pole alongside Henry. "That's a fascinating pole you have there."

"Am I allowed to make an inappropriate joke about that?"

She groaned but couldn't help laughing. "I'd say you already have."

"You'll have to forgive me," he sighed. "My last four clients have all been under the age of thirteen, and I was in dire need of saying something PG-13."

"I'm glad I could help you recalibrate," she said. "Well, if that's all you need from me . . ." Grace turned to leave.

"How do you do it?" he asked in a small voice, almost a whisper.

Grace turned back. Henry looked adrift, like a young child waiting to be chosen last for a game of kickball.

"That auction," he said, shaking his head. "I still don't understand what happened."

"I'm not sure I can explain it."

"Thank God. I'm not sure I really want to know." He watched the older Latino man walk by, wearing a smile as wide as his poster was tall. "But that," he said with envy in his eyes. "I'd love to be able to do that." Henry's constant smile, that wicked twist of irresistible charm, had been wiped clean from his face. This mattered to him, deeply.

And so, thought Grace, reaching for the celestial globe. *It matters to me.*

And the globe was warm. And Grace knew it mattered to it as well.

"We'll teach you then," she said. "*I* will, I mean."

"Teach him what?" asked another expert, who had drifted over from his table. "Inquiring minds want to know."

Grace heard a few others chime in from behind her, and she turned to find herself surrounded by three other eager experts.

"It appears you are on your way to assembling a harem, Ms. Schaffer," said Jerome, forcing his way into the circle. "But before you retire to the Appraisal Boudoir, there's something you need to see back at your table."

Grace froze. "What kind of something?"

He nodded. "*That* kind."

Six

Robert Bedford stood hunched over at the front of the line, shuffling from one foot to the other as if he might bolt for the exit at any moment. He had pulled a weather-beaten Red Sox cap so far down over his head, Grace could not see his eyes until he lifted them to greet her.

"Hello, Ms. Schaffer," he said, in the smallest whisper, as if someone might recognize his voice and sound the alarm.

"It's good to see you, Rob," said Grace, sliding behind her table. "But I thought we agreed you would call me Grace?"

He nodded. "Sorry."

"That's perfectly all right."

He forced a weak smile into the corners of his mouth. "I brought you something."

Grace's breath caught in her throat. She was afraid to stir, afraid to do anything that might make him reconsider. Robert placed a large rectangular object on her table, masked within a black sheet. Grace bit down on her lower lip, nearly breaking the skin. She didn't want to appear too eager, too desperate to lay her eyes upon it once again.

Robert drew back the sheet.

Grace nearly burst into tears. The rich bouquet of colors, the river, the sunset, the sensual immediacy of the object, radiated off the surface—she could feel it, vibrating the space between them, filling it with such intense beauty it hurt to look upon it. To be so close, less than a breath away; to know her entire life had been leading up to this moment. Ever since that first day in her father's backyard, she had been excavating, churning up dirt, tunneling through mountains of scholarship, inching ever closer and closer, but never able to reach out, never quite able to grasp it.

My Grail.

But she had to be sure. She needed confirmation, from someone she trusted; someone who would verify her suspicions either way—that she had found a Lost Grail, or that she had completely lost her mind. But the only pair of eyes she trusted for something this momentous belonged to Jerome Zwick, and he had denied her.

"You weren't actually thinking of appraising that alone, were you, Ms. Schaffer?" whispered Jerome, who had snuck up behind her.

Grace nearly leapt into his arms, and might have if she wasn't worried she might tackle him to the ground. "I didn't think I had a choice, Mr. Zwick."

"You do now," he said, eyeing the painting as if it were some kind of exotic serpent—poisonous but irresistibly hypnotic. "And now that I'm face-to-face with it, you might have a devil of a time shooing me away."

Grace turned back to Robert. "Do you mind if I include a colleague?"

Robert shrank back and his hand scrabbled for the sheet, as if to cover the painting.

"I trust him, Rob," she said, placing her hand over his. "I've trusted him with some of my deepest secrets."

The boy hesitated, still uncertain.

"And I'm dead old, Robert," said Jerome, stepping up beside Grace. "I have the memory of a Labrador on mushrooms."

Robert laughed, in spite of his simmering anxiety. "I had a Lab. Not too sharp."

"But dependable," said Grace, ruffling Jerome's hair. "In a sweet, scruffy sort of way."

"I admit the dependable," Jerome said, smoothing back his hair. "But I deny the scruffy."

Robert laughed again, and Grace knew their duet had just become a trio. She turned the painting clockwise so Jerome could view it. He leaned over it, hovering an illuminated magnifying glass above the spire and the sunset, down the babbling river, and across the stone bridge. He paused over the figure of the hesitating woman at the crest of the bridge. He leaned forward, even farther, close enough to smell the varnish.

He sees her! thought Grace, and a million sparkling possibilities careened about inside her, lighting her thoughts on fire—the show would explode, the experts would prosper, Robert would be free, and Grace, Grace would be free, too, free from the pain and loneliness and humiliation, free enough to finally pick up a phone and make a call. And maybe they'd take her call. Maybe now they'd have to.

Jerome stood up, returning the glass to his suit jacket pocket.

"I don't see it," he said.

Grace blinked, unable to compute what he had told her. He didn't *see* it?

"It's right there," she said, waving her hand over the tactile surface of the oil. "Look at the sunset, the water... that *woman*."

"I'm sorry, Grace," he said. "You're seeing something I don't see."

Grace's knees buckled, and she placed a hand upon the table to brace herself. She had been so sure, so absolutely confident. But she'd been confident before, hadn't she—in her husband, in her position in the field, in the time she had left to bridge the yawning chasm to her father's affection. But Victor had betrayed her, and the field had forgotten her, and her father... Her father was gone.

And so was the dream of her Holy Grail.

It had teased her, tempting her with a shimmering reflection of her own possibility, instead of the sunken mask of capitulation that mocked her from the mirror. She felt it trickle out of her, drop by drop, like the relentless drip of an IV.

"It's not..." she sighed, lost in darkness. "It's not there?"

"I can't see it," he said.

No one does, she thought. That's why it was sitting behind a wall of cobwebs. That's why Stuart Bedford gave it so freely to his son. Only Grace saw, but that was not enough.

She turned to Robert, expecting the worst. Instead, his face was devoid of recrimination; in fact, he looked relieved. "I'm so sorry, Robert," she said. "I thought we had something here."

She reached for the black shroud, but Jerome stayed her hand.

"You're not listening to me," he said. "I can't see it...so you have to see it for me."

Grace let the sheet drop. No expert had ever put that kind of faith in her, not even when she was at the very pinnacle of the profession. Why was Jerome Zwick? He wasn't a particularly charitable fellow—no one had ever accused him of that—nor had he ever allowed emotion to cloud his judgment. He was by the book, by the numbers, no wing, no prayer.

"Come on then, Ms. Schaffer," he said with an encouraging grin. "Tell me what I'm missing."

Grace smiled back. No, Jerome Zwick could not be swayed by whim or intuition, so he had seen something, too—just not within the painting.

He saw *her*.

Her father had noticed her, he was aware of her, but he didn't see her, not like this. Victor had once, but his eyes had drifted, and then so had he. Grace had grown accustomed to magic, it hung about her neck, but there was an alchemy in Jerome's words, in his faith, that turned her doubt to twenty-four-carat inspiration.

Now it was time to earn it.

"Let's take a look," she said, leaning over the oil. "I don't see a signature, and I can't find a date, but I see an Impressionist painter at work here—maybe early, very early in their career."

"Where?" asked Jerome, challenging her, nudging her forward.

"We're outdoors, not indoors," she said, her fingers hovering over the trees on the riverbank. "The paint is laid down in these heavy, diffuse strokes; and the colors—look at them—alternating, back and forth in such stunning contradictions, they leap off the canvas."

"Go on."

"The textures—shifting between soft and sharp, making the entire landscape so immediate, so intense, it seems to rise up from the frame, almost in three dimensions. The combination of all this leads me to believe... we are looking at the brushstrokes of a master."

"Yes, but who?" he asked.

Grace paused. "I don't know." She turned to Robert. "Tell me again, Rob—how did you originally come across this?"

"It was in the attic when we moved in, like I told you."

"And there was nothing to identify it? No letter or bill of sale?"

"Nothing," he said. "I'm sorry."

Jerome looked closer at the frame. "So clean. No marks anywhere. Are there any on the back?"

"Not that I could see," said Grace.

"Supplier marks on the canvas?"

"No. It was too—" Grace stopped. The light was horrible in Robert's room, and canvas marks could be notoriously faint. She leaned the painting up and Jerome handed her his illuminated glass. "No, nothing here."

Her light passed over a slight gap between the inside edge of the wooden stretcher and the canvas beneath. She pressed lightly against the canvas to expand the gap and shone the light inside it, peeking under the old wood in the desperate hope she might find something, anything. And then, she did.

"Oh my God, Jerry—look!"

She handed the glass to Jerome, and he peeked through it.

"Bull's-eye," he said.

"What?" asked Robert, leaning in. "What did you find?"

Jerome passed the magnifying glass to Robert, and he peered

through it. Although the mark was upside down, it had not faded, due to the protective wooden frame above it:

PREPARED BY
WINSOR & NEWTON
Limited
38, RATHBONE PLACE,
LONDON, W.
42675

"Winsor & Newton?" Robert asked. "What's that?"

Grace took the glass from him and checked again, just to be sure. Her heart doubled its pace. "Winsor & Newton produced canvas for British painters all the way back to the 1830s."

"How does that help?" Robert asked. "This could have been painted anytime between 1830 and yesterday."

"No." She grinned. "It was painted between 1883 and 1905."

Robert gawked. "How can you tell?"

"The stamp has changed over the years. 'Prepared by' began to show up around 1860. That tiny image of a Griffin at the top began about ten years later." Grace paused for effect. "But the addition of 'Limited' only appeared between 1883 and 1905."

"Making it Impressionist?" Robert asked.

Grace turned to Jerome. "What say you, sir?"

"It is indeed," he said, giving her a Victorian bow. "I stand enlightened. But you still have not brought us any closer to the artist in question, Grace."

"Oh, you *men*," sighed Grace with mock indignation. "Will you never be satisfied?" She set the painting back down, leaning back to take it all in. Yes, there were the hallmarks of Impressionism, but nothing immediately came to her in terms of the voice of the artist. Even the horizon itself—usually blurred by Monet and the painters of the time—told no tales, as it was surprisingly present in the landscape.

Grace reached for her necklace, and it immediately calmed her, clearing her mind, turning it into a blank canvas. She didn't fear their partnership anymore; it was beginning to feel as much a part of her as her own consciousness. But still it amazed her, that mysterious something pulsing beneath the polished sparkling surface of the lapis lazuli.

Yes, it said. *Something beneath.*

There was something beneath the painting.

Coursing beneath the pigments and the oil, a subterranean current Grace sensed as much as saw, rippling within the paint, turning it viscous, alive. She felt as if she were looking through someone else's eyes; as if she were being transported, not only by the light and the colors and the strokes and the shadows, but by the ecstasy of another's experience of the work. To Grace, it felt operatic—multiple strings and voices stacked high, one on top of another, and it all rushed over her, thrilling her to the point of exhaustion.

"What are you seeing?" asked Jerome; not a challenge, but pure distilled jealousy.

Grace opened herself to the painting and it broke free from the canvas, the river rising and falling, the hills folding over one another, the sun's rays crashing down from the heavens in crescendo after crescendo, and the woman...

"Her," Grace said. "I see her." Because *he* did, she could sense him now—the artist himself—and they gazed at the woman through the same eyes. "She's the soul of the piece. She's his Aria."

"The woman hesitating on the bridge?"

"Yes. But I don't think she's hesitating." Grace traced the outline of the woman with the tips of her fingers: the gentle sweep of her head, the soft swirl of her dress, the bounce of the hem—so light, so buoyant, as if it were weightless. As if time itself has stopped.

"He's hesitating," she said, and the realization thundered inside her like the peal of a Gothic bell. "The artist. He's drawing out the space between the seconds, this infinitely tiny pinpoint in his life when he teetered at the very summit of whatever True Beauty meant to him."

Grace hesitated, overwhelmed not just by the beauty, but by the crushing loss its passing must have been. "He'll never see her again, so he bars the gates with his brush, straining against the hands of time. There's so much sadness here, because he knows the strike of midnight is fast upon him, but so long as he dabbed and swirled and brushed—"

"He had her," said Robert. "But not *just* her. There's more to it."

Grace stood up, unlocking herself from the majesty beneath. "How so?" she asked, intrigued. "What do you see?"

He tried to look down but did not dare. "The End," he said quietly. "Something's dying."

Grace took the boy's hand; it trembled in hers. She smiled at him warmly. The painting was now, truly, his.

"The boy is on to something," said Jerome. "Look at her feet."

Grace and Robert followed Jerome's finger, which circled beneath the figure. "They're blurred, faded, like an apparition's." His finger traced the far bank of the river. "But take a look at the passing couples."

"Shoes and flats," said Grace.

"Indeed," said Jerome. "She's a woman, yes, but a spirit, as well."

"Of what?"

He threw up his hands. "Your appraisal, my dear. I'm just along for the ride."

Grace laughed, but Jerome did not—something else had caught his eye. "But don't leave her—not just yet," he said. "There's something odd about the way the sun is framing her."

He was right. The woman was facing the artist, and the sun was setting far off behind her, just over the church spire. Her face was shaded as it should have been (without a hint of the stunning illuminated visage that had flashed before Grace in the attic), but her body glowed brightly, wrapped in the swirling ribbons of the distant setting sun. Grace followed the beams, round and round, as they whipped around the woman like the fiery contrails of a comet, until she leapt on the back of one of them, tracing it all the way back to the place from whence it had come—from the sun.

"The sunset!" she cried. "Look at the sunset!"

It had once been a molten globe of brilliant yellows, reds, and oranges, but its oils had cracked badly over the years, fracturing the colors into a scaly crust like the impact of a meteor.

"Tough to see anything," said Jerome. "The *craquelure* is so intense. They must have used a weaker varnish in this corner, because I don't see damage anywhere else."

"No, just here," she said. "Covering the sunset."

Grace hesitated. *The sunset.* It echoed within her, over and over, like rippling waves against a sandy beach. And then it all fell into place.

"*His* sunset," she said. "That's his sunset, Jerry."

Jerome stared back, utterly confused. And then, his eyes grew wide. "That's impossible."

"I know."

"All his works are accounted for."

"I know."

"He was retired by then, long retired!"

"Who?" said Robert, desperate to get back on the whirling coaster that had swept the other two away.

Grace turned to the boy. "I hope you own a very large suitcase, Robert."

He blinked, confused. "Why do you say that?"

"Because you're moving out of your father's house."

"Sure thing." He laughed. "When?"

Grace took his hands and placed them on the frame.

"When you sell this unknown William Kent masterpiece for a hundred million dollars."

Seven

Victor Karlin sat in his favorite green Victorian armchair, drinking his favorite Scotch whiskey, watching the evening news on his favorite ninety-inch television—the only three things he had managed to grab during the tumultuous exodus from his marriage. He figured he didn't need anything else, for he had set sail for a land of milk and honey, and now he would rebuild his life from the ground up in a new home.

He had not realized his mistress would build it for him. Victor might have been able to make a few decorative decisions when Julie Robinson was The Other Woman, but once he placed that three-carat boulder on her finger, she became The Fiancée, and their home became a repository for her twenty-eight-year-old whims, which had been well fermented in the milquetoast milieu of social media. The sparse furniture in the living room was swathed in an endless array of grays and creams. There were plants (none living, of course), and not one but two Loloi pattern rugs (in an astonishing array of brown). Digitally enhanced conceptual photographs of the many tropical resorts she had "taken him" were arranged in tight geometric shapes on the walls, broken up by the occasional faux-chic French bistro poster—as if that might somehow lend *Je ne sais quoi* to a room that more resembled an HGTV rerun than the curated retreat of a renowned art historian.

Julie lay center stage in the room, draped over a dove-colored Bellini chaise lounge like some Ptolemaic princess, a sheer formfitting ankle-length dress clinging to every curve, her expertly manicured feet rubbing up and down against each other like the slow-motion symphony of a butterfly's gossamer wings. After a few moments, she glanced up from her flickering iPhone and met his glance, flashing him a dazzling pearl white smile. Victor smiled back, knowing full well if he did not, he would reap the whirlwind of one of Julie's lesser smiles, spoiling a physical perfection that still unmade him.

"I'm staying in tonight," she said, sitting up to begin the painstaking process of painting her toenails. "Wouldn't you like that?"

"Of course." Victor muted the television. "I love it when you stay in."

"But not tomorrow," she said, blowing on a glistening toe. "There's a pampering party at Vanessa's."

"I thought you hated Vanessa."

"I do." She held up her phone, its screen locked in the electronic death grip of a Facebook evite. "But everyone will be there."

"Well, in that case, 'tis a *fait accompli*, my dear."

She wrinkled her nose. "Is that Spanish or something?"

"What would you like it to be?"

She thought—or suspended speaking in such a way it appeared she was thinking. "I'd like it to be Spanish."

"Spanish it is," he said. "By way of the *Champs-Élysées*."

She blinked a few times, trying to piece together the clues, but it proved too taxing and she lost interest, her eyes instinctively wandering toward yet another blinking screen, this time the television.

"What's up with your ex?" she asked.

Victor scoffed. "I couldn't tell you."

"Then turn up the volume, Vic."

Now it was Victor's turn to blink. He grabbed the remote and turned toward the television. Grace was being interviewed for a local affiliate report from FOX 44 NEWS in Vermont. She was beaming (aggravatingly so), beside a fidgeting, awkward young man. Victor thumbed up the volume, his face a mask of neutrality.

Grace walked the spellbound reporter through the miraculous discovery on the easel behind them. It was a forgotten masterpiece, she said, a never-before-seen painting created by William Kent, one of the nineteenth century's greatest artists. It had been found in the young man's attic, among moth-eaten clothes and boxes of rubbish—the find of the decade, perhaps the century. A large banner flashed at the bottom of the screen:

LOST TREASURE DISCOVERED IN
BENNINGTON ATTIC

Victor's eyes descended, locking on to the image of the modestly framed painting that stood between her and the boy. Even miniaturized on his television screen, Victor could see it. He could see it well enough.

"Vic?" purred Julie.

With his eyes glued to the screen, he patted the arm of the recliner until his hand grasped his phone.

"Victor?"

He picked it up, thumbing through his contacts.

"Who are you calling?" Julie asked, her voice inching up into a full-fledged whine.

"Tricia Elroy."

Julie placed her well-manicured hands against her tiny hips. "I didn't stay home tonight to watch you work, you know."

"It'll only take a second."

"But Vic-ky," she said, her whine turning to sex-kitten pout.

He raised the phone to his ear.

"Sweetheart!"

Victor hung up the phone and turned to Julie, who was reclining on the purple zebra-patterned couch—naked.

She was impossible to resist. She was beautiful. And sexy. And perfectly proportioned in every way, shaming every Titian and Correggio, every Rodin and Botticelli, even the great Venus de Milo herself.

And she couldn't hold a candle to what he saw on that television.

"Are you going to take your pill, or what?" she asked, turning back to admire the *Fairest of Them All* on the screen of her iPhone. "I'm not going to wait all night, you know."

Victor sighed. He had made his bed, he had wet it, and now he was doomed to lie in it. "Yes, dear," he said. He reached over and opened the top drawer of the end table, removing a large vial of diamond-shaped blue pills. He shook one out and swallowed it.

For the briefest of moments, he wished to God it was cyanide.

Eight

The reports of the death of the Appraisal Experts Roadshow had darkened the mood of similar shows all across the country; the rumors of its resurrection felt like a reprieve from the gallows. Due to the shocking news of the William Kent discovery and the rapid spread of online chatter about their sky-high appraisals (verified at auction after auction), the Roadshow's next stop in Saratoga Springs was a near sellout. The following one in Pittsfield's Lakewood Park did sell out, and a few despondent guests were turned away. Elaine worried they might need to buy a larger tent for future shows, but Grace noticed her eyes swim with tears of joy when she said it.

The experts arranged their tables for the Lakewood show in a giddy daze. It was a shocking and sudden twist of fortune, and it had knocked them off their feet like an unexpected gust of wind. They had held each other's hands as the tour had been taken off life support, but a miracle had happened. And everyone knew exactly from whence that miracle had sprung.

In the beginning, Grace had felt like the tour's resident leper—aside from Jerome Zwick, all the experts had kept their distance. Now they clung to her as if she were Florence Nightingale, carrying with her the elixir to all their troubles. And so Grace moved from table to table, spinning her necklace, spreading the mysterious fingers of the celestial globe out over the entire show, and wherever they touched sprang hope and happiness, gratitude and joy.

And then, Grace began to sense something else. A dissonant sound; a single flat note in a sprawling symphony. At first, she thought it was her imagination, that part of her that sought the sour in things. She wandered to the very center of the tent, and the long serpentine lines of the crowd rotated around her in a frenzied orbit, like the thundering bands of a tropical storm. Grace stood within the eye wall, closed her eyes, and listened. Her hand instinctively went for the globe. Its warm, calming pulse had become irregular, hesitant, as if it were listening, too.

Something's wrong, she thought.

It was just a tiny splinter, a pea buried deep within the mattress, but it was there, embedded in the soft tissue of the show.

It's here, she thought. *But it's small.*

Suddenly, Grace gasped and clutched her chest; the air squeezed out of her by some monstrous force. She felt herself being pried open and flooded full of something white hot that vibrated deep within her, shaking her ribs with such violence, she feared they would shatter. Grace gave in to it, allowed it to fill her completely and the pain disappeared, but something else remained in its place. She heard it as a voice, because it allowed her to.

Yes, it's small, it said. *But it won't be small for long.*

"Penny for your thoughts?" asked Jerome, who had snuck up beside her.

"Careful with that penny," she said, forcing a laugh. "I might appraise it for a dollar."

"You're troubled," he said. "I could see it from the other side of the tent."

"I'm fine," she said, waving it off. "It's nothing, really. I've always had a problem seeing the rose behind the thorns."

Jerome's eyes narrowed as he surveyed the babbling crowds. "Well, the entire show appears to be blooming, so I'm sure they're both here in equal measure."

Grace noticed a slight chill had edged into his voice. "Penny for *your* thoughts?"

"Better not," he said. "I am worried, just a little, that you might indeed turn it into a dollar."

Grace was stunned, and a little hurt. Jerome had urged her to wield the globe for good, and so she had. Maybe it was just his usual irascible self, rearing its pessimistic head. Maybe he was jealous? "And what would be so wrong with that?" she asked.

"A penny's not a dollar," he said, glancing around the tent. "I'm beginning to worry we might be on the verge of losing sight of that, just a little bit."

"You're worried *I* might be losing sight of that?"

Jerome paused, treading lightly. "There was one call at Saratoga..."

Grace took a step back from him. "Which call?"

"The Grunberg Brooch—there was just a little... topspin on it."

"Maybe," she sighed, agreeing. "Maybe a dollar or two, you know, we had a news crew on that one."

"Of course. Perhaps that affected things a bit."

Grace flinched. "Affected what?"

"I've been hearing some of the appraisals today—the Sheipo silver set, the U-Fly-It Aircraft Carrier."

A thin needle of anger pricked the back of her throat. "You think I'm wrong?"

"No," he said, carefully choosing his words. "You're helping everyone find a value, a different sort of value, and I think, in many ways, a truer value, a humane one." He took a deep breath and released it. "But I think, Grace, just as you're beginning to feel stretched a little too thin, I think the elastic around these values—these new values—is beginning to stretch a little, too. Just a bit, you see, nothing too troubling—just a few extra dollars here, twenty or so there, but at some point, if we keep going like this, that band might break."

It landed like a cold sharp slap on the side of her face. And it hurt. Not the words themselves—she had heard those and far worse—it was hearing them from him. It surged up, filling her mouth like bile. "These are my values, Jer. You're saying I'm overvaluing."

Jerome let his silence speak for him.

"Every value I've given is exactly what these things are bringing at auction," she said, her voice trembling. "You think I'm wrong? Well, half a dozen auction houses around New England confirm I'm right." Grace waved her arms over the massive crowd. "And these people, this sellout, the coverage, the presale for Boston? They say I'm right, too."

Jerome fell silent for a long moment. "Then who am I to argue?" he said. "I must have been mistaken." Without another word, he disappeared off into the surging crowd.

Of course he's wrong, she thought. Dead wrong. The more she thought about it, the more it infuriated her. How dare he? He wasn't just arguing with her; he was arguing with the celestial globe. Grace reached for it protectively but could not find it at first. Her heart fluttered, and she felt around in desperation, but she could not lay her fingers upon it. She reached for her throat, and the necklace beads were there, but still no sign of—

It was behind her neck. She exhaled with sweet relief. It had somehow gotten spun about on the string. She fished it around and placed it above her heart. But the celestial globe was cold as a corpse.

And so was I.

Grace cursed herself. Jerome had pushed a button, a button she didn't even know she had, and she'd let her ego kick back. He was only trying to be a friend—and my God, she had so few. She felt the fever break, and cold sweat dripped down her forehead. *What's happening to me?* That wasn't her. It was the exhaustion, the pressure, the responsibility.

"There's my Crown Jewel!" said Elaine, poking through the crowd.

"Oh, Lainy, I feel anything but."

"What's wrong?"

Grace waved it off. "Just little old me tripping over my big old tongue."

"Welcome to my world," Elaine said, her voice taking an unusually serious edge. "I think your tongue's about to fall out a little bit farther, though." She unfolded a printed email, holding it against her chest. "Before I give you this, I need to ask, and you need to answer me honestly—you're not leaving us, are you?"

Grace laughed. "Not unless those are my release papers."

"I'm not sure *what* this is." Elaine handed her the email.

Grace scanned the paper, and the words seemed to levitate off the page, swirling around her like the sweet breath of a fading dream. Only this wasn't a dream, and the words—as wished for as words could be—were real: an invitation, a first-class plane reservation, five-star accommodations, assurance of a speedy return.

"Crazy, huh?" asked Elaine.

Grace agreed. It was crazy. It was shocking. It was absolutely terrifying. And she had dreamt of nothing else for the longest time.

Grace's prayers had been answered—not in thunder or writ large against the night sky, but there in the pixilated printout of Elaine's email.

She would accept, of course. She would do as they bade. She would fly to Indianapolis. She would willingly be thrown overboard, as Jonah had been, and allow herself to be, once again, swallowed whole by the Leviathan.

She was about to return to the belly of the beast.

She was going to *Antiques Roadshow.*

Part IV
Form

One

It stood bestride the narrow world like a Colossus, and every other show, every gallery and flea market, every blogger and vlogger, every podcast and website walked under its huge legs, feeding off the scraps of its success like pilot fish. Its empire spanned nine British prime ministers and eight US presidents, spawning a worldwide sensation over which the sun, quite literally, never set.

Seven years after the show premiered on the BBC, a sparse three hundred curious souls wandered into an old armory building for the first US taping in Concord, Massachusetts. Within a decade, over six thousand guests were attending each show, with as many as thirty thousand others denied entrance (who then consoled themselves before their television alongside eight million other viewers each week). It had struck a chord that resonated across generations, across racial and income gaps, it survived multiple wars and shrinking attention spans and Covid and "reality" TV. It would not die because it could not die—it lived and thrived within all of us.

What is it worth? What am *I* worth?

Unlike the minor league shows of the antique diaspora, *Antiques Roadshow* did not arrive in passenger vans and perform in tents. It descended in a Blitzkrieg of eighteen wheelers: an expeditionary force of forklifts, stanchions, light trusses, and giant wooden crates, securing beachheads within the massive halls of municipal convention centers. Police shut down entire zip codes to route the traffic; helicopters buzzed back and forth over the invading horde of pilgrims that flooded the streets. Any city brave enough to host may have found itself in the limelight, but it was also under siege.

Grace had seen it all before, of course, but she nearly swooned from the immediate flood of anxiety that hit her the moment she left the leather cocoon of the town car. The sheer pressure of the surging humanity struck her full force in the chest, wobbling her legs. Robert Bedford peeked out the open door behind her, his face frozen in a marble mask of terror.

"Are you okay?" she asked, hoping for his sake she sounded calmer than she felt.

"This is a lot," he mumbled.

"I know," she said. "We don't have to do this, Rob." Grace was ashamed of how hollow it sounded. Maybe Rob didn't have to do this, but she did. Yes, this was his call, but it was her summit—she had been inching toward it since her little red shovel struck stone all those years ago. She had raced through her youth, missing her chance at childhood; she had devoted herself to study with a Benedictine focus, denying herself the simple pleasures that everyone else enjoyed; she had weathered success and failure, divorce and death, and the crumbling of every foothold she had dug into the hard rock of her profession, only to begin the climb once again from what felt like a graveyard, up the mountain, into thin air, until she stood on the uppermost ridge within a few steps of the peak. She hadn't come this far to take a rain check.

"I'm okay," Robert said, giving her his own impression of a smile. "Promise. Let's go." He stood up and Grace saw him wobble, just as she had.

"Can you take my arm?" she asked, offering it. "The show always makes me a little woozy."

Robert perked up, happy to have a task to focus on, rather than the crushing sea of humanity around him. He took her arm just as an *Antiques Roadshow* staffer threaded her way through the crowd to them.

"Eyes on the Prize," the staffer barked into her walkie-talkie as she gave Grace's hand a quick shake. "Nice to see you again, Dr. Schaffer."

"And this is Rob," said Grace, introducing him.

The staffer held up her hand, silencing Grace. "On our way," she snapped, clipping the walkie-talkie back onto her belt and hustling Grace and Robert through the surging crowd as if they were rock stars bolting for the stage door.

They emerged into a small clearing, face-to-face with the lumbering glass towers of the Indianapolis Convention Center. Instead of taking them through the massive entryway, the staffer slammed through a service door; Grace and Robert followed, rushing through a maze of hallways and offices, passing an endless line of empty crates. Staffers and technicians raced past at a frantic clip—the show ran on such tight allowances, even a moment's delay could jeopardize that one explosive appraisal that could make or break a season.

They turned another corner, and a final stretch of hallway lay before them, ending in a closed access door marked HALL H. Grace could feel a distant rumbling beneath her feet, like the rolling tremor from a far-off detonation deep belowground. She could hear it, too, echoing off the floors and walls, enveloping her in the basso vibrato of the *ambo*—the ambient excited chattering of thousands. The staffer placed her hand on the bar of the hall door and turned back to them, hesitating. She looked different—gone was the cold, stony countenance of procedure. She looked younger, childlike, full of wonder.

"Welcome to *Antiques Roadshow*," she said.

The door swung open, and they walked into another world.

The cavernous main hall reared up fifty feet above their heads, its latticework of light towers and electrical grids cracking open like monstrous metallic jaws. Grace felt the intake of its very breath pulling at her gut, drawing her forward like the updraft of a cyclone. She stepped forward into the maelstrom and immediately felt that familiar crackling energy surge through her, as if her blood had been replaced by a million tiny shocks of static electricity that nibbled and pricked. For Grace, it was an exquisite pain, an unbearable pleasure.

She was home.

Twenty-foot-high royal blue fabric "walls" ringed the space, turning the hall into an enormous velvet jewelry box. Twenty-five bright orange marquees for each appraisal station were spaced out evenly around the edges of the "box," each manned by the foremost authorities in every field. There were PhDs and multiple masters, specialists from Sotheby's and Christie's and Skinner's, representatives from every major gallery in the country, draped in colorful arrays of silken bow ties and chiffon neck scarves with knots so tight, they appeared painted on.

The guests, too, had come from different stock. Those bestowed with Golden Tickets had not traveled such great distances for a simple roll of the appraisal die. They came prepared—they had scoured the internet for the curious inlaid marks on their pottery, they had researched the auction histories of clockmakers, they had painstakingly assembled the genealogy of their objects back through the shaded corridors of time. But when the revelation came, when the veil of true provenance was drawn aside, their poker faces crumbled, their vocabulary was reduced to a series of pants and gasps, their eyes brimmed over with tears, or they simply froze over, a blushing slack-jawed monument to shock and awe. They had placed not their objects, but themselves on the appraiser's block, and for their courage they were rewarded with the undeniable proof that they mattered, when the world had told them time and again that they did not.

But Grace knew that gift opened in two directions—one flap toward the guest, the other toward the expert. As she scanned the appraisers at their posts, the throbbing din of the masses died off into a peaceful silence and she allowed herself to be hypnotized by the elegant dance of pointer and provenance. She marveled at them, the stout pillars of the House of Antiquity. None of them had to be here.

They'd seen it all; they'd probably written the book on it, or at least the foreword. Their careers were complete. Their bellies were full.

But their eyes were hungry.

It humbled her. And it made her so goddamn proud to be a tiny cog within the machinery of this business, even in such a remote and desolate place as the Appraisal Experts Roadshow. She might not belong here, not anymore, but at least she hadn't lost the fire in her belly.

God, had she missed it.

But *Antiques Roadshow* had not missed her. It was only natural—they had all wanted to move on, to avoid the unpleasantness, and so long as Grace remained, she would be a constant reminder of it. She didn't blame anyone (some nights after a third glass of wine, not even Vic), but she feared the looks and the volumes of vitriol they'd speak.

Now, she was trespassing once again—yes, she'd been invited, but only because they couldn't coax Robert out here on their own. She was a necessary evil, and they'd all swallow their bile, but Grace would smell it. If she could just avoid—

Oh, God, she thought. *Not her. Not Jeanette.*

Jeanette Lackey made a beeline for Grace, looking as if she would finish it with a hard right cross to the jaw. Jeanette was physically imposing for an art appraiser—perhaps it had to do with a life in Arms and Militaria and a backbone as stiff as a drill instructor's.

Grace stepped away from Robert—she was terrified the poor kid would be caught in the crossfire. This was Robert's day, and she had no intention of doing anything to jeopardize it. She would take her medicine like a big girl. She was resigned.

And then she was hugged; so tight, the air was accordioned right out of her.

"Grace Fucking Schaffer!" crowed Jeanette. "They kept it under wraps until the Appraisers Session last night," she said, releasing Grace from the bear hug. "It was like *Close Encounters* in there—everyone ooh-ing and aah-ing like you'd be arriving by flying saucer. The whole crew's tickled super pink—'cept *Karloff*, of course. Poor Vic was silent as the grave."

"It was nice of Victor to set this up," said Grace, not wanting to rub salt in any wounds. "And do the appraisal himself."

"Well, it's paint," Jeanette said. "And it's you."

Grace tried to laugh it off. "It's Kent, Jeanette. I'd jump out of my deathbed for that appraisal."

"You almost had to. Bunch of us are right pissed at you, Gracie," she said. "Where the hell did you go?"

Grace paused, shocked. "I'm sorry?"

"You left us," said Jeanette. "Without a word, without an explanation. Just . . . poof."

"It was better that way. For everyone, not just me." Grace glanced around the hall, feeling the same flush of anxiety. "I knew what people were saying. I saw the looks."

"What looks, Grace?"

Grace laughed—that one was easy. She looked through the crowd, seeking out the cold shoulders of her former colleagues. And everyone was staring at her, just as she expected.

But everyone smiled, and everyone waved.

Was this Tricia's doing? Had she demanded they play nice to ensure a successful taping? Had everyone forgotten the excruciatingly awkward tapings between her and Victor? The snapping, the side-eyed looks, the paper-thin eggshells beneath everyone's feet? Grace could not fathom an answer. And then Jeanette handed it to her.

"Miss you, Gracie," she said. "Everyone does. Whether you like it or not."

And there it was. It had been unendurable for Grace—the hooded looks and the unrelenting nauseating pity—and Grace had seen them; she knew that she had.

But she'd been looking in the mirror.

"Glad to have you back," said Jeanette, giving her a peck on the cheek and rushing off.

Robert slid back beside Grace, reattaching himself to her. "Can't she do our appraisal?"

"No," said Grace. "You want the best for this one, Robert. Trust me."

And Victor was the best. Not always the best husband, but he was the Stradivarius of appraisers. He could pluck an old canvas or board, and no matter the state of tune, tease out notes long forgotten. Grace had always worried his talent was being diluted by hosting the show, but she never dared say anything. Hosting did something for Victor—it filled a place that art could not; that Grace could not. She wondered if Julie Robinson had filled that gap. Grace hoped she hadn't, for what would that say about Grace? It wouldn't just trumpet the tired old tale of forbidden, riper fruit; it would be a scarlet mark of her own accountability in their breakup. But she was tired of lugging grudges alongside the rest of her baggage. If Julie had filled that gap, well then, good for Victor.

But would Victor be good for Robert? Grace feared her own association with the boy would influence Victor, would muddy the lens through which he viewed the William Kent. Robert needed this. But, more than that—

I need this.

Grace cleared her throat and her eyes watered—some acrid bubble of anxiety had burned the base of her throat, but it soon passed.

She nodded to the *AR* staffer to soldier forth, and the three of them threaded through the crowd toward the Green Room door at the far corner of the hall. As they passed the expert at the Musical Instruments Table, he leaned over it to give Grace's hand a hearty high five.

"Miss Midas got her groove back," he said. "Good for you, Grace."

Miss Midas. Far better than Miss Medusa, which was how she had felt the last time she had seen him. Yes, she could get used to *Miss Midas.*

Something sharp stung her throat again, harder this time, nearly stopping her in her tracks. She swallowed, trying to force it back down into her stomach. *Relax*, she thought. *Just a little anxiety.*

She couldn't help it. She had expected to be terrified, and she was, but she hadn't expected the thrill of being recognized. Of being missed. Being relevant again. Of being (well, why not?) just a little bit famous.

Suddenly, something pinched her, hard, right at the base of her neck. She felt it grab hold and twist, and she knew what it was, and she knew it meant well, but she didn't have the time, not right then, so Grace ignored it, even as it grew more insistent, until the pinching finally gave up.

Tricia Elroy, the show's head producer, waved them over to a gap between two of the blue fabric walls. For all the leaping insanity that swirled about her, Tricia was the eye of the storm—calm, placid, immune to the violent emotional swings of *Antiques Roadshow*. She and Grace had never been terribly close, but they had always enjoyed a tight working relationship.

"Here they are," Tricia said. "Our guests of honor. Thank you for delivering them." She waved off the staffer and turned to face Robert. "Are you excited, Robert?"

He nodded. "Yeah. I think so."

"Don't be nervous," she said, and Grace thought that request as ridiculous as telling rain to dry off. "And don't worry about the Kent. It arrived in perfect condition, and we'll be shipping it back with the very same care, I assure you." Before he could thank her, she waved over another staffer. "Please take this young man to makeup."

Robert followed the staffer behind the walls to the Green Room, glancing back one last time at Grace, looking every bit like a nervous child going off to his first slumber camp.

Grace noticed Tricia was looking closely at her. Evaluating her.

"How are you, Grace?" she asked.

"I'm good." Grace hesitated, thinking of the gut punch of the affair, her messy exit, the weeks without sleep, the empty bottles of zinfandel and Zoloft. "I'm better."

Tricia laughed. "You're more than that. Bloody fabulous work you're doing with that show. You must be very proud."

"I am."

"Too proud to leave?"

Grace paused. "Too proud to be unemployed. You know what these shows do for our galleries, Trish."

"You found a William Kent," she said. "A *Kent*, for Christ's sake. That's pretty much Kryptonite to unemployment, Grace. I'd say it's a one-way ticket to wherever you want to go."

Grace hesitated. Did she mean . . . ? "Wherever?"

Tricia smiled. "You left *us*, remember? The door's still open. But I don't poach, Grace. You'd have to be a free agent."

"Of course. I understand completely."

"We'll talk after?"

"I'd like that," said Grace. Jesus, she'd *love* that.

Tricia's headpiece crackled with information. "Copy that," she said. "Just waiting on talent." She pushed the mic away from her mouth. "Your boy—he'll step up to the plate, right?"

"He'll be fine."

Tricia laughed and Grace was reminded of her clairvoyant ability to see through bullshit. Grace had just thrown her a shovelful, and they both knew it. *But does she see through Victor's?*

"Why Victor?"

"He pitched it," said Tricia. "He wanted it."

"You don't think . . ." Grace paused. "You don't think he's after it, do you?"

"The Kent?" She took a moment. "No. I don't think so. He's been by the book all week—head in his laptop, researching, typing up copy."

"Have you seen it?"

"Victor's copy?" She laughed. "I'd sooner get the keys to his Porsche, and you know it."

Grace laughed, but it wasn't funny, not to Grace. Victor was researching.

Victor didn't have to research. He knew every master, every school, every revival; he knew them blindfolded, he knew them from the back. So why was he researching?

"It's time," said Tricia. "Let's get to set." She led Grace through the crowd into a circular clearing in the center of the hall where only the cameras roamed.

The star of today's show stood on a large easel in the middle of the center stage. The fluorescents in the grid above burst to life, and four cameras lumbered forward like a battery of siege cannons. Many of the guests gave up their places in line to gather around the set. Experts paused appraisals, rushing over to the nearest monitor. Every eye, every word, every thought anchored on the jewel-like setting that glimmered before the cameras. And in the very center of that setting, the finest jewel of all—a shimmering emerald of oil and pigment, of river and bridge and sunset.

The William Kent.

Its time had come. And so had Grace's.

The curtain to the Green Room parted and Victor Karlin stepped forth, an antique gladiator armed for blood sport. He jerked on the lapels of his suit jacket and the crisp snap of fabric ricocheted across the hall, drawing the eyes of all those around him. Little by little the news spread, and a tense hush circled the hall. Victor made the tiniest adjustment to his silk crimson necktie and waded into the crowd as the bodies parted to either side.

Finally, he arrived at the William Kent, standing before it as if he were sizing up an opposing gladiator. His eyes scanned down the painting, braille-like, prodding every brushstroke. Every now and then his eye fastened upon a particular shade or color, categorizing some crucial something, some strength or weakness to be exploited.

Then he turned, and Grace felt the full force of Victor upon her.

He inclined his head, inviting her to approach. Grace had no choice—it was not a neutral field—so she walked over, joining him beside the Kent. Although hundreds of lights and thousands of eyes were upon them, Grace felt a curtain descend, shielding them from the crowd. Victor could do that.

"Hello, Grace," he said.

They had not spoken since they had signed the divorce papers. His voice should have sounded so harsh, so jagged in her ear, but it didn't. It was the sensation of hearing an old tune, dearly loved but long forgotten. There was so much Grace wanted to say. How dare he. How could he. Did he have regrets, second thoughts, sleepless nights? Did he ever... did he miss her? She settled for:

"Hello, Victor."

"Ah." He smiled, and her skin closest to him melted a little. "Victor, is it? Not Vic?"

"Would you rather 'Dr. Karlin'?"

He laughed. "Touché, Grace. Victor it shall be."

Grace clamped down on a smile, but a hint of it creased her lips. Even after all the hurt he had caused, the core essence of Victor—his charm, his panache—still swept her off her feet. And what was worse, he looked good—disarmingly so. His wavy, espresso brown hair still showed no sign of receding, he was trim and toned, and his blue pinstripe suit fit tautly over his frame like fabric gilding. There was the occasional cosmetic scaffolding, of course—a few teeth whitened here, a few hairs colored there—but he had aged well. If only their marriage had done the same.

"How's the kid?" asked Victor, sneaking a quick glance behind her.

"A fucking mess."

"Naturally."

"Don't make it worse."

He paused, hesitating, about to speak. The thought passed. "I'll take good care of him." He leaned the barest inch forward. "Just please, take care of you, okay?"

"Don't worry," Grace scoffed. "I've had a lot of practice with that lately."

Victor nodded—he had walked into that one. He turned back to the painting. "It was gracious of you to bring it here before you took it to auction," he said, his voice flat as the horizon. "I am in your debt for allowing me to inspect it."

Grace knew, even though Impressionism had never been Victor's guiding passion, he had always had a soft spot for William Kent. This discovery would open a bright new chapter in the public's appreciation of Kent's works. Victor was clearly pleased with that.

He was not pleased by the cacophonous interruption of a man bounding toward them, a small retinue of handlers in tow.

"Mrs. Schaffer!" crowed Glenn Kennedy, swooping in close enough she could smell the cellophane from his freshly dry-cleaned double-breasted suit.

"*Dr.* Schaffer," said Victor, and Grace silently thanked him for it.

"Pardon me, of course," said Glenn, undeterred by his faux pas. "I'm Glenn Kennedy."

Grace recognized him immediately. Glenn's face may not have launched a thousand ships, but it had launched a flotilla of "reality" TV shows. Grace feared he was here to launch another. Grace shook his offered hand, and her fingers brushed over his pampered cuticles. "Pleasure to meet you, Glenn," she said. "I recognize you. Aren't you on—?"

"*Antiques Roadshow!*" he crowed. "I'm the new host."

Grace's jaw dropped. Victor hadn't breathed a word. Then again, of course he hadn't—she knew exactly what hosting had meant to him.

"You ready to muster up some Must-See-TV Magic for us today?" asked Glenn, flashing her a smile that must have cost a small fortune.

Grace tried to share a glance with Victor, but he had turned away.

"Well, Glenn," she said, thinking of all the ways she'd like to respond, knowing there was only one. "I can certainly try."

"That's the spirit!" He shook her hand once again, and Grace marveled at how eerily similar his grasp was, as if it had been programmed by computer for just this specific interaction.

"Wish I could chat more, but duty calls," he said. "You know how it is, right, Vic?"

Victor turned. His face was a mask of tranquility, but the pulsing veins in his neck looked ready to catapult across the room and wrap themselves neatly around Glenn's throat. "Indeed I do, Glenn," he said, his words the temperature of dry ice.

"Well, cheerio, then, folks." Glenn marched off, calling over an assistant to tease back the one or two eyelashes that had been thrown out of sorts by the thirty-second conversation.

Grace turned back to Victor. "I had no idea," she said, searching for the words. "I'm so sorry, Victor."

He spun on her, face hard, eyes cold. "You'll have to excuse me, Dr. Schaffer." He gestured to Tricia, who hustled Robert into position beside the painting. "We're about to roll."

"Of course," said Grace. "Talk to you aft—"

But Victor had already turned away, walking over to the edge of the set, where Julie was waiting for him with open arms and waxed armpits. Grace had no desire to see anything pass between them other than a venereal disease, so she retreated off the set, taking a spot beside Tricia at a large video monitor.

Tricia's monitor cut from camera to camera, and she barked out a few final adjustments to the initial framing for each shot. The final image was a full screen shot of the William Kent.

Of my William Kent, thought Grace.

And it was too late for Victor Karlin to do anything about it.

"In your attic?" asked Victor, eyebrows arched.

"That's right," said Robert, his hands locked so tightly behind his back, Grace half expected a finger to break off and tumble to the ground.

"Anything else in there we might want to take a look at?" asked Victor. "Like Blackbeard's Treasure or a cement block in the shape of Jimmy Hoffa?"

Robert laughed and his limbs unlocked. Grace shook her head in reluctant wonder—when the camera rolled, Victor could calm a grand mal seizure.

"So no clue at all how it came to be in that magical attic of yours?" asked Victor.

"None," Robert shrugged. "Sorry."

"It's not signed. But you have an idea who painted it, right?"

Robert's eyes flashed over to Grace. "Yes," he said. "It's a William Kent."

The crowd gasped, but Victor shot them a stern look and they fell silent once again. He turned back to Robert with a wide smile. "Well, that's quite a journey for Mr. Kent—all the way from nineteenth-century London to Bennington, Vermont. How much do you know about him?"

"He's an Impressionist, right?"

"One of the first," Victor said. "Some regard him as the Claude Monet of British Impressionism. He started painting right about the same time as Monet, with a nearly identical brush technique and color palette. In fact, some authorities are still unsure exactly who gave rise to whom. What else do you know about him?"

"I read somewhere that his mother was a singer."

Victor nodded, as if Robert was his star protégé. "She was indeed. Kent attributed the melodic interplay of his colors to the hours he spent as a child listening to her practice. His parents were of modest means, so they originally wanted him to be a physician, but they scrapped their plans when it became obvious they had a prodigy on their hands. Fortunately for William and the rest of the art world, they put him in art school, and at the tender age of sixteen—have you heard this story?"

Robert shook his head.

"Well, late one afternoon, Kent was on the Thames working on his homework—copying *View of Westminster Bridge* by James Francis Danby. An elderly gentleman stopped by to admire it, particularly the stunning three-dimensional quality of Kent's sunset, which the man thought superior to the original, a copy of which stood beside the boy's easel for reference. Kent said it wasn't better, not even close, but the old man disagreed. 'You're past copycatting, boy,' he said, and offered William his card. But as he walked off, he called back over his shoulder: 'Just don't forget my yellow tree on the north bank.'"

Robert grinned. "That was Danby, right?"

Victor nodded. "Danby's signature was his sunrise—it's what separated him from all the other landscape painters of the time—and in time, he taught William how to create a signature all his own." Victor waved his mahogany pointer over the setting sun in the upper-right corner of the painting.

"The Kent Sunset."

Victor looked closer at the brilliant, if fractured, burnished celestial giant that dominated the oil. "It's a pity the piece has sustained such pinpoint *craquelure*," he sighed. "Particularly here, of all places. It makes it difficult to truly place this as a William Kent."

Grace's stomach balled into a tight fist. Where was he going with this?

"But that's not all we have to go on, is it?"

Grace released a few fingers within her abdomen—but not all of them.

"With your permission, we tested a microscopic flake of the painting and found the usual pigments and oils of the Impressionists, but also surprising traces of egg yolk, which is highly unusual for the time. Kent was one of the few artists who still mixed yolk into their oils, which he did to highlight individual brushstrokes"—he pointed to the canvas—"as we can clearly see around the outer edge of the painting. It gives the work a rustic framing, accelerating the eye into the center of the piece—a hallmark of Kent's technique."

Grace took a relieved breath. Victor was just building the tension, that's all. Grace just wished he wasn't building it around her throat.

Victor's pointer danced over the canvas as he teased the hidden mysteries out of the swirling oils. "The location is another Kent signature. He loved riverbanks, particularly the River Arden, which this might possibly be." His pointer caressed the outline of the church spire. "This could be St. John's in Fladbury, or Tewkesbury Abbey, site of his most famous work, *Elbow of Avon*, but I'm not one hundred percent certain." Victor hesitated; something about the spire had drawn his interest, but he was unable to bring it into focus. "Regardless, we can clearly see another Kent signature in the detailed nature of the horizon. Monet blurred it, creating a world without directional perspective, but Kent worked cinematically, using the horizon to direct our eyes into closer and farther focus, depending on what he wanted us to see."

Victor tapped the side of the frame with his pointer. "And we have an idea of the date of the work's completion, thanks to the Winsor & Newton canvas stamp you uncovered behind the stretcher: sometime between 1883 and 1905—the very prime of William Kent's career."

The hall erupted in a low rumble of breathless murmurs. Victor let it build, stoking it. He stood back from the painting, swiveling toward Robert, matching the precise speed of the close-up camera, which rolled toward him for his final *coup de grâce.*

"So," he said. "We have a match with time, we have a match with location, we have a match with the quality and content of oils."

Grace's heart began to pick up speed, galloping to Victor's crescendo toward climax.

"We have a signature horizon, and even with substantial *craquelure*, I doubt anyone would argue that we are looking into the brilliant beams of a William Kent Sunset."

Grace would sob, she could feel it rise, stinging her sinuses; she would make an absolute blathering fool of herself.

"Although we see so few of them at auction these days—buyers tend to hold his paintings for generations—we have seen William Kents going for six, even seven hundred thousand dollars when they do come up."

Tricia grabbed Grace's arm in a vise, but she didn't feel it. She didn't feel anything.

"But a fresh Kent?" Victor asked. "An unknown? That's a million-dollar painting."

Victor smiled the smile of his life.

"But this isn't William Kent."

The entire hall froze. No one dared blink. The only sound was the vibrating thrum of the air-conditioning vents overhead.

Victor inhaled deeply, savoring the moment. "This painting is the work of a lesser-known contemporary of Kent's." Victor sneered at it, as if he had spotted it at a swap meet. "And he was lesser known for good reason. His first known painting was a knockoff of *Elbow of Avon*, a juvenile art school project that somehow captured the dull, desperate imagination of 1899 London. Kent had retired by this point, and this imposter cashed in, cloaking himself in Kent's fame to establish himself as the new voice in London art."

Robert shook his head, seeking equilibrium from the atmospheric shift of elation to despair. "So then, who painted it?"

"Ay, that's the rub," said Victor. "The artist—and I use that moniker lightly—the artist that painted this is, without a doubt... James Davies."

Grace—frozen solid in a block of ice-cold shock—broke free, her thoughts tumbling out: *James Davies?* It was inconceivable, an absolute impossibility. Davies was a footnote at best—notorious for using the legacy of older masters to bolster his own paper-thin reputation. He skyrocketed to fame right around the turn of the century, and just as suddenly skyrocketed out, never being heard from again.

Victor spun back to the painting with a flourish. "My first clue was the similarity in style to *Avon's Elbow*—Davies' sampling of *Elbow of Avon*. Davies also mixed egg yolk in with his oils—copying Kent—but unlike the master, who used just enough of it to create that inner framework, Davies used far more." He pointed at the clear brushstrokes that stood out like pigmented ridges near the outside of the landscape. "As you can see, these strokes are too defined, but Davies wanted you to see his work. That's the mark of an artist seeking plaudits, not perfection."

Victor snapped his pointer over to the cracking, scaling sunset. "My second clue was a more grievous mistake. The *craquelure* only occurs in this one corner of the canvas. When we tested this area, we found traces of not one, but two kinds of varnish. It appears the artist accidentally sealed this corner with a water-based varnish first, and then covered up his mistake by applying an oil-based one over it. Over time, the tension between oil and water fractures the painting, creating just this type of scaling. If Davies were any more competent, one might think he did this on purpose. Perhaps he did—perhaps this was his way of thumbing his young nose at the famed 'Kent Sunset.' The Sunset he would never achieve."

Grace bit down hard on the inside of her cheek. She had been careless with the *craquelure*; in her excitement, she had assumed it was due to the humidity of Robert's attic. Still, that was not damning, in and of itself. Victor's master stroke, however, would be.

"My final clue was the signature," he said, pointing to the fractured orange sun. "Kent always signed his work with his initials, most often somewhere in the sun or the clouds around it. James never signed his canvases, at least not in the few pieces of his that went to market." Victor paused and the entire hall held its breath.

"But he always signed."

He whipped an illuminated magnifying glass out of his inside jacket pocket and handed it to Robert. "Look at the bottom-right corner of the frame, on the very edge."

Robert leaned closer, peering through the glass. The cameras pushed in. Grace put her nose to the monitor, but even the most aggressive zoom yielded nothing but the ornate gilded flowers of the wooden frame.

"I don't see anything," said Robert.

"Inside the fold of the bay leaf that connects the joints."

Robert strained, running the glass up and down the open joint between the two angles of the frame, still unable to spot it. And then—

"Wait!" he said. "I think I see..."

Oh God, please no.

"It's tiny, but I see two letters."

Grace braced herself for the kill shot.

"JD," said Robert.

"James Davies," said Victor. He turned to face the camera, but Grace knew he was looking directly at her. "I'm sorry to disappoint you, Robert, but I can certainly see why you—and your previous appraiser—mistakenly identified this as an unknown Kent. It's certainly very similar to his later work, and much of the technique has been patterned after the master's, although a poor shadow of it, to be sure. That's the bad news."

"There's good news?" asked Robert.

Victor laughed. "Indeed, son," he said. "It's a Davies, but it's an unknown one. I couldn't find a single reference to it coming up for sale, nor any mention of it in any private collections. He's come up for auction once or twice over the past fifteen years—at smaller boutique houses, of course—and the values have been consistently in the three-to-five-thousand-dollar range."

"Okay," said Robert, disappointed, but not crestfallen.

"On the other hand, this is an unknown, as we said. If you can get another expert or two to confirm my suspicions, you could be looking at five to seven thousand, maybe more."

"Oh!" said Robert, pulling himself off the mat. "Well, that's something, at least."

"It is indeed," said Victor, smiling at him (and for the camera, of course). "What a workout—thank you for putting me through my paces!"

Robert laughed, the crowd laughed, the crew laughed.

Not Grace. Everything seemed to move in slow motion for her—the cameras cut, the audience applauded, the stage managers rushed over to Victor, crowing with congratulations, nearly hoisting him in the air like a victorious Super Bowl coach.

Tricia turned to her with a look that made Grace question whether she had a bubonic boil on her forehead. "Tough break, there, Grace," she said without a hint of pity. "Thought it might be too good to be true."

"It still could be." It sounded as desperate as it felt.

"I have to set up the next appraisal," said Tricia, starting off.

"Talk later?" asked Grace.

Tricia turned. "I'm sorry?"

"We're still talking later... right?"

Tricia checked her watch. "We're running late. I'll ring you tomorrow, okay, Grace?"

"Sounds good," said Grace, who knew it sounded anything but good. There would be no reaching Tricia tomorrow, or the next day, or the week after that.

Grace would not be returning to *Antiques Roadshow.*

There would be no triumphant return, no profile in *The New Yorker*, no book deals, no interviews, no national tours with the brightest names in the business. All gone, like an exotic dream snuffed out by daybreak. Grace scanned the hall, making note of every crowded station, every appraisal, every expert, for there would be no repeat performance. She remembered the first time she'd had the nerve to invite her parents to the show; her mother looking like a wide-eyed tourist gazing up at a pyramid, her father silent, his face unreadable, his eyes glassy—from exhaustion, he said—but a slight quiver in his voice betrayed him when he said: *My daughter.*

Sorry, Dad.

But Grace knew she had far more to be sorry for. Through the mass of scurrying stage managers and rolling cameras, Grace noticed Robert shuffle over, shoulders slumped, head down, as if coming over for a paddling.

"I'm sorry," he said, beating her to it. "I'm so sorry, Grace."

"Oh dear, why?" She took his hand and gave it a gentle squeeze. "You were absolutely marvelous, Robert."

"I let you down."

"You did nothing of the kind," she said, staring straight into his misty eyes. "I'm the one that brought us all the way out here for nothing."

"Well, it's not nothing, not by a long shot," he said, finding his smile. "Five thousand dollars is five thousand more than I had this morning, right?"

Grace smiled back. She needed more of this kid in her.

"That's more than enough to get me out of my dad's place. I can't thank you enough."

Grace nodded. Robert was free, free to begin a new life. But what about the painting? Grace watched the crew remove the frame from the easel and lug it back to the production headquarters with far less care than they had brought it forth. It seemed cruel to Grace. To put something under the lights, make it feel so special, then trash it and drag it out a side door.

Like me.

Grace's hand patted her chest until her fingers wrapped around the celestial globe. It was so comforting to her, like the soft purr of a sleeping cat. She could feel it, alive within her grasp, rising and falling with her own breath. It was so reassuring.

But the globe had been wrong. Grace had been wrong.

Victor walked over, victory writ large upon his smiling face. "What drama!" he said, shaking Robert's hand. "You did spectacularly well, Robert. I think you'll be pleased with the final cut."

"And the five thousand dollars," Robert said.

Victor laughed. "Well, of course. Wish it was worth more."

"It is!" Grace said, surprising Victor—and herself—with the outburst. It made no sense. She had lost fair and square. It was not a Kent; Victor had proved it beyond a shadow of a doubt. Every single person in that convention hall—amateur and expert alike—knew it.

Everyone except Grace.

It's not right, she thought. She had no idea why, but the feeling was unmistakable—like the sound of a midnight floorboard creaking in the dark; she could not shake it. *This painting is worth more.*

"Well, sure," said Victor, "in the hands of the right restorer. Perhaps another thousand, two thousand dollars with the right buyer."

He's wrong, she thought, and a voice whispered back.

We are right.

"It's a Kent," Grace said, before she could stop herself.

A few crew members halted their work and looked over at them.

"It's not," said Victor. "If you were listening—"

"I heard what you said," said Grace. "But you're wrong. That painting is an unknown William Kent."

"Your proof?"

"Frames can be recycled; you know that. If we take that out of your appraisal—"

"It removes Davies, but it still doesn't add up to a Kent. What's your proof, Grace?"

"I don't need proof," she said. "I can feel it."

Victor glanced around at the small crowd that had gathered to eavesdrop. "Oh, you can *feel* it," he said, loud enough for everyone to hear. "Well, why don't you take that feeling to market, Grace? See how far it takes you."

"We will," she said. "We're going to Sotheby's."

Victor's eyes bulged. "Sotheby's?" He edged closer, lowering his voice. "Don't do this, Grace. Run it online or at a smaller house. Sotheby's—that's suicide. It'll destroy you."

Grace looked into his eyes, and instead of confrontation, she saw honest concern. But there was also something else in those eyes.

"What are you afraid of?" she asked.

"You losing your gallery."

"I'm prepared to, if I have to."

"For a James Davies?"

"For a William Kent."

"It's not, Grace."

"What if it is?"

He paused. "It's not," he said. "I know it's not."

"How?" she pressed. "How do you know it's not?"

"Because." He stared at her for an eternal moment. "It *can't* be."

Grace saw it spark and crackle once again—an anger deep within him, a rage. If she could just get a closer look at it, just tease it out of him...

Victor reared back, sensing the intensity of Grace's gaze. "No you don't, Ms. Schaffer," he snapped. "Save it for your next appraisal."

He shook Robert's hand, but his eyes remained on Grace. "Good luck at Sotheby's," he said, storming off.

Robert joined her, and together they watched Victor disappear into a crowd of guests clamoring for his autograph. "Are you sure it's a Kent?" he asked.

"Yes," she said. "I have absolutely no idea why, but yes. I'm sure."

Robert smiled. "Then, so am I."

Grace gave him a shaky smile back. That sweet boy had taken her at her word. Would she punish him for it? She had assumed the celestial globe was an instrument for good; was it now lighting the path to their destruction?

Would she know the difference?

Grace watched the painting disappear back into its crate. The William Kent.

Not the James Davies, she thought.

Because who the hell was James Davies?

Two

29 September, 1899

My Dearest Mother,

I have made my mark, just as you said I would! A hit, a very palpable hit!

It began as a simple apprentice exercise; my perspective on William Kent's first masterpiece, 'Elbow of Avon.' I set out copying Kent's usual hallmarks—the burnished sun, the soft cushioned hills, the shimmering face of the water—and as my brush spoke, his voice crackled through it. But then I heard a sweeter voice, my own voice, muzzled too long in the dungeon of that eternal apprenticeship, tortured with the rote repetition of old forms and precedents, as if I were learning a court dance Cadenza and not the Mysteries of Art.

I turned instead to my own instruction, reimagining his landscape, painting over his old, withered strokes with wider, bolder, brasher colors. Where Kent whispered, I thundered, where he suggested, I declared, conscripting his tired strokes into the service of my story. A story for today, Mother; not for the corpse of tradition, but for the beating heart of a modern audience.

I could go on, but to do so might earn me a well-earned rebuke from Father. Then again, perhaps I shall, as it appears rebuke is all we two share these days. It is of great sadness to me that he is unable (or unwilling) to share in my success, as you have. Perhaps it is my proving him wrong that has soured him, perhaps the company I keep.

But, oh, what company, Mother! Lady Judith Bonner herself not only purchased the piece (at a shockingly stupendous sum), but thereupon threw a celebration in my name, inviting the entirety of London Society to view its debut at her home in Kensington. Alas, my dear Alexandra was unable to accompany me. She claimed an illness, but I fear the suddenness of things is to blame. Without her on my arm, I felt I was listing a few degrees to starboard, and the constant bowing of heads and shaking of hands, while delicious, began to feel too rich for my young stomach. I fled to the drawing room, as if seeing my own work on the wall before its reveal might steady me, and suddenly found myself in the most awkward of encounters. The butlers were in the process of removing, of all things, an imprint of Kent's 'Stratford Shore,' which had, until now, claimed the place of honor in the room. They handed it to a porter of some type, a slovenly, slap dashed man, who I surmised had been hired by Kent to convey it home on its unceremonious return. He passed me in the foyer, and as I gazed upon the once proud work, I could not prevent myself the slightest chuckle of disapproval at its well-trodden shapes and colors. The porter must have heard me, for he lowered the painting enough for me to see him for who he was.

The Great William Kent himself.

Well, a part of him, Mother. He looked as if he had been carved out of himself, and all that was left of him was the shriveled rind before me. His eyes were glassed over and sunken, and his hair was greased and mussed about upon his head like waxen straw. He might have recognized me—I think he did—for he quickly raised the painting to hide his embarrassment as he shuffled off down the long hallway and out the door to obscurity. His time, it appears, is past.

But my time has come, Mother, as you knew it would! I only wish you could have seen 'Avon's Elbow' at full sail with that buzzing multitude about it.

The work is good, Mother, it truly is. And it's better—better than all that has come before. So very much better.

Because it is New.

Your Disgustingly Famous Son,
Jim

Three

The Appraisal Experts Roadshow had always been the Bruce Banner of the Antique World—quaint, mild-mannered, perhaps even frail—but in a few short weeks, it shredded through the shirtsleeves of its hospitality tents like the Incredible Hulk. Elaine had originally scheduled their Portland, Maine, show on the lawn of the McKernan Hospitality Center, but early presale suggested she'd have a riot on her hands if she didn't find a larger space. Fortunately, she found one at the last minute at the James Banks Exposition Center, which would double their footprint from twelve to twenty-four thousand square feet.

It was not enough.

Over one thousand hopeful pilgrims had queued up the night before, and the long line of folding chairs, sleeping bags, and camp stoves that stretched a mile down Park Avenue made the crowd appear like a reincarnation of Woodstock—minus the LSD. The carnival atmosphere of the night before had evaporated with the morning sun; now the crowd was on edge. Even in this larger venue, not all of them would enter, perhaps hundreds of them, and so money changed hands, as it always does, until the speculators had taken their usual spots at the front of the line.

They stood out like sore thumbs, carrying the objects they wished to appraise like stock portfolios, not family heirlooms. Grace could pick them out of a lineup as easily as if they had robbed her in broad daylight, which was exactly what she feared was about to happen inside the Banks Center. These were the scavengers of the Antique World—they pecked through garage sales, estate sales, any old carcass they could nose their beaks into, snuffling out the "bargains" that promised exponential returns at the expense of desperate, uneducated sellers. The stunning news of the show's appraisals had spread across their message boards; there was blood in the water, and the frenzy had begun.

I see you, thought Grace, glaring at the smirking profiteers at the front of the line. She wanted them to know her eyes would be on them for the duration of the show.

But the eyes of everyone else were on Grace. The moment she slipped out of the hotel shuttle with the other experts, a thunderous roar rose from the multitudes. They surrounded her, some for autographs, others shoving objects into her face, begging her for a quick appraisal. Grace was pleasantly surprised—either they had not heard the news from the fireworks at *Antiques Roadshow*, or if they had, they had taken Grace's side against Victor's appraisal.

My fans, she thought, chuckling to herself. She'd never had them before, not even at the height of her notoriety at the Roadshow, and she was tickled bright pink at how silly and ridiculous it all felt.

And how glamorous.

But what a boon to the show, to the experts, to their galleries. Her surging notoriety might even allow them to expand the tour, maybe even film it.

She realized she'd fallen behind the other experts, who had rushed into the center like John, Paul, George, and Ringo in *A Hard Day's Night*, and the crashing waves of desperate fans now pressed in at her from all sides. The furor reached such a pitch, Grace feared one of them might accidentally draw blood and the rest would fall upon her, tearing her to pieces; when from behind her, a voice boomed out like an oil tanker's foghorn:

"LET THAT WOMAN GO!"

The crowd parted, and Jerome Zwick shoved his way through, jabbing his pointer into the spleens of those unwilling to step aside. He grasped Grace's arm with surprising strength, dragging her through the narrow path to the front entrance. A staffer waited until they were mere inches from the door before he jerked it open, hustled them through, and slammed the door back again with a metallic clang.

Inside the safety of the lobby, Grace and Jerome attempted to catch their breath, each of them bent over at the waist. "My knight in shining armor," Grace gasped. She had never played the damsel in distress, never needed a hero, but she had never known how sweet it was to have a Jerome Zwick. "If this keeps up, I'm going to need a bodyguard."

"You're going to need a Seal Team," he panted. "This is getting out of hand."

Grace stood up and gazed out the doors, where a score of faces had pressed up against the glass, still shouting and cheering. It was surreal, like watching a film of some celebrity's life, with you playing the celebrity. But this wasn't a movie, and Grace wasn't acting.

And I'm not a celebrity, she thought.

Then again, isn't this what it looked like? The screams, the adulation... the love? For she could feel it, draped about her like a warm blanket. And it had been so long since she'd felt it. So long she'd convinced herself she'd never feel it again.

Maybe I am, she thought. A celebrity. Not that it mattered, of course. Although if it had this kind of effect on the show, then Grace would have to make peace with it.

"It's a bit nutty," she said, "That's for sure. The sweet curse of success, I suppose."

"Yes, but at what cost?" He groaned his way up to a standing position, teetering with exhaustion. "This is getting to be too much for us."

"Then we expand," she said, her smile fading. She wondered if the glass Jerome looked through was no longer half empty, but completely drained. "We're going to have to, Jerry. Once the Kent sells at Sotheby's, we'll be a sensation. It's okay. We can handle it."

He waved at the chaos outside. "That's not for handling. You saw the mercenaries out there. You think—" He pointed at the celestial globe that hung from Grace's neck. "You think that's why it's here? That's why it chose you?"

Grace felt her cheeks ignite. She snatched the globe off her chest, grasping it in a tight fist. "Whatever this thing is, it's *mine*, okay? And I know what to do with it."

Jerome reached toward her. "Grace, please."

She swatted his hand away. "Don't tell me what to—"

"GRACE!" Jerome's voice brooked no argument, and Grace immediately hushed. "You're bleeding," he said.

She looked down—a small rivulet of blood dripped from the base of her fist. She opened her hand and the globe dropped out, swinging back down to her chest. She was cut, the flesh split down the middle of her palm.

Jerome fished a handkerchief out of his suit pocket and pressed it against the wound. Grace stood there in silence, wide-eyed like a child watching a parent make the hurt disappear.

"Thank you," she said.

He nodded, examining the wound. "I think it's stopped."

They checked her hand, but their thoughts remained on the lapis lazuli around her neck.

"Jerome . . . ?" she asked, her voice quivering.

"Shhh," he said, wrapping the bloody handkerchief around her hand. "You must have cut yourself on the way in."

"Yeah. Must have," she said, repeating the lie. "I'd better go clean up."

She noticed Jerome was still sweating from the melee outside. She found a clean spot of the handkerchief and gently wiped the perspiration from his pasty brow. "You better clean yourself up, too, Mr. Absent-Minded Professor," she said. "You look like death."

The James Banks Exposition Center had often thundered with the fisticuffs of the local roller derby, but it had never played host to a more raucous crowd. Delirious squeals of laughter and joy ricocheted from one side of the hall to the other like the call and response of cannon fire, swirling into a cyclone of sound that wound all the way up to the trellis roof, causing the fluorescent light cans to sway as if a tectonic fault had ruptured beneath the parquet floor below.

There was a thickness to the air; humid, like a hot blast of aromatic steam, and Grace breathed it in, deep, all the way to her belly as she patrolled the appraisal stations, encouraging the experts, entertaining the guests. At each table she twisted her celestial globe, and if it felt perhaps a little cooler than usual, she pressed on anyway, knowing the globe would catch up soon enough. She dare not delay—everyone clamored for a little touch of Grace, and she did not wish to disappoint. Everyone was thankful, of course, effusively so, and even though Grace still stung from the setback at *Antiques Roadshow*, her fellow experts assured her that Victor had been wrong, dead wrong, and she'd prove it to him in front of the entire art world at Sotheby's in less than one week's time.

It was an unusual sensation—to have so many in her corner. Only Jerome steered clear of her, and as she finished her tour of the hall, she watched him trudge his way through a half-hearted appraisal at the Antiquities Table. Grace refused to let his gloom infect the celebration. For that was what it was, a revival—of tour, of expert, of Grace, of Jerome, too—if he'd just open his heart to it. She settled back behind the Paintings, Prints, and Posters Table, and immediately her spirits soared. Her line was naturally the longest—the strange rumors that were initially only whispered about in secluded online chat rooms had now risen to a dull roar:

Grace Schaffer is an alchemist.

She had turned canvas into gold, Velvet Elvis into Emerald Elvis, garage sale discounts into college tuition.

What can she do for me?

Grace glanced over the small framed watercolor on her table and made a quick check of the owner: middle-age, middle-class, forearm tattoo of an anchor, a sailor of some kind.

"Okay, let's talk value," she said, and the anchor on his arm fluttered with anticipation. "In a retail store—which may be your best bet with a lesser-known artist like this—I'd say you'd be looking at a value between four to five hundred dollars."

Grace twisted the globe around her neck, and for a terrifying moment, nothing happened. She wrapped her fingers around it, seeking its warmth, but it was cold—so cold it pricked her skin—and oddly smooth, as if the golden pyrite inclusions had been polished flat. She twisted it again, harder now, and nearly cried out in relief when it pulsed, faintly (weakly?), which was all she needed. She wasn't asking for much—the piece was worth very little on the open market, perhaps fifty dollars. Five hundred would be a windfall for this man. Her heart raced once again with the thrill of bringing joy to one in dire need of it.

But the man just stared at her, as if he had not heard the appraisal. "Five hundred?" he asked, shaking his head as if he might jumble the numbers into a different amount.

"Yes." Grace smiled again, thinking she must have truly shocked him. "Surprised?"

He nodded, disappointment washing over him. "Just five hundred?"

"Well," said Grace, an odd sensation hatching in her belly. "Maybe five twenty-five?"

He sighed and the anchor on his arm drooped into the inky sea below. "Nothing more?"

"I'm sorry." That truly was the limit; beyond it. "That's all."

He glanced down at the watercolor, his heart broken, as if it had been unfaithful to him. As if it had betrayed him.

As if I betrayed him. The ingratitude—it infuriated her. She had given him more, far more, than he deserved, and this was her thanks?

She bit down on the sharp stream of anger that rose from deep within her lest she say something, lest she (well, she could, couldn't she?) lower her appraisal and teach the man a lesson he'd not soon forget.

The man picked up the frame and turned to his wife, who placed a comforting arm around him. "I told you, doll," she said. "She's an appraiser, not a miracle worker." She looked to Grace for help. "Right, ma'am?"

Of course, thought Grace. But she couldn't say it.

Because I'm both.

"Just a moment," Grace said, reaching out for the frame. The man handed it back and Grace set it on the table before her. "That value was for the painting itself. In my excitement, I left out the carved white frame, which is of the most exquisite craftsmanship. The frame alone adds another five to seven hundred dollars."

The couple's eyes popped simultaneously. "Twelve hundred dollars, then?" he asked.

"At least." Grace twisted the globe hard enough she could feel the beginnings of a blister. "Maybe even more, in the right gallery."

"Wow! Thank you, thank you, thank you!" he said, shaking her hand with gusto. "Twelve hundred dollars!"

The handshakes quickly turned to hugs, and as Grace watched them disappear into the crowd, she felt a huge weight lift from her shoulders, and all was once again right in the world.

Then, someone screamed.

Grace spun around; a huge commotion had erupted at Jerome's table. Elaine flew by her, barking into a walkie-talkie, "I don't care about the lines outside! I need Security at Tribal Art—now!"

Grace leapt after her, grabbing her sleeve. "What's going on?"

"Jerry caught a counterfeit. The guy's getting belligerent."

Grace's throat clamped shut, but she screamed inside: *Jerome!* She broke into a panicked run, past Elaine, rushing over as fast as her legs could carry her.

As she punched through the crowd, she saw them struggle in the distance—Jerome and a large man, at least a foot taller and half again as wide. The man shoved Jerome back, and something silver appeared in his hand—

"GUN!" Grace yelled.

The shot boomed out across the hall, people screamed, the wooden floor rumbled with the frantic stampede of a thousand feet. Grace pressed forward against the shrieking tide, desperate to catch a glimpse of Jerome through the thrashing mass of people. She saw an elderly man shoved aside; another crashed to the floor in a fetal position as he fell underfoot. Shopping carts filled with the dearest family possessions were overturned, their contents trampled to splinters. Through a gap, Grace saw two security guards converge on the shooter, tackling him to the ground, one easily wresting the gun from his grasp

"It's a starter pistol!" the guard yelled. "Just blanks!"

Thank God, Grace sighed. But the terrified herd had whipped themselves into a frenzy, clawing and stumbling out the exit doors in a giant chaos of flailing limbs. Grace could only stand in the middle of the hall and watch, buffeted by the storm.

By my storm, she thought, despair clogging her throat. But the despair was about to choke off her throat completely.

The celestial globe lay at her feet, necklace snapped, globe split right down the middle, sheared in two. The once brilliant constellations of the lapis lazuli had ceased to sparkle, their golden fires extinguished.

The Great Stone, which had endured millennia, could no longer endure Grace.

She fell to her knees and gathered it up in her hands as if it were the limp body of a beloved friend. "What have I done to you?" she said, stroking the scuffed shards of the stone. "What have I done?" She didn't sob; she refused to give herself that relief. The tears just poured down, drenching the gift she had so abused.

Grace heard another commotion and glanced up. Four EMTs burst through the tattered remains of the crowd, wheeling in a gurney. She stood up, and Elaine backed into her, her face white as fresh canvas.

"Is someone hurt?" asked Grace.

"No," said Elaine, shaking her head in denial.

"Elaine!" Grace yelled, grabbing her shoulders. "WHO IS IT?"

Elaine turned, her eyes frozen in shock. "Brace yourself, Grace."

Grace tried.

But she knew some things were not for bracing.

Four

"Hey, Dad."

Grace eased herself down on the hospital bed beside Albert. The bed creaked, but her father did not stir. The only sounds in the room were the slow, whispered breath of the ventilator and the soft chimes of the IV, which pumped useless medicine through his ruptured veins. She smoothed the hair back from his forehead, careful not to disturb the electrodes.

"Can you hear me, Dad?"

Shirley spoke up quietly from a chair in the corner. "He can't, sweetheart."

Grace ignored her, leaning ever closer to her father. "I have some news, and you're the only person in the world who understands what it means." She glanced away for a moment to collect herself. "I'm getting the Excellence in the Arts Award, Dad. Twenty-five years since you did—almost to the day, isn't that something? I thought we could hang it in your office, if you like, right beside yours. Father and—"

The respirator sighed.

Grace fell silent. She was speaking to no one. That was not her father in that bed, just tubes and wires. He had left her.

Not now, she thought. *I'm so close, Dad.*

One more step and she'd be there, right beside him on the summit that only he stood upon. And he'd smile, and she would take his hand, and they would look out.

Together.

"Grace," said Shirley.

Grace looked up but couldn't see her mother through the tears.

"I'm so sorry, sweetheart," said Shirley. "It's not fair."

"No, it's not." Grace cupped her father's limp head in her hands. "I thought we had time."

"I know." Shirley rose but kept her distance. "I know you always hoped he'd..."

Grace turned to her mother, confused.

"When you were older, I mean," said Shirley. "I know you thought, maybe then he'd—"

Grace stood up, facing her mother. "He'd what, Mom?"

Shirley took a few hesitant steps toward Grace until only the motionless body of her husband separated them. "Grace. I don't think time—more time—I don't think it would have made any difference, sweetheart."

Grace flicked the tears from her eyes, her cheeks flushing. "Meaning what, Mom?"

"I'm just saying," said Shirley, choosing her words with care. "Your father was—well, he was who he was."

"He *is*, Mom. We're standing right over him."

"I know, dear, I just hate to see you beat yourself up."

Grace's tears were gone now, burned off by the fire in her eyes. "My anger has a pretty clear target right now, Mom, and it's not me."

"Grace," said Shirley, refusing to back down. "Your father was—is—he's a very complicated man."

"Too complicated for you?"

Shirley bit down, her own anger rising to the surface. "You're not listening to me."

"Because you're talking nonsense. You didn't know him like I did."

"Oh, Grace."

"You didn't." Grace gazed down at her father. "We talked about everything—about work, about art. We shared the same dreams, the same jobs, the same path, the same passions, the same awards, for God's sake!"

"You shared, Grace."

Grace sucked in a deep breath, steadying herself. "Every word you say right now, every one of them, is another nail in the coffin, do you understand?"

"I do. But you need to hear—"

"Not another *word*, Mom. I mean it."

Shirley fell silent. The two women stared at each other over Albert's comatose body. The respirator sighed, but neither of them breathed.

Then Shirley spoke. "I loved your father, Grace. And he loved me. But I knew what that meant, and I hope one day you will too. Albert was an extraordinary man, but his whole life was fueled by one thought and one thought only—that he would die in front of a blinking cursor before he had the chance to fill it." She gazed down at the empty husk of her husband. "That's what he saw at the end. Not you, not me. Just that relentless, tormenting cursor."

Grace looked up, eyes simmering. "Well, at least he saw *something*. What do you see, Mom—other than a lifetime of empty promises and missed opportunities?" she said. "I'll take the cursor."

And so, the coffin closed.

They would not speak for months, not even at the funeral two weeks later.

But when Grace left the gravesite, her head resting on the shoulder of a man who had already fallen in love with another, Grace felt her own eyes begin to blur. Soon she could not even see her own cursor, blinking back at her. Without her father, and soon mercifully enough without Victor, nothing blinked back at Grace. No cursor, no partner, no one to meet her at the top of the summit, which crumbled beneath her feet. And so she fell; all the way to the bottom, and then into the darkness below. It was so cold, so terribly cold, as if she'd been marooned deep within a subterranean cavern, no sound but that awful dripping echoing in the darkness—Art, Albert, Victor, all draining out of her, dripping away like tears, until those stopped, too. And then, there was only Grace, and nothing else.

And the shadows grew, and the walls closed in, for Grace was not enough.

Five

Jerome Zwick died.

The Maine Medical Center was only a few blocks away, but the ambulance struggled to carve a path through the stampeding hordes. Three blocks had taken the time of thirty, and Jerome had been subjected not once, but twice to the savage shock of the defibrillator in an attempt to restart the rhythm of his failing heart. It held on as long as it could, through the emergency room doors and into the operating room. But while the doctors raced to bypass the malevolent mass blocking his coronary artery, his heart flatlined, and nothing could bring it back; not medicine, not his reputation, not the riches he'd discovered, nor the gratitude of thousands over a career that spanned half a century. None of that could bar the door that opened before him.

Death had come to Jerome.

But Jerome was just as cantankerous with Death as he was to any other unwelcome guest at the Antiquities Table, and rather than prolong the heated argument that raged between them on the operating table, Death demurred.

As far as Death was concerned, Life could have the son of a bitch.

And so the EKG beeped, and the cardiologist jumped, and a nurse crossed herself, and Jerome slept on, dreaming the most magnificent dream—that he had finally given the medical profession the kind of scare they had been giving him for the last twenty years.

Once Jerome regained consciousness ("with the worst acid reflux this side of chicken vindaloo"), Grace allowed the well-wishers in, one at a time, for exactly five minutes each. She stood guard at the door, and the brimstone in her eyes was of such ferocity, even the nurses deferred to her wishes.

Once she had gently—but firmly—shown Elaine out, Grace shut the door to the ICU and tiptoed across the reflective floor to Jerome's bedside. She did not take the padded seat beside it as the others had. She stood over him, hands gripping the white plastic rails, protecting him lest Death regain its nerve and return for a rematch.

His eyes were closed, and she couldn't tell if he was momentarily resting or had slipped back into a sedated sleep, so she watched him silently; his features sagging, drawn, so thin, so frail, like the mirthless bony grimace of a skeleton.

Not you, too, she thought. *Please stay.*

He blinked open his eyes, and they lit upon her. "Shocked 'em all, didn't I?"

"How so?" she asked, lightly stroking his arm.

"Who knew I had a heart to attack?"

Grace laughed, but it turned quickly to tears.

"It's okay," he said, soothing her. "It's okay."

"I did this to you," she sobbed.

"You did not." He gripped her wrist with surprising strength. "I did this—with a lifetime of flank steak and Keebler cookies. The gunshot didn't hurt, I guess." He suddenly lifted his head, concerned. "Was anyone hit?"

"It was a starter pistol."

"Fucking amateur," he scoffed. "Should have known by the Pier 1 *schmatta* he tried to fob off as a Chimayo rug."

Grace laughed, mucus cascading out her nose, which sent them both into hysterics. They calmed, and his tight grasp loosened into a caress. Grace looked down at his fingers, stroking the back of her hand.

"I was so wrong, Jer," she said. "So very, very wrong."

"Then go back to the show and make it right."

"I can't." Grace reached into her purse and withdrew the shattered remains of the once celestial globe.

He sat up on his elbow and gazed into her hand. The inclusions had disappeared, the lapis faded to a cold, dull gray.

"It's dead, isn't it?" he asked.

"I think so." She turned the pieces over in her palm, looking for some tiny speck of life, finding none.

He looked up, troubled. "What does this mean for Sotheby's?"

"The William Kent?" She looked down at the destruction in her hand. "I don't know." She thumbed one of the shards. "Maybe it'll be okay. I made the appraisal before it broke, right?"

Jerome winced. "I'm not sure that's how it works."

She nodded. "Me neither."

He put out his hand, and she placed the two halves of the globe in his palm. He worked them around as if he were trying to leach the answer from the stone. "Do you think it's a Kent, Grace?"

"Not without that."

He snapped his fist closed, hiding the globe.

"Do *you* think it's a Kent?" he asked.

Grace listened for the voice—their voice, hers and the stone's—but no trace of it remained. "I'm not sure, Jer," she said, pointing to his closed fist. "I can't answer without that."

Jerome reached over to a starch white paper trash bag attached to the bedrail and gently placed the remnants of the shattered stone inside, laying it to rest. "You're going to have to, Grace. It's gone."

The tears returned, and Grace gave in, sobbing. "Everything's gone," she said. "Dad, Vic, the stone... thank God you're coming back to the show—so long as we still have a show to come back to."

Jerome nodded, but his eyes betrayed the lie.

Grace shook her head. "Don't you dare—"

"I can't go back, Grace."

"Bullshit. The doctor said—"

"I'm saying it, Grace." He smiled up at her, not a sad smile, but a firm one. "I'm done."

Grace leapt up and paced the room, hyperventilating. "No," she said. "No, no, no, no, no. I ruined everything."

"Grace."

"You still had a chance."

"Grace, please—"

"It's out there!"

"GRACIE!"

Grace froze, eyes wide, chest heaving up and down as she teetered at the very edge of hysterics.

"Sit, girl, before you give me another heart attack."

Grace nodded and wiped her nose with her sleeve. She shuffled back over to the bedside. Jerome lowered the plastic rail and tapped the mattress. Grace eased down beside him.

"It's time," he said. "My whole life I've been digging in the ground, searching for clues. I just got a huge one, and it's written all over my chest."

"But your Grail," she moaned. "Maybe it's close. Maybe it's at the next show, or the one after."

"No," he said, shaking his head. "I won't find it there."

"How can you be so sure?"

He smiled up into her eyes with more love than Grace had ever seen.

"Because I already found it."

She turned away. That was too much, much too much to handle. "You lie," she said. "I'm anything but that."

He reached up, turning her face to his. "You just need a little restoration, that's all," he said. "Scrape off the varnish, Gracie. The thing you seek—it's not in some stone." His hand descended down the curve of her neck, resting over her heart.

"It's right here."

Six

It was High Noon on the Upper East Side.

Grace arrived outside the entrance five minutes early, hoping to give Robert a familiar face to focus on, rather than the monstrous ten-story glass leviathan that reared up behind her. Grace heard the sharp snap of fabric and looked up. Five giant flags—United States, Great Britain, France, Switzerland, and China—billowed above her like the great sails of a military armada. And so it was—what began in a cramped London office in 1744 had mushroomed into the largest auction house in the world, with offices in over forty countries spanning the globe. The sales, once measured in guineas, now tallied in the tens of millions: $21 million for a seven-hundred-year-old copy of the *Magna Carta* in 2007; $63 million for Picasso's *Femme Assise* in 2016; and in 2019, $110 million for Claude Monet's *Meules*, the unassailable record for an Impressionist work. It was an artistic juggernaut, a nation unto itself.

It was Sotheby's.

The wind-whipped flags waved at Grace as they fluttered in the Manhattan breeze, mocking her from their perch forty feet above the sidewalk. Grace did not need the reminder—she was quite aware it could have been her armada. When Grace left Christie's to found her own gallery, climbing the auction house ladder was the path not taken—the scales of her career would have tilted from art to commerce, and that was not the life she was seeking. Then again, she certainly hadn't sought out this ten-car pileup of a life either, so she figured the flags had every reason to mock.

A taxi skidded to the curb. Robert clambered out, stretched, looked up at Sotheby's, and froze: a five-foot-ten solid block of ice in a Suit Spot blazer.

"You look good, Robert," she said, taking him gently by the elbow.

He mumbled something unintelligible, but Grace did not need subtitles—perhaps only a stretcher to carry him inside. They approached the revolving doors, which flashed about like the whirling blades of a slaughterhouse.

"Are you excited?" she asked, her voice far steadier than her pulse.

"Guess so," he said. "You?"

"Catatonic."

Robert laughed, which was medicine to Grace, who laughed along with him. The laugh lasted a full fourteen feet—all the way to the shiny black Salvatore Ferragamo heels of Annette Neiman.

"Grace Meredith Schaffer, as I live and breathe," she crooned, leaning against the edge of the stately reception desk as if she had been waiting for them at the local watering hole. Grace knew an ambush when she saw it.

"Madam Vice President," said Grace, greeting her former colleague as if they were the oldest and dearest of friends. They embraced in the middle of the foyer, and Grace wondered if the bad vibrations would shatter the glass doors behind them.

"Madam *Senior* Vice President," said Annette, with a peroxide white smile.

"Oh, that's fabulous, Annie," said Grace. "I hadn't heard."

"No, of course not," she said. "Must be hard to stay abreast of things when you're out touring, right?"

Grace struggled to maintain her smile. "That's right."

"You came straight from—where was it, Portland?" She had said *Portland* as if it were fish wrapped in yesterday's newspaper. "Heard you had a little turbulence up there."

Before Grace could return fire, Annette introduced herself to Robert, who gushed a bit, slightly starstruck. It was a natural response to Annette, irrespective of the svelte, sophisticated curve of her figure, which slithered about beneath a jet-black Giorgio Armani dress. Annette appeared more like a sculpture than an actual living, breathing woman. She did not gesture—she posed, her arms flowing from one position to the other with the grace of a ballerina.

"Your piece has been making quite the stir here, Robert," she said, still holding his hand. "We placed it in the seventh-floor gallery for exhibition this week, just around the corner from the auction hall. No one knows quite what to make of it, which should make for an interesting sale. Not sure it will meet your reserve, maybe not even close, so you might consider lowering it before we begin."

"We're good with that number," said Grace. She had set their minimum at twenty million dollars. A William Kent had fetched that in Sotheby's London a few months back, but that was a known Kent. An unknown, well, twenty was the least they'd accept.

"How about you, Robert?" Annette asked. "Are you good with that number?"

Robert shot Grace a nervous glance. "Yeah. I'm good."

"Because if you don't get twenty, you don't get anything."

"But it'll get twenty, right?"

"Possibly," said Annette, "if the buyers have faith in Grace's appraisal."

"Were you able to get it into the catalogue?" asked Grace.

"Just." Annette grinned. "It was past the deadline, but I snuck them in."

"Thank you," said Grace with a relieved sigh. The Kent was a last-minute addition, so many buyers might have missed seeing it online, but the printed auction catalogue would be on every chair in the hall. So long as they read Grace's appraisal—

"Wait," she said, confused. "I'm sorry, '*them*'? As in multiple appraisals?"

"Of course," said Annette, smiling thirty-two well-flossed stilettos. "My hands were tied, Grace. When we were alerted to the alternate appraisal at *Roadshow*, I was forced to solicit one from Victor. Don't worry. I made sure to list yours first."

Annette lifted a colorful brochure off a stack at the reception desk and passed it to Grace. Grace thumbed through to Lot 86. A small image of the painting was printed on the left side of the page, and on the right, the first of two pages of textual information with the heading:

-86-
UNNAMED OIL ON CANVAS
Artist Contested
William Kent (?) James Davies (?)
[England, 1885–1901]
Estimate: $10,000–$50,000

Grace slapped the brochure closed. "Your estimate is off, Annette."

"My estimate is high, Grace," she said, still smiling, but her voice dripped with hydrochloric acid. "Did you read Victor's appraisal?"

"No, but I did notice it had mysteriously leapfrogged in front of mine."

"Oh dear," said Annette, twisting the knife. "That *is* a mystery."

Grace held her tongue. She had expected the shiv, so she let Annette twist away. They had both been highly regarded up-and-coming specialists at Christie's, but they had never fought over work. They had fought over a certain dashing fellow specialist.

"Victor!" said Annette, spotting him on the atrium escalator.

Victor Karlin descended from the second floor, a vision of Rembrandt's *Ascension* in reverse, his slicked-back hair illuminated like a petroleum halo. He was dressed in an immaculately tailored double-breasted suit—in stark contrast to his fiancée, Julie Robinson, whose miniature black dress may have featured a double breast, but very little fabric to cover it. As they stepped off the escalator, Julie locked her arm around his, fusing them together.

"Hello, ladies," said Victor, nodding at Robert, "young Master Bedford." He reached out to shake Annette's hand, and Julie's grip on his arm ratcheted even tighter, immobilizing him.

"It's okay, dear," said Annette. "We'll only borrow it for a second."

Julie barked out an awkward giggle and released his arm. Victor reached out and shook Annette's hand with a firm grip. "Good to see you, Annie."

"Don't look too close at me," she said, eyeing Julie. "Might get you in trouble with The Law."

"Oh, I wouldn't worry about that," Vic said. "Julie knows you're anything but trouble."

Annette grew stiff as a petrified tree. Grace suppressed a laugh.

"Shall we?" asked Victor, allowing Julie to retake his arm.

"Allow me," said Annette, bolting in front of them. "I'll show you to your seats."

Annette led them around the registration desk to the escalator, stepping aboard. She turned around once her step had risen above Victor's, pointing out the rotating digital marquis that ringed the lobby, her long sinewy arms sailing this way and that.

Grace wasn't sure she knew Victor, not anymore, but he certainly didn't look pleased—not by Annette's attention, nor the garbage compactor grip of his fiancée. It surprised Grace; Victor had always basked in just this type of glow, but it now seemed a distraction. Was he merely focused on another glow—the glow from the bonfire of Grace's reputation? That seemed petty, even by Victor's standards, but something was troubling him, and whatever it was, it was aimed squarely at her.

They circled the second-floor atrium, and Grace looked through the windows at the whirling world below. It felt higher than it looked, and so did she. Grace had dragged herself off the mat; she had been left for dead but now she was nearing the pinnacle once more, and this time she'd stay there. When the world saw what she had seen, when they saw the William Kent...

They'd see her, too.

Grace's hand searched for the celestial globe necklace around her neck, but her fingers only found the creased lapels of her suit jacket.

It's gone, she remembered. *I broke it.*

Jerome had mercifully laid the shattered remains to rest. The miraculous globe was no more; there was only Grace. And it terrified her.

As they rounded the atrium to ascend to the seventh floor, the rise of the escalator felt to Grace like the final steps to a guillotine. Soon, the entire art world would know her head had been lopped off; and as it fell, so too would the legacy of her father, for she had been its standard bearer, and with her failure she would drag it into obscurity with her.

The massive double doors of the auction hall materialized at the top of the escalator; soon they would swing wide and swallow her whole. The digital marquee outside the door read, IMPRESSIONIST & MODERN AUCTION DAY, but to Grace, it was the writ to her execution. As she neared the double doors, the vibrato hum of anticipation grew louder and louder, like an angry swarm of vengeful bees—and they were coming for her. They would read her appraisal, they would read Victor's, and then they would decide. The news would flash across the tickertape of an entire industry. Grace was mistaken. Grace was wrong. Grace was not enough.

"STOP!" she yelled, halting six feet from the door.

Annette hesitated, her hand on the knob. "Too late to lower the minimum now, Grace."

"We're not changing the minimum," said Grace. "We're not going to auction."

Victor plucked Julie's talon off his arm and stormed over, temples pulsing. "What the hell are you doing, Grace?"

"I need more time."

"For what?"

Grace took a steadying breath. "We're not ready."

"That's not up to you, is it, Grace?" said Victor, spinning hard on Robert. "You don't need her, son. I can help you with the other side of the sale myself. I won't even take a commission. Not a penny."

Grace scoffed. "When have you ever waived a commission, Victor?"

His jaw locked. "I'm waiving it now."

"Why? Because you're that desperate to wreck me?"

"BECAUSE THAT IS NOT A WILLIAM KENT!"

It echoed across the atrium, down the escalators, and if the doors had been opened, it would have reverberated right onto York Avenue. Annette, Julie, and Robert all took a step back, shocked, but Grace did not. She'd seen it peek out at *Antiques Roadshow*, that wildfire behind his eyes. And she'd seen it in their marriage, at the very end.

But before she could pry into it, Victor clamped down on his fury, and the mask of Victor the Magnificent returned.

"I just want the truth, Grace," he said, his voice as even as the horizon.

"So do I," she said. "Just let me look."

"There's nothing there. Trust me."

"We're holding up the show, lovebirds," said Annette. "Yes or no?"

Victor turned to Robert. "What do you say, kid? Ready to make a killing?"

The boy lit up, and Grace could not blame him. Ten, maybe twenty, thirty thousand dollars? He could move out of that familial prison. He could start a new life.

"We need more time," he said.

He could also stop a guillotine.

Robert walked over to Grace and took her hand, squeezing it. "I trust Grace," he said. "If she says we need more time, then that's what we'll do."

The mask slipped off Victor's face. "Very well," he hissed, spinning on Grace. "You take all the time you want. I'll do the same. Let's see who finds what, shall we?"

He stormed off, down the escalator.

"I'd better go after him," said Julie.

"You'd better hurry, dear," Annette called after her as she rushed off. "Meal tickets that large don't come along every day, you know." She then swiveled the turret of her ire back to Grace. "I thought that might be tasty, Grace, but it was truly delicious—surprisingly so. Who knew, after all these years, the Third Wheel would be the only wheel still rolling?"

She yanked open the huge door to the auction, and the sonorous tenor warble of the auctioneer wafted out. "We have an Impressionist Evening Auction in two weeks," she said. "If you intend to entertain me with a repeat performance."

"We'll be there," said Grace.

"Very good." Annette smiled, the predator grin of the Serengeti. "I'll be waiting."

She slammed the door and Grace was left alone with Robert in the empty atrium. They stood in silence, listening at the double doors to what might have been. As the initial bids ballooned from overpriced to outrageous, the pleasant buzz from their defiance waned, leaving them stone-cold sober.

"Just a little more time, right?" he asked.

"That's right," said Grace. *And a great big fucking miracle.* Victor had been so sure it was not a Kent. He was confident.

And I'm a fool.

"Robert," she said. "I'm calling this off."

"Off?" He shook his head as if the words were a foreign language. "Why?"

"I can't take the chance that Victor might find something that would jeopardize your sale."

Robert took a moment. "The money's important, Grace, yeah. I'd love to get the hell out of that house, believe me. But there's reasons I'd stay."

Grace tilted her head. "Name one."

"You," he said. "I'm not used to kindness, Grace."

It made her heart swell. "Then let me do this kindness for you. Let's walk through those doors right now. I can still fix this."

"You asked for time," he said. "So take a little. We can still call it off before he starts messing with our auction, right?"

Grace couldn't help but smile. He was right, and a bit shrewder than she'd given him credit for. "You'll make one hell of an appraiser one day, you know that?"

"I'd prefer organized crime," he said. "Fewer knives in your back."

Seven

There was no time to lose. Grace knew it was dangerous to delay more than a few days—once Victor had employed the Jaws of Life to extract himself from Julie's grip, he would board the first plane to London. To prevent disaster, Grace planned to raise the white flag no later than the end of the week. She needed something to distract her until then, so she ordered up a good old-fashioned helping of familial anxiety.

"There's my girl," said Max, rocking back and forth in his wheelchair on the breezy veranda of Mary Elwood Estates.

"I thought you said your eyesight was getting worse." Grace laughed, leaning against the railing beside him.

"I didn't say anything about my sense of smell."

"Oh? How do I smell?"

"Like beauty incarnate."

"You better get your eyesight back, Max—I think you're getting cataracts in your nose."

Max chuckled. "I'd take that trade, my dear. Gladly." He squinted at the drooping, late afternoon sun. It was only a matter of weeks before the pale gray curtains obscured his pupils completely. Grace adored how he refused to give up. She hated that it wouldn't make any difference.

"Well, maybe I can do something about that," she said. "Why don't we put your nose on consignment—maybe we can scare up an eye or two at auction."

Max lit up with the very thought of it. "What's the commission on something like that?"

"That look on your face," said Grace, kissing his cheek and walking inside.

"She's in the Activity Center," Max said, calling after her.

Grace chuckled to herself and wondered what sort of activities she might encounter in such a center. Her mother loved gin rummy, so perhaps a card game or two. Scrabble, Boggle, perhaps even backgammon if she was feeling frisky.

The cavalcade of Shirley's favorite pastimes could not distract Grace from the foul aroma of embalmment that wafted down the Mary Elwood corridors. It was overwhelming to her, as were the ghostlike specters roaming the hallways. They shuffled on, without destination, just bobbing up and down in the stale waters at the end of their journey.

Is this it? she shuddered. *Is this my next stop?*

Or am I already here?

Grace wasn't getting any younger; just ask anyone who compared her to Victor's (soon-to-be) second wife. Her career was sputtering, her love life a left swipe away from its dying gasp. She considered asking Dr. Lee if there was some sort of multi-room discount as she rounded the bend to the Activity Center and wound up smack in the middle of an art class.

The room had been converted into a studio. Twenty tall desks were arranged in a perfect circle in the center of the room. Twenty residents—men and women alike—sat poised, perched atop their stools, their hands arcing back and forth between palettes of watercolor and the pigmented landscapes that dripped from their brushes.

Max had to be mistaken. Shirley had never, would never take an art class—Grace and her father had seen to that when they callously belittled her first and only attempt. Grace glanced around the circle from resident to resident but could not find her mother.

Until she looked at the teacher in the center of the room.

Shirley fluttered from desk to desk, steadying hands, refining brushstrokes, complimenting the good, commiserating the bad.

Teaching? Grace thought, and it could not have shocked her more if she had found her mother scampering across the ceiling like an arachnid.

Grace noticed a sign on Shirley's easel in the center of the circle: BEGINNING WATERCOLOR; each letter stenciled in the shape of an exotic bird—toucans, parrots, finches, puffins—all masterfully wrought in vibrant hues.

It was not just improbable; it was impossible.

Her mother was an artist.

"*Mom?*" asked Grace, as if Shirley were in disguise.

Shirley briefly glanced up, waved, and returned to her conversation with a struggling student. Grace squeezed through a gap in the desks and approached her mother with care, as if she and everyone else in the room were teetering on a psychotic break, rather than Grace.

"When did you become an *art* teacher?" she asked.

Shirley laughed. "Not sure I am, dear. Just something to pass the time."

Shirley sidestepped toward the next desk in the circle, but Grace took her arm. "Mom, I'm serious," she said. "Where did you study art?"

Shirley hesitated. "I didn't," she said. "Must have picked it up listening to you and your father."

"It doesn't work like that, Mom."

"Well, that's what happened," Shirley said, her mouth tightening.

Grace noticed the dog-eared copy of *Drawing on the Right Side of the Brain* on her mother's easel. "That's not from the library, is it, Mom?"

"Sure it is."

"I can check on my way out."

"Go ahead. I have nothing to hide."

But Grace knew she did. There was something there, lurking right behind her mother's eyes. Grace leaned in, seeking, searching, fingering the lock, but Shirley closed whatever book had accidentally been left open and Grace felt it shut against her.

"Look at the time, folks!" Shirley announced. "Better clean up or they won't let us back." She spun back to her easel, flipped over her portfolio, and dumped her supplies into a large bag, sealing it tight. She had done all this without a hint of Parkinson's. Something within her had taken precedence—something far more powerful than the Parkinson's.

What is she hiding? Grace wondered.

And what had this strange woman done with her mother?

Eight

The crowds had all disappeared without a trace. The Appraisal Experts Roadshow, which had streaked across the firmament like a comet, had fizzled out, falling to earth with a sickening thud. Less than a fortnight before, Elaine had guzzled champagne over a two-week contract with the James Banks Exposition Center. Now she shared a bitter concoction of lukewarm coffee and room temperature regret with Grace, Henry, and Pat outside the front doors in a few tattered picnic chairs. Jerome had been discharged from the Maine Medical Center, but was still too weak to make the pilgrimage, so they had toasted him in absentia. Considering her recent misadventure at Sotheby's, they were all pleasantly surprised Grace had flown up, but she would not have missed it. It was a wake of her own making.

Although word had gone out, a trickle of people had shown up anyway, hoping that news of the show's demise had been exaggerated. The four remaining experts took turns apologizing to the disappointed, thanking them for their support, and deflecting questions about the tour's next stop because there was no next stop. This was the end of the line.

Pat raised her coffee cup, saluting the group. "To bitter things, but better friends."

"Hear hear," said Henry. He flicked a few drops of coffee off his mustache and turned to Grace. "This must go down extra hard for you, Grace."

"Not at all," she said, taking a whiff of her cup. "Pat made sure to spike mine first."

All laughed, save Henry. "I envy you," he said. "I'd be so...I don't know what I'd be if I'd lost what you've lost."

"Hmm," mused Grace. As brutally rapid as the fall had been, she hadn't had the time to consider it. She had certainly risen all the way to the top once again, maybe beyond the place she'd been before, and she'd felt so full, so blissfully full, but the funny thing was—"I'm not sure I've lost anything at all," she said. "Looking back on it—if I'm honest—it all felt so flimsy, like cotton candy. It was sweet, of course, and it felt so full in my mouth, but the second I started chewing..."

"It was gone too soon," said Henry.

"No," Grace sighed. "I'm not sure there was truly anything there to begin with."

Henry laughed. "Oh, there was something, Grace. Just ask my gallery manager."

Elaine raised her cup. "And mine."

"Y'all have managers?" Pat gasped in mock indignation. "I have a brother-in-law, and the sonnavabitch is robbing me blind!"

They all laughed, even Henry this time, and Elaine reached out, taking Grace's hand. "Well," she said, giving it a loving squeeze. "Flimsy or not, it was awfully sweet having you around, Gracie."

Pat and Henry nodded, and no jokes were made.

Grace would miss them dearly. This odd, magnificent band of outcasts had not just given her their friendship, they had given her a home. It would ache to leave, but she would carry with her what she could. She hoped they would, too. The show was dead, of course, but their galleries had soared on the wings of the tour's success. Things would slow now, without the constant fuel of publicity and word of mouth, but Grace prayed not all of it would turn to cotton candy. If only she had cleared the cataracts in her mind's eye in time, if only she still had the celestial globe.

What miracles we'd make, she thought. And it didn't feel insubstantial, didn't feel flimsy at all. It didn't feel achievable either, but the desire to help—no, to serve—these proud, purehearted, crusading champions of the art world filled her quite completely.

Full, she thought, bottling it up for the famine ahead. *I feel full.*

And then, she felt nauseous.

A young girl and her mother walked up Park Avenue wearing their Sunday best, untroubled by the empty sidewalk outside the center. The girl held a small box aloft in her tiny hands as if it contained a diamond tiara.

Grace and her friends dreaded their approach in silence. They had broken open many a box of tissues that morning, but this was a child. This would break hearts.

"Dear God," said Henry, setting down his cup. "I'll go to Hell for this one."

"I'll go," said Grace groaning out of her chair. "This one has my name written all over it."

"So will my firstborn," said Henry. "Thank you."

Grace touched his shoulder and walked toward the couple, meeting them a few feet outside the sealed entrance of the center. "Good morning," she said. "Here for the show?"

"Yes, ma'am," piped the girl. "Are we too late to get in?"

Grace paused, just for a moment, and the mother read her mind. "It's gone, isn't it?"

"Unfortunately, yes," Grace said. "I'm so sorry."

The light dimmed in the girl's eyes, but she refused to give up. "But you'll come back, right?"

"I, uh..." Grace sighed. "I don't think so."

"That's a pity," said the mother, eyeing her daughter. "Emily was really looking forward to this."

"I'm so sorry," said Grace, fishing a business card out of her pocket. "I'd be happy to give you a recommendation for an appraiser in your area."

"No, she wanted—" The woman paused. "No offense. She wanted Mr. Zwick."

"Oh," said Grace, kneeling down beside the girl. "That's so smart of you, Emily. Jerome's the best."

Emily looked past her. "He's not here, is he?"

"No, I'm sorry. He's a little sick right now."

"Oh no," said the girl. "I hope he's okay."

Grace smiled and stood up. "I'll tell him you said that."

Emily nodded, and the two of them started off down the sidewalk. Suddenly, the girl stopped and turned back, returning to Grace.

"Would you give him something for me?" she asked, placing the small box in Grace's hand. "It might make him feel better."

Grace tried to respond, but she could not find the words. "Of course," she said, gazing down at it. "This might be just the thing."

"It's an arrowhead," she said.

Grace froze.

"I found it in our backyard."

Grace fingered the box in her palm. It felt warm, so very warm. "Could I take a look at it?" she asked, voice trembling.

"Sure."

Grace lifted the cover.

A tiny white arrowhead lay nestled in a bed of fresh soil. Grace inhaled deeply, and her nostrils tingled with the intoxicating scent of fresh earth. She reached out, brushing flecks of dirt away from the carved face of the stone with her fingernail...

And suddenly she was back, digging through the dirt in her backyard, the flinty rock buried for centuries, right there where only she could find it, waiting for her, all that time.

Waiting for her to live.

For this was her life. Art, history, discovery, loss, success, failure, marriage, divorce. All of it. She had been absent from herself, a walking shadow, but she could feel the very heart of her return. It beat so strongly, she feared her chest would not contain it.

This is my life, she thought, cradling the arrowhead. *This is me.*

How she had missed it. It had been so long since she'd felt herself, since she'd seen her reflection in the mirror, rather than the sad, sunken-eyed counterfeit she'd become. Somewhere along the way, when her life crashed down around her, she had turned on the autopilot to get her through the storm. And maybe, maybe for a time that was good; that was safe.

But Grace was tired of safe. Safe had sedated her, lulling her to sleep with the solemn promise that no pain would ever come to her, and for a while, no pain had. But she had slept enough. It was time to wake up.

Grace closed the box and placed it back in the young girl's hand, wrapping her tiny fingers around it. "This is yours, Emily," she said. "I think you're going to need it."

"Really?" she asked. "Why?"

Grace looked into the girl's eyes. The curtains were wide open, and it was easy to see inside.

"Because," Grace said, "it's going to be your life one day."

A rouge sunrise broke across the young girl's face. "How did you know?"

"Because I've seen that look before," said Grace.

And I'm going to see it for the rest of my life.

Grace thanked the girl—assuring her she'd pass on her well-wishes to Jerome—and walked back to her friends, snatching her purse from beneath the chair.

"Where are you going?" asked Pat.

"London," said Grace.

"Take me with you," sighed Elaine.

"Can't," said Grace. "You have work to do."

"Yeah," Elaine scoffed. "Liquidating the Appraisal Experts Roadshow."

"Better not," said Grace, walking off. "In fact, you'd better rent a bigger space."

"Why the hell would I do that?"

Grace smiled.

"Because I'm coming back with a William Fucking Kent."

Part V

Texture

One

31 October, 1899

My Dearest Mother,

If you receive this and I have not imagined writing it, please book a seat on the next train to London. When you arrive, pray make your way to Shoreditch and wake me from the most peculiar dream I have ever had.

My new work had stymied. Perhaps it is the new studio. Working in my own space, appointed as it is with the latest technologies and innovations, has felt a little—well, lonely, Mother. Without a muse to guide me, I admit that I have become rudderless. The star of 'Avon's Elbow,' which I thought would shine for years, has already dimmed, not two months in; the lifespan of a work of art is all too brief. So, too, I fear, is the life of the artist if he is unable to throw another scrap of fish into the mouth of this insatiable monster, Fame.

My loneliness has been compounded by the tide of Alexandra's affections, which have begun to ebb away from me. I am mystified, Mother. I had assumed that the higher my star in the firmament, the deeper her love. My downcast state was to blame for what followed. At the first knock at my studio door, I threw aside my brush and ran for the door, my arms yearning for the comforting embrace of Alexandra. I was greeted instead by a dark specter of a man, drawn, haunted, weakened to the point that I fully prepared to catch him if he collapsed across the threshold.

It was William Kent, or what used to pass for him. Our last awkward meeting had shown him in a weakened state; now he was dangerously frail. I rushed him inside and poured a kettle of tea into him, and his spirits brightened enough to remark upon my fancy new studio. "So this is where Art goes to die," he said. Considering the pulse of my output, I did not argue the point. But he had not come to accuse. He had come to hire me.

For an exorcism, Mother.

Kent asked if I would mentor him—to exorcise the 'Old' from his work, so he might recover a morsel of his former glory. The man was in mourning—not for his career (which I found stranger still), but for the woman who had left him since its demise. I admit that Kent and I stand across an abyss of aesthetic, but my present circumstances have awakened a kind of empathy that has been difficult to shake.

And yet, fear of contagion prevents me. The eyes of London are upon me and the door to greatness remains ajar for only an instant. Will my way through it not be hampered by dwelling on an aging footnote to my own development? Should word of our partnership spill out, will my name not be infected with the rank humour of his?

But even as the denial crept to my lips, I could not help but notice a faint sparkle in his eye. There is life left in that corpse, Mother, I am sure of it. If I ignore the risk, if we pursue our mission in secret, perhaps I might drain the last of his genius into my own lifeblood. Perhaps that is the very thing that will launch me into orbit, finally and forever.

What say you, Mother? Is there any agency in this? Please write as soon as you are able. I do so wish I could speak to Father about this. I wish I could speak to Father about anything.

I'd even settle for an argument.

Your Bewildered Little Boy,
Jimmy

Two

Grace rolled up her shade and glanced out the airplane window. She was hoping for a hint of Ireland but saw only an endless expanse of Atlantic. The flight was crossing the pond so slowly, she wanted to get out and push. Victor had surely been let loose in London by now, but he had always been excruciatingly meticulous with his research, so Grace might be able to make up a little time once she landed at Heathrow. She wouldn't make up the stagger, but they were working from the same treasure map, so even if Grace couldn't get ahead of him, hopefully she wouldn't be too far behind.

He'd start at the Tate Museum and their extensive archives, but he'd have a tough time extricating himself. Grace had called it his Black Hole: Victor could spend days wandering the Pre-Raphaelite galleries, which were among the largest in the world. And if someone recognized him from *Antiques Roadshow* (and a few someones would), he'd be sidelined once again—signing autographs, sharing stories, basking in the glow the show had stolen from him.

They were fools to replace him.

Victor may have failed her as an honest partner, but Grace refused to allow it to cloud her faith in his work. His fidelity had tobogganed down a slippery slope, but his artistic integrity was unshakable; it was foundational to him. She loved that in him.

So, yes. Grace loved him still.

But there was something so savage about his outburst at Sotheby's, something so primal, Grace wondered if, near the end of their marriage, he had been hiding more from her than Julie's studio apartment in SoHo. Grace had seen a nasty glimmer of it at *Antiques Roadshow*, and the wound had spread wide at Sotheby's. She had tried to peel back the flaps of it, but Victor had sealed it tight. Whatever it was, he was guarding it with his life. Grace sensed it was a crucial piece of the puzzle, but she would have to fit it later.

The plane had begun its descent into Heathrow.

Three

The Gothic spires of Westminster Palace, the majestic seat of British Parliament, have spanned the banks of the Thames for a thousand years. Its towers have been etched, sketched, painted, and photographed in sun, rain, fog, fireworks, and Blitz. But in all its millennium of life, it had never looked more beautiful than it did astride the canvas of Claude Monet. Six of Monet's Westminster masterworks ringed the Room 7 gallery of the Tate Museum. In each painting, the shadowed towers of Parliament breached the London fog like biblical leviathans, their ghostly silhouettes marking the horizon between Heaven and Earth.

Grace joined a small group of museum guests as they passed from painting to painting. Her eyes were on the Monets, but her ears were tuned to the crowd. They spoke in hushed tones, of color, and haystack, and light, and lily; not a single breath wasted on price, or pound, or sale, or auction, but a communal gasp at the emotional impact of the art itself.

In all the hustle and high stakes, Grace sometimes forgot to stop and listen for that sound, and she let it wash over her, a soaring symphony of unpretentious, honest awe that took her back to why she had fallen in love with art in the first place.

She followed the group into Room 8 of the exhibition. The other rooms had all been lined with French expatriates, but the gray walls of the eighth were hung with British Impressionists.

With William Kent.

The entire crowd was drawn toward his corner, as if his works exerted some sort of gravitational pull that had arrested their eyes. They shuffled past his earlier pieces with their lips parted, as if they might breathe in the lushness of his landscape, as if they could swallow his sunset. And then, their jaws dropped.

It was *Elbow of Avon.*

Exquisite in print, it was breathtaking in person. The quilted green bank, ringed with downy willows, their gossamer branches floating like feathers in the afternoon breeze; an infinite stretch of cotton clouds—throw pillows for your imagination while you gazed up into a seascape sky of the brightest blue; and in the far corner, the sun—*his* sun. It erupted from the canvas in a pyroclastic fountain of orange, singeing the sky in thick strokes of crimson and yellow. The colors streaked down from the heavens, from dark red to orange, until its fading yellow fingers fell upon a small figure in the distance.

The ghostly spirit from the unnamed Kent!

She stood upon another bridge, on another river, but it was unmistakably her. Even at such a distance, the woman's features were revealed, not masked by the shadows of the unnamed work. Her open, kind face shone out like a beacon; her eyes twinkled with the sharpest blue, matching the gentle ripples of the river below. This, then, was neither a model, nor a mistress, nor even an inspiration. This was his Muse.

But still, there was mystery in the air. This may have been twin to the faceless woman of the unnamed Kent, but she was not the spectral apparition that had momentarily revealed herself to Grace inside Robert's attic. Like her, but not her. And unlike the shaded figure in the unnamed Kent, the woman in *Avon* was not hesitating on the bridge. Her knuckles were stippled white from the effort of gripping the railing, as if she had staked her claim to the bridge, to the water, to the steeple behind her. As if she had staked her claim to William Kent.

Elbow of Avon was the birth of their love. The painting back home was their death.

Could there be any question now? If Victor had walked past this, he'd have instantly known, as she had. So why hadn't he called off the search? What new clue had he found?

Grace's eye was distracted by some nuisance beside it. It felt like a fly buzzing back and forth in the space to the left of the painting, not insistent enough to look at, just annoying enough to ruin the moment.

It was *Avon's Elbow.*

James Davies's one and only painting of renown hung a few feet away. Beside Kent's masterwork, *Avon's Elbow* sulked like a child held back at recess. Davies had called it his reaction to Kent, but to Grace, it was much closer to regurgitation. Instead of having the courage to put his own head on the chopping block, James had taken the age-old shortcut of the amateur—avoiding the agony of original creation by "improving" the work of another. In his time, they called such work *In the Style of*, but Grace knew it by its modern names: Refresh, Reboot, Reimagine, Sample, Subvert. As far as Grace was concerned, they were all Names of the Beast.

But she was riveted—not by the painting, but the framed description beside it. The work had been added to demonstrate how often Kent was copied by his young contemporaries. There was a bit about Davies's sudden rise to prominence (and his even more sudden fall), and a bit about a few of his other pieces. But near the bottom of the page, Grace found the clue that would have sent Victor scurrying to the Tate Archives. It was the mention of a posh London society party, a celebration of the changing of the guard from Davies to Kent. The two artists were rumored to have met there in 1899 during the reveal of *Avon's Elbow* and entertained an artistic partnership soon after.

How close a partnership? Grace wondered, holding her breath. Close enough for Kent to have purchased one of Davies's used frames? That would close the book on Victor's discovery of the Davies frame signature.

Leaving it open for William Kent.

Grace read the last line of the description and finally took a breath. The information had all come from a letter—from a James Davies letter housed in their archives.

There was no time to waste—Victor had certainly seen the description, perhaps even the letter—but Grace felt welded to the spot. If she made a single misstep, if she stumbled, not only would her own career come crashing down, the aftershocks would decimate the fortunes of her friends, the show they loved, and the hopes and dreams of thousands.

But Grace knew what it was like to be left for dead, and she had not clawed her way out of that pit to climb back in and, God forbid, drag everyone else down with her. The gates had opened and the race was on, and even after all she'd been through, Grace was still in it.

It was time to kick off her shoes and run.

Four

Grace flew down the winding rotunda stairs, down to the basement of the Tate, emerging at the entrance to the Archive Gallery. It took every ounce of her willpower to push past the stunning displays of diaries, sketchbooks, and letters on her way to the library doors at the rear of the hall, through which a dozen researchers silently pored over the entire history of British culture from the polished desktops of a dozen pinewood desks. Artists, historians, professors, and critics came from all over the world to feast their eyes upon the million documents the Tate had amassed. Grace had come for just one—that letter.

Hopefully it would reveal the clue that would disqualify Davies from being the artist in question. It was a stretch to think they would finger Kent as the creator, but Grace was in the mood for reaching.

"Good afternoon," she said, approaching the librarian sitting behind the registration desk just inside the entrance.

The librarian looked as if her head had been dipped in orange paint—not just her hair, but her face as well, which was oddly sunburned for a denizen of London drizzle. "Name?" she droned. Clearly, 5:00 p.m. could not come soon enough.

"I'm sorry," said Grace. "I don't have a reservation."

The librarian sighed out her frustration with Grace, the job, and half the English-speaking world. "You'll have to book one for access, miss."

Grace checked her watch, and it told her the obvious—she was behind and falling farther back with each fork in the road. "Are there any slots left today?"

The librarian grumbled something mercifully unintelligible and clacked away at her keyboard. "Nope," she said, with perhaps her first smile of the day. "Booked solid."

Grace was so close. She eyed the archway on the far side of the reading room that led into the shadowed archives themselves. Just inside, an archivist spun one of the spidery arms of a large handle, and a massive, ceiling-high metal file cabinet rolled apart from another, revealing an aisle thirty feet deep. To each side, dozens of shelves were stacked high with hundreds of marked boxes; in each box, the paraphernalia of genius. And hidden in one of those aisles, within one of those cabinets, stuffed inside one of those boxes, was the letter she sought—the letter Victor had already read—and without a reservation, the letter she might never see.

"I'm Grace Schaffer," she said, working up her most pitiful smile.

The librarian was not impressed. "Hello, Ms. Schaffer."

Grace swallowed her pride and belched up her reputation. "You might have seen me on *Antiques Roadshow*," she said. The words tasted even worse in her mouth than she had feared.

"Not likely." The librarian frowned. "I only watch the real version."

Grace bit her tongue. Apparently, the librarian's residual annoyance with the American victory in the Revolutionary War precluded her from watching anything but the BBC show. Using the *Roadshow* card had felt beneath Grace's dignity. She was about to limbo far lower. "I believe my husband Victor was here earlier this week."

"Yes." The librarian chuckled. "He was just as mystified that I didn't recognize *him*."

"Oh," said Grace, daring to hope. "He didn't get in?"

"Not the first day," she said. "But he made a reservation yesterday."

Thank God, thought Grace. *Only a day behind.* And Victor liked to cover his bases. "Did he happen to make multiple reservations?" Grace asked. "Did he have one today?"

"He did," she said. "And he said you'd try to use it."

"I don't suppose you'd let me?"

"I don't suppose you remarried him since he was in?"

Grace laughed. "I had that coming, didn't I?"

For the first time, the librarian smiled—an honest one. "You did," she said. "But I can't say I blame you. I'd probably have tried the same myself." She arranged herself in her chair, tucking in her blouse. "Besides, he's quite a looker, so I wouldn't have been surprised if you *had* remarried him."

There she is, thought Grace. The librarian had let her cards down, and Grace stole a look at her hand. It was the way she had fidgeted in her seat, gaining height; the way she'd tucked in her blouse to make herself more svelte. Grace knew that move all too well.

She leaned over the registration desk, dropping her voice to a confidential whisper. "I've thought about it, believe me. I'd even knock off a few months of his infidelity."

The librarian nodded, clearly from experience. "Anything to stay out of that dating pool," she sighed. "Bunch of piranhas in there."

"And so hungry," Grace groaned. "First time I stuck my toe in, I lost an ankle."

"And even if you find one, good luck striking up an actual conversation."

"In anything more complicated than an emoji."

The women cackled. One of the researchers shushed them, which only sent them both into a harmony of giggles.

"You know the worst thing?" asked Grace, catching her breath.

"They're just as lonely as we are."

Grace nodded—no one understood misery like the miserable.

"Come on," said the librarian, sliding back her chair.

"Sorry," said Grace. "Are we disturbing the readers?"

"Probably," she said. "But let's disturb them from the Archives."

Grace blinked back at her. "Don't I need a reservation to copy a document?"

"Not anymore," she said. "I'm your reservation." She led Grace through the room and over to the arched entry into the archives.

"This is unbelievably kind of you," said Grace. "I'm looking for a specific letter."

"No you're not," she said. "You're looking for five."

Five

11 November, 1899

My Dearest Mother,

If Father and I do not speak until the Rapture, I fear even that may be too soon. His visit to meet my new 'pupil' (how exquisitely odd to call him that) was, of course, expected—I know how Father worships Kent, and I was only too eager to use him as bait. Kent was lovely, regaling Father with whimsical stories about his long and arduous road to fame. Unfortunately for me, Kent's history of struggle became an instrument of torture in Father's hands—a means to accuse me of sloth and privilege. I must cultivate a TRADE, he said, even if it was Art. It must be honed, pursued, the same as medicine or law or even haberdashery, like Father.

I expected Kent to argue, that Art cannot be learned or studied—that it is innate, born with you—but the man was silent. Perhaps I should not have expected him to come to my aid. He and Father are both cut from the same moth-eaten cloth.

I raised my voice, Father his, and the visit ended in fireworks and recriminations.

But there were more explosions to come. Alexandra is gone. In my stead, she has installed another artist. A hack, Mother, a rank amateur. She freely admitted this, that his lack of ambition was one of his greatest attractions. How can she prefer this, Mother—a life of mediocrity to one amongst the stars?

At least the first steps of my partnership with Kent have gone well. He seems willing to learn the New Ways, and most eager to dispense with rusty structures. I have instructed him after my own technique—to be tethered to none at all. Just paint, no stifling sketches or outlines or drafts. We work as one—much must be exorcised in him—so my hand guides his over the canvas. I am under no delusion—he is battling not the changing shape of the market, but the loss of his dearest love. I understand the fire and fear that motivate him all too well.

But time is short. I must cure him of his malady before his love, too, is lost forever. He has suggested we leave the studio and embark upon his new work immediately, so we are off to scout the length of the River Avon. It is near the site of his breakthrough work (and therefore the site of mine), so there is poetry in it.

Pray there be poetry in what we create, for both our sakes.

Your Fatherless Son,
Jimmy

Grace looked up from the photocopied letter, placing it atop the first two in the train seat beside her. It was riveting—a window into William Kent through the clouded lens of another. But still, even after three letters, Grace was no closer to the truth. Who had truly created the painting? Was it one, the other, or a duet between master and amateur?

Grace had leapt on the first train to Birmingham, scanning the letters as she flew. The Avon was a long river, running nearly the entire beltway of England. The painting had been created somewhere along its banks—that, so far, was the only clue Davies had left for her. She rested her eyes for sixty seconds, as that was all she could spare, and placed the final two letters in her lap.

17 November, 1899

My Dearest Mother,

Please forgive me for not coming around to see you. It is not fear of Father that prevents me, but the work has begun, and we both hear the ticking of the hangman's clock. It is unconscionable of me, I know—we are within a short carriage ride of home. Perhaps you can hear us shouting at the sunset to delay its descent each evening?

And what a sunset he is creating, Mother. Kent begins with it, in all his works, but it has never been more iridescent. To place your hand above it, you might be forgiven for believing you could feel the celestial fire upon your fingers.

But that is not the Modern Way. It is not the viewer's experience but the artist's that sells paintings. So, I have stayed his hand, cloaking his in mine. It is a trial for us both: I propel him forward; he lingers in preparation. He sketches, he discards, he contemplates, he repeats—it's exhausting, Mother. And it is not Art—it can't be—it feels far closer to childbirth. Still, when I'm all alone at night in my room above the Inn, a small haunting voice keeps me from slumber:

Am I improving upon perfection? Or distorting it altogether?

Your Lost Boy,
Jim

Grace set the fourth letter aside. Davies had begun to reveal the mechanism of the painting's creation, but so much still remained behind the curtain. It was up to the fifth and final letter to pull the drawstring back, or Grace's train ride would end, not in Birmingham, but in disaster.

17 November, 1899

Dearest Mother,

The curtain rises at sunset! A strange anxiety has overwhelmed me—I feel as if we are drawing back the veil on my own work, not William's. And just between us, Mother, it very much is. His hands were guided by mine down every line, his colors chosen to my exact specification. At certain points, he stood back completely and begged me to take the brush myself. So, yes, I feel invested in its revelation. It is superb, Mother, a true masterpiece. But will it be enough to reclaim his lost Naomi?

She has agreed to meet William on the Stratford bridge across the Avon. He will bring two gifts—the first, an elegant gold bracelet we purchased on Chapel Street; the second, our painting—of this very spot. For Stratford was not just the birthplace of 'Elbow of Avon' and the midwife of his bright star's breach, it was the place of their first kiss before the mighty storm of his career swept them both away.

I hope our creation will reverse the cruel sickle of time and win Naomi back to him. Either way, I am proud of the spell we have spun within these oils and pigments.

May there be Magic in it.

Your Son, Come What May,
James

Grace laid the final letter atop the others and hailed a passing conductor. "Excuse me, sir. Does this train stop in Stratford-upon-Avon?"

"It does," he said. "One stop after Leamington."

Grace thanked him and he went on his way. Leamington was the next stop, so she had discovered her destination a few stops early. But she hadn't uncovered the mystery.

Who truly painted it?

Was it Kent? Or Davies, as he believed? Both? If so, how much of each? Grace needed tangible proof. Without the painting's true history, Victor's appraisal would be the only one that mattered, snuffing out her last chance to save her friends, to free Robert from his father's prison, and stay the death knell of her career. But she knew something far more precious would die with it.

For it was not just a job to Grace. Yes, it was her life's great passion, and to be denied it, she would die a little death, every day. But her work, and the way in which she pursued it, was one of the only things—perhaps *the* only thing she had ever truly shared with her father, and with his loss, it had now become her eulogy to him.

And Grace Schaffer had more to say.

She steadied herself and cleared her mind—she had to stay focused on what she could do, not the disaster that would befall them all if she could not. She had boarded the train in London blind and in haste, wondering if she was headed to Bradford or Avon Park. Both those bends in the Avon had bridges and churches like the ones in the painting. But she would exit the train in Stratford, and she would hurry to the Tramway Bridge, which overlooked the Avon and the great spire of Trinity Church.

But she was still so confused. William Kent had never returned to paint the same vista twice, so why would he have this time?

Probably because he didn't, she thought with dread.

James Davies had.

Six

Grace had no time for the taxi queue. The moment she left the train station, she set out on foot for the riverbank that ran through the center of town. She cursed herself for not packing a pair of blinders—stately Victorian homes built upon the thatched floors of sixteenth-century inns and taverns beckoned from either side of the street, tantalizing her with the possibility of the precious heirlooms hidden within. She crossed onto Henley Street, and halfway down the cobbled road an old Tudor two-story home blocked her way. Not physically—the crumbling wooden structure stood to the side of the road—but spiritually. The yellow-and-black coat of arms that hung above the entrance was the only surviving mark of the boy who grew up there. When he left to join a traveling troupe of actors, William Shakespeare would make a far more indelible mark upon his age, and all that followed.

Parting was such sweet sorrow, but Grace hurried on, once more into the crowded breach of Henley Street. The way was crammed with chattering tourists; legions of vendors sang out to them, hawking Bard-themed treats and souvenirs from a battalion of colorful carts to either side. Grace's stomach bellowed in rage when she passed the *Midsummer Night's Cream* cart, but if Shakespeare could wait, so could Rocky Road.

Grace emerged from the two-story kill zone of bakeries and sandwich shops into a large roundabout plaza. A light tree had been erected in the very center, atop a circular pedestal. She had hesitated at Shakespeare's birthplace, but the blue sign at the base of the tree froze her solid:

LIGHT UP A LIFE

Light up a life in memory of your loved one and
sponsor a tree light.
Join us here, or online, for our special remembrance.
5th of December.

Oh, Dad, she thought. *I wish you were here.*

How he loved the chase, the shrouded mysteries, that one clue that uncovered a passageway into undiscovered country. And when the hunt was on, he *was* a light, as bright as any Grace had ever seen.

She made a mental note of the website. When all this was done, win or lose, she would light up her father's life, mere feet from the birthplace of *Elbow of Avon.*

If only he'd tried to light up hers, just a little bit.

Grace set off through the plaza onto Bridge Street and her heart began to race—not from the exertion, but from what she could just make out in the distance.

A shimmering blue-green sheet of water appeared at the end of the street, sparkling in the late afternoon sun. Grace picked up the pace, faster and faster, until walk became run, and run gave way to all-out sprint. The buildings to either side blurred as she scampered across the final street against the traffic light, waved at the honking cars, and flew right by a bronze sculpture of Shakespeare without even a passing glance.

A meandering cloud of white swans beat their wings in fury, squawking avian curses as she scampered through their conference at the mouth of Bancroft Gardens. But on she ran, her flats clacking an ever-increasing tempo on the stones of a small inlet harbor.

Faster, faster, out of the harbor, up the steps, and over a short metal walkway.

Two flights left.

Down the other side, gasping now, out of breath, nearly tripping, through the middle of a grass amphitheater, newly mowed, kicking up the clippings, a thick green cloud in her wake. And suddenly it rose above her, its stony shoulders rearing up like the hump of a giant whale.

Tramway Bridge.

It was just as he had painted it, as she had seen it in her dreams. She felt the history, the very spirit of it caress her like the gentle stroke of an invisible paintbrush. But on she ran, up the final stairs, two at once, onto the bridge, one hand on the brick railing, another on the wrought iron lamppost. She spun around it, giggling like a young girl, like Gracie, her body slamming into the brick railing, her eyes blasted with:

The Avon.

It stretched out beneath her, powder blue waters rippling in concentric circles, an undulating cosmos of gentle currents swirling across the smiling face of the Avon. To her left, an infinite phalanx of green willows guarded the eastern bank, their identical twins reflected in the river below. Beneath their moping branches, lovers traded secrets across the delicate current of a kiss, artists threw off their shackles, poets' pens bled indescribable beauty, and old men reunited with old feathered friends by the grace of breadcrumbs.

And there it was, shimmering in her tears.

The Elbow of Avon.

The banks had ebbed, the skyline had shifted, but the soul remained unchanged. The lovers, the lonely souls, the birds, the river, the great spire of Trinity Church looming above the trees on the western bank, pointing the way to Heaven; it was exactly as Kent had painted it. How had he captured paradise in pigment and yolk?

He had been here, in this very spot, a mere century and change ago. Grace sucked in the air around her, filling up her chest. Was part of him still here, mixed in among the bricks and mortar of Tramway Bridge? Grace believed he was. No passing trains would have disturbed his spirit—by Kent's day, Tramway was for ambling only. Perhaps that encouraged the mysterious female figure haunting both paintings to materialize in this very spot, right beneath the lamppost.

Grace swung around it again, briefly catching sight of Clopton Bridge in the distance. Its arched stones were choked with traffic, as they would have been in Kent's time. Once over the Avon, the road turned north away from Stratford, into the British countryside. Even today, it was easy to see why Kent had set his easel upon Tramway.

So Grace set hers directly atop his. She looked out over the water, peering through Kent's eyes, awaiting the clues to yawn up from their slumber. This was the precise vantage point of *Elbow of Avon*; Kent had painted the original from this very spot. In her mind's eye, Grace could line up the Trinity Spire and the leftward bend of the river perfectly to his painting.

But something was off.

She sensed it, but the thought refused to come into focus. It was a feeling only, and Grace had no use for feelings. She needed more.

Grace spun about once more, gazing back down the Avon at Clopton Bridge, but that was a dead end. The crude ancient stonework was no match for the elegant masonry of the unnamed work. It had to have been painted on Tramway—the Eden of Kent's career. But what was *east* of his Eden?

The Woman.

The ghostly figure, illuminated by an auburn sunset, floating on the bridge like an apparition, suspended in the ether between coming and going, her face turned toward the artist. But her body twisting, turning away from him.

Grace closed her eyes and conjured the painting to life. It broke upon the darkness like a sudden sunrise—the church, the water, the trees, the woman, facing east...

Toward town!

In the bottom-left edge of the painting, shrouded behind a curtain of willows lurked a building—an inn, perhaps. Kent (it *had* to be Kent) was pointing Grace somewhere, somewhere very specific, somewhere just over the bridge.

She spun toward the eastern bank of the Avon and opened her eyes to the exact spot in the painting. The Inn had been burned in her retina, so she laid the pulsing red outline of it directly over the landscape, but nothing appeared in its place. No inn, no tavern, no house, no building, just the grassy open field of the Stratford Sports Complex. Whatever Kent had painted was long gone, just dust beneath the field.

The woman was on her way somewhere—but where? Grace could taste the answer, tickling the very back of her throat. If she could just find that last piece of the puzzle, if she could hear that *snap*, it would reveal itself. She reached for her necklace, for the stone that wasn't there, but her fingers felt nothing, save her own quickening pulse. There would be no voice to guide her, no hand to draw her. But it was so close, so very close, as if it were waiting for her to reach out, just one more inch and she'd be there.

But try as she might, Grace could not grasp it. She felt it ebbing away, trickling through her fingers like mist, dissolving into thin air.

She should have known. Grace was not enough.

She collapsed against the cold mossy bricks of the railing and hung her head over the water, which reflected her despair in a sickly green grimace. As she lifted her eyes, a cloud passed over the Avon and the life drained out of it. The waters grew still, the trees wilted, lovers quarreled, poets surrendered, old men winked off into the sleep of the nearly dead. The River Avon looked its age, and as Grace turned back to her reflection, so did she.

Grace looked away and noticed another figure bobbing to and fro in the murky water. It wasn't a friendly looking figure, not by a long shot, but it was a familiar one.

Victor sat upon a wooden bench at the edge of the river, gazing into the Avon.

Grace pushed herself away from the railing and walked back down the ramp. She had skipped up the steps to the landing; now she took them one at a time, her hand on the railing to prevent her from tumbling down. She approached him from behind and hesitated. He had come here to destroy her, to rip the Kent from her grasp, and he—like her—had failed. Why on earth should she give him even the mildest of hellos?

Because you know exactly how he feels.

Grace took another step toward him, and without turning, Victor spoke in a low, hollow moan. "There's nothing here."

"I know," she said, walking around the side of the bench and sitting beside him. "You could have told me that and saved me the trip."

His mouth arched up in a half smile. "I figured you could use the miles."

"I have nowhere to go," she said. "Why don't you take them—for the honeymoon, or something. I don't think she'll let you off with a weekend at the Boston Museum of Art."

He laughed. "What honeymoon?"

Grace finally turned to face him directly. Victor had always shined through, but his skin was a pallid, colorless hue. "No honeymoon?"

"No honey," he said, releasing a huge sigh. "Well, not my honey. Who am I kidding?"

"She's gorgeous."

"She's a fucking infant."

Grace laughed. "Have you told her yet?"

"Just made the decision," he said, nodding at the elbow of the river before them. "Failure will do that to you."

"You're not a failure, Victor."

"*Victor?*" he groaned. "C'mon, Gracie. Please."

"Okay," she said, "Vic."

"Thank you." He turned back to the river. "But I am a failure, a spectacular one."

"You won, Vic," Grace said. "They'll take your appraisal over mine in a heartbeat."

"I didn't chase you halfway around the world for a better appraisal." And there it was, once again, that open door behind his eyes—the rage from *Antiques Roadshow*, the stone-cold finality at Sotheby's.

Victor noticed her leaning in, but this time, no doors closed. "Go ahead," he said, leaning back against the wooden bench. "Tell me what you see."

Grace opened her mind to him. The adolescent girlfriend was easy—the false mirage of younger women stranding middle-aged men in the desert was a tale as old as time. But this was not about a woman, or even the number of candles on his cake. Grace looked closer and he opened himself to her. He was not angry, not anymore, he was just…

"You're so sad," she said.

He nodded. He had lost something, something dearer to him than Grace or Julie or even hosting *Antiques Roadshow*. Something so precious, the very thought of it sliced through him.

"You've lost your Treasure Box," she said.

He shook his head. "I lost that ages ago, Grace. When we moved to New Jersey."

Where Victor went, the little box had followed—ever since seven-year-old Victor found a 1913 Type II Buffalo nickel in his grandparents' basement. His grandfather had given him an old Ben-Hur cigar box to keep the discovery, and Victor placed the building blocks of his love for antiquity within it. And when his discoveries grew so numerous the box refused to close, Victor brought that box inside, deep within him, where it could grow as wide as his imagination. Every new painting he identified, every lost masterpiece he uncovered, stretched the sides of that box, but it never broke. There was always room for another misidentified masterpiece.

Until there were no new masterpieces to find.

"It's gone, isn't it?" Grace said. "There was nothing left to fill it, so you threw it away."

Victor shook his head, but her aim was true.

He had lost his Treasure Box. It had been withering for years, draining the life out of him. It swallowed up their marriage, and then it swallowed him. Grace's first true love, her dear sweet husband, had thrown away the most precious part of himself. The final Grail had been found, so there could be no other.

Victor Karlin had not come to find James Davies. He had come to bury William Kent.

"It couldn't be a Kent," she said. "You had no place to put him."

He stared ahead, but a single tear broke free, running down his cheek. "I wanted it to be nothing," he said. "I *need* it to be nothing."

"I know," said Grace. "And I need it to be everything."

He turned to Grace and the fury broke like a fever; it was gone, leaving Victor, Vic—*her* Vic. "I'm so sorry, Grace," he said. "I've hurt you in unconscionable ways. I never meant to, I didn't. I was just so—"

"Lost," she said.

He nodded and brushed aside another tear. Grace reached into her purse and emerged with a tissue. He took it, laughing.

"How do you do that?" he said, wiping his face. "Pull these out of thin air?"

"Tissues?"

"Appraisals."

Grace paused. She had always been able to do this, to peer inside an object or its owner. So had her father.

Or had he?

Albert could tease the story out of any object—but people? He had a human-size blind spot for anything that breathed.

But Grace had learned it somewhere; she had *seen* it. She dropped her head, gazing once more into the river, into her own reflection. It was still in her eyes—the look that had peered into Victor, into painting and print and people at show after show. She knew that look.

Because she had seen it across the dinner table—in her mother's eyes. The way Shirley had looked at her father when he tried so earnestly to apologize and failed. She had looked past his failure, past the fortress behind his eyes, and returned with the elixir to forgive him.

My eyes, she thought, seeing the pearl sparkle within them. *They're Mom's.*

"You're something else, Gracie," Victor said, blowing his nose. "You still got it."

Grace turned and smiled. "And you never lost it."

She reached out and grasped his hand, and the two old, dear friends looked out over the same view for the first time in far too long.

After a silence, Victor perked up with a thought. "Are we supposed to go back to the hotel and sleep together?"

Grace considered it, and it sounded awfully good. But awfully wrong.

"I don't think so, Vic."

"Thank God." He laughed. "I didn't think so either, but you're so lovely, I felt like asking anyway."

Grace smiled at the love of her life to this point. "God bless you for saying so."

She scooted closer, laying her head upon his shoulder. The connection felt good to her—they would never again be husband and wife, but they would always be together.

So together they watched the Avon flow by. A different Avon—no longer sick, but the richest blue, like thousands of tumbling, tiny sapphires. The entire world shimmered, and the setting sun spread across the waters in the shape of something achingly familiar.

Grace chuckled when it came to her: It looked like an orange arrowhead—her arrowhead from all those years ago. She followed the base of the arrow as it tapered back toward the setting sun, down the river as it bent this way and that, winding its way to Trinity Church. The sun disappeared off behind the great spire, its last rays reflecting off the limestone, shadowing the bell tower below.

Suddenly, she sensed it: some whispered secret, some clue, just out of focus. But it was diffuse, blurry; she couldn't tease the threads of it together. And then her stomach dropped—it was staring right at her.

The tower is off!

Not for *Elbow of Avon*—Kent's sun pinged off the steep edges of the looming spire in the exact same way, dominating the building below. But in *Elbow*'s mysterious unnamed twin, the tower was less extreme, standing bolt upright against the sky, the last rays of the sun just kissing the very tip of the spire. Almost as if...

"He didn't paint it from here!"

Victor shook his head, lost, and then his eyes grew wide. "Oh my God," he gasped, grabbing her hands. "Of course!"

They leapt up as one and flew up the staircase onto Tramway Bridge, splitting the lamppost, peering out at the bony finger of Trinity Church and the towering spire above—which arched toward the sky at an incrementally different angle than the one in *Elbow*'s twin.

"He wasn't here," Grace yelled in triumph. "And neither was *she*."

She spun around to Clopton Bridge—a mere hundred yards behind them.

"There!"

They ran back down Tramway, through the park, past silent Shakespeare, onto the thin walkway of the A3400, which led them right onto the ancient stones of Clopton Bridge.

The traffic whizzed by but on they ran, oblivious to anything but the view down the Avon. A small overgrown island of dead trees blocked their view, so they rushed farther onto the stone bridge until the view opened up before them.

"Look at Trinity!" she cried.

The last rays of the sun reached out, caressing the very tip of the Trinity bell tower—exactly as it had in the painting.

"He painted it right here," she said. "In this exact spot."

"But this isn't the bridge," said Victor, running his hand over the jagged railing. Clopton was far older, and looked it; nothing like the soft chiseled stones of Tramway.

Grace sighed. Vic was right. The perspective was perfect, but the bridge was dead wrong. Kent had painted it from here, she was sure of it, so why had he used the other bridge's perspective? She thought of that final letter: Stratford Bridge was *not just the birthplace of 'Elbow of Avon'* but *midwife to his bright star's breach.* It was Kent's first kiss with Naomi, *before the mighty storm of his career swept them both away.*

Snap. Grace felt it—the final piece of the puzzle.

Vic saw it on her face. "What do you see?"

"Kent," she said. "I see William Kent." She could feel him, too. She pulled him tight about her shoulders, wrapping herself in his final stroke of genius. "He wasn't painting Tramway, and he wasn't painting Clopton," she said.

"He was painting both."

She pointed to the lamppost on the edge of Tramway. "That was the beginning—not just his relationship with Naomi, but the birth of his inspiration; the first full breath of his Art." She ran her hand over the jagged rocks of Clopton. "This was his end."

Grace looked out at Tramway and saw her—the ghostly Specter in the painting, floating weightless in the instant before coming and going. She locked eyes with Grace, and Grace recognized her, finally.

"I saw her in Robert's attic," she said. "Only for a moment, but I think she's still there in the canvas, buried beneath the pigments and the oils. But it's not a woman."

The Specter smiled at Grace—so sad, so infinitely barren.

"He wasn't saying goodbye to a woman," Grace said. "He was saying goodbye to Art." She released a tremendous sigh, which gave way to sob after sob. Grace let it flow—it was the funeral for a master. He deserved it.

Victor fished into her purse and pressed a tissue into her hands. She wiped her face and smiled. "Still think it's James Davies?"

"Who the fuck is James Davies?"

They laughed, cried, and embraced. Cars slowed as they passed, confounded by the contradictory displays. It all made sense to Grace, and that was all that mattered.

And then, something else made sense. She stood back and looked down Clopton Bridge, into the small clump of buildings on the other side of the Avon.

"Kent disappeared into obscurity," she said. "But Naomi went somewhere else."

Vic paused. "The Inn."

"It's not off Tramway," said Grace. "It's off Clopton."

Vic stood back and wiped his nose on his shirt, squinting at the block of buildings. "Where is it, Gracie?" he asked. "Can you see it?"

"Of course." She grinned. "I can see anything."

Seven

The historic Swan's Nest Hotel stood on the site of an older establishment, The Bear Inn, which had overlooked the Avon since the seventeenth century. Originally the main living quarters of the Inn, The Bear had since been converted into the Swan's dining room. The polished wooden floors of the walnut-paneled tavern were all that remained of Naomi's Inn, but the bar was stocked full with Scotch whiskey. Soon after they took their seats at the bar, so were Grace and Vic.

"Need another round?" asked the bartender.

"How much do you have left?" asked Grace, squinting at the bottles behind him.

"As much as you need, miss."

Grace turned to Vic. "He's gonna need a bigger bar."

Vic tried to chuckle, but it sounded more like a death rattle. They had flown in on the wings of inspiration but, like Daedalus, had flown too close to the sun and crashed to earth, directly onto the thinly padded barstools.

There's nothing here, she thought. Grace couldn't feel anything, not a hint—the history had been stripped out of the Inn, panel by panel. She swiveled around on her stool, peeling back the years of the freshly painted walls around her, searching for anything that might lead them out of the dead end drain they were circling.

"You looking to buy the place?" asked the bartender.

Grace laughed. "No. Just looking for clues."

"Ah, of course," he said, filling both their drinks. "CIA, right?"

"*AR*," said Vic. "*Antiques Roadshow*. The Colonies version."

The bartender shrugged. "Never seen it. Any good?"

"Used to be," said Grace, eyeing Vic, "till they let their host go."

Vic raised a toast to her, and they both downed their drinks.

"So," said the bartender, refilling them, "you two location scouts?"

"Something like that," said Grace, scanning the nooks and crannies of the bar.

"You should talk to Margaret," said the bartender. "She's the resident historian."

Grace followed the bartender's gaze to a slight wisp of a woman at a small table in the shadowed corner of the bar. She was lit only by the glowing embers of a small fireplace, a delicate snifter of pale green liquid in her long, thin fingers, her eyes hidden beneath the brim of a knit red fascinator hat.

Grace swiveled back to the bartender. "Is she a tour guide or something?"

He laughed. "She should be. She's been coming here as long as, well, ever, I think."

Grace laughed and spun her stool around...

And slapped her hands on the seat bottom, freezing the chair. She felt it—only a breadcrumb, perhaps, but the trail lay there.

"What's she drinking?" she asked, her eyes riveted on the delicate figure.

"Absinthe."

Vic laughed. "My kind of tour guide."

"Let's buy her one," said Grace.

Vic laughed again until he saw the laser in Grace's eye. "I'll grab it," he said. "Go."

Grace slid off the stool and walked across the wooden floor past dozens of tourists, all dressed for their evening pilgrimage to the Royal Shakespeare Theatre. At the rear of the dining room, a two-sided ceiling-high fireplace separated the diners from the darkened nave of the tavern. As she turned the corner to the other side, it was as if Grace had stepped across the threshold of time itself. The walls had not been painted a modern gray like the bar—they were wood paneled, and the oak had splintered like an old palm. The furniture was older too, and sparse—just one wooden bench built into each corner wall, joined together in a wobbly "L." The brash lamps of the dining room had been banished from the walls, leaving the flickering fingers of the fire as the only source of light. Grace felt as if she'd climbed right into an oil painting.

"It's so beautiful," she whispered.

The old woman glanced up from beneath the brim of her hat, and Grace caught the flickering reflection of the fire in her bright emerald eyes. "How kind of you to say so," the woman said, as if Grace had complimented her. "This little corner of the tavern is all that's left of the old Bear Inn."

Grace ran her hand over the wood paneling. "Are these walls original?"

"Not to 1660," she said. "But that panel's at least a hundred years old."

Grace lifted her hand, hovering it over the wood, hoping to feel some sort of resonance, some whisper from the distant past.

"I'm Margaret," said the woman.

"And I'm unconscionably rude." Grace offered her hand. "I'm Grace."

The woman's hand felt tissue paper thin. Grace feared it might crumble.

"You can shake it, dear," said Margaret. "If it's survived this long, it'll probably make it to dinner."

Grace laughed and shook her hand. "Mind if I join you?"

"Not at all," she said, patting the bench beside her. "Far easier to stare at me from here."

Grace flushed. "Oh, I'm terribly—"

"And tell your friend at the bar to make it a double."

Grace laughed and gestured to Vic, before sliding down onto the bench across from Margaret. Now that she was closer, Grace found herself hypnotized by the fire's reflection in the old woman's eyes.

That's not the fire, she thought. *That's her.* There was magic in Margaret, Grace was sure of it, from the delicate float of her long arms to the way she adjusted the folds of her dress as if it were a royal train. Margaret looked royal—there was gravitas to her, and Grace could not help but feel a little awed in her presence.

"I fear you're already a few moves ahead of me," said Grace.

"Age does that, my dear," she said, lifting her glass. "Age and absinthe." She sipped the green liquor, and Grace marveled at how closely it matched Margaret's emerald eyes.

"They call it *La Fee Verte*," she said, savoring the taste. "The Green Fairy."

Grace smiled. "I could use a fairy myself right now."

"You've found one." Another flicker. "How may I enchant you?"

She already had—Grace wanted to take Margaret home in her luggage. "I'm on a quest."

"A quest?" asked Margaret, leaning forward. "I'll need fuel. Tell your friend to hurry."

"Ask and you shall receive," said Vic, sliding down beside Grace and presenting the snifter of absinthe to Margaret. She smiled at him and took the glass, letting her long fingers linger on his for just a moment. Vic blushed as she took the snifter, cradling it in her palm as if it were Baccarat.

She's sex incarnate, thought Grace. Margaret must have broken hearts the way pastry chefs break eggs—by the dozens. And her age—eighty years at least—could not dampen her. She shone through, lighting up their tiny cove with her wit, the elegance of her every gesture, her eyes...

"Tell me about your quest," said Margaret, sipping her absinthe.

"We're looking for a ghost," said Grace.

"A ghost?" she gasped. "I regret I left my wolfsbane at home." She turned to Vic. "Be a dear and go fetch it for me?"

Vic instinctively stood, mesmerized by her.

"He's delicious," Margaret said to Grace. "You must have shared the most unforgettable times together."

Grace laughed, pulling him back down. "We did, didn't we, Vic?"

"Wouldn't have changed a thing," he said. "Just me."

Margaret laughed. "A man who learns," she said. "Bless you."

She took another slow slip of the sparkling liquid. Grace sat back and studied her—her thin lips, her long neck, her fingers—perfectly posed around the glass, like a dancer's legs.

Snap. Grace felt it—another piece had fallen. She pressed her knee into Vic's thigh, and he took his cue like the brilliant host he was, chattering with Margaret about *Antiques Roadshow*, about the history of The Bear, while Grace . . . appraised.

Speak to me, she thought. Margaret had money; that was a given. The elegance of her every move suggested training, pedigree, and a lifetime to pursue it. Perhaps she had been a model at some time, or an actress—but she didn't have any of the insecurities of the aging *Grand Dame.* She had married, many times perhaps, the proof of which sparkled from the fine jewelry that bedecked her every curve. The teardrop Tahitian black pearls in her ears, the blood red ruby pendant that hung above the swell of her bosom, the platinum sapphire brooch, the rings—aquamarine, indigo berry, diamonds of the purest white. Margaret tilted the snifter once more to her lips and her sleeve slid back, revealing an antique bracelet. Unlike the museum of precious stones that wrapped around Margaret's every extremity, the bracelet was just plain, simple gold—faded, chipped, scratched from a lifetime of use. From life*times.*

"That's a beautiful bracelet," Grace said.

Margaret stared at Grace for a moment. "Thank you."

"Have you ever had it appraised?"

"Why would I?"

"For insurance value," said Grace. "Or if you'd ever want to sell it."

The sparkle in Margaret's eyes grew sharp, cold. "I'd never sell this."

"Really?" asked Grace. "It holds a special value to you?"

Margaret smiled, but it was thin as a blade. "Thank you for the drink and the delightful company," she said, standing. "I'm missed elsewhere." Without another word she floated off, disappearing out the back exit of the tavern.

"I pressed too hard," sighed Grace. "Sorry about that."

"Don't be," said Victor. "I was plumb useless myself. That woman turned my brain to Cream of Wheat."

Grace laughed. "Mine too, I think."

Vic leaned around the fireplace, checking the bar. "Looks like we haven't cleaned them out yet." He stood up and offered her his hand. "Buy you a bottle, my dear?"

"What did you see?" asked Victor, swirling a glass of absinthe.

"I'm not sure," Grace said. "But it felt important."

"You clearly hit a nerve, so you were on to something."

"Maybe," she sighed. "Who knows? Not that it'll give us what we need."

"We know it's a Kent."

"*We* know," said Grace. "No one else will. Ever." Grace finished her glass, and the bartender refilled them both. Then, for good measure, he slid a third glass across the bar, right between the two of them.

"What are we supposed to do with that?" Vic asked. "Arm-wrestle for it?"

The bartender laughed. "Nope." He glanced past them. "But you might have to arm-wrestle her."

Margaret had returned. She was seated as before, in the far corner of the old tavern, her wide-brimmed hat tilted just so.

Fearing she might dissolve into thin air, Grace swiped the extra glass of absinthe off the bar and walked over, Victor close behind. They lowered themselves onto the L-shaped bench, slowly, carefully, lest they scare her off once and for all.

Margaret did not seem to acknowledge or even notice their presence, so Grace slid the glass of absinthe across the polished wooden table. Margaret raised the glass to her lips and took a long sip, luxuriating in its exotic burn. Then she set the glass down and finally locked eyes with Grace. "Why are you here?"

Grace checked with Vic; he nodded—there was nothing to lose.

"We're trying to prove authenticity for an unsigned Impressionist painting," she said. "I found it in an attic, forgotten for at least a century." She paused. "I think it's a William Kent."

The glass hesitated mere inches from Margaret's lips. "Are you sure?"

Grace paused—was she? "Yes," she said. "I'm sure."

Margaret took a deep breath. "Is it of the Avon?"

"It is," said Grace. "And a woman."

Margaret fell silent, her eyes blank. She set her glass down on the wooden table and stared at it, unable to look up at Grace. "Do you have a picture?" she asked.

Grace fumbled around in her purse and fished out her phone, thumbing open a picture of the painting and placing it in the middle of the table. Margaret pulled the phone close but could not bring herself to look at the painting. Finally, a decision was made, and she tilted her head down, gazing upon it.

Grace could not see Margaret's emerald eyes beneath the brim of her hat, but she didn't need to.

She could see them in the painting.

"You know her, don't you?" asked Grace.

Margaret nodded.

"A relative?"

"My grandmother."

Margaret stroked the screen, as if her fingers might caress the face of the woman beneath the oils. Her hand trembled, and the gold bracelet around her wrist sparkled in the firelight.

"That's her bracelet, isn't it?" Grace asked. "The one Kent gave her on the bridge?"

Margaret nodded, unable to tear herself away from the image. "It didn't make a difference," she said, her voice bitter. "Naomi was already gone, the poor fool. And she knew it, eventually. She died so unbearably sad." Margaret sighed and placed the phone back on the table, face down. "But that's not her."

Vic stirred, troubled. "Not her?"

"Not quite," she said. "I knew her—when I was very young, of course—she died when I was only seven. But I remember her. She was a striking woman." She nodded down at the phone. "Although that's not *quite* her."

Grace leaned forward. "What makes you say that?"

Margaret looked into her eyes, testing her to see if she was worthy.

"Please, Margaret," said Grace, taking her hands. "We've come halfway around the world to meet her."

"No, you haven't." Margaret smiled—a kind, sad smile. "You came for this."

She gently removed her hand from Grace's and it disappeared beneath the table, emerging with a tattered faded envelope. Grace reached out for it, but Margaret intercepted her, grasping her hand with surprising strength.

"My grandmother broke many hearts," she said. "Prepare yourself—she's about to break yours."

Eight

26 November, 1899
Miss Naomi Chambliss,
The Bear, Stratford-upon-Avon

Dear Miss Chambliss,

I come not to chide you for the events of Wednesday last, but in explanation of them—and in hopes you might hear my prayer and take pity upon me.

When you met William at Clopton Bridge, I was a secretive observer upon the western bank, but the primary instigator in the row that unfurled between you. He had come to my studio in London for guidance, in hopes that my tutelage might provide him the means to regain your fancy. We toiled together on the Avon, but William chafed at the New Forms required by our modern society. Still, he forced his hand to the canvas without bitterness, desperate to recover your affections. I helped, of course, guiding his brush, and I blush to admit a piece of my own heart beats within the painting he revealed to you that day.

It was difficult to watch from afar—his earnest plea, the

agony of your discomfort. You had moved on, that was clear even from my vantage. What William offered, I suppose, was a poor bauble compared to the sparkling new life you have begun with young Master Munnings—a man rising to dizzying heights no less splendid than my own.

I know it was a consolation to him that you kept the bracelet, and it will, I believe, one day be of great comfort to you. Whatever you may think of William, I can tell you without the slightest hesitation that he is a genius, nonparallel in this world. No, he cannot parlay with a voice sweet in modern ears. But I tell you, at great risk to my own ego, his eye sees things... within things. He sees what we can't. And when he paints his visions upon the fabric canvas, I tell you, it glows.

But it haunts me, Miss Chambliss, to my very core—which is the true reason I write.

When you walked off the bridge with neither his heart nor his painting, I expected William to rage, to tear his hair, to shred the canvas to tatters. But he was quite the opposite. It was as if he expected your denial and had come armed to Clopton Bridge. He reached down behind the stone railing and reemerged with his easel and a box of oils. He placed our creation upon the easel and gazed out at the Avon: from Tramway to Clopton, from water to spire, from Past to Present. His hands moved with such shearing speed I lost sight of them in the white-hot blur of his shirtsleeves. Across the canvas, from palette to page, he seemed possessed, astride the wings of invisible angels. His hands slashed against our former creation, opening wounds with his own inspiration, burying our painting a full fathom beneath his. I inched forward through the weeds, desperate for a closer view. I had to know, Miss Chambliss, what furnace had opened within him.

I wanted it. I admit that. I wanted it for myself.

As the last ray of day winked off behind Trinity Church, he finished the work, but he did not linger. It had all timed out to perfection—your denial, the sunset, his final painting. He closed his box of oils, secured the latch, and tossed it into the surging Avon. He did not spend a single moment to follow its progress; he simply turned and walked off down the far side of Clopton. I thought he meant to follow you to The Bear, but he turned north, walking still, disappearing into the night. I have not heard from him since. I fear none of us will, ever again.

I rushed onto Clopton, fearful a passing carriage would knock the easel into the Avon but dared not touch it—the varnish was still glistening, and I feared the slightest disturbance would destroy the absolute perfection before me.

It was stunning, Miss Chambliss. A mixing of colors that I had never seen, but it was so much more than that—it was a mixing of Time itself: the promise of Youth, the flower of Invention, the ache and ecstasy of Fame. It was Love and Loss in equal poise, and a life well-lived between the sweet pangs of each.

It was Goodbye.

But it will never sell. It's too experiential, it asks too much from an audience. And most damning of all—although his spirit courses through every pigment and oil, you cannot see him suspended above them; he calls no attention to himself—and our modern audiences crave stars above stories. Of that I can bear particular witness.

I carried the painting back to my lodging across the Avon and placed it beneath the window in the pale blue moonlight. It haunted me for days, refusing to give up its secrets. And then, this very evening, a window in Heaven opened, and the answer revealed itself:

I should paint it.

That is my only way forward from my purgatory. I will use his masterpiece to ignite my own. I will set it beside my easel, there upon Clopton, and I will transfuse its spirit from his canvas to mine. I will see through his eyes, yes, but then I shall emerge from them, reborn, and see more clearly than I ever have before!

But you are the key to my prison cell, dear Miss Chambliss. His oils will be my lifeblood, but your figure haunts both Alpha and Omega of the work. I need you there, upon Tramway, as you were. Only then may I truly submerge myself beneath William's skin and emerge reborn.

When we have finished, I will destroy his creation, for only one can survive; his Cain will not abide my Abel. Only my work—our work—will see the light of day.

And I promise you light, Miss Chambliss, so much light! I have already written to my patrons in London, and the guest list for the reveal is already overflowing with a pantheon of the most high.

Your modeling for me is your invitation.

This letter is my prayer.

Your Hopeful Partner,
James Davies

Nine

Grace gazed out the airplane window into the blackness below. It was an abyss beyond her imagination, and even if the plane climbed out from it, she would not.

James Davies, she thought. It had always been Davies. How could she have been so unforgivably wrong? And Grace would have to cop to it before a standing-only crowd in Sotheby's. The word would spread like a pestilence, laying waste to them all—Robert, Jerome, Elaine, the Appraisal Experts Roadshow.

Me.

Grace had heaped her entire happiness on the back of that painting and her desperation had cracked it in half, crushing the hopes of everyone she knew. Except Annette Neiman, of course. She'd need a bib to keep all the Schadenfreude off her blazer.

Goodbye, William Kent, she thought.

She had felt so full with him beside her, and now that he had disappeared, she had never felt so empty.

"I'm so sorry, Gracie," said Vic, placing his hand atop hers.

Grace turned from the window with a sad smile. "Me too." She laced her fingers in his. "Thought I'd found something for that little lost Treasure Box of yours."

He laughed. "For a few moments there, it didn't feel quite so lost." He squeezed her hand. "Thank you."

Grace nodded and turned once more to the bleak sky below.

Vic caught her reflection in the window; her pale, lifeless eyes floating in the void. He sighed, frustrated—struggling for something, anything to say or do that might ease her pain. And then he found it.

"I'm not going to the auction," he said.

"Yes you are."

"I'll have to authenticate the Davies. It'll be the end of you, Grace."

She turned back, pleading. "One of us has to authenticate for Robert or he'll get nothing," she said. "I can't be there—I just can't. I'm tired of disappointing people." She squeezed his hand. "Please, Vic. Do this for me."

Vic paused, then grinned. "I never could deny you."

"You never could deny anyone, and you know it."

He laughed, and she did, too.

Grace savored it. It would have to last her a very long time.

Part VI

Value

One

SCHAFFER & SCHAFFER, Ltd.
Fine Arts, Auctions & Appraisals
Est. 2005

"You can't be serious, Grace. That's our *name* on that sign."

"Dad's gone," said Grace, placing her arm around the slumping shoulders of Jeff Tangeman, her gallery manager. "It's a bit maudlin to see him up there, don't you think?" She noticed Jeff's shoulders lying particularly low—the sudden rush of gallery walk-ins had him crooning his trademark (and much beloved) operatic arias of anxiety, but their equally sudden exodus after the triple misfires of *Antiques Roadshow*, Sotheby's, and the James Banks Exposition Center had left him uncharacteristically morose.

"But that name's our reputation—it's all we have left right now," he said. "I'm not sure changing it is going to stop the bleeding, Grace."

She grinned. "Not even 'Schaffer & Tangeman'?"

He roared out a magnificent laugh, loud as a sonic boom, and it rippled up and down his belly like a flesh xylophone. "Your funeral, boss," he said. "Just say the word, and I'll throw it up there so your father can haunt me for all eternity."

Grace laughed—she knew the experience and didn't wish it on anyone, least of all Jeff.

He tossed open the front door with the dramatic flourish of Madame Butterfly, hesitating in the entrance. "Oh—you have a package. Andersen's Moving and Storage. I'm assuming that's not a Qin Shi Terracotta Warrior?"

"Not unless it's wearing one of my mother's muumuus. It's just a little stowaway from Mom's move. They found it hiding in the back of the truck after they got back. Mom said it was just a bunch of junk, so I'll probably just trash the thing."

"Well, if it's a muumuu, I get first dibs," he said, starting inside. "I'll put it in your office. Can't promise I won't peek."

"If you find a Terracotta Warrior instead, let me know. We're going to need it after word gets out from Sotheby's this weekend."

Jeff spun around, framing himself perfectly between two cast iron Corinthian columns. "Got a date to watch the carnage Saturday night?"

"I'm not going."

"We can watch it online."

"I'm not going anywhere near a computer this weekend."

"I'll bring the tequila."

Grace sighed. "I love you."

"Tell it to the accountant when you give me a raise."

He blew her a kiss and disappeared inside, leaving Grace alone on Spring Street. Her gallery was one of many on West Broadway, each vying for the attention of passers-by. But Schaffer & Schaffer was the outcast—an antique gallery lost in a sea of Modern and Avant-Garde. When Grace opened it in the early 2000s, she made most of her sales off foot traffic. Now the majority of her sales were over the internet, and most of the people who poked inside the two-story gallery sought air-conditioning, not Cassatt.

She gazed back up at the wooden gallery sign swinging gently in the breeze. Even the Gothic font looked old, rare, as valuable as the pieces within. Grace had been so proud to pull her hands away from her father's eyes when she had revealed it to him at the grand opening. She had expected a little wink of pride from him at the very least, some rupture in his hardened shell. Instead, he just stared at it, his face blank as fresh canvas. No wiping of the eye, no sniffle, no clearing of the throat, just—

"That's nice, Grace. We appreciate it."

Albert had a royalty complex, and both Grace and her mother had chided him for speaking of himself in the second person, but this was different.

We appreciate it.

Whispered, almost under his breath. As if he were trying to tell her a secret, one he was forbidden to tell.

Tell me what, Dad?

But the trail was cold, and if Grace was honest, she had never made it very far with that appraisal, try as she might. Her father was a fortress; immovable, inscrutable, glacial.

Grace gave up and walked into the gallery, easing the door closed behind her. She leaned back against the glass and let the sweet bouquet of walnut, maple, and varnish wash over her. It warmed her nostrils—the aroma of Pissarro and Tiffany and Queen Anne; how she had missed it. She stepped out onto the carpet pathway, and the old hardwood groaned beneath her—the only acceptable soundtrack for an antique gallery as far as Grace was concerned. There were a few empty spaces where tall clocks, highboys, and porcelain had stood, and many of her favorite oils and pastels had disappeared from the walls—the word of mouth from her adventures with the Appraisal Experts Roadshow had clearly given her business the steroid shot it needed. But since the disaster in Maine and its encore at Sotheby's, the phones had gone silent, and emails had dwindled to the usual duet of spam and scam. After the auction on Saturday, she'd need more than an adrenaline shot to bring the gallery back to life. She'd need a necromancer.

She walked deeper into the gallery, past sculptures and crystal and display cases glowing with jade and jewels. It was her collection, her eye—and her vision had been so clear. Where had it gone? *Antiques Roadshow*, the divorce, the Kent—the *Davies*, of course.

She came to a small door at the rear of the gallery, her nameplate across the top:

GRACE SCHAFFER
OWNER/APPRAISER

Some appraiser. Grace laughed out loud. She could look past centuries of varnish, inside paint and pastel, into the shrouded corners of history, but she couldn't look into herself.

Grace opened the door to her office and closed it behind her, sealing herself in the vault-like silence. Jeff called it her rat trap, and although it made her chuckle, she knew it was a pretty accurate description. It was tiny—gallery space was astronomically expensive, and any square feet taken up by anything other than an antique was wasted space. There was a pine wood Ikea desk with a laptop, a creaky leather chair on wheels so chipped they'd become as square as dice, a few boxes of things Grace would file "*Tomorrow, I promise*," and a small bookshelf stocked with frayed antique guides.

Jeff had placed the package on her desk. It was small and light—no wonder it had been overlooked by the movers. It was an older box, and the tape was fraying, so Grace easily peeled it back with her fingernail, expecting to find nothing more than a few odd cookbooks and empty jars, but when she drew back the flaps, she saw something inside that made her heart flutter.

She reached in and removed a plain, dust-coated 4-by-6 frame, placing it on her desk. It had come from her father's home office; she had seen it many times in the deep recess of the bookcase behind his desk. It was a black-and-white photograph of Albert in his office at Columbia, taken for a *New Yorker* article on a Pre-Raphaelite exhibition at the Met. Grace had always admired the photograph from a distance, and seeing it up close felt forbidden, as if she were viewing her father's most guarded secret.

But her father had always been guarded, visor down, shield up—even to his own daughter. Grace had never pushed him, had never demanded anything, even as the mystery festered within her, gnawing holes that nothing—not her career, nor her marriage, nor the midnight march of bedroom guests—had filled.

It's time, Dad.

Grace settled back into her chair and let her mind wander over the black-and-white picture. Her father behind his desk, a meticulously curated exhibition in itself. To his right, illustrated collections of works by the Pre-Raphaelite titans. On his left, stacks of scholarly criticism. And in the middle, a pristine copy of his latest publication, *The Medieval Victorians.* His hands rested atop the virgin cover, fingers laced just below the elegant curves of his own scripted name in the event anyone had missed it in the title of the article.

How exhausting, thought Grace. Even taking a simple picture required the effort of a lengthy tenure process.

The bookcase behind him was similarly arranged for effect, down to the complementary colors of each book's spine. There were diplomas, of course; awards of brass and ribbon from least to most impressive. And buried far behind them, deep in the shaded recesses of the bookcase, dwarfed by the books and the plaques and citations, a tiny silver oval object peeked back at her.

Grace gasped. She had never noticed it from the back of his office, but suddenly it was all she could see. It was an antique silver frame: a faded portrait of a little girl, her face and fingers covered in dirt, holding out her hand to the camera, and within that hand, an arrowhead.

The other neighborhood parents wrote their child's most inconsequential adolescent accomplishments in sky-high towers of neon and gold. Gracie had been so jealous of her friends, for she knew they were loved, and she was not. But she was wrong. And she had never been so ecstatic in all her life.

Albert loved her.

Maybe not in the way she wanted, but in the only way he knew how. He loved her in pigment and shade and line; he loved her in the books they read together, in the discoveries they shared.

An awful memory swept over Grace—that disastrous dinner when she and her father were so dismissive of Shirley's desire to take an art class. But as she forced herself to look closer, Grace saw something else behind the thick veil of her own regret—her father cringing at his terrible cruelty, his stuttered apology, the sweat beading across his face; struggling to emote, to comfort, to care.

And as Shirley turned to him, her mother saw—not the totality of his failure, but the earnestness of his attempt. And that was enough for her. She took him—she chose to take him—not at his word, but at the soul imprisoned beneath.

Grace picked up the frame with trembling hands and pulled it close. She looked again at her own tiny portrait behind him, lost among the acres of his accomplishments. But it was *there*, wasn't it? He had carved out a space for her.

And that, after all those years, was finally enough for Grace.

She drew the photograph to her lips and kissed her father's forehead, that gorgeous masterpiece of a brain, and set the frame within her own crowded bookcase. But she set it in front, for that was the space she had carved out for him.

As she leaned forward to turn on her laptop, she noticed one last item nestled in the very bottom of the box. It was a small hardcover book, and splashed across its cover in yellows, oranges, and the deepest blues was a reproduction of William Kent's *Elbow of Avon.*

It was her book, purchased with her very first paycheck. In her haste to leave home for her freshman year, she had neglected to pack it. Thrilled by the surprise reunion with her old friend, Grace reached in to pull it out, but it fell from her hand, ricocheting off the desk and tumbling onto the floor. As it fell, a folded piece of yellowed parchment slipped out from between its pages, fluttering to the ground.

Grace let the book lie and picked up the folded parchment instead. It was old, maybe decades old, and the folded edges were badly frayed. The paper smelled fresh, though; it had been entombed straightaway.

But who had buried it?

Grace placed the parchment on her desk and unfolded it, leaf by leaf, until it lay before her, revealing its thunderclap of a secret. She read it, reread it, and then read it again until she leaned back to catch her breath; the power of the thing made her dizzy.

It was the most astonishing thing she had ever seen, and it opened a fissure in her understanding of everything—most of all herself. Even the date upon the parchment accused her.

Nineteen ninety-three? she thought.

"What the hell took me so long?"

Two

"Not bad for someone who never took an art class."

Shirley looked up from her easel in the middle of the Activity Center. "Gracie." She broke out in a huge smile. "How'd you know I was here?"

Grace walked through the crisscrossing lines of residents as they packed up their art supplies. "I have a lookout on the veranda," she said. "Need help schlepping this back to the apartment?" She leaned in to grab the easel.

Shirley's hands were shaking worse than ever, but they moved with sudden urgency, flipping the portfolio closed. "I'll take this and the pastels," she said. "If you can get the easel."

Grace nodded and they walked the halls, back toward her mother's apartment. Shirley waved as they passed an octogenarian making the rounds with his walker. He stood up that much taller, as if preening for her.

"Say, Mom," said Grace. "I think he was flirting with you."

"Don't be silly."

But it wasn't silly. The residents all seemed to know Shirley. And Shirley seemed to know them—from the names of their grandkids to their next orthopedic appointment. Grace and her father had called

Shirley a closed book. Grace wondered if they'd simply never opened it up.

The image tickled Grace, and she laughed, not caring her lungs would fill once more with the choking humid musk of age and antiseptic. Grace waited for the usual surge of nausea, but oddly enough, it didn't come.

Grace took another breath, much deeper, but there was no sting of ammonia, only the fresh scent of dewy wildflowers floating through the open veranda doors. And strangest of all, although there was age all about her, there was no death. No, this was the sweet smell of life. Grace held her breath, savoring it.

Shirley noticed the goofy smile on her daughter's face. "All right, kiddo," she said, opening the door to her apartment. "You going to let me in on the joke or not?"

"Oh, Mom," said Grace, wrestling the easel through the tiny entryway. "I'm pretty sure you're already in on it."

Shirley shrugged and closed the door behind them. "Just leave that anywhere, dear. I'll put it back in my bedroom later."

"Like you ever let me get away with leaving *my* toys out."

"I knew that'd come back to haunt me." Shirley chuckled as she led them into the bedroom, placing her portfolio on the bed. She turned back to Grace, but something on the wall behind her daughter stopped her cold. Even her hands' helpless vibrato suddenly ceased.

It was an antique frame, and within it, the parchment from Grace's gallery.

Shirley was quiet for a long time. "That's a beautiful frame, Grace."

"Not half so beautiful as what's inside."

They stared up at it in silence.

"Did Dad know?"

"I never told him," Shirley said. "But you know Albert."

Grace did, but she was just beginning to know her mother. "Why didn't you tell us?"

"That was your bond, not mine. The one string that tied you two together. I was so happy for you when the gallery opened. It was yours, Grace. But he was part of it, too—not just a name on the sign next to yours."

And finally, Grace understood.

"We appreciate it."

Her father had tried to tell her a secret, but it was not his to tell.

"Yes, Mom," Grace said. "That's his name on the sign. But it's not beside *mine*."

Shirley tried to speak, tried so many words, but not a single one would do. The tears would have to be enough.

Grace took her mother's hand, turning them both back toward the frame:

By authority of the Board of Trustees of
UNION COLLEGE
in the town of Schenectady in the State of New York
and upon recommendation of the Faculty
SHIRLEY GRACE SCHAFFER
has been admitted to the Degree of
BACHELOR OF FINE ARTS

"Congratulations, Mom," said Grace. "Can I peek at your portfolio now?"

"Sorry, dear." Shirley winked. "That's mine."

Grace laughed. "Fair enough."

Both women's faces were striped with tears. "Look at us," said Grace. "We're a salty mess."

"Oh dear," gasped Shirley, rushing to her nightstand for a box of tissues. "We have to clean you up—didn't you tell me you have an auction this evening?"

"Oh, no," said Grace. "I'll take this beating online, thank you very much."

Shirley stared at her daughter.

"What?" asked Grace.

"That's not like you."

"It's a drumming, Mom. I'm not bringing a noodle to a gunfight."

Shirley's eyes sparkled with a sudden inspiration. "What if you went armed?"

Grace was tempted—not that she wanted to kill Annette Neiman, maybe just wing her. "Thanks, Mom. But I'm not sure gunfire's enough."

"Then let's send you with something a little bit stronger." Shirley lowered herself onto her hands and knees and pulled a small shoebox out from under the bed, handing it to Grace.

Grace smiled—what was this? Old pictures? Grade school ribbons? She yanked off the top, tossing it aside . . . and froze. There it was, not lost, not forgotten, but packed with a mother's love in a soft bed of shredded newspaper.

A tiny red shovel, its tongue still caked with the brown dirt of their backyard.

Grace eased it out of the box and held it in her hand, turning it this way and that, admiring it as if it were a bejeweled Arabian scimitar. "It's so beautiful, Mom," she said. "I had no idea you kept it all these years."

Shirley shook her head, as if Grace should have known better. "Even if little girls don't know what's for keeping," she said, "mothers do."

Grace sat on the bed, cradling the tiny shovel in her lap. Shirley eased down beside her, draping a thin arm around her shoulders. Grace noticed how still and strong her mother's hand was, as was her voice.

"Your father and I let you dig outside because we were certain there was nothing out there." She placed her hand over Grace's, squeezing it against the red plastic handle. "But you knew something was there, Gracie. You marched right into the backyard, past the swings, out there where nothing grew, and you dug, right down into the earth, through mud and rock and soil, through century after century until you hit that arrowhead."

Shirley raised her hands to each side of her daughter's face, holding it tight.

"You didn't guess, Gracie. And you weren't lucky," she said. "You *knew*."

Grace shook her head. Her mother was wrong; it hadn't been like that. Not then, not ever. Grace had been lucky, she'd been fortunate; she'd had her father and her education and her experience and the awesome power of the celestial globe.

She hadn't known anything.

But she looked into her mother's eyes, and there, reflected within them, was the girl her mother saw—so confident, so sure, so full of faith.

And that girl was for keeping.

Three

The jagged metal teeth at the top of the escalator bit down with the relentless metallic clang of a slaughterhouse as Grace rose toward the open doors of the auction hall. She knew this time there would be no going back—not down the other escalator, nor away from the doom that lay before her on the seventh floor of Sotheby's.

The escalator ejected her into the middle of a swirling dirt devil of three-piece suits and cocktail dresses. Grace pressed her hands against her thighs to stop her shaking legs, but realized it was the vibrating thrum of the standing-only crowd. She ran her hand back up her body, smoothing the wrinkles of her anxiety as well as the pressed lines of her pantsuit. It was her three-alarm fire red suit, one she rarely wore, but the color made her feel as if she had snuck her little red shovel into Sotheby's for the battle ahead.

"Grace!" Robert Bedford squeezed his way through the cummerbunds and hugged her tight, swaying her back and forth like a long-lost sibling. "I thought you couldn't make it?"

"I was being an awful coward, Rob. I'm terribly sorry."

"Don't be, please," he said. "I'm just glad you're here."

Robert looked anxious, but oddly excited. Grace feared she had not prepared him properly for the slaughter ahead.

"You do understand what I said on the phone, right?" she asked.

"Uh-huh." He bobbed up and down, as if she had brought him back a Golden Ticket and not a poison one. "Mr. Karlin's going to confirm it. It's a James Davies, for sure!"

He's choosing, she thought. *And James Davies is enough for him.*

Grace lurched forward and hugged him close. "Thank you, Robert," she said. "I'm so glad I came."

He grinned and took her hand, leading her toward the open doorway. The cocktail tempest within had ceased, and now Grace saw them for what they were. Just people—perhaps the richest people in the world, sure—but they weren't her executioners.

No, Grace saw her executioner at the far end of the hall, standing between Vic and Annette Neiman on the raised dais—a tall, wiry skeleton in a suit. She recognized him immediately.

Shaw. His name crawled across her skin like a midnight chill.

Thomas Shaw, Head of Auctions. If the face of Sotheby's shone with the millennia of the finest art ever created, its voice was Shaw. The auction audience—from the seats to the phones to the internet—sat atop a mountain of money larger than the gross national product of many nations, but the bidders did not part gently from their mutual funds. They had come to acquire, yes, and to acquire, they knew they must pay.

But Shaw told them how much.

When Shaw spoke, they opened to him like an oyster, and he plucked pearls from their throats by the billions. And he would bury Grace. Annette might pass the sentence, but Thomas Shaw would lower the blade.

"Sit by me, Grace," said Robert. "I have an open seat in the back row."

Grace blew out a huge sigh of relief as they crossed the threshold into the yawning hall—she could easily disappear back there, among the casual observers and the looky-loos. No one would recognize her, and after Robert got what he needed (hopefully a little more than he needed), she could slip out the back and lick her wounds in peace.

"Oh dear," said Robert, gazing down at his open seat—the only one left. "The whole row was open when I went to the bathroom."

"That's okay." Grace eased Robert into his seat. "I can stand."

"Take my seat, miss," said a friendly voice. "I could use the exercise."

Jerome Zwick stood beside a chair one aisle down.

Grace threw herself at him, nearly knocking him over.

"Easy, Grace." He laughed, embracing her. "One heart attack's more than enough."

She jerked back, eyes narrowed in sudden fury. "What on earth are you doing here? You're still on bed rest, mister."

He tilted his head, stymied by the question. "I'm not exactly sure," he said. "I certainly didn't expect to see you here."

"I wasn't expecting to be seen—particularly by you," she said. "You didn't answer my question, Jer."

He tilted his head, amused by his inability to respond. "I suppose I was just curious."

Grace stared at him. Jerome wasn't lying; she could see that. His eyes had lost some of the *Zwick Focus*, for sure, so he was probably still a little confused from his sojourn in the ICU.

He leaned in, lowering his voice. "I heard you have confirmation on the painting."

"Yes." She paused. "It's a Davies."

A wry grin cracked the side of his lips. "You're not sure."

"We have proof."

"You're not sure."

"Facts are facts, Jer."

"Yes, they are." He placed his lips an inch from her ear. "But you're not sure."

He kissed her cheek, and his eyes shone like two Sabbath candles, blessing Grace with such unconditional love. With such faith.

This man, she thought.

"If I were twenty years older," she said.

"And it wasn't completely inappropriate."

"I'd be giving you that second heart attack."

Jerome laughed. "Thank God I'm seventy," he said, gathering his overcoat from the chair.

"Not on your life, Prince Charming," said Grace. "I'll stand."

"That won't be necessary," said a voice—this one anything but friendly.

Annette Neiman stood in the aisle, hands on surgically sculpted hips, armed with a venomous smile of peroxide white knives. "We need you in the front row, dear," she said. "In case you wish to add anything to Victor's presentation."

Grace was startled. "It's not printed in the program?"

"It came too late, unfortunately," she said. "And we can't postpone a second time—it might lower confidence that the piece is an authentic Davies."

She had put a gleeful little twist on *Davies*, and Grace flinched at it.

"It's unorthodox, to be sure," said Annette. "But let's stop the bloodletting, shall we? Thomas is on his usual lavaliere, but we've added a wireless mic for Victor at the lectern. He'll announce his confirmation of authorship when we transition to your lot number."

She turned to Robert, and Grace had to restrain herself from sliding between them and brandishing a wooden cross in her face.

"Enjoy the auction, Robert." Annette grinned, with perhaps more teeth than were necessary. "Remember—you win, we win."

Robert opened his mouth to thank her, but Annette had already spun on her stilettos and dashed off. Grace followed in her wake as they threaded down the still-teeming aisle of the Sotheby's Evening Auction Hall. To Grace, it felt like she was being led through the sacred sanctuary of a medieval Gothic cathedral. The coffered ceiling buttresses towered thirty feet high above her. A glimmering latticework of light towers hung down, bathing row after row of the shrewdest collectors in the world in luminous glory. She'd been here before of course, many times, but there was still something so awesome about the space—something holy. She forged ahead, passing a long white-paneled bandstand; behind it, a small army of Sotheby's staff were already jabbing away at their keyboards, welcoming a staggering proportion of the world's wealth into the proceedings.

Grace floated forward in a daze, drawn toward the raised altar at the front of the hall. To the right, another two dozen staffers stood behind another white-paneled bandstand: the cathedral choir, singing their hymns into a bank of telephones on the pedestals before them.

And at the far end of the tabernacle, it rose—the auctioneer's podium, hewn from the richest crimson mahogany, sanctified by a gilded Sotheby's plaque. It towered over the congregation like a papal throne, and the auctioneers walked not up to it but into it, cloaking themselves in the unassailable power of an artistic empire.

"Coming, Grace?" asked Annette, jolting Grace from her stupor.

Grace nodded and followed Annette the last few feet to the front row, to a seat right beside Victor.

"You two know each other, right?" Annette took in a deep, pleasurable breath, as if savoring their discomfort. "I'll let you catch up. I have an auction to start." She walked around the dais and huddled with Shaw, giving him last-minute adjustments to the program, which he notated in his copy.

Grace sat down next to Victor. "Surprised to see me?"

"Not really," he said. "But good on you, Gracie." He patted a page of typewritten notes in his lap. "I'll take care of you, okay?"

"I know you will," she said. "Thank you."

He smiled at her, but she could see the strain behind it. This would hurt him, too—it would close the coffin on his little lost Treasure Box once and for all.

Poor Vic, she thought. She leaned over to whisper one final encouragement, but a sudden rumble of excitement rolled over the crowd like an approaching thundercloud.

Thomas Shaw stepped onto the altar and the lights dimmed, cross-fading into a deep, lush purple. The crowd settled; people took their seats, laughter ceased, voices hushed. Shaw looked out over the audience, taking measure of their worthiness. He waved to those who had earned the honor, his balletic arms gliding through the air like Monet's *Water Lilies* atop the River Epte. And as he clamped his bony hands down upon the massive podium, his lithe frame seemed to expand like a silken lung, engorged with the power of the mahogany shrine. He took in a mighty breath, and the room held theirs.

"Good evening, ladies and gentlemen, and a very, very warm welcome to Sotheby's!" The sumptuous cello vibrato of his rich English voice sang out over the crowd, rising and falling in operatic arias. He was both orchestra and conductor, drawing his bow across the strings with elegance and ease, seducing the crowd with the music of the Market's Spheres.

"My name is Thomas Shaw, and I will be your auctioneer for tonight's Impressionist and Modern Art Evening Sale. As representative of the House, I may open the bidding by placing a bid on behalf of the seller, and I may further bid up to the amount of the printed reserve."

Grace's heart clutched at her throat. Had she set their reserve too low? When she returned from her British disaster, she had advised Robert to set his minimum reserve at $10,000. But the lots this evening had the makings of a world-class museum—there were paintings by Voorhees and Cassatt, exquisite drawings by Gauguin and Sargent, and seminal works by Chagall and Matisse. The reserves were in the millions, in the tens of millions. Would poor little James Davies even get a second glance?

But it was too late. Shaw grasped the ebony handle of his auction gavel and the entire audience leaned forward as one, like stallions at the gate. He unlatched his suit coat button and his tie swung free, waving a silken purple flag at the ravenous throng.

"Lot Number 1!"

The section of the wall to Shaw's right glided open with a well-oiled whisper, and a raised pedestal rotated onto the dais. Upon it, a black-aproned staffer displayed a small, framed sketch with white-gloved hands, deftly balancing it upon a white easel. A spotlight shone down from above, bathing the elegant Spanish *jaleo* dancer in the drawing in soft brilliant light. Grace smiled—she knew her well.

"John Singer Sargent," said Shaw. "*Sketch After 'El Jaleo,'* 1882. Ink on paper. Signed by the artist on the lower left. Provenance can be traced back to George Berhaim, Paris, France, 1924."

Shaw surveyed the slack-jawed faces of the crowd from his perch high above them. "I'll begin the bidding at *two hundred and fifty thousand dollars.*" He let the number settle over the crowd. With his opening bid, Shaw had laid waste to amateur and bargain hunter alike.

"Two hundred and fifty thousand dollars—"

A bid paddle in the front row shot into the air.

"Two seventy-five," Shaw said, prowling back and forth in his podium. "Two seventy-five, I have—"

A second paddle, eighth row.

"Three hundred!" His eyes swiveled back to the front row, locking the initial bidder in his sights. "Try another."

It was not a question. The man raised his paddle, but another quickly answered.

"Three hundred fifty now!" Shaw dipped his chin, fixing both barrels of his eyes on the man in the front row.

"*Against* you, sir."

The man smiled and shook his head. Shaw pressed forward into the soft flesh of his denial. "A solid three hundred and fifty behind you. Try another."

The man's arm betrayed him, thrusting his paddle into the air.

"Three seventy-five!"

A massive digital screen on the wall to Shaw's left, well over a story high, flashed out the skyrocketing bids in dollars, pounds, euros, yen, and yuan like the departure board at Grand Central Terminal. They came from every corner of the room—the phone banks, the computers, the pneumatic arms of the bidders themselves, jackhammering up and down at ever-increasing speeds. Shaw writhed about as he caught each one, slithering above the podium like a cobra; up, down, side to side, until he shot forward for one last strike at the original bidder:

"The bid is five hundred and seventy-five thousand dollars." Shaw leaned out over the podium, looming over the bidder in the front row. "Say six," he said. "Five hundred and seventy-five thousand dollars—say *six*."

The man's eyes glazed over. He was up above the limit of his finances, and the thin atmosphere unmade him.

"Five hundred and seventy-five *against* you."

The man opened his mouth, and Grace thought he might beg for mercy.

"I'm going to sell it. Fair warning…"

Shaw raised his gavel.

The man dropped his head in shame.

"Sold!"

Shaw slammed the gavel down with one hand as his other hand opened, palm up, offering the spoils to the victor in the third row. "Thank you very much indeed," he said, turning to an assistant at the phone bank. "That's Paddle 528."

Shaw turned the page of his program with a flourish, and the losing bidder stumbled to his feet, shuffling up the aisle toward the exit. That single sketch had drawn him from miles, perhaps oceans away, just for the opportunity to measure the sum of his life's great works to a piece of human perfection, and although he left with his finances intact, his spirit was broken.

How will I leave? Grace shuddered at the thought, but the auction rumbled forth, churning out lot after lot by the thousands and tens and hundreds of thousands, by the millions. She tried to prepare herself for the inevitable, but terror crawled out of her stomach like a long-legged spider, its chitinous fangs clamping down around her throat, choking off her breath.

What have I done? she thought. Why had she insisted on Sotheby's? Why hadn't they pivoted to a smaller house, like Bonhams or Swann?

Thomas Shaw held up his hand, and the crowd fell silent.

"Lot Number 12." He called it out as if it were the name of the condemned.

Here we go, she thought. *Judgment Day.*

The rotating wall behind Shaw swung open, and the raised platform rumbled forth, bearing the painting Grace had discovered in the dusty corner of Robert's attic. It looked so lonely upon the stage, so savagely displayed. Grace had brought it all this way, from the rolling hills of Vermont to the highest summit of the art world, only to desert it, leaving it alone atop the pedestal to fend for itself.

Grace noticed the bidders around her turn the page of their brochure to Lot 12, where a small slip of paper alerted them to the peculiar process ahead.

"Lot Number 12," said Shaw. "Late Impressionist painting. Oil on canvas. Presented as is—unrestored by owner. British, dated 1885 to 1905." He hesitated, reviewing his notes. "Authorship contested."

A low rumble rolled across the crowd. Grace felt nauseous. Her failure felt so inevitable, so public.

Shaw read on: "However, to assist the bidders this evening, we can provide an addendum to the primary appraisal in your brochure." He glanced over the podium at Victor. "It is, in fact, a precise authentication, is that correct?"

Grace felt Victor tense beside her. He nodded, staring straight ahead.

"Very good," said Shaw. "I yield the floor to Dr. Victor Karlin for his expert report."

Victor turned to Grace, but he could not bring himself to look upon her. She reached out, grasping his hand.

It's okay, Vic, she thought, sending it through her fingers into his. *I forgive you.*

I forgive you for everything.

His hand relaxed and a sigh escaped his lips. He nodded, leaning forward to stand. His foot faltered, striking something, perhaps the leg of his chair, and he glanced down for a moment. Grace feared his resolve had broken, but suddenly he stood up, striding around the side of the stage, up the stairs, and onto the dais. As he entered the docket of the massive podium, he placed his notes down and stared at them—but he didn't speak. He didn't breathe.

He looked up, eyes wide, haunted, his pupils dilated in shock. He opened his mouth, silent for a moment, and then the words tumbled out in fits and starts. "I've—I've been tasked by Sotheby's to . . . well, to report my authentication of my . . . of my original appraisal of Lot 12. And I have uncovered irrefutable evidence that compels me . . ." He trailed off, and his face went blank.

The bidders fidgeted but kept silent, unsure if they were witnessing a complete mental break. Shaw remained just off-stage right, poised to intervene. Annette stepped out from the internet bank, whispering into her lapel microphone, alerting the staff to prepare the next lot. She nodded to Shaw, but as he stepped forward, something broke across Victor's face, some great peace, some submission, and he raised his notes once again.

And then he ripped them in two.

"That compels me to withdraw my original appraisal."

The hall fell silent as a stone tomb.

"I am, therefore, unable to authenticate the work in question," he said. "Thank you."

He folded his shredded notes with a perfect crease, tucked them into his suit jacket, and walked off the dais, sitting back down beside Grace.

Grace looked at him, mouth agape.

"Close your mouth, my dear," he said with a grin that wrapped all the way around his head. "You're up."

Shaw stepped back toward the podium. "Well, that's interesting," he said, genuinely intrigued. "On a cold night, we could use a little drama to keep us warm."

The audience tittered nervously, but Shaw fed off it. "We have lost our primary appraisal for Lot 12," he said, his spirits returning to full bloom. "But we do have a secondary appraisal of authorship on the following page in your program."

As the bidders turned their programs to Grace's appraisal, Jerome Zwick suddenly realized what had compelled him to come to the auction that night. He leapt to his feet and called out, "Can that appraisal be confirmed?"

The crowd shouted their approval.

Shaw turned to Grace. "Madam Schaffer," he said. "I yield to you."

The room contracted around Grace like an iris. All she could see was the podium above; everything else was a blur. She stood on shaking legs and felt herself floating forward, around the stage, up the stairs, and into the open gate of the podium. The crowd before her was a mumbling shadow, an alien mob of unshapen expectation—all of it focused on her.

She had nothing to say. She would not lie. Not for Elaine, or Jerome, or Robert, or the show, or her gallery, or her career, or even the legacy of her father.

James Davies had painted that picture. James Davies was a fact.

Grace turned to the easel. The white-gloved hands of the staffer holding it had disappeared, and all she could see were the shapes and colors of the painting she loved so dearly.

Her painting.

For they were One. They had reached out to each other in their solitude, two discarded artifacts, and found themselves reborn in the other's eye. Grace had brought it into the light, but the painting had done the same for her. And in that moment, on the stage of her greatest failure, the complicated masterpiece of Grace's life rose before her eyes in luminous oils and pastels and watercolors. And Grace knew the time had come for her final appraisal.

Herself.

She surveyed the canvas of her life: her little red shovel, thrusting into the pebbled void; her teenage arms, reaching out for a father unable to grasp them; her mother, a blank cover, teeming with color in the pages beneath; Victor at the altar, how he loved her, how he hurt her; the gallery, the Roadshow, the exile from everyone and everything she knew; the celestial globe, fractured to pieces by the unchained rage of her ego, let loose upon the world like a pestilence, laying waste to everything in its path.

Click.

The last piece fell into place, and finally, Grace could see it all.

Yes, Grace had failed, as her father had before her, as her mother had, as dear Victor had. She had ruined Robert's auction, she had fled *Antiques Roadshow*, she had destroyed the Appraisal Experts Roadshow, she had pushed Jerome to the brink of death, she had shattered the very gift of Heaven. And she had done it all to see her reflection glimmer more brightly in the eyes of another—of the profession, of her father, of Victor, of a one-night stand. All of these had been choices, just like this one, the one before her. But it was so hard, so agonizingly hard for Grace to choose Grace.

For Grace to be enough…for Grace.

Her appraisal done, she turned back to the painting upon the easel. And even though every eye in the room, every eye in the entire world saw the unimaginative oils of James Davies, they looked so achingly beautiful to Grace. The brilliant orange *craquelure* sun, hesitating in its descent for one final flicker in defiance of night, the infinite banks of the Avon, the spire of Holy Trinity arcing toward infinity, the spectral woman floating in the sacred instant between inspiration and obscurity, her face alight beneath the parasol, caressed by the finger of God, for her face shone with all the colors of Creation. She was the reason artists toiled in obscurity, that actors gladly starved. She was the wind in the musician's flute, the wrap on the dancer's point, the ink that flowed from the poet's pen.

And regardless of what anyone else saw…Grace saw her.

And suddenly, something within the painting ignited.

The oils peeled away like flaming petals, a new image bursting forth from beneath the pigments and varnish and an entire century of neglect: the masterpiece she had seen in Robert's attic, and in her weakness, what she had *un*seen. It shone with the light of a thousand suns, but her eyes remained open, and for once, Grace Schaffer refused to flinch.

She had found her Grail. It was time to reach out and claim it.

"Since my initial appraisal," she said, "I have discovered compelling, physical evidence that proves this to be the work of James Davies..."

She looked out over the hall and the entire crowd held its collective breath.

"But it is not."

Grace smiled, for she saw. Damn experts, damn auctions, damn value, damn market, damn the entire Art World, Sotheby's and all. Grace *saw.*

And that, finally, was enough for her.

"This is a William Kent!" she cried. "I stake my very soul on it!"

A flash bomb of indignation erupted from the crowd in a mushroom cloud of disbelief. Grace inhaled it as she walked back to her seat, savoring it on her tongue like the finest ambrosia. She sat down beside Victor, and he whispered in her ear:

"Good on you, Gracie."

But it was not good on Annette, who raged hot crimson in the corner, barking curses into her lapel microphone. No one seemed to be listening to her, so overwhelmed were they by Grace's napalming of the proceedings. Annette bolted toward the dais, yanking Thomas Shaw to the stage by his silken sleeve, nearly spilling the glass of water in his hand.

"Get back up there," she barked. "I'm canceling the lot."

Shaw plucked her hand from his arm before she tipped water all over his seven-thousand-dollar suit. "You can't do that," he said.

"I'm head of sales," she snapped. "I'll do whatever I want."

"Look at them." He pointed at the riveted throng. "The game's afoot. Let it ride."

She hesitated, and it was enough for him to get free. Shaw swung open the low gate to return to his podium, but Annette grabbed his collar, yanking him back.

Time slowed for Grace, and she saw it all. So many things had to happen, so many *ifs*: If Annette grabbed Shaw and he hadn't ripped free; if he'd ripped free but held on to his glass; if he'd lost the glass, but it hadn't tilted just so. But she did grab him, and the glass did fly, and it tilted just so.

And a single drop of water fell like a tiny tear upon the *craquelure* of the setting sun.

With every eye on Annette and Shaw, only Jerome Zwick, still standing in the back of the hall, saw it.

"The painting!" he thundered, pointing at the easel behind them. "The *paint!*"

Grace rose to her feet as the entire congregation stood behind her, every neck craning for a better view. Annette and Shaw turned toward the easel, following the stunned stare of two hundred eyes.

A single droplet of water had struck the painting, a perfect bull's-eye in the center of the *craquelure* sun. But water could not harm it, Grace knew. Not the oils, not the thick varnish that sealed them for over a century. Paint feared no water.

But somehow, water had stripped the varnish, and the paint, pulling back a hundred-year veil on a sun brighter and more luminous than the one in Heaven's sky. And Grace and Victor and Shaw and Annette, and everyone in the entire room knew that sun.

Annette crumpled to the floor in a babbling heap of disbelief, freeing Shaw, who approached the painting with a religious reverence. He had spied something within the sun, something too small for anyone to see, and he turned to the audience, walking toward the lip of the stage, gazing down at Grace with a giddy smile that filled her with so much joy, she feared she would surfeit.

"Dr. Schaffer," he said. "I now see a tiny, faded signature within the sun. Can you please tell our bidders what it says?"

She did not need to see it, for she knew.

"William Kent," she said.

"Indeed," Shaw said. "Thank you for authenticating the piece." He gestured for the crowd to take their seats, and they dropped as one. He put his hand out to Annette, still a crumpled mess on the floor. "If you'd be so kind," he said, raising her to her feet. "I have an auction to run."

Annette walked offstage as if entranced, resuming her spot behind the internet bank.

"Well, ladies and gentlemen," Shaw said, spreading his wings once again. "We asked the gods for drama this evening, and they did not disappoint. It appears we have inaccurately attributed this work to James Davies, but it is, in fact, an overpainting of a previous work." He deferred again to Grace. "Dr. Schaffer—do you wish to remove the piece for a full X-ray radiograph of the work before auction?"

Grace knew Robert would do as she advised. He had faith in her.

And Grace had faith in Grace.

"We are comfortable moving forward with the auction," she said with a wink. "Let it ride, Mr. Shaw."

He nodded to Grace, saluting her. "Very well," he said. "Barring objection, I will start the bidding on this authentic, unknown masterwork by William Kent, at *five hundred thousand dollars.*"

Grace had been wrong. She had told Robert the Kent would sell for one hundred million dollars.

It had sold for one hundred and one.

The buyer, a wealthy British widow, would be bringing the Kent back home—for a full, complete restoration to reveal the totality of Kent's creation, of course. Grace was not an expert restorer, and caution had guided her hand before the sale, but she did alert the widow that she'd noted something odd about the varnish in the upper-right-hand corner of the painting where the water had wreaked its havoc, something only an expert examination might uncover.

Or perhaps it wouldn't.

Robert had been shocked to silence, but regained his voice in time to ensure Grace received her representative fee when the auction had concluded. Grace wasn't concerned. It wasn't her money anyway. She intended to sign the check over to Elaine before the ink was dry. The Appraisal Experts Roadshow would rise from the ashes, and Elaine and Pat and Henry and Grace would all rise with it.

Jerome would not. He had disappeared before Grace could thank him. But Jerome was not comfortable with goodbyes, so Grace would not trouble him with them. She intended to hound him forever anyway.

As the hall cleared, Grace noticed Victor still seated in the front row, gazing at the podium with a strange, far-off look on his face. She walked over, plopping down beside him with an exhausted sigh.

"Not a bad auction," she said.

"No," he said, his voice a blank monotone. "Not bad."

Grace elbowed him playfully, but he stared on.

"You okay?" she asked.

"I'm not sure." He paused. "I need you to be honest with me."

Grace nodded. "I always have, Vic. You know that."

"Then tell me," he said, voice trembling. "How long have you had it?"

She paused, confused, "Had what?"

He spun on her, eyes wide with fear. "You didn't have it?"

"Have *what*, Vic?"

He took a deep breath and reached under his chair, to the spot he had kicked before he ascended the stage. He emerged with a small cigar box, its faded cover a stampede of Roman chariots. Grace gasped.

It was Victor's Treasure Box.

"You didn't put this under my chair?" he asked.

She shook her head.

He set the box in his lap and laid his hands over it. "Well, however it got here, I have it now," he said. "And I'll never let go of it again."

He kissed her cheek. Grace leaned into it.

"Thank you, dear, dear Grace," he said, and stood up, his heels clacking off down the aisle and out the exit.

The door slammed behind him, and Grace was left alone in the shadowy hall. She sat there for several minutes, her thoughts swirling around something impossible but true.

She reached under her seat and grasped the handles of her purse with trembling hands. She placed it in her lap, peeled the flaps open, and drew out a long unbroken string of polished white onyx, orange carnelian, and Nubian gold. Fastened between two crimson bloodstones was a single spherical stone of the finest lapis lazuli, mined in the ancient limestone beds of Pakistan. The smooth, walnut-size sphere did not appear to have been carved or fashioned by human hands, and the golden pyrite inclusions shimmered like starbursts across the deep blue face of the stone, illuminating Grace's face with the sacred light of the Cosmos.

She had known it was somehow with her at the end, that it had made itself whole, for she had been made whole. And she was so happy to be reunited, but so terrified, for she knew there was one final question to ask of it. The two of them had plumbed the depths of so many, had excavated their worth, not their value. But Grace had not fully completed her final appraisal, and she needed its help, for she could not do it alone. The stone shimmered, ready to answer.

Ask, it said.

I'm so old, she thought. There was still time, of course—years, decades even—but for the first time in her life, Grace could see the end of her in the distance. And although she lived in fear of the answer, it was time she asked the question.

"I know what I was," she said. "I just don't know what I am. Not anymore."

She grasped the globe in both hands.

"What am I worth?"

The celestial globe ignited, throbbing, a starburst in her hands. Grace felt it pierce her through, fastening upon something deep within her, drawing it up, up and out of her.

And then a man walked to the podium, gazing down at her with a love beyond her comprehension.

"Hello, Grace," said her father.

She slumped back against the chair, convinced she had lost consciousness.

"You're not real," she said.

Albert smiled and he was beside her; she could feel his bony shoulder against hers, smell his aftershave.

"Don't be afraid, Gracie," he said. "Please don't fight it. I can't be here for long."

Grace gave in to the dream—for that was what it was to her, as anything else might have broken her—and laid her head upon her father's shoulder.

"That's my girl," he said, stroking her hair.

"I'm so lost, Dad," she said. "I can't see my way out. What am I supposed to *do*?"

"The thing you're most afraid of."

She nodded and the tears fell. "But I'm so tired, Dad," she said. "To start again, all over again, career, relationships . . . I just don't have the strength anymore."

"But you have something else. Something far more powerful." He lifted her chin to his, and she saw such constellations in his eyes.

"There is Magic in us, Grace," he said. "Not at first, no. It hatches over the course of our lifetimes, and sometimes we're so tired, too tired to do anything about it. It stumbles to its feet just as we're falling from ours. But only then are we ready for it. Only then are we old enough to see. And it's so beautiful, Grace. The sun is at its most profound as it sets, and so too are our lives. At sunset we kiss, at sunset we sigh over deep blue waters, at sunset we break hearts, and our hearts are broken. At sunset, dear Grace . . ."

"The Universe is ours."

He stood up and took her hands, pulling her to her feet.

"But it's a choice, you know. What you do with it. What you're worth."

He kissed her hands and looked into her eyes, his shining one last time.

"Choose Magic, Gracie."

And he was gone.

Grace nodded, so pleased with the answer. And so challenged, thank God.

A challenge to last a lifetime.

Perhaps more.

Epilogue

Color

"Learn to look—only then will you see."

—Claude Monet

One

James Davies hated it.

He had painted in a fever. No food, no drink, nothing but oil and brush. And the *canvas.* God, he despised that canvas—the blank stare, mocking his every stroke. It laughed at him like a cruel lover. It unmanned him.

James tore it from the easel and hurled it into the corner of the room. It landed face up, still grinning, so he retreated to the open window, seeking solace from the Avon as it made its serpentine progress through the arched legs of Clopton Bridge.

He couldn't shake the image: Kent straddling the cobblestones, the blur of his brush, the ignition of color that surged across his canvas. When he had finished, the fool had simply walked away, leaving it as offal for buzzards to pick at. But James had rescued it, stashing it away in his temporary Stratford studio until it revealed its secrets to him.

But the Kent was silent.

James kept it near, imprisoned in the corner while he worked. It joined him at mealtime, it overlooked his bed; it was his constant companion. But it told no tales. James could trace the exact outline of Kent's tree on his own canvas, but no tree would grow. He spent hours modeling Kent's Naomi—weightless and buoyant as a cloud—but her spirit never materialized. Not even after she sat for James at Tramway, just as she had for William Kent. She had lain in bed beside him in much the same way. Neither had aroused his inspiration.

Despondent, James threw himself against the easel and sobbed, his chest heaving against the empty wooden frame. The transplant had failed, and both patients had died on the slab. Perhaps it would be better to bury the paintings together—at least their ashes might marry in the earth, and through that, James would be reborn.

"Of course!" he gasped. The answer was so simple. James would not destroy Kent's work after completing his own.

I will revive it.

He leapt across the room and grabbed Kent's canvas off its easel, returning to his own, wrenching it down tight. He set his oils beside him, but mixed each color a deeper, thicker hue, almost in a soup. It would need to be stout.

It would need to hold down William Kent for an eternity.

His hands moved with extraordinary speed, heaping the boldness of his own brash colors over Kent's. And with each covering stroke, James stole a drop of Kent before he laid it, like the slight withdrawal of the physician's needle before the elixir's injection.

And for a while, it was good.

But as the Kent slowly disappeared beneath his brush, his soaring spirits fell to Earth, and then to the Pit below. Overpainting Naomi's spectral figure had taken hours. His hands shook as he filled her floating skirts with lead. He suffocated her with his brushstrokes; her luminous face disappearing into the murky shade beneath her parasol. He paused, contemplating it like a death.

Like a murder, which it was. William Kent had captured his Goodbye in paint and pigment—the barest, most naked moment of any artist, and he had opened his soul and shared it with the entire world. And James Davies had killed it.

He sobbed again, but there was no rage this time. His tears had cleansed him, and his eyes were opened. He found the courage to look upon the canvas, and his eyes inched upward until he saw Kent's Sun shining down in glory, breathing life into James's own wretched work below. It hung among the clouds, still unmolested, the last gasp of a master.

James rushed to his palette of oils and grabbed a bottle of toluene, meaning to strip away his own abomination, but inches from the painting, he froze. Who in London would care? Kent had been exiled; only James saw the magic in his pigments and paste. If there were a way to pull the scales from the eyes of a future generation, they might see, as James now saw, God's light upon that bridge. For that was the source that lit Kent's eye.

And it will never light mine.

James would leave London. He would seek a trade, as his father had. He would break every one of his brushes and bury them in the forgetful silt of the Avon.

But he was not done. James Davies had a masterpiece to paint.

The revelation took hold, and something strange and magnificent began working within him—a dizzying euphoria. He stumbled to his oils, combining his oranges, reds, and yellows with a dangerous swirl of zinc oxide white. Such a combustible marriage would shatter and crack over time like *craquelure*, expanding out in waves like fractured halos, weakening the varnish coat above. And in the very heart of Kent's Sunset, directly above his final signature, he laid his timely trap, and over it a thin and weakened varnish, with resins sure to fail against the passing glance of even *one single drop of water.*

When they are ready, he thought. *William Kent will be waiting.*

And James Davies would be his midwife.

When he had finished, he stood back to survey his masterpiece. James would not sign the canvas—it was not his to sign—but he would sign the frame and sell it, sending it off on its long journey. He wondered what foreign shore would welcome it, whose eyes it would bless.

He peered through his creation into Kent's one last time, and saw it quiver and glow beneath the thick layer of oil. It was sleeping, but it was still very much alive.

More than that, it was good. It was so very, very good.

Perhaps even perfect.

Because it was Old.

Two

Max Kreisberg tilted his face toward the warmth of the setting sun. His eyes were fully closed, as they were no longer of any use to him, but as the golden glow of the fading day fell across his face, he broke out in a contented smile.

"Enjoying the sunset?" Grace said from the lower landing of Mary Elwood Estates.

Max angled his face to her, and his smile grew wide. "Hello, my dear," he said. "You better hurry or you'll miss the start of the lesson. Shirley's a bit prickly when we're tardy—like Medea with a paintbrush."

Grace laughed. "Oh yes," she said, climbing the stairs to Max's perch. "She perfected her technique on me, so I take full responsibility."

"Whatever horrors she exposed you to, you appear to have turned out all right."

"I'm still turning, Max."

He tilted his head, savoring her answer. "Yes," he said. "I can tell that you are. Keep turning, my dear—just keep turning toward the Activity Center or I'm going to get an earful."

"Mom can wait," Grace said, opening the drawstring on a small Macy's plastic bag. "I came to see you."

She removed the tattered sweater from his shoulders, draping it over the arm of his wheelchair, and pulled a blue cashmere cardigan from the Macy's bag. She placed a gentle hand on his back, and he leaned forward while Grace draped the cashmere around his slender frame as if she were robing a king. And to Grace, he was. She could *see* it. Oh yes, she could see it quite clearly. She had that power. She chuckled and corrected herself.

She had that Magic.

Max reached across his belly, rubbing his fingers over the delicate fabric. "It's beautiful," he said. "As are you, dear girl."

Grace blushed.

"You're blushing."

Grace laughed. "How can you tell?"

"I can feel the heat."

"You're a liar."

"I'm an actor."

She laughed again. "Still performing, are you?"

"Always," he said. "I'm still turning, myself."

Grace had another turn to make, but it made her so very, very sad. She sat down on the top step and laid her head against the arm of his wheelchair. He reached down, gently stroking her hair.

Grace gazed out over the orchard. It stretched into the distance, bound only by the darkening sky. Orange honey sunbeams drizzled down over the juniper trees and the dewy grass, enveloping the world in Day's final embrace.

Max turned his cheek to the warm glow. "I could look at this forever."

Grace smiled. "Things are always at their most beautiful right before sunset, wouldn't you say?"

"I did say, my dear. You're stealing my line."

Yours, among others. She thought of her father.

A challenge, he had said.

Grace feared she wasn't up to this one.

She reached beneath her blouse and drew out the necklace, laying the deep blue lapis lazuli of the celestial globe upon her chest. She wrapped her fingers around it, and it wrapped itself around her. They had seen such sights together, such dazzling vistas, for they had seen into the mysteries of the multitudes, into their sacred core, and there they had unlocked the answer to the elemental question that makes Human of Beast.

What Am I Worth?

Grace's worth had been in her father's eyes, in her marriage, in her career, in the size of her name on an article; most of all, it had been in her youth. And for the past few glorious months, her worth was in her hand, sparkling within that stupendous granite and gold Elysium. But Grace had been challenged to find it somewhere else.

To find it in her future.

Goodbye, she thought.

Farewell, it answered.

As she removed the necklace, the globe dragged across her skin, taking for itself the memories of Grace that would forever be a part of it.

She held the lapis lazuli up to the fading rays of the sun, and as she looked at the golden constellations, a single star burst forth, overwhelming billions upon billions before fading into place, into *her* eternal place within the celestial globe.

Grace smiled—for that was more than enough for her.

"I better go in," she said, rising to her feet.

"Thank you for the gift," he said, hugging the cardigan. "I shall cherish it."

She looked down at Max, his face still angled to the setting sun. "I brought you one more gift, if you'll allow me."

"But of course, my dear."

"Close your eyes."

He laughed.

"Please."

He paused, then nodded and closed his eyes.

Grace guided the celestial globe around his neck, resting it against his heart. He reached up and took it in his hands, rubbing his calloused fingers over the ancient face of the lapis lazuli.

"Oh," he gasped. "It's *warm*."

Grace leaned down and placed her finger beneath his chin, lifting it toward the golden horizon. She kissed his cheek and moved her lips to his ear.

"I'm going to go inside now, Max," she whispered. "And when you hear the door close behind me, I want you to open your eyes."

Max nodded.

Grace lingered, but only for a moment.

She walked across the wooden veranda, opened the door, and went inside. The door closed behind her.

Max paused, for a great joy and terror was upon him.

And then he opened his eyes.

Acknowledgments

All of us stand on the shoulders of giants. This novel stands on the love, generosity, and support of the following:

My wife, Laura, my muse, who comes first, last, and everything in between. My mother, my first editor, for hounding me to write a novel since I was old enough to hold a pencil. My father, who showed me what hard work was, and how to do it. My sister, for laughing at my stories when we should have been doing our homework.

My friend and agent, Michael Signorelli at Aevitas, for his eye, his ear, and the chance he took on me. My brilliant editor at Grand Central, Jacqueline Young, for her never-ending passion and artistry throughout this entire process. The army of artists and creators at Grand Central Publishing, for conjuring a manuscript into a novel: Joan Matthews, Bob Castillo, and Susan Gutentag for their laser-edged, fine-tooth combs; Jim Datz and Sam Green for capturing the mystery and whimsy of the book in such vibrant colors; Taylor Navis for the stately elegance of her interior design; and Victoria Lustbader for hypnotizing me into believing this was possible.

My artistic father, Joel Zwick, for reading nearly every draft of everything I've ever written and always finding at least one thing (and sometimes twenty) to make them better. Jack Clay, for tuning my ears to the musicality of language. John Bouchard, for seeing the writer in me long before I did. Cornelius Carter, for teaching me the difference between past successes and new challenges. David Saltzman, for being someone I could laugh with and look up to at the same time. And Karen "Dragon Lady" Stephens, for the short story class that started it all.

You, the reader, for bringing Grace to life. Nothing I write is truly real until you read it.

Last, I should be remiss if I did not thank one of the main inspirations for this novel—the experts, appraisers, creators, producers, and guests of *Antiques Roadshow*. I cannot watch that legendary show without laughing, crying, and learning something new about the art within us all.

About the Author

Antique is Seth Panitch's first novel. His plays—*Dammit, Shakespeare!*, *Hell: Paradise Found* (Broadway Play Publishing, Inc.), *Alcestis Ascending*, and *Separate and Equal*—have all been produced Off Broadway, and his films—*Service to Man* and *The Coming*—are distributed by Freestyle Entertainment Studios and Terror Films. Seth is also Professor of Theatre and directs the MFA Acting Program at the University of Alabama. More important, he is married to Laura Earnest Panitch, who does not seem to mind when he creeps upstairs to write at odd hours, or when he lets their dog Moses use him as a jungle gym. Seth is a proud member of the Author's Guild, the Dramatists Guild of America, the Society of Directors and Choreographers, and the Illuminati—although he has steadfastly refused to have their names tattooed on his chest.

Reading Group Guide Questions for Discussion

1. Each character expresses affection differently. How does Grace's father express love? How does this differ from Grace's mother and Grace herself? Are there people in your own life who love you in ways you, too, might have initially missed or misinterpreted?

2. Jerome Zwick admires Grace's ability "to set the value—not by a bidder's whim, or the cold calculating machinery of the market—but by the *worth*." Do you see this distinction between value and worth in the world around you? After reading *Antique*, how might you address that distinction in your own life?

3. Consider Grace's appraisals of the celestial globe and William Kent's painting. Why do you think the novel focuses on color and light? What do you value in art? What makes artwork beautiful and *meaningful* to you?

4. Reflect on Grace's choice to pull out of the *initial* auction at Sotheby's. How do you feel about this decision? Would you have done the same? If not, what would hold you back? Might the

outcome have been different if Victor's appraisal wasn't the one contradicting hers?

5. By the end of the novel, Robert Bedford, despite not having known Grace for long, deeply trusts her judgment. What sets Grace apart from her appraiser peers? Why do clients feel comfortable and confident in her presence? Would you trust Grace in the same way? Why or why not?

6. It's clear that Grace doesn't truly understand her mother, Shirley, until the end of the novel. How has this affected their family dynamic? Was Grace a good daughter? Was Shirley a good mother? What advice would you give to this mother-daughter duo to move forward? How has their relationship encouraged you to think about your own relationship with your parents or children?

7. Consider Grace and Victor's post-divorce dynamic. How did seeing Victor again affect Grace? What feelings did the reunion stir up? How does their relationship change as the story moves toward climax? Have you revisited or restored past relationships of your own? If so, why, and what was different about them the second time around?

8. Grace wishes that she be enough for herself in her final appraisal. How has the celestial globe guided her to this moment? What might have happened to Grace if she hadn't found the globe? Have there been moments in your life when you, or someone you care about, have strived for something similar?

9. Jerome Zwick, after the devastating loss of his Holy Grail, claims that his work now has become inertial. Do you agree that Jerome is just treading water in his career? If you were in his situation, how would you wrestle with such a loss? Would you continue searching for the Grail? Why or why not?